# Three Weeks in Washington

*a novel by*

**LUANA EHRLICH**

This book is a work of fiction. Names, characters, places, and incidents either are products of the author's imagination or are used fictitiously. Any resemblance to actual persons, living or dead, events, or locales is entirely coincidental.

**Visit the author's website at www.luanaehrlich.com**

**All Titus Ray Thrillers can be purchased on Amazon.**

ISBN-10: 153078574X
ISBN-13: 978-1530785742

To Ray Allan Pollock,
for giving an eleven-year-old girl
permission to read adult spy novels.

# PART ONE

## Chapter 1

*Monday, June 22*

The shooter was just around the corner from me. To get to him, I would need to cross N Street. If I crossed N Street, he would have a clear shot at me.

I decided to wait him out.

He had already eluded several SWAT teams in the Washington Navy Yard, the home of U.S. Naval Operations, and now he was hunkered down inside the entryway of Building 175. I suspected he was trying to find an exit out of the former shipyard.

If I remained at my present location, at the corner of Building 172, he would walk right into my waiting arms when he crossed N Street.

I stayed put.

I wasn't exactly sure how the shooter had ended up at the Navy Yard in Washington, D.C. on a summer morning in June, but I'd arrived at the location after driving non-stop from Norman, Oklahoma.

♦♦♦♦

Douglas Carlton, my operations officer, and the head of the Middle East desk at the CIA, had called me the day before and given me the surprising news I'd been restored to active duty status by the stroke of a pen from Robert Ira, the Deputy Director of Operations at the CIA.

Three months earlier, the DDO had placed me on medical leave after the two of us had engaged in a very public spat regarding his competency. I'd questioned him about his ability to run Operations, because I'd discovered his political games at the Agency had brought down my network in Tehran.

Needless to say, things had not gone smoothly for me after that, and, except for a brief run into Caracas to capture a Hezbollah assassin, I'd spent the last two months in Norman, Oklahoma on medical leave.

Ostensibly, I'd been there trying to recuperate from shattering my leg while trying to escape the clutches of VEVAK, the Iranian secret police. But, in reality, everyone at the Agency knew my medical leave was simply Ira's way of punishing me for berating him in front of two division heads during a debriefing.

Immediately after Carlton had called to let me know I'd been reinstated, I'd gotten in touch with my property manager in Norman. After that, I'd reluctantly said goodbye to Nikki Saxon, a detective in the Norman Police Department, and I'd made my way across the southern states to the east coast.

An hour before arriving at Building 172, I'd been cruising along the interstate outside of Fairfax, Virginia. That's when I'd called Carlton to let him know I'd be in his office at Langley within the hour.

My boss didn't sound happy.

"Don't bother," he said. "There's been a shooting at the Washington, Navy Yard and all federal agencies within a fifty-mile radius of Washington, D.C. are on lockdown."

"Are you telling me you're not allowed to leave the grounds?"

"Not just the grounds. We're being told to stay inside the buildings."

"Doesn't that strike you as a little strange? You're supposed to be providing intel for any threats to the homeland. How can you assess threats when you're not allowed to leave your own backyard?"

"We're being told it's for our own safety. The feds believe the shooters could be part of a coordinated attack against all government agencies in the area. The CIA is an obvious target."

He was quiet for several seconds, and I imagined him aligning the corners of the pile of papers in front of him—a compulsive habit and one of his many idiosyncrasies.

"One of the shooters at the Navy Yard has already been taken out, but the feds believe the other one is still somewhere in the compound."

"What nationality is the dead guy?"

"He wasn't from the Middle East, if that's what you're thinking. He's been identified as Reyes Valario, and he's been here on a student visa from Venezuela for at least a year. The FBI is sifting through the intel on him as we speak, and our own analysts are scanning the data banks as well."

"Did they call Salazar for his input?"

Carlton made some kind of strange noise at the back of his throat.

I didn't think the timing of his guttural utterance was coincidental with the mention of Salazar's name.

C.J. Salazar was the head of the Latin America desk at the Agency. He wasn't known for his astute grasp of the region. Instead, his focus was on the drug cartels operating in his territory, and, for that reason, everyone around the Agency called him Cartel Carlos.

Not to his face, though.

I'd experienced his ineptitude firsthand on my recent run into Caracas during Operation Clear Signal. Both Salazar and Carlton had been part of the Clear Signal team directing Ben Mitchell and me as we tried to stop a Hezbollah assassin from murdering a high-profile government official in Caracas, Venezuela.

Carlton said, "The Department of Homeland Security called C.J., but he didn't give them anything."

"Nothing at all?"

"Well, he did have our analysts run down Valario's prints and the origins of his visa. He also called Ben Mitchell, who was in D.C. at the time, and sent him over to the DHS Command Center in the Navy Yard. He said since Ben had recently been in Venezuela, it made sense for him to serve as the Agency's liaison with DHS."

"Ben's over at the Command Center? I might head over there myself. I'm not that far away."

"You haven't been reinstated yet, Titus. Officially, you're still on medical leave."

"I'll keep my head down. It won't be a big deal."

It wasn't.

But then, it was.

♦♦♦♦

Thirty minutes after talking to Carlton, I arrived at the Navy Yard, but, due to the area being blocked off, I parked my car several blocks away and walked over to the Patterson Avenue gate off 6th Street.

However, one look at the chaos in front of the gate, and I immediately realized getting inside the compound wasn't going to be easy. The place was swarming with policemen, not to mention SWAT teams, FBI, and a whole host of other law enforcement personnel. Most of them were decked out in bulletproof gear.

All of them looked jumpy.

From news reports I'd heard on the way over to the site, I knew eight people had been killed. Two of the victims had been policemen. However, one of them had managed to take out the Valario guy before dying of his own wounds.

With another gunman on the loose, I realized all members of law enforcement had good reason to be a little nervous, but that meant every male not in uniform was going to be under intense scrutiny. Since I had no official ID on me, talking my way inside the Navy Yard didn't appear to be an option.

As I considered other possibilities, I saw a uniformed officer taking an interest in me.

I quickly walked over to a news van and grabbed a piece of equipment out of the cargo compartment. After fiddling around with it for a few seconds, I glanced up to see if my actions had made any impression on the curious cop. I was relieved to see his eyes were once again on the crowd of onlookers.

As I looked past him to a group of feds off to his right, I spotted

Frank Benson.

Benson was FBI; not exactly a friend, but if he could get me inside the compound, our past relationship wouldn't really matter.

At least, not to me.

I walked over and tapped him on the shoulder. "Hey, Frank, long time no see."

It took him a second or two to recognize me, and when he did, he didn't exactly give me a bear hug. "Titus Ray. What are you doing down here?"

Benson had light brown hair and a prominent square jaw. Clarice Duncan, a Level 2 female operative, had once told me women found Benson very appealing. She said it was the square jaw that did it.

I had to take her word for that.

I said, "I'm supposed to meet a guy down here. I was told he's over at the Command Center."

"The Command Center is at 7th and Elm, but access to it has been blocked off from here. You'll have to go over to the 9th Street gate and come in that way. The buildings in that sector have been evacuated already, so you just need to show them some ID at the gate."

"Any sign of the other shooter?"

Benson shook his head and pointed at the entrance to the Navy Yard. "He's still in there somewhere. We have SWAT teams clearing the buildings, but finding him may take some time."

"Give me a description of the guy in case I run into him."

"He was last spotted near Building 197. That's in the opposite direction of the Command Center."

"Humor me."

Benson frowned. "You haven't changed, have you? You're like a dog in heat when it comes to wanting information."

"Where's all that cooperation between the agencies I keep hearing about, Frank? We're supposed to be sharing intel these days."

He shrugged. "He's of average height, brown hair, moustache, probably Hispanic. He's dressed in jeans and a green shirt, and he has a dark-colored backpack with him."

"Weapons?"

"We know he has an AR-15 assault rifle on him. But I doubt his backpack is full of books, so I think it's safe to assume he has access to even more firepower."

"Any chance I could hitch a ride over to the 9th Street gate with one of your people? I'm parked at least a mile away from here, and a long walk doesn't sound too good in this heat."

He motioned toward a woman standing beside a Crown Vic. She was wearing a dark blue shirt with F.B.I. printed in big yellow letters across the back of it.

"Renee was just leaving; she could give you a lift."

"Sounds good."

When he called Renee over and told her I needed a ride over to the Command Center, he didn't identify my employer.

That didn't surprise me.

Benson was ex-CIA, and he'd sworn to keep the identity of Level 1 intelligence officers a secret. Because Benson had never been a person who ever broke the rules—even when he should have done so—I knew my secret life was safe with him.

I thanked Benson and followed Renee over to her vehicle.

As I walked away, Benson called out, "Hey, big guy, you may need to return the favor someday. And remember, I have a very long memory."

"Sure, Frank. You've got my number. Call me anytime."

He didn't have my number, but he managed to contact me anyway.

♦♦♦♦

Renee didn't have very much to say on the drive over to the 9th Street gate, and that was fine with me.

I hated small talk.

By the time I'd made up my mind she must be a loner like me, we were pulling up to the 9th Street gate. Moments later, she flashed her creds at the cops guarding the gate, and, just like that, I was inside the compound.

"We'll have to park somewhere around here and walk over to the Command Center," she said. "The SWAT teams aren't allowing vehicles past O Street."

Although I'd told Benson otherwise, I assured Renee a long walk wouldn't bother me.

The moment I got out of the vehicle, a flash of something in my peripheral vision caught my attention.

It had been off to my right, near Building 175.

I gestured over to a nearby building. "I need to take a little detour, Renee. All that coffee has finally caught up with me. I'll see you over at the Command Center."

"Sure. See you there."

I watched as Renee walked down the block toward 7th Street. A few minutes later, I saw her take a right turn onto Elm and disappear from sight.

Although I spotted a cadre of uniformed police officers entering a three-story structure at the opposite end of the block, the street in front of me appeared to be deserted. I was guessing the buildings off to my right had already been cleared.

That was the direction I was headed—off to my right, where something had flashed in my peripheral vision.

Something like the barrel of an AR-15 assault rifle.

## Chapter 2

About five minutes after taking up my position alongside Building 172 in the Navy Yard, I saw the missing shooter slip underneath the overhang of Building 175 and disappear from sight.

He appeared to be a slightly built Hispanic male, wearing a green shirt and a pair of blue jeans. Besides the rifle, I'd also caught a brief glimpse of a dark blue backpack.

If the guy had plans to get out of the Navy Yard through the 11th Street exit, then I knew he'd have to cross N Street. Instead of making myself a target and going after him, I'd made the decision to hold my position and wait for him to make a move.

Now, that time had finally come.

The shooter made a dash across N Street. After creeping along the exterior wall of Building 172, he rounded the corner and ducked inside the building's recessed doorway.

That's when the two of us came face to face.

He looked surprised to see me.

Maybe it wasn't me, though.

Maybe it was the gun I was holding.

At any rate, he was slow to react when I placed the Glock against his temple.

"Put it on the ground," I said.

He hesitated for a moment, and then, he slowly bent his knees and placed the rifle on the ground.

"And the backpack."

As if he hadn't understood my order, he stared at me for a few seconds.

I touched one of the straps on the backpack and said, "Drop the backpack."

I said it in Spanish this time, and he immediately shrugged it off.

As I watched the careless way he allowed it to slip from his shoulders and fall to the ground, I decided his movements probably meant the bag wasn't full of explosives.

However, just in case my instincts were rusty from two weeks of inactivity, I grabbed the rifle off the ground, pushed the shooter out towards the street, and put some distance between the two of us and the backpack.

When nothing exploded, I immediately regretted having to leave the shooter's backpack behind.

After we'd gone about fifty yards, I motioned for him to enter Building 220. The sign on the outside of the structure indicated it was the Navy Fitness Center.

Since the occupants had already been evacuated, there was no one inside the building.

From the look of things, everyone had left in a hurry. Weights were sitting out, towels were strewn across the carpet, and a treadmill in the middle of the room had been abandoned with its motor still running—traveling along the road to nowhere.

I told the shooter to take a seat on the floor and motioned for him to put his back up against the wall. He did as he was told, and I got the impression he was used to taking orders from people.

I sat down on a weight bench opposite him.

He pulled his knees up to his chest, put his head down, and locked his hands together in front of him, almost as if he were expecting me to cuff his hands in that position.

If I'd had any zip ties on me, I would have done exactly that.

Instead, I kept my gun pointed at him and showered him with kindness.

"You're in a lot of trouble. You know that, don't you?"

His head popped up, but he didn't say anything.

When I repeated myself in Spanish, there was an immediate look of recognition in his eyes.

He nodded and said he understood. *"Sí, lo sé."*

I explained—with a slight degree of exaggeration—what the federal authorities would do to him once they locked him up. My colorful description portrayed the type of punishment inflicted by a drug lord on a courier who failed to follow orders.

He grew more agitated with each horrific adjective.

"But," I paused a second or two for emphasis, ". . . if you're willing to cooperate with me, I won't allow any of this to happen to you. You won't be harmed."

It didn't take him long to make a decision. Within a few seconds, he was agreeing to do whatever I told him to do.

After I'd finished these negotiations, I called Ben Mitchell.

♦♦♦♦

"Can you leave the Command Center and get over to Building 220 without drawing anyone's attention?"

"Titus?"

"Yeah, it's me. There's someone I want you to meet. He's at the Navy Fitness Center, but it's best if this introduction stays between the three of us."

"What are you doing here? The last I heard you were still in Oklahoma."

"I'll explain later. Can you get over here?"

"Who's this mysterious person you want me to meet?"

"That's not important right now. How soon can you get away from there?"

He sighed. "I'll need at least ten minutes."

"That works. When you turn onto 10th Street, stop off at Building 172 and grab the backpack in the doorway. As far as I can tell, it's not hot."

"As far as you can tell?" He lowered his voice. "Any chance that item belongs to the person I'm about to meet?"

"There's a very good chance of that, and now you know why I want you to meet him."

"Are you sure about this?"

"I am."

"On my way."

"Before you leave the Center, grab one of those blue shirts with the big yellow letters across the back of it and bring it with you."

"Oh, sure. Are you looking for any particular size? Would you prefer cotton or polyester?"

He hung up before hearing my answer.

♦♦♦♦

While I waited for Mitchell to arrive, I had the shooter empty his pockets and answer a few questions.

He had nothing of significance on him—no ID or cell phone—and he responded to my grilling with a minimum of prodding.

He said his name was Felipe Arcos, and he was originally from Mexico. He told me he and Reyes, the other shooter, were students at the University of Arkansas in Fayetteville. When I asked him about what they were doing in Washington, he gave me some nonsensical story about visiting his aunt.

I decided not to press the issue.

I knew he'd eventually tell me the truth.

After a few minutes, I had him move over to a spot on the floor by the front windows. I wanted to keep him in my sights, while I kept an eye out for Mitchell.

Although I'd only known Mitchell a short time, I fully expected him to arrive at Building 220 without bringing the feds along with him. I didn't believe he was the type of guy to betray a fellow operative.

While I was pretty sure I was right about that, I didn't know the guy well enough to be certain of it.

Mitchell had been my contact at the embassy in San José, Costa Rica, when I'd arrived there to do a snatch and grab of Ahmed Al-Amin, a Hezbollah assassin who had recently gunned down a fellow operative in Dallas, Texas. Unfortunately, things hadn't gone exactly as planned in Costa Rica, and Ahmed had eluded my grasp and boarded a yacht for Venezuela.

After Ahmed had made his getaway, his bodyguards—a couple of members of a Mexican drug cartel—had tortured a CIA asset who knew Mitchell was an employee of the CIA. Because the Agency couldn't take the chance Mitchell had been burned by the asset, they'd pulled him out of Costa Rica and brought him back to Langley.

Once Mitchell had arrived stateside, I'd convinced Carlton to vet him for Level 1 status—even though he'd only been with the Agency a short time and wasn't really eligible for a change in status.

My motive in moving him to Level 1 status was to have him assigned as my partner for the run into Caracas to capture Ahmed.

Carlton had agreed to assess him for a status change, but he'd been surprised at my willingness to accept Mitchell as my partner.

My request had surprised me as well.

Usually, I preferred to work solo.

I'd found it was a lot less messy, and, if I ended up getting killed, I wouldn't have to answer to anyone for losing an operative during a mission.

However, from the moment I'd laid eyes on Mitchell, I'd seen something of myself in him—he was also a good-looking guy—and I'd observed several characteristics indicating he had a natural talent for doing clandestine work.

He wasn't perfect, though, and he had several strikes against him. Besides his immaturity, the biggest obstacle he had to overcome was his father.

I'd been clueless about Mitchell's genetic makeup when I'd first laid eyes on him in San José. However, when we'd met up again at Langley, I'd discovered his father was Senator Elijah Mitchell, the Chairman of the Senate Select Committee on Intelligence. He was also a member of several other congressional committees, including the Senate Armed Services Committee.

The Senator was a controversial figure, able to annoy both parties with equal enthusiasm, and he was known for his biting sarcasm and caustic wit. Controlling people appeared to be a passion with him, and the younger Mitchell had once told me he'd joined the CIA because he was certain his father's reach couldn't extend into the bowels of the Agency.

That wasn't necessarily true, and I'd never told Mitchell what I'd discovered about his father's influence at the Agency. Nor had I mentioned I'd actually met the Senator once in the Situation Room of the White House—not a pleasant encounter for either of us.

Now, as I glanced at my watch and realized fifteen minutes had passed since I'd last spoken with Mitchell, I was beginning to get a little worried about that trust issue.

♦♦♦♦

Another five minutes passed—probably more like four—and then I spotted a Chevy Suburban slowly making its way down the block toward the Fitness Center. The windows were tinted black, and it was difficult to see inside.

It drew to a halt outside Building 172.

I immediately relaxed when I saw Mitchell jump out and grab the backpack from the doorway. Seconds later, he pulled up outside Building 220.

As he emerged from the vehicle, I noticed he'd recently gotten a haircut. On our run into Caracas, his dark brown hair had always looked disheveled, as if he'd just gotten out of bed. Now, his hair was shorter, making his boyish face appear more mature.

When he came through the doorway of Building 220, he was carrying a dark blue shirt in his hand. Presumably, FBI was spelled out in yellow letters across the back of it.

He quickly surveyed the area, taking in Felipe, the AR-15, and the treadmill going full speed in the middle of the room.

"Now would be a good time to tell me what you're doing."

"What *we're* doing," I said, "is getting out of here."

I pointed toward Felipe. "He gets the shirt. You do the driving, and I'll give the orders from the back seat."

Mitchell tossed the shirt toward Felipe. "Let's hope there aren't any CCTV cameras around here."

I said, "We're clear. I've already checked."

I wasn't sure how much of the conversation Felipe had

understood, but, as soon as Mitchell threw the shirt at him, he put his arms through the sleeves and started fastening the buttons.

When he'd finished, I warned him. "Remember what I told you. If you cooperate with me, I'll get you out of here alive, and *los federales* won't be able to touch you. Just keep your mouth shut and try to relax."

He assured me he was very relaxed. *"Estoy muy tranquilo."*

That made one of us.

# Chapter 3

Getting through the 9th Street gate was a breeze. The cops barely glanced inside the vehicle. If they'd done so, they might have questioned why a skinny young Hispanic kid, barely out of his teens, was wearing an official FBI shirt.

But they didn't, and we cleared the compound easily.

The hardest part came next.

I called Carlton.

Communication Services put me through to him almost immediately, but when he came on the line, he sounded irritated.

"We're still on lockdown, Titus."

"I wasn't calling to check on your status."

"If you're calling about additional intel, there's not much of that either. The only thing I can tell you is that Katherine's office has identified the second shooter. He's—"

"Felipe Arcos. I know."

"Yeah, that's the guy. How did you know that?"

"That's why I'm calling."

I heard him take a deep breath. "I'm listening."

"Ben Mitchell and I are with Mr. Arcos right now, and the thing is, we need a quiet place away from the crowds where the three of us can have a nice little chat."

Carlton didn't respond for several seconds, and when he did, I had to hold the phone away from my ear.

"Have you lost your mind?"

"That's always up for debate. Listen, Douglas. I believe there's a connection between the shooter at the Navy Yard and what we discussed a few days ago. For obvious reasons, I can't go into those details right now."

I saw Mitchell glance at me in the rearview mirror. From the look on his face, I thought he might be questioning my sanity as well.

Carlton said, "Well, in that case, Titus, what you're doing is perfectly acceptable, and I'm sure the feds will see it that way and not haul you off in handcuffs."

"I'm not unaware this sounds crazy, Douglas, but bear with me. I'll give you a fuller explanation later, but right now, the most pressing issue is to find a location where we can sort everything out."

I heard a rhythmic tapping noise, and I knew Carlton must be drumming on his desk with his Century Cross pen, the gold one he always carried with him, the one engraved with the words "special edition" on it.

I felt sure the irritating sound meant he was considering my request, so I tried to ignore it. A few seconds later, he said, "Head out toward Arlington, and I'll call you back in five minutes."

When I hung up, I told Mitchell to get on the Beltway and take the Arlington exit. I wasn't about to tell him anything else until we were alone. Even though Felipe didn't seem to have more than a rudimentary grasp of the English language, I decided not to take any chances.

As promised, Carlton called me back within five minutes. However, he asked to speak to Mitchell instead of me.

I wasn't sure what that meant.

♦♦♦♦

As I listened to Mitchell's side of the conversation, I paid close attention to his responses and tried to get a clue as to what Carlton might be telling him. All I heard were one-word answers and a bunch of "uh-huhs" strung together.

His facial expression also left me clueless.

Once Mitchell had hung up, he handed me back the phone without saying a word.

"What gives? Where are we headed?"

"He told me not to tell you anything until we got there."

"Did he give you a reason for that nonsense?"

Mitchell laughed. "He said you probably wouldn't agree with the location."

There were times when Carlton tried to control his operatives by means of psychological games, and I wondered if this was one of those times.

On the other hand, Carlton could be so furious with me for snatching the shooter out from under the feds' noses, he was about to turn me over to them.

I tried to get more intel from Mitchell. "What are your thoughts about where we're going?"

"The place sounds perfect to me, but it'll take us at least forty-five minutes to get there."

As Mitchell merged onto I-66, I calculated where we might be in forty-five minutes.

My thoughts were suddenly interrupted by Felipe announcing he was hungry. *"Tengo hambre."*

Before I could say anything, Mitchell replied in Spanish. "Well, tough, kid. We don't provide meals on this tour."

Whether Mitchell wasn't in the mood to coddle a shooter, or he'd decided to use his bad cop routine on Felipe, I wasn't sure.

At any rate, I opted for the good cop role. "Hey, the guy's hungry. Let's stop somewhere and get him something to eat."

Mitchell shrugged and took the next exit off the freeway. A few miles down the road, I spotted a truck stop, and he pulled in.

As I waited in the car with Felipe, Mitchell went inside to grab some burgers.

When I began assessing our surroundings, the synapses suddenly fired and the cerebral cortex went into overdrive. Something about the place looked familiar, and I remembered purchasing gas at the same truck stop several years ago. It was around Thanksgiving, and I'd just come in from a run into Pakistan.

Now, I knew exactly where Carlton was taking us.

♦♦♦♦

When Mitchell returned, I told him I needed to make a phone call and left him in the car with Felipe.

After walking a short distance away, I leaned against the bumper of an older model Buick and called Carlton's personal cell phone. It was a number I seldom used, except in an emergency.

The phone rang four times before he finally answered it.

"Titus?"

"Yeah, it's me."

"So you worked it out?"

"You're sending us out to The Meadows, aren't you?"

"It was the only place that made sense."

The Meadows, as Carlton always referred to it, was his ten-acre farm outside of Fairfax, Virginia. It was located about fifty miles from Langley.

After he'd gone to work for the Agency, he'd purchased the property for his wife Gladys when she'd refused to live anywhere in the D.C. area. At the same time, he'd also bought a townhouse near Langley to use when an operation was running hot, and he had to be on call.

However, after Gladys had suddenly passed away of a heart attack, Carlton had moved into the townhouse permanently.

He'd never sold the house in Fairfax, but, as far as I knew, he seldom spent a night there, leaving its upkeep in the hands of his live-in housekeeper and her husband.

Once a year, usually at Thanksgiving, he threw a big bash at his country estate, inviting Agency personnel, as well as a few academic types from Georgetown University.

I'd been on his guest list a few times, and although I hadn't especially cared for the company, I'd always enjoyed the food.

I'd also visited The Meadows on one other occasion for an entirely different reason.

I said, "No, Douglas. The Meadows makes absolutely no sense. You need to find me a safe house, and, preferably, it needs to be one the feds can't connect with you. Otherwise, when they realize I was the person who grabbed the shooter, you'll be forced to take an early retirement."

"What makes you think they'll connect you with Felipe Arcos?'

"There were CCTV cameras all over that place, and I ran into Frank Benson before I spotted Felipe. It was because of Frank I managed to get into the compound in the first place."

This revelation didn't seem to faze him.

"All the more reason for you to get out to The Meadows and question the guy as quickly as possible. Once you get that done, I'll make arrangements for Homeland Security to take custody of him."

I could tell there was no talking him out of it, so I told him I'd call him back once I'd finished interrogating Felipe.

When I got back inside the Suburban, Mitchell handed me a large drink cup.

"They didn't have any lemonade, so I just got you some ice water and a ton of lemon slices."

"Thanks, I can improvise."

"Isn't that what you've been doing all day?"

♦♦♦♦

The Meadows was located off Fairfax County Parkway, about ten miles southwest of Fairfax and a mile from Piney Branch Creek.

The first time I'd seen the property had been back when Gladys, was still alive. It was in the summertime, around this same time of year, and even now I could remember how unassuming the house had looked when I'd first seen it from the access road.

The view had been spectacular as I'd driven up to the house with the sunlight breaking through the canopy of foliage. However, as I'd pulled into the circle drive in front of the two-storey brick monstrosity, I'd remembered Gladys' phone call and the way she'd described the place to me when she'd invited me out for a visit.

"Come out to my magnificent house at The Meadows," she'd said. "We'd love to have a visit from you."

When I'd arrived on that summer morning, the house had hardly appeared magnificent to me.

Big, yes.

Imposing, yes.

But hardly magnificent.

Nevertheless, once inside, magnificent had been the perfect word to describe it.

Each of the rooms, from the living area to the den to the study, was oversized and lavishly furnished, and the tall ceilings and dark draperies gave the place a kind of manor house feel. Carlton's study, with its dark wooden accents and elaborate stone fireplace, contributed to this old world look.

When I'd arrived in Carlton's study, he'd been seated behind a massive desk with a wall of bookshelves at his back. To his right, a set of French doors led out to the patio, and, on his left, in front of the stone fireplace, was a small seating area.

He hadn't been expecting me, so when he noticed me standing in the doorway, he looked surprised—and also very angry.

"What are you doing here?" he demanded.

I'd never seen him look so disheveled.

He was wearing a dark green, button-down cardigan, with a white shirt and a pair of dark, ill-fitting slacks. There were stains across the front of his white shirt.

"I'm here to let you off the hook," I said.

He stared at me with impassive eyes, revealing nothing.

I continued, "None of it was your fault. Baker shouldn't have gone in there. He should have called the whole thing off."

He suddenly pushed his chair away from his desk and stood to his feet."Did Gladys call you? Is that why you're here?"

"Yes on both counts."

He shook his head. "That wasn't necessary. I'm just taking a few days off."

"It's been two weeks."

He walked over to the French doors and looked out towards the pool.

"She thinks I'm depressed, but I'm not."

"Good," I said, joining him at the French doors. "I'm glad to hear it. Stanley Baker wasn't a very nice man, and he wasn't someone to lose any sleep over."

He turned towards me, his bald head shiny with sweat. "Why would you say something like that?"

"Stanley was arrogant and insufferable."

"I could say the same thing about several people."

He walked back over to his desk and stood there for a few seconds, staring down at a stack of papers.

Without looking up, he added, "Even you."

"You're probably right about that, but I wouldn't have put the whole team in jeopardy when my asset didn't show up."

He jerked his head around. "I was the one who gave Stanley the go-ahead. I was his handler. That was my call."

"No, Douglas. It wasn't your call. I was there. You gave him permission, but, ultimately, you said it was up to him to decide whether to go in or not. His death was his own fault. It wasn't yours. None of the team blames you for what happened to him."

He sat down in his leather desk chair again. "I doubt your opinion matters much to the wife and kids he left behind."

"If you're trying to convince me you're not depressed, you're doing a lousy job of it."

He pointed his finger at me. "Are you forgetting something? In addition to losing Stan, the entire mission was a failure."

"Listen, Douglas, I'll tell you something a very wise man once said to me after a blown operation."

"I don't want to hear this."

"Just because there's been a mission failure doesn't mean the mission's a failure. Every disaster holds the key to the next successful operation."

His dead eyes came alive with anger. "You can go now."

As I walked out the front door, I told Gladys I wasn't sure my visit had done her husband any good.

Whether that was true or not, Carlton had come back to work the next day.

Neither one of us had ever mentioned that visit again.

Ever.

# Chapter 4

The moment Mitchell pulled into the circle drive at The Meadows, I thought I heard Felipe say, "*Magnífico*."

When I asked him to repeat what he'd said, he shook his head and denied he'd said anything at all. Maybe that was true. I hadn't had much sleep in the last twenty-four hours, and I was beginning to feel a little punchy.

After Mitchell had shut off the engine, he gestured toward the house. "Does this place have some kind of basement dungeon where we can question this scumbag?"

Felipe didn't react to Mitchell's remark, giving me even more reason to believe the shooter wasn't that fluent in English.

But, if that were true, why did he claim to be a student at the University of Arkansas? Didn't the school require some kind of English language skills in order to be enrolled in their institution?

I decided I'd ask him that question when I interrogated him in the basement dungeon.

Before I had a chance to respond to Mitchell's question, Arkady Orlov opened the front door of the house and stepped outside.

I realized just the sight of him might prompt Felipe to start giving up his secrets.

Arkady had been the Soviet Union's 1988 gold medalist in weight lifting. He and his wife, Millie, were permanent residents of The Meadows and served as its caretakers for the absent Carlton.

The day after Arkady had won his medal in Seoul, he'd entered the American Embassy and formally declared his desire to defect to the United States. One of Arkady's escorts back to the States from Seoul had been Millie Durkin, a Level 2 Agency employee. She and Arkady were married six months after his arrival in America.

Because Millie had been Gladys' roommate in college, Arkady and Millie had been frequent guests at The Meadows, and a few weeks after Gladys' death, Carlton had asked the couple to come and live at The Meadows permanently and become its caretakers.

Even though both of them had responsibilities at The Meadows, Arkady and Millie continued to do contract work for the Agency—Arkady as a Russian translator and Millie as a consultant on Korean politics.

This turned out to be a perfect arrangement for everyone, especially Carlton, who didn't have to worry about keeping his own employment a secret from them, nor did he have to hire a vetted caterer whenever he wanted to entertain Agency personnel.

Arkady was a large man, all of it muscle, and when he jerked open the passenger's side door to let me out, I was surprised the door hadn't come off in his hand.

"Welcome. Welcome," he said in heavily accented English. "We've been expecting you. Come inside."

When Arkady held the front door open for Felipe, he hesitated, eyeing the giant suspiciously. Mitchell, who was standing behind Felipe, shoved the shooter inside the foyer.

Ignoring Mitchell's behavior, Arkady continued playing the role of the gracious host. "Is there anything I can get for you? Something to eat? Perhaps a cold beverage?"

I declined his offer. "We're fine, Arkady. I just need to borrow the study for a few hours, and then we'll be out of your hair."

He pointed off to his right. "Help yourself."

As Mitchell took Felipe by the arm and pushed him down the hallway, Arkady added, "I almost forgot. When Douglas called, he had Millie lay out a few things for your visit. She left them on the table by the fireplace."

I thanked Arkady and followed Mitchell inside Carlton's study.

After locking the door behind me, I immediately walked over to the fireplace. On the table, were a couple of zip ties, a roll of duct tape, some white cord, and several bottles of water.

I knew Mitchell would be disappointed to learn Millie had forgotten to bring up the implements from the basement dungeon.

♦♦♦♦

I tossed the zip ties over to Mitchell and told him to handcuff Felipe. By the smile on Mitchell's face, I could tell he was looking forward to putting the restraints on the guy.

However, that feeling was not reciprocated.

Once Felipe realized what was happening, he began protesting, and I ended up slapping several strips of duct tape across his mouth.

Felipe managed to make some disparaging remarks about me before I silenced him. Among other things, he pointed out I'd betrayed his trust.

Whether that was true or not, it hardly mattered to me.

All that mattered was where this thing was headed now.

Once Mitchell had secured Felipe's legs to the chair, I left the shooter to stew in his own juices for awhile and ushered Mitchell out the French doors and onto the patio.

As I shut the door behind me, Mitchell said, "Has the Oklahoma sun fried your brain or do you really know what you're doing?"

"I know what I'm doing."

Mitchell gestured toward the French doors.

"Are you aware Felipe and his buddy shot up a bunch of people this morning? If you'd seen the body of that kid they killed, then maybe you wouldn't have been so quick to get him out of there."

"Is that right?"

"Yeah, that's right. If it were up to me, I would have turned him over to one of the SWAT teams and let those cops administer a little pre-justice before questioning him. That's the kind of treatment he deserves; not this kumbaya stuff you're giving him."

"While that may be true, I don't ever recommend those tactics. More importantly, those cops wouldn't have asked Felipe the right questions. As to the justice he deserves, he'll get it eventually. I'm sure of that."

Mitchell plopped himself down in a patio chair. "Yeah, but that's years away. Justice is sweeter when it's delivered on day one."

I wondered if those were Mitchell's own thoughts or if he were simply repeating something he'd heard his father say.

After what I'd observed of Mitchell's behavior in Caracas, I thought it might be the former instead of the latter.

I pulled a chair away from the patio table and angled it so I could keep my eye on Felipe.

"So, you weren't just mouthing the bad cop script back there? You'd really like to take a few swings at our shooter right now?"

He stared at me for a second. "Look, Titus. I don't need another lecture from you about getting involved with the players." He gestured toward the study. "As you can plainly see, I'm not in there beating Felipe to a bloody pulp, am I?"

There were times when Mitchell let his emotions get the best of him. It was something I'd occasionally seen on our run into Caracas for Operation Clear Signal.

"I guess that proves you've learned your lesson after Clear Signal," I said.

"So now you're bringing up Clear Signal? What happened to your promise never to mention it again?"

"I don't believe I ever made that promise."

♦♦♦♦

Operation Clear Signal had come to an unsatisfactory conclusion in a safe house in Caracas the moment Ahmed Al-Amin, the Hezbollah assassin, had been killed.

I hadn't been the man behind the trigger, nor had Mitchell, but with the possible exception of Carlton, no one at the Agency knew that.

Officially, I was listed as Ahmed's executioner in the files stored in the Agency's archives.

However, the person who had sent Ahmed Al-Amin off to his hellish fate had been Roberto Montilla, a high-ranking official in the

Venezuelan government.

Roberto Montilla hadn't shot the assassin in self-defense, nor had he killed Ahmed because the man had murdered hundreds of people on behalf of the Iranian government.

Instead, Roberto had secretly entered the safe house—where I'd been preparing to interrogate Ahmed—and shot the Jihadi terrorist multiple times in the chest because Ahmed had killed his only son, Ernesto.

Roberto had learned the details of Ernesto's death after the Agency had made arrangements for Mitchell and me to interrogate him away from his family. Once we'd told Roberto what we knew of Ernesto's murder, he'd been more than willing to tell us why he thought Hezbollah had hired Ahmed Al-Amin to come after him.

He'd confirmed what Carlton and I had suspected all along—Hezbollah had wanted Roberto Montilla dead because of what he knew.

Roberto had told us he'd been working with Hezbollah to facilitate the construction of a couple of warehouses for a Syrian export business in Venezuela. He said he'd changed his mind after realizing the two warehouses weren't being built to store baubles and beads.

Instead, he'd discovered the storage facilities would be used to house canisters of sarin gas. Such canisters had once been part of Syria's stockpile of chemical weapons, but instead of being destroyed, they'd been turned over to Hezbollah in direct violation of the agreement Syria had made with the U.S. to get rid of its chemical weapons.

As disturbing as that was, Roberto also said Hezbollah was making plans to use the sarin gas on American cities.

Although the details had been sketchy, Roberto's disclosure had caused quite a stir back in the Ops Center. In fact, Roberto's admission had almost caused my field officer, Olivia McConnell, to take her eyes off the goal of Operation Clear Signal; namely, the capture of Ahmed Al-Amin.

Because Roberto had told us the weapons were being stored aboard ships and weren't due to arrive in Venezuela until much later,

I hadn't been as concerned about Hezbollah's plans to use the chemical weapons as I had been about my own plans to lure Ahmed to a place where I could grab him without alerting the Venezuelan authorities.

Those plans had finally come to fruition when Roberto had called Ahmed and invited him to a meeting. Once that phone call had ended, Olivia had given Mitchell the responsibility of getting Roberto out of the house, while I stayed behind to make the acquaintance of Ahmed.

Operation Clear Signal had gone south the moment Mitchell and Roberto had walked out of the safe house.

According to Mitchell, as soon as he and Roberto had driven away from the safe house, Roberto had asked him to make a stop along the way. When that occurred, Roberto had knocked him out, stolen the car, along with his gun, and returned to the safe house, where he'd placed several bullet holes in the torso of Ahmed Al-Amin.

The only part of Mitchell's story I could verify was the part about Ahmed being killed by Roberto.

I'd been there; I'd seen it happen.

As to the rest, it could have happened that way.

But, I had my doubts.

Despite my misgivings, I'd taken the blame—or the glory—for killing Ahmed.

I did this because I'd already made an agreement with Roberto to help him relocate his family to Argentina in exchange for his help in capturing Ahmed.

If I hadn't admitted to killing Ahmed, the DDO wouldn't have allowed Roberto to leave Venezuela, and I knew I couldn't let that happen, because I knew Hezbollah would come after him again.

Admittedly, Roberto's safety hadn't been the only reason I'd put my name down as Ahmed's killer.

I'd also falsified the record because I knew Olivia McConnell.

I knew she wasn't a very nice person, and I knew she would use her position at the Agency to have Mitchell demoted to an analyst for the rest of his career because of his failure to stop Roberto from killing Ahmed.

Moments after Roberto had killed Ahmed, the CIA's chief of

station in Venezuela, Sam Wylie, had shown up, and the two of us, along with Mitchell, had conspired together to adopt the story we'd eventually told Olivia and our handlers back at the Ops Center.

The short version—the one everybody totally bought—was that I had shot Ahmed when he'd gone for his gun and neither Mitchell nor Roberto had been present at the time.

Later, I became convinced Mitchell had lied to me about what had actually happened after he and Roberto had left the safe house that morning.

Whether he'd deliberately helped Roberto get back to the safe house in order to shoot Ahmed, I wasn't sure.

What I did know was that Mitchell's emotions had gotten the best of him, and I was pretty sure Roberto had exploited Mitchell's emotions to carry out his revenge on Ahmed.

Now, as I sat on the patio and considered Mitchell's attitude toward Felipe Arcos, I wondered if his present feelings weren't further proof he'd been complicit in helping Roberto Montilla carry out his own form of justice on Ahmed Al-Amin.

However, knowing what might be at stake in the days ahead, I decided I couldn't let that happen to Felipe.

♦♦♦♦

When Mitchell didn't respond to my statement, I had to assume he was trying to remember whether or not I'd actually promised him I wouldn't bring up Clear Signal again.

For my part, I was betting it was only a case of wishful thinking on his part.

"Yeah, okay," he finally said. "Maybe you never made me that promise."

"Look, Ben, we have to talk about Clear Signal because I believe what went down at the Navy Yard today is connected to what Roberto told us back at the safe house in Caracas."

"How could they be connected?"

"Think about what Roberto told us. He said Hezbollah was recruiting students like Ernesto Montilla, and then paying their educational expenses so they could attend college here in the States. In effect, he said Hezbollah was building a network of terrorists on college campuses. Do you remember that?"

"Of course I remember. He said they plan to use those recruits to bring the chemical weapons into the U.S."

"Exactly."

I waited a second to see if he might put it all together himself.

Instead he asked, "How does their agenda relate to the shooters at the Navy Yard?"

I gave him another hint. "Douglas said Reyes Valario, the dead guy, was here on a student visa, and Felipe told me both of them were enrolled at the University of Arkansas."

Mitchell sat back in his chair. "Are you kidding me? That's all you've got? You kidnapped Felipe out from under the feds' noses and risked our careers because both the shooters happened to be college students from Latin America?"

"No, that's not all. As usual, you've jumped to a conclusion without having all the facts."

"Is that right? Well, my father told me the exact same thing just a few hours ago. And I might as well tell you, when the Senator presented me with the facts, I still came to the same conclusion."

I remembered Carlton had told me Mitchell had been in D.C. when the shooting occurred at the Navy Yard. If he'd been spending time with the Senator, then I certainly understood why he might want to take out his frustrations on Felipe.

"Were you enjoying some quality time with your father?"

He gave a short laugh. "Enjoyment is not a word I'd use to describe the breakfast my father and I had together this morning."

"Did the Senator give you a hard time?"

He nodded. "Somehow, he'd heard the DDO had offered me a position as an analyst, and I'd turned it down so I could remain in Operations. Naturally, he still tried to convince me to reconsider."

"I'm guessing he didn't convince you."

He shook his head. "No, and before I left his office, I made sure he knew I was on my way over to Langley to be briefed on a new assignment. It was gratifying to see how much that information galled him."

"What's the new assignment?"

"I never made it back to Langley to find out. Salazar called me a few minutes after I left the Senator's office and told me to get over to the Command Center and hook up with Homeland Security."

"Did Cartel Carlos give you any hints about your new assignment?"

"No, but . . ." A look of understanding suddenly appeared on his face. "Does my new assignment have anything to do with why you're back at Langley?"

"It does."

"Did the DDO reinstate you?"

"He did."

"Did Carlton give you some new intel about Clear Signal?"

"He did."

"Does this new intel have anything to do with students running around Washington shooting people?"

"It does."

## Chapter 5

Douglas Carlton had called to tell me about the new intel less than a week after my arrival back in Norman. His phone call had interrupted an intimate dinner with a very beautiful woman.

"I'm calling about The Caracas Document."

That had been it.

No greeting.

No "how are you?"

Nothing.

I didn't have a clue as to what The Caracas Document was, but I wasn't about to let him know that. Had I been alone, I might have tried harder to make a connection, but when he'd called, I had been preoccupied by the sight of Detective Nikki Saxon sitting across from me.

When I finally realized he was calling about Agency business, I quickly excused myself from the table and walked out on the patio.

"What about The Caracas Document?" I asked.

"I found it very troubling. Didn't it disturb you when you read it?"

"Yes. Yes, it did."

Just then, Stormy, my yellow lab, came over and dropped an orange tennis ball at my feet, and I picked it up and threw it out towards the lake located on my property. Afterward, I sat down in one of the Adirondack chairs on the patio and tried to concentrate on what Carlton was talking about.

He said, "I'm not as concerned about Roberto Montilla's

statements not matching up with the document, as I am by what he's saying in the document itself."

Finally, I realized The Caracas Document he was referencing must have been the name the Agency analysts had given to the statement Roberto had typed out for me at the safe house in Caracas.

Even though my interrogation of Roberto had been recorded, I'd given him a laptop and asked him to type out everything his Hezbollah contact, Rehman Zaidi, had told him.

Zaidi, who was a member of Hezbollah's inner circle, had told him a lot.

He'd bragged about his relationship with the Iranian regime, and he'd claimed to know all about their plans to attack the U.S. with the chemical weapons Hezbollah had acquired.

When I'd given Roberto the laptop, he hadn't put up much of a protest, and the last night at the safe house, he'd even stayed up late editing his document.

The next morning, he'd mentioned he'd added a few more details to his account, but since I'd been preparing for Ahmed's visit, I hadn't bothered reading a word of what he'd written the night before.

In the rush of wrapping up the operation, I'd given the laptop to Wylie, who'd promised to send the encrypted file to the Ops Center for analysis.

Evidently, according to Carlton's statement, once the analysts had transcribed the tapes of Roberto's interrogation and compared them with what he'd said in the written document, they'd discovered some discrepancies.

I decided it was time to confess I hadn't actually read The Caracas Document.

"Full disclosure, Douglas. I never did get around to reading Roberto's written record."

"You didn't read it?"

He sighed. It was a deep breathy sigh, and I felt certain he'd wanted me to hear it.

"I admit that surprises me, Titus. You've always been so insistent on knowing the minutiae of an operation."

"Events got a little crazy at the safe house towards the end."

"Oh, you mean when Ahmed was killed?"

"Yeah, that."

"Then maybe your failure to read the document is understandable. Sometimes things get overlooked when situations go sideways during an operation. Of course, there was also that equipment failure when the Ops Center didn't get an audio recording of what went down when Ahmed got shot."

"That was regrettable."

"It was."

"I appreciate your understanding, Douglas."

"I do understand, Titus. Make no mistake about that."

At that moment, I knew Carlton wasn't just talking about my failure to read The Caracas Document. Somehow, he'd figured out I hadn't been the one to pull the trigger in the Ahmed shooting.

He knew I'd lied to him about the operation.

Stormy arrived back on the patio clutching the orange tennis ball in his mouth. He was soaking wet, and he gave me an accusatory look, as if he knew I'd deliberately thrown the ball in the lake.

Now, I regretted my actions and wondered how I could make it up to him.

I felt inside my pocket and pulled out a treat.

Once Stormy saw it, he quickly forgave me.

I doubted Carlton would do the same, with or without a treat.

♦♦♦♦

Mitchell listened carefully as I told him about the new intel I'd received from Carlton, but every once in awhile, I saw him glance over at the French doors just to make sure Felipe hadn't managed to free himself from his restraints.

Although I told Mitchell about The Caracas Document, I didn't mention I was having dinner with Nikki Saxon the night Carlton had called me. No one at the Agency knew about Nikki, and I planned to keep it that way as long as possible.

After summarizing the discrepancies the analysts had uncovered in The Caracas Document, I said, "When Roberto told us Hezbollah was embedding Muslim extremists in cities across the United States, Roberto failed to say why they were doing this."

Mitchell shook his head. "I disagree. I distinctly remember Roberto saying the recruits had been trained in chemical weapons at that phony youth camp on Margarita Island, and Hezbollah was planning to use them to smuggle the canisters across the border and into the United States."

I nodded. "That's what he told us verbally, but then he added more details to that statement in the document itself. He said some of those recruits would be used to perform other tasks before the chemical weapons were used on the population."

"What did he mean by that?"

"He said a few of them would be asked to make dummy runs as passengers on airlines, while others would be told to probe security reactions when a city's power grid went down or when a bunch of people were killed in a movie theater. And then, in order to test law enforcement's potential reaction to the event itself, some would be asked to make the ultimate sacrifice before a major operation."

Mitchell thought about what I'd said. "You mean they'd be asked to give their lives in order to carry out a dress rehearsal?"

"That's what Roberto wrote in the document."

Mitchell glanced over at Carlton's study again.

"Is that what you think Felipe and his friend were doing at the Navy Yard this morning? They were there to martyr themselves at Hezbollah's request?"

"That's what I think."

He shook his head. "I can't believe—"

"Wait a minute, Ben. Before you disagree with me, hear me out. The other big discrepancy found in The Caracas Document was what Roberto told us about Hezbollah using chemical weapons on several key cities in the U.S. In the document, Roberto said they weren't targeting several cities. He said they had their sights on just one city. That city was Washington, D.C."

Mitchell thought about what I'd said for a moment, and then he slowly nodded his head. "Okay. I get it now. When you heard about the shooting at the Navy Yard this morning, you thought the two shooters were part of some advance team being used to gauge how law enforcement would react to a terrorist event around the Beltway."

I nodded. "You saw the massive response to the shooting incident this morning. There were hundreds of officers from Naval Security, the Metro Police, Capitol Police, FBI; not to mention all their SWAT teams, plus the helicopters and tactical teams on the rooftops. Didn't you notice how all of them were concentrated within a six-square block perimeter?"

He shrugged. "Yeah, I guess. Are you saying it was overkill?"

"I'm saying anyone watching the news feed this morning was given a lesson on what might happen if a couple of shooters showed up anywhere in the D.C. area."

Mitchell rubbed his forehead as if he had a massive headache. "You're right. The response teams this morning would have been sitting ducks if someone had decided to introduce sarin gas into that scene."

"And think about—"

Before I could finish my thought, my Agency phone vibrated, and when I saw the caller ID, I answered it immediately.

"They're looking for you," Carlton said.

"Already? They must have found my Range Rover."

"No. I took care of your vehicle. It's sitting over here in the Agency's west parking lot right now."

"Did they identify me because of the CCTV cameras in the area?"

As soon as I mentioned the cameras, Mitchell gave me a disgusted look and got to his feet.

"No. It was Frank Benson."

"Benson? He actually took some initiative? Good for him."

"I was told the agent who got you through the 9th Street gate phoned Frank when you didn't show up at the Command Center. She said you'd made some flimsy excuse to stay behind once your were inside the compound. Evidently, she also told Frank you weren't very friendly toward her."

I decided to ignore what Renee thought about my personality. It wasn't relevant, and besides, Carlton knew what she said couldn't possibly be true.

"How much time do we have?"

"You need to wrap things up there pretty quick. I'm bringing some friends of mine from DHS out to The Meadows in about two hours."

"Two hours? How can I possibly extract all this man's secrets in two hours?"

"Use your winsome personality."

♦♦♦♦

The moment I hung up, I told Mitchell the Department of Homeland Security would be arriving at The Meadows to take Felipe into custody and escort him back to Washington.

Mitchell, who'd been pacing back and forth in front of the patio table, looked over at me. "Are you sure they're not coming out here to take us into custody?"

"I'm sure."

"Weren't you also sure there were no CCTV cameras at the Navy Yard?"

"Right now, the only thing we need to be concerned about is how to get Felipe to talk to us before Carlton and his company arrive."

"Did I hear you say we've only got two hours to get that done?"

"That's right. Anything about Felipe jump out at you?"

On our run into Caracas together, I'd observed how good Mitchell had been at reading people, and while it had been disconcerting when he'd pointed things out about me, his ability had been useful when we'd interrogated Roberto Montilla.

He shook his head. "One thing's for sure. He doesn't seem to be grieving over his partner's death."

I walked over and stared at Felipe through the small glass panes in the French doors. He appeared to be extremely uncomfortable in the wingback chair where Mitchell had restrained him.

However, unlike most Jihadists I'd seen in similar situations, he looked defeated, and there was no fire in his eyes when he saw me staring at him.

I walked back over to Mitchell.

"There's not much fight in him. When you were at the Command Center with DHS, did you pick up anything about the other shooter?"

He shook his head. "Not much. They put me over in a corner of their trailer with a couple of FBI guys and told all of us to stay out of their way. The only thing I heard them say was that Valario had probably had some weapons training, and he was a good marksman."

I thought back to when I'd first seen Felipe with the rifle. "I'm not so sure that's true of him."

"Maybe it's time we took a look at the backpack he was carrying."

I nodded. "You're right. While I'd prefer one of the guys from the bomb squad examine it first, there might be something in there we could use to get Felipe to talk."

Both of us were quiet for a few seconds.

Finally I said, "Give me the keys to the Suburban. I'll go take a look at it."

Mitchell dangled the car keys in front of me and didn't say a word.

Apparently, he wasn't about to volunteer to handle the backpack himself.

Had he offered, I wouldn't have let him do it anyway.

He probably knew that.

That's what I told myself.

# Chapter 6

I took some precautions before opening up Felipe's backpack. First, I drove the SUV away from the house and parked it further down the road. Second, I made sure I had a clear pathway away from the vehicle, just in case I saw something inside the bag—something with a timing device attached to it—and I needed to make a quick run for it.

Although I hadn't jogged in years, I knew I could set a record in the 100-meter dash, especially if I were trying to outrun an exploding backpack.

Having done everything I could to protect Gladys' magnificent house and my fragile body, I placed the backpack in the drainage ditch beside the car and loosened the straps.

Seconds before lifting the flap, I voiced a short prayer.

It wasn't an instinctive act on my part, and, until recently, I'd never uttered a single prayer in my life.

However, while hiding out from the Iranian secret police in Tehran, I'd been forced to live for three months with some Iranian Christians. That experience had changed my life. Their faith and commitment to the teachings of Christ had sparked a feeling of discontentment in me and fueled my own desire to have the same sort of peace they exhibited.

Shortly before being smuggled out of Iran, I'd made my own decision to follow Christ, and the first prayer I'd ever prayed had been the words Javad, my host, had told me to repeat after him.

Now, my words were just as simple. *"God, I'd like to go on living, but if it's my time to go, please make it quick and easy."*

I lifted the flap and peered inside.

Seconds later, with one quick motion, I turned around and started to sprint away.

But then, I stopped and took another look inside the bag.

What I'd assumed were bricks of Semtex—a pliable plastic explosive—turned out to be several large bags of compressed heroin. Ultimately, though, what had caused me to take a second look inside the backpack had been something I hadn't seen there.

I hadn't seen a cell phone or a trigger device.

While it was entirely possible for someone to detonate Semtex using a different device, most terrorists used a cell phone to trigger the explosive material. There wasn't a cell phone inside the bag, nor had Felipe had one on him when I'd frisked him at the Navy Yard.

In addition to the missing cell phone, I'd also noticed items in the shooter's bag that didn't seem to belong there.

There were at least a dozen small bags of cookies, a box of crackers, some potato chips, and an assortment of oranges, apples, and bananas, plus several bottles of water.

I lifted one of the packs of heroin—wrapped in yellowed wax paper—out of the bag and looked it over. It probably weighed about a kilo. I quickly estimated the street value of the four packs of heroin at around a million dollars.

Had I been wrong about the shooters? Was the Navy Yard shooting just another drug deal gone bad?

My gut said no, and my gut premonition—as Carlton liked to call it—was seldom wrong.

It wasn't always right either.

♦♦♦♦

I drove back up to the house, and, as I entered the foyer, I found Mitchell just coming out of Carlton's study.

I nodded towards the door. "Everything okay in there?"

"Everything's fine. I told Arkady to keep an eye on Felipe while I came out to check on you."

He gestured toward the backpack in my hand. "I see you survived."

"It was a harrowing experience, but I made it through." I tossed the backpack over to him. "Take a look inside."

He sat down on a wooden bench in the entryway and placed the bag on the floor between his legs.

He looked up at me after examining its contents, and I could tell he was beginning to question whether my suppositions about the two shooters were correct.

"Looks like it's time for a little reassessment."

"No. It's time we found out why a Hezbollah recruit on a suicide mission had a million dollars worth of drugs in his possession."

"So you're still sticking with your theory? You think Felipe and his partner were sent here by Hezbollah to scout out the venue before the main event?"

I nodded. "I still believe they're connected to Hezbollah, but I have to admit I'm not exactly sure how those drugs fit into their agenda. Remember though, the Zeta drug cartel in Mexico has an ongoing relationship with Hezbollah in Syria, and it was the cartel who helped Ahmed Al-Amin cross the Texas border and enter the U.S. a few weeks ago."

Mitchell handed me the backpack. "The only way to know for sure is to get Felipe to talk, but when I was in there just now, he wouldn't say a word to me."

I wanted to point out he hadn't exactly exhibited a caring attitude toward the guy, but instead, I opened up the backpack and pulled out a box of crackers.

"I think we can use this as an incentive to get him to talk to us."

"Crackers?"

"What's the one sentence Felipe uttered during our forty-five minute drive over here?"

Mitchell thought for a second. *"Tengo hambre."*

"Correct. He said he was hungry. I'm guessing either this guy loves to eat or he's one of those hungry-all-the-time kind of people. Maybe he could be induced to talk if we bribe him with some food."

Mitchell looked skeptical and grabbed the crackers out of my hand. "You think we'll get him to crack if we give him some . . . crackers?"

He chuckled at his own joke.

"As amusing as that was, Ben, I really don't think it's going to take much to get Felipe to talk."

Mitchell glanced down at his watch. "Let's hope you're right. Carlton and his entourage will be here in less than ninety minutes."

♦♦♦♦

Mitchell returned to the study and sent Arkady out to the foyer so I could make arrangements with him for a food delivery from Millie's kitchen.

Arkady didn't question me about my odd request, nor did he seem the least bit curious as to why Felipe, who was still wearing the FBI shirt, was tied down in an armchair in Carlton's study. His attitude made me wonder how often Carlton had used The Meadows for an off-the-books enterprise.

Although I doubted Felipe was a practicing Muslim, as Arkady headed out to the kitchen to confer with Millie, I told him, "Be sure and leave off the pork."

Arkady waved his hand at me without looking back and disappeared down the hallway.

Meanwhile, I grabbed Felipe's backpack and reentered the study.

When Felipe saw the bag in my hand, his eyes widened, and the duct tape around his mouth appeared to move a little, as if he might be trying to smile.

I realized it was the first time Felipe had seen the backpack since I'd ordered him to drop it at the entrance to Building 172. Once that had happened, he'd probably thought he'd never see the bag or its contents again.

Now, for the first time since grabbing him, I detected a measure of hope on his face.

I motioned for Mitchell to join me at the small square gaming table in a corner of the room. The tabletop consisted of a solid wooden chess board, and even though there appeared to be a game in progress, I'd never heard Carlton talk about playing chess before.

He was excellent at recognizing patterns, thinking ahead, and analyzing weaknesses, so it didn't surprise me he was also a chess player.

After sweeping the chess pieces into the drawers at the sides of the table, I set the backpack on top and started pulling out the drugs. Mitchell followed my lead, and we made a big deal about finding the drugs inside and discussing what the value of the heroin might be on the streets of D.C.

Although our exchange was in English, I felt sure Felipe was picking up the gist of what we were saying.

After putting on this little show for several minutes, I walked over and ripped the duct tape from Felipe's mouth, demanding he tell us about the drugs.

He moved his jaw up and down a few times, as if wanting to make sure everything was still working properly. After that, he said he was thirsty.

I twisted the cap off a bottle of water and allowed him to drink about half of it before removing it from his lips and putting it back down on the table.

"What were you planning to do with the drugs at the Navy Yard?"

He held his handcuffed wrists out in front of him and said, "Take these off, and I'll tell you everything."

I didn't believe him, but I took the fact he was trying to bargain with me as a good sign.

"Explain what you and your friend were doing at the Navy Yard this morning. Once you do that, I'll remove your restraints. That's the way this works, not the other way around."

He frowned. "Reyes was not my friend."

"No? Then why were you with him this morning?"

He nodded his head in the direction of the table, where four packets of heroin, stacked two across, were on display in front of Mitchell.

"I have a solid buyer for those," he said. "Take me to him, and I'll split the money with you."

After seeing the look on Felipe's face when he'd spotted the backpack, I wasn't surprised he was trying to work out a deal with me now.

I shook my head. "Tell me about your relationship with Reyes. What were you doing at the Navy Yard? Why did you shoot all those people?"

There was a knock on the door, and Mitchell quickly tossed the heroin inside the backpack before Arkady walked in the room.

The smell of onions wafted in after him, and I spotted slabs of sizzling steaks, fried potatoes, and onion rings on the large tray he was carrying.

After placing the tray on the gaming table, Arkady looked over at Felipe. "Shall I bring in a plate for him?"

Mitchell, who was already devouring an onion ring, immediately spoke up. "That won't be necessary."

There was no mistaking the look of disappointment on Felipe's face. As soon as Arkady had left the room, I pulled up a chair, and sat down across from him.

"There's a lot of good food over there, Felipe, and I don't mind sharing it with you. But first, you'll have to tell me what you and your partner were doing at the Navy Yard this morning."

His eyes narrowed. "I told you. Reyes was not my partner."

"You said Reyes was not your friend. You didn't say Reyes was not your partner."

Felipe raised his voice. "He wasn't my partner or my friend. He wasn't anything to me. Don't you get that? I barely knew him."

"Okay, so you barely knew him. If that's true, then why were you at the Navy Yard with him this morning?"

This was it. My interrogation of Felipe had reached critical mass.

Either Felipe was about to clam up, or he was about to start giving us some answers.

I was betting on the latter.

## Chapter 7

Felipe didn't answer my question. Instead, he turned away from me and stared out the window.

Just when I'd made up my mind to try a different approach with him, he turned around and said, "I was with Reyes this morning because his roommate, Alejandro, couldn't make the trip with him. He said Alejandro was in the hospital with a ruptured appendix."

Although I was eager to learn more about the absent Alejandro, I didn't want him to know that, so I asked him again, "If you barely knew Reyes, what were you doing in D.C. with him?"

Felipe glanced over at Mitchell.

I was betting it was the food commanding his attention and not Mitchell, and I decided to put that theory to the test. "Look, Felipe, tell me about your relationship with Reyes, and I'll untie your hands and let you eat steak until it makes you sick."

He glanced down at his shackled wrists for a moment, and then he looked up at me and said, "Reyes came over to my place three days ago. He said he wanted to buy some reefers from me, but after we'd made the transaction, he asked if I'd be interested in making a delivery to the East Coast with him. After he told me how much he'd pay me, I said yes, and that's when he went out to his car and brought in the backpack."

When Felipe paused, I jumped in. "Had you met Reyes before he showed up at your place?"

"He was at my apartment with some other guys once, but I didn't actually talked to him then. One of the other students made the purchase. After that, whenever I saw him around campus, he always spoke to me."

"So I'm guessing he knew you as the local campus drug connection?"

Felipe nodded. "I guess so."

Mitchell asked, "Reyes was a drug dealer then? That's what he was doing at the Navy Yard this morning?"

"Reyes isn't . . . wasn't a drug dealer. He said he'd agreed to help a friend in Mexico get the heroin to a buyer on the East Coast."

"Was this buyer at the Washington Navy Yard?" I asked.

"No. I'd never heard of that place until this morning when Reyes drove us over there. He told me the buyer lived in the Royal Courts Apartments on 4th Street, but instead of turning in at the apartment complex, he turned in the opposite direction and drove us onto that military base. I couldn't believe what he doing because I could see there were guards at the gate, and I knew they might search the car and find the drugs."

"He drove you right up to the gate?"

He shook his head. "No, instead of driving up to the gate, he pulled off onto the shoulder before we got there. When the guards started yelling at him, he got out of the car, opened up the trunk, and pulled out the backpack. That's when he took out the two rifles."

Felipe bowed his head. When he looked up again, he said, "I had no idea the guns were even in there. He handed me one and told me to follow him or I'd end up dead. When he grabbed the backpack, I followed him. What else could I do?"

"You could have said no," Mitchell said."You could have refused to go with him."

Felipe shook his head. "No, I couldn't. He would have shot me the way he did those guards."

Mitchell was out of his chair and up in Felipe's face within seconds. "You're responsible for the deaths of all those people today, whether you pulled that trigger or not."

I grabbed Mitchell's shoulder. "Back off."

He turned and walked away.

Whether role playing or not, Mitchell's bad cop routine bordered on perfection.

In contrast, I apologized to Felipe for Mitchell's behavior and offered him a drink of water.

After taking a swig, he handed the bottle back to me. "Since Reyes took the backpack out of the trunk to begin with, how did you end up with it?"

Felipe looked down at his wrists. "You promised to take these off if I told you about him."

"I'll do that as soon as you explain why you were the one carrying the backpack instead of Reyes."

He sighed and laid his head back against the chair for a few seconds. When he looked up again, his speech was hurried, as if he might want to get the whole thing over with quickly.

"After Reyes shot the guards, we ran over to the next building, where he herded everyone inside an office. There were two women, a young kid, and an old man in there. Reyes found a small closet inside the office and locked them all inside. I kept asking him why he was doing this, but all he'd say was that he was doing it for Allah. When I—"

"Allah? He said he was doing it for Allah?"

He nodded. "A few hours after we left Fayetteville, he told me he was a practicing Muslim. He had a prayer rug with him, and we had to stop several times so he could perform his prayers."

Mitchell asked, "Did he tell you why Allah wanted him to kill people?"

Felipe ignored Mitchell and spoke directly to me. "Once he shot the guards, he refused to tell me anything, and he kept threatening to shoot me if I didn't stop asking him questions. As soon as he put those people in the closet, he turned on a television set, and he got very excited when he saw all the policemen and ambulances arriving. That's when I decided I had to get out of there. I knew it wouldn't be long before the cops arrived and tried to rescue those people."

Felipe sounded breathless as he began reliving that moment. "Reyes had dropped the backpack when he'd entered the office, so when he turned his back to adjust the volume on the TV, I picked it up and ran out of the room. He followed me out in the hallway and shot at me a couple of times, but I ducked inside a stairwell."

He shook his head. "A few minutes later, I heard the two women screaming and some other shots being fired, so I guess he must have gone back inside the office and shot those people." His voice trailed off. "He shot them all, even the boy."

No one spoke for several seconds.

Finally, Mitchell said, "That's the reason the SWAT teams decided to go in. They heard shots being fired."

I asked Felipe, "When the SWAT teams arrived, how were you able to get away?"

"As soon as they entered the building, Reyes immediately came out of the office and began firing at them. I used the opportunity to escape through the fire exit door underneath the stairwell."

Mitchell sounded skeptical. "How were you able to make it all the way over to the other side of the Navy Yard without being caught?"

"I found an empty building and slipped inside it for awhile. I decided there had to be another way off the base, so I just started walking in the opposite direction of the front gate."

I nodded toward the backpack. "And the drugs? What were you planning to do with them?"

He looked surprised at my question. "Sell them, of course. I told you. I have a buyer. If you let me go, I'll split the profits with you."

I shook my head. "I don't believe Reyes had a buyer for the heroin. He was lying to you about that."

Tiny droplets of moisture appeared on Felipe's upper lip. He sounded desperate. "No, he wasn't lying to me. The guy called him several times on his cell phone. I have his number."

"What's the number?" I asked.

"I wrote it down."

"Where?" I asked. "I didn't find anything in your pockets. You didn't even have a cell phone on you."

"I wrote it down on a bag of potato chips. It's in the backpack. Give it to me."

I didn't give Felipe the backpack.

Instead, I dumped the contents on the floor at his feet, and Mitchell and I sifted through the stuff until we came across a snack-size yellow bag of potato chips.

Felipe said, "That's the one. See? There's the phone number. He's the buyer."

The writing was faint, but I could make out some numbers.

I handed the bag to Mitchell.

"That's a D.C. area code," he said.

I asked, "How did you manage to get this number from Reyes?"

"The day before yesterday, while I was waiting in the car for Reyes to come back from his midday prayers, I noticed his cell phone had been left on the front seat. He'd been talking to his contact before we stopped for lunch, so I took a look at the last number he'd called and wrote it down on the bag before he got back inside the car."

I asked, "What were you planning to do with the number?"

Felipe shrugged. "I considered it insurance, just in case Reyes decided to double cross me or wouldn't fork over the money he'd promised me."

Mitchell said, "Weren't you afraid Reyes would find the number when he decided to have a snack?"

Felipe shook his head. "He only ate healthy foods. Those apples and oranges in there belonged to him, and he didn't touch the other stuff."

I said, "Tell me about Reyes' friend, Alejandro, the one who got sick and couldn't make the trip."

"I never met him."

"Reyes never mentioned him?"

Felipe thought for a second. "He said the two of them went through school together in Caracas. He also said Alejandro was the person who'd invited him to check out the mosque where he was converted."

"So Alejandro is also a Muslim?"

"Yeah, I guess so."

There was a knock on the door. When Mitchell opened it, Arkady stuck his head in and motioned for me to join him in the hallway.

I stepped outside and closed the door behind me.

"Mr. Carlton just called. He'll be arriving in ten minutes."

"Thanks for the heads up."

When I turned to go back inside, Arkady grabbed my arm. I was sure his grip had bruised my arm.

"I don't think you understand, Titus. Mr. Carlton doesn't allow anyone to eat in his study."

I attempted to reassure him. "Okay, Arkady. Give me a minute, and then you can come in and clear away the dishes. Douglas doesn't have to know we broke his rules."

I should have known better.

♦♦♦♦

As soon as I went back inside the study, I told Mitchell I needed to make a phone call before Carlton's guests arrived, and he came over and helped me untie Felipe's restraints and take off his cuffs.

Once Felipe was on his feet, I handed him the plate of food Arkady had left for me and pointed him toward the patio. "Enjoy your food."

Mitchell took out his handgun and said, "Make the phone call. I've got this."

As soon as I closed the French doors behind them, I scooped up all the stuff I'd dumped out of Felipe's backpack and put it back inside.

Everything, but the yellow bag of potato chips.

A few seconds later, when Arkady came in to clear away the dishes, I walked over and handed him the bag of chips.

"Tell Millie to put this away for safekeeping. When I get hungry later, I'll come and get it."

He placed the bag on his tray and left the room without a word.

Once he was gone, I took out my phone and punched in Katherine's number.

Katherine Broward was one of the Agency's top intelligence analysts. I'd worked with her on several occasions, including Operation Clear Signal, and although we'd attempted to have a more-than-just-friends relationship several years ago, it had never gone anywhere.

She answered her phone the way she always did—by repeating her phone number.

"Hi, Katherine, it's Titus."

"They're looking for you."

"It's taken care of."

"What were you thinking?"

"According to Carlton, I wasn't."

"I'm inclined to agree with him."

"Please don't tell him that. He has way too much self-esteem as it is."

"You know, Titus, something tells me this isn't just a social call."

"As always, your analysis is right on target. So, here's the thing. I have a phone number, and I'd like you to run it for me."

"Off the books? Are you serious? That would be—"

"Strictly speaking, it won't be off the books."

"What's that supposed to mean?"

"It means someone will eventually ask you to check out the number anyway. What I want you to do is to run a preliminary data dig on it. Like right now. Do it as a personal favor to me for old times' sake."

As I waited for her to respond, I could hear Arkady speaking to someone in the hallway.

Katherine said, "Okay, this goes against my better judgment, but give me the number. "

I gave her the number I'd memorized from Felipe's yellow bag of chips and disconnected the call.

Seconds later, the door to the study suddenly swung open and Carlton walked in.

He was followed by four men dressed in suits.

All four were serious looking guys.

Well, counting Carlton, all five of them were serious looking guys.

# Chapter 8

Within a few seconds, Carlton assessed the situation and started issuing orders. First, he directed the men in suits, who were from the Department of Homeland Security, to take Felipe into custody.

The moment he gave that order, two of the suits went out on the patio and grabbed Felipe, placing handcuffs on him once again. As that was taking place, Carlton had me open up the backpack and show him its contents. The other two DHS guys also walked over to take a look inside.

When the younger of the two saw the heroin, he let out a high-pitched whistle, while the older guy uttered a curse word.

Carlton didn't say anything.

The older guy appeared to be in charge—Carlton called him Arnie—and he demanded I tell him where I'd stashed the AR-15.

When I told him it was out in the Suburban, and I offered to go get it, he gave me a you've-got-to-be-kidding-me look and told The Whistler Guy to go retrieve it.

Arnie appeared to be distrustful of me.

I thought I knew why.

A few minutes later, they brought Felipe in from the patio. The look on his face was one of resignation, and he never even glanced in my direction as they marched him out of the study.

Once this drama was over, Arnie wanted Carlton's assurance any information I'd obtained from Felipe Arcos would be turned over to the Secretary of Homeland Security within twenty-four hours.

Carlton looked sincere as he gave him that assurance.

Before leaving, Arnie turned to Carlton and said, "We're even now, Douglas. I don't owe you anything."

"Understood."

Arnie nodded in my direction. "The FBI may still want to question him, though."

"Quite possibly."

Carlton walked out in the hallway with Arnie, reentering the study a few minutes later. After closing the door behind him, he came over to the fireplace where Mitchell and I were standing.

I'd already prepared myself for his tongue lashing about Felipe.

"Which one of you brought food in here?" he asked.

♦♦♦♦

Even though both of us feigned ignorance of any food infraction, Carlton kept sniffing the air and insisting he smelled onions.

I offered to open up the French doors and let in some fresh air, but when Carlton sat down at his desk, he forgot all about discovering the culprit who'd created the stench in his study.

Instead, he wanted to know what intel Mitchell and I had on Felipe Arcos and Reyes Valario. He pointed his finger at Mitchell. "What did you learn over at the Command Center?"

Mitchell hesitated for a second.

Since Carlton was head of the Agency's Middle East division, he wasn't Mitchell's boss, at least not technically.

Mitchell's boss was C.J. Salazar, head of the Latin America division. Thus, according to the rules governing Agency protocol, Mitchell didn't have to answer Carlton's question because he was operating under the Latin American division.

An exception to this organizational structure had been made during Operation Clear Signal, when Ahmed Al-Amin, a Middle Eastern operative, had been traveling in Latin America. Both divisions had been involved then, and the DDO had ordered Carlton and Salazar to work together, which meant Mitchell and I had found ourselves answering to two bosses.

I knew Mitchell didn't have much respect for his own boss, so it didn't surprise me when he responded to Carlton's question a few seconds later.

"When I was over at the Command Center, their analysts were still running the threads on Valario. All they had on him was pretty much what the Agency had given them—he was here on a student visa from Caracas, and he was enrolled at the University of Arkansas. One of the feds said he thought Valario was a good marksman just by the way he took out those guards at the gate."

Carlton nodded. "We've determined Valario attended Hezbollah's training camp on Margarita Island two years ago. That's probably where he got his training."

My pulse quickened. "Really? You've confirmed this?"

"Why are you surprised? A few hours ago, you sounded certain this shooting was tied to the Clear Signal operation. You insisted it was the reason you grabbed Arcos in the first place. Was that true or were you just blowing smoke?"

"When I saw the response to the shooting, I knew it fit the scenario Roberto had outlined in The Caracas Document. Let's face it, Douglas, all the news outlets this morning were providing Hezbollah a video lesson on how law enforcement would react to a terrorist event in D.C."

Carlton nodded. "That's true. But—"

"As to the rest . . . well, I'm not exactly sure why I decided to grab him."

Carlton rubbed his hand back and forth across his baldhead a couple of times. "Knowing you, I can understand that, but I need something more concrete than just your gut premonition to explain your behavior. Did you at least get some intel out of Arcos? Otherwise, . . ."

His voice trailed off.

I knew what Carlton was implying, so I immediately summarized what Felipe had told us about Reyes Valario and why he'd made the trip to Washington with him.

The only part I left out was the phone number on the potato chip bag.

The moment I began reciting this narrative, Carlton pulled out a legal pad from his desk drawer and started making some notes. When I ended my account, he lifted the lid on his laptop and started typing.

A few minutes later, he looked up and asked, "Did Felipe give you a last name on this Alejandro?"

"No, but that shouldn't matter. He's a student at the university, so—"

He waved his hand dismissively. "No, no, it doesn't matter. I just wanted to make sure you hadn't forgotten to tell me something."

"Not likely."

Carlton went back to his screen, and, after a few more keystrokes, he closed the lid and said, "I just sent the Ops Center a summary of your interrogation of Felipe. I've also scheduled a meeting with the entire operations team for ten o'clock tomorrow morning. Nolan is drawing up some possible scenarios on the reasons behind Valario's actions today and gathering information on his Hezbollah connections."

"Nolan's directing the team? Where's Olivia?"

"She called in sick this morning."

Carlton didn't elaborate, but I wasn't surprised to hear about Olivia McConnell's absence.

Olivia had breast cancer, something she'd revealed to me in a safe house on Margarita Island the night before the Clear Signal team had flown into Caracas.

She'd also indicated she didn't plan on having a mastectomy, even though that's what her doctors had advised her to do. Her mother and sister had both died from the disease, but she told me she wasn't going to put herself through the turmoil they'd gone through trying to fight the inevitable outcome.

I'd tried to convince her to change her mind about having the surgery, but Olivia wasn't known for changing her mind about anything—especially if the person doing the coercing happened to be a man.

Olivia had issues with men, or at least with those who didn't treat her as an equal.

I said, "Olivia won't be happy with any scenario put forth by Nolan."

Carlton nodded. "When she's back at work tomorrow, I'm sure Nolan will get an earful of her revisions."

Olivia was not at work the next day.

Nor was she at work the day after that.

♦♦♦♦

Carlton pulled his cell phone out of his pocket and glanced down at the screen. It was difficult to tell if he'd just received a text, or he was ignoring a caller, but after returning the phone to his pocket, he looked up at Mitchell and told him to check in with Salazar as soon as he got back to Langley.

Mitchell appeared to get the hint Carlton was dismissing him and said, "I was just leaving,"

Carlton looked over at me. "There's no need for you to ride back with Ben. I drove your Range Rover out here to The Meadows."

Mitchell got him and nodded at me. "I guess that means you can make it back to Langley on your own."

"Right. I'll see you tomorrow."

"What about the . . . ah . . . stuff you left in the Suburban?"

I had to believe the imaginary stuff he was referring to was his way of letting me know he wanted to have a private conversation with me before he left, so I said, "Yeah, I better get that stuff out of your car. I'll walk out with you."

Carlton said, "Don't be long, Titus. There's several things we need to discuss."

"I won't be but a minute."

I took longer than that, but it wasn't Mitchell's fault.

♦♦♦♦

I'd been right about Mitchell. I hadn't left anything in his car; he had just wanted to talk. As soon as we walked out of the house, he started bombarding me with questions.

"What about the phone number Felipe gave us? I didn't expect you to show it to the feds, but why didn't you at least mention it to Douglas?"

I didn't say anything until we were further away from the house.

Once we'd walked over to the Suburban, I said, "Information is a powerful commodity in this business, Ben. If you come across something important, something no one else has, you should view it as an unexpected windfall and stash it away somewhere for a rainy day. One day, when a storm pops up on the horizon, you'll be glad you did."

He nodded. "Okay, I get that. But sooner or later, Felipe is going to tell the feds about that telephone number."

"I'm sure he will, but I think Felipe has a hard time remembering numbers. More than likely, he can't recall that phone number, and he'll tell the feds he wrote it down on the bag, the same way he told us about it."

"But won't they—"

"By the time the DHS guys show up in Carlton's office and demand we share that bag of chips with them, the Agency will have already figured out whether the number is connected to Hezbollah or not. That way, no matter what happens, we'll be one step ahead of them, and when you find yourself sharing the roadway with the feds, that's a good place to be."

"Is that why you made the phone call before the feds showed up? Do you have someone tracing that number right now?"

"That's right."

As if on cue, my phone vibrated.

"But what if—"

"Sorry, Ben," I said, heading back towards the house, "I need to get back inside and see what Carlton wants."

When I walked back inside the house, I took the first left and entered the living room.

Gladys had always called it the great room instead of the living room, and, with its multiple seating areas, it had obviously been designed for entertaining large groups of people.

I didn't care anything about the room's design. All I cared about was whether the room was far enough away from Carlton's study to prevent him from being able to overhear my conversation with Katherine.

I pulled out my iPhone and looked down at the caller ID before accepting the call.

However, the call wasn't from Katherine.

It was from Nikki Saxon.

♦♦♦♦

Nikki and I had met in Norman, about a month after the DDO had forced me to take a year's medical leave. My initial encounter with Detective Nikki Saxon had not been an auspicious one.

She had been assigned to investigate the death of a young woman I'd recently met. Since I'd been the person who'd discovered the woman's body, the detective had conducted an extensive interrogation of me and had even considered me a possible suspect in the murder investigation.

Because of those suspicions, and also because Ahmed Al-Amin could have been involved in the woman's death, I'd made the decision to break Agency rules and reveal my true identity to the detective. Although she'd been skeptical of my assertion, after verifying my CIA employment with a mutual friend, she'd allowed me to work with her to find the woman's killer.

Despite the circumstances surrounding our introduction, I'd been captivated by Nikki from the moment we'd first met. Admittedly, in the beginning, I was drawn to her beautiful face and incredible figure. Later, after getting to know her better, I realized the hidden qualities she possessed were equally appealing.

Such an attraction was unusual for me because I considered myself a loner, and, with my lousy track record with women, I'd made it a practice never to get too close to the opposite sex.

In spite of this, Nikki and I had established a connection, and our fledgling relationship had been one of the reasons I'd purchased a home in Norman and left Stormy in her care when I'd gone after

Ahmed.

Having Nikki look after Stormy had been an ideal situation when I'd been on assignment in Caracas. Now, however, Nikki had been invited to attend the FBI's sixteen-week Law Enforcement Training School in Quantico, Virginia, and her classes were due to begin in less than a week.

After Carlton had ordered me back to Langley, I'd discussed with her what we should do about Stormy. She'd agreed the only thing we could do was to board him somewhere, and she'd offered to find him a suitable kennel before she left Norman.

Even though I knew she was probably calling me about Stormy's care, when I accepted the call, I felt a twinge of excitement at the thought of hearing her voice again.

"Hi, Titus. I hope I'm not calling at a bad time."

I walked over to the windows facing the west side of Carlton's property and looked out on the backyard. It was a peaceful setting.

"No, Nikki, it's fine. Nothing's happening around here right now."

As I gazed out on Carlton's country garden, with its trimmed bushes and blossoming flowers, I suddenly had a vision of Nikki and me walking hand in hand down the sloping path toward the swimming pool.

"Were you able to get some rest after you got there?"

Nikki's question brought me back to reality.

I couldn't very well tell her I'd been busy kidnapping a young Hispanic kid, smuggling him out of a hot zone, and transporting him to a magnificent country estate. Nor could I tell her I believed this same kid was involved in a Hezbollah plot to use chemical weapons on the nation's capital.

Since the truth wasn't an option for me, I did what I did best and lied to her.

As I stared out at the perfectly manicured grounds, I assured her I'd spent a restful afternoon at a Residence Inn in Arlington, Virginia. After spinning my tale, I changed the subject and asked her if she'd had any luck finding a kennel for Stormy.

"As long as it's okay with you, I think I've come up with a better solution. I've asked my captain to let Stormy stay out at his farm again. I believe I told you he has two labs of his own, and when I went out there to pick Stormy up after your mother's funeral, he seemed reluctant to leave his new playmates behind."

In the middle of the Clear Signal operation, I'd been forced to fly home to Flint, Michigan to attend my mother's funeral. The day after I'd arrived there, Nikki had surprised me by showing up at my hotel.

She'd explained her presence by saying she was there because that's what friends did for each other. I hadn't argued with her. In fact, I'd been so happy to see her, I'd been speechless.

Later, after spending several days with her, I realized I wanted Nikki to be more than just a friend who showed up at funerals.

"That sounds like the perfect arrangement. What about you? Are you leaving for Quantico soon?"

"I'm planning to leave in a couple of days. I should be there by the end of the week. Will I be able to see you then?"

Although I was happy she'd asked the question, I knew I couldn't make such a commitment, so I brushed her off. "I doubt it, Nikki, but you'll be so busy at Quantico, you won't have time to think about me."

Suddenly, I knew I wasn't alone, and I instinctively grabbed for my gun as I turned away from the window.

Seconds later, when I saw who was standing in the doorway, I released my grip on the gun and immediately told Nikki goodbye.

Carlton asked, "Who's Nikki and why is she coming to Quantico?"

# Chapter 9

I thought of several bogus responses I could give to Carlton's question, but before I started spinning an answer, I reconsidered.

It was one thing to lie to Nikki because I'd sworn not to divulge Agency secrets to anyone without the proper clearances, but it was an entirely different matter to lie to Carlton about my personal life.

I hadn't always felt that way, but since making a commitment to follow the teachings of Christ, I'd felt increasingly guilty about my tendency to be less than truthful about personal matters.

"Nikki Saxon is a woman I met in Norman. She's a detective in the Norman Police Department, and she's been taking care of Stormy while I've been out of town."

I tried to deliver this information as dispassionately as possible, hoping against hope Carlton wouldn't pursue the matter any further.

"If she's a local detective, why's she coming to Quantico?"

Obviously, he was going to pursue the matter further.

"She was selected for the FBI's Law Enforcement Training School. It begins next week, and since we'll both be out of town, we were just discussing where I should board Stormy."

Carlton sat down on one of the sofas and gestured for me to join him. I reluctantly walked over and sat down in a chair opposite him.

He said, "That's quite an honor. You know the Bureau is very selective about who gets invited to that course."

"Yes, I knew that."

"If she's fortunate enough to graduate, she'll be part of Homeland

Security's national defense team. It's a tough course, though, and not everyone makes it."

"Nikki mentioned that."

Carlton looked off in the distance for a moment, and then, as if he'd suddenly remembered something, he pointed at me and said, "Wasn't she the detective involved in the discovery of that Hezbollah sleeper cell in Norman? You remember? The one Danny Jarrar uncovered not long after you moved down there?"

Danny was a former CIA operative who'd gone to work for the Oklahoma Bureau of Investigation (OSBI). I'd made contact with him shortly after arriving in Norman, and when Nikki and I had needed help on the murder investigation, I'd called on him for backup.

Later, when I'd stumbled across a nest of Islamic terrorists operating out of north Texas, Danny had used his OSBI credentials to prevent both the Agency and the FBI from learning I'd taken part in a domestic encounter—something the feds didn't take lightly and the Agency didn't tolerate. Instead, Danny had attributed the discovery of the sleeper cell to Nikki Saxon, one of Norman's finest detectives.

Now, as I observed Carlton's body language, I wasn't so sure Danny had been successful in keeping my association with Nikki a secret from him.

"Of course I remember, and you're right, Nikki worked with Danny to bring down that Jihadi network."

Suddenly, he leaned forward and stared at me as if he wanted to drill a hole straight through to my brain. I immediately recognized Carlton's interrogation stance, the posture he assumed when he was questioning the bad guys.

Seconds later, he hit me with a barrage of questions.

"Did Danny introduce you to Detective Saxon?"

"No, he wasn't—"

"Is your legend good with her? Does she think you work for the Consortium?"

Like all covert operatives, the moment I'd joined the CIA, I'd been given a public cover, something the Agency referred to as a Career Legend.

According to my Career Legend, I was an employee of the

Consortium for International Studies, a think tank based in College Park, Maryland. Among the staff listed in the CIS directory was Titus Alan Ray, a Senior Fellow in Middle Eastern Programs.

That would be me.

Everyone in my family, and the few friends I had outside of the Agency, thought I was a nerdy pundit who worked at a scholarly think-tank. I knew they must picture me laboring away at a desk all day writing papers and doing research.

A few months after I'd gone to work for the Agency, I'd driven by the Consortium's building just to make sure it really did exist.

It did.

However, after years of being listed as one of their employees, I had yet to set foot inside their building.

I said, "Danny didn't introduce us, but yes, when I met Nikki, I told her I was employed by CIS."

"If Danny didn't introduce you, how did you meet Detective Saxon?"

For whatever reason, the moment I'd spotted Carlton standing in the doorway, I knew he would eventually back me into this corner, even if it took him all night to do it.

Nikki once asked me what the Agency would do if they found out I'd violated their sacrosanct rules and disclosed my true identity to her. At the time, I'd assured her it wasn't going to matter as long as I shared it with my handler before taking my next polygraph.

Now, I was about to find out if that were true or just wishful thinking on my part.

I looked Carlton in the eye. "When I met Nikki, I was being detained as a possible suspect in a homicide investigation."

Carlton pursed his lips, glanced up at the ceiling, and then leaned back against the sofa and said nothing for several seconds.

Finally, he nodded and said, "I believe that statement requires an explanation. I suggest you make it a good one."

I gave him an explanation, but whether it was a good one or not wasn't relevant. It was the truth.

♦♦♦♦

After describing the circumstances of how Nikki and I had met, I revealed why I'd made the decision to disclose my true identity to her.

At first, Carlton appeared skeptical of my choice, but when I mentioned that some of the early evidence in the murder investigation pointed to a connection between the victim and Ahmed Al-Amin, he seemed less doubtful. Then, by the time I was wrapping up my narrative, he was nodding his head.

When I finally finished, Carlton said, "Okay, now that you've told me exactly what happened, Danny's account makes a lot more sense. His story was chocked full of holes."

Hoping Carlton and I might share an inside joke about Danny, I laughed and said, "Danny's stories usually are."

There was no humor in Carlton's reply.

"You'll need to file a Disclosure of Personal Information form, and, in this case, it has to be the long version."

If a CIA employee inadvertently revealed personal classified information, the filing of a DPI was always mandatory. However, when the disclosure was deliberate, not just an inadvertent slip, the long form was required.

In other words, filing a DPI-L meant an employee had intentionally blown his cover to an unauthorized person, which was pretty much what I'd done with Nikki.

Still, I decided to argue the point with him.

"Nikki is a member of law enforcement. I thought that might—"

"No, that doesn't matter. You gave an unauthorized person classified information. In doing so, you revealed your standing with the Agency. That constitutes a criminal offense."

"Technically that might be true, Douglas, but I only gave her the barest of details about my status with the Agency, and, of course, I never disclosed anything operational."

Carlton nodded. "I'm sure of that, and I can understand why you made the decision to tell her you were with the Agency, but that doesn't negate the law."

I couldn't think of anything to say.

After a few seconds of silence, Carlton looked over at me, and smiled. "You know, it's fortunate Detective Saxon was chosen for the FBI's specialized training. A few months from now, she'll have a higher security classification than when you told her you were CIA."

I mulled over Carlton's statement for a moment.

Finally, the fog dissipated, and everything became perfectly clear.

"Let me see if I've got this straight," I said. "If I don't file the DPI for a few months, my breach of security won't really matter?"

"Quite possibly," he said, nodding his head. "Quite possibly."

"Then, if it's all the same to you, Douglas, I'll contact Legal *after* Nikki completes the FBI course."

Carlton didn't respond to my statement. Instead, he got up from the sofa, straightened his jacket, and said, "Meet me in my study in thirty minutes. We have more important things to discuss than Detective Saxon."

Before leaving the room, he looked back and said, "Don't forget, Titus. Your detective has to pass that course in order to get her security clearance."

I assured him. "Nothing to worry about there."

It was an FBI course.

How hard could it be?

♦♦♦♦

When Carlton left the room, I walked back over to the windows and gazed out at the tranquil garden scene once again.

For one brief moment, I tried to imagine myself living at The Meadows with a wife and a couple of kids. I tried to picture waking up every morning unaware of the threats facing America.

Unable to get my head around that scenario, I gave up after a few minutes and turned my thoughts to Carlton and the psychological game we had just played out in Gladys' great room.

I wasn't sure if Danny had deliberately told Carlton I'd revealed my identity to Nikki, or whether Danny had accidently let that information slip from his sometimes loose lips.

But, however it happened, I felt certain Carlton knew about my relationship with Nikki before he ever walked in the room and overheard my conversation with her.

I thought back to the letter Nikki had shown me when I'd returned from Caracas, the one inviting her to attend the FBI classes. At the bottom of the letter, Danny Jarrar's name had been listed as the person recommending her for the training. Now, I suspected Carlton had been responsible for getting Nikki's name added to that training course roster.

Had Carlton done this in order to keep me out of trouble with the Agency's Legal Division?

Probably.

Did he have some other motive for doing so?

Probably.

♦♦♦♦

The moment I decided to head off to the kitchen in search of a snack—perhaps a bag of potato chips—Katherine called me.

This time, I kept my eye on the doorway as I answered the phone.

"Have they put you in handcuffs yet?" she asked. "Or have you escaped already?"

"Nothing happened. As always, Carlton worked his magic."

"That magic is going to run out one of these days."

"Let's hope not."

I tried coming up with some small talk to add, since Katherine always seemed to like that sort of thing, but nothing popped in my mind, so I said, "Tell me about the phone number."

"Of course, right to the matter at hand. Well, I'm not sure what you were expecting, but the phone number is registered to a photography business."

"Not an individual?"

"Not exactly. It's WK Photography, but the WK stands for Walid Khouri."

"And what do you know about Mr. Khouri?"

"He's originally from Jordan. Arrived here about ten years ago with a pocketful of cash supposedly from a family inheritance, and he's been in the photography business ever since. On the surface, he appears to be an upstanding businessman running a legitimate business."

"But you suspect otherwise?"

"There are definitely a few red flags there, but unless I have some context, I'm not sure what data I should be investigating. Is Walid connected to the shooters at the Navy Yard this morning? Did someone call you from WK Photography? Context. I need context."

"Try this for context. Did any of your red flags involve Khouri and illegal drugs? Perhaps some money laundering?"

Katherine was quiet for a moment, and I thought I heard her tapping away on her computer keyboard.

"No, and no. If that's your context, Walid Khouri is not your man."

Katherine's information made no sense to me. Why would Reyes Valario have been communicating with a photographer before he embarked on his suicide mission at the Navy Yard? Did Felipe simply fail to write down the number correctly?

I asked, "What were the red flags on Walid?"

"No, Titus, I'm not going there. Once I get an official inquiry on this number, then I'll do some more digging on Walid Khouri. Until that happens, it was nice talking to you."

When Katherine hung up, I headed to the kitchen to get that snack.

## Chapter 10

The kitchen at The Meadows had dark wooden floors and pale yellow cabinets. The contrast in colors gave the room a warm, rustic feel, although the appliances were stainless steel and the countertops were made of granite.

Carlton still called it Gladys' kitchen.

A multi-tiered pot rack hung from one of the exposed wooden beams in the ceiling. The pot rack was centered over a kitchen island made of white stone. It reminded me of a beautiful piece of artwork and served as the room's focal point.

When I walked in, I found Millie sitting at the island studying a tattered, food-splattered cookbook.

She smiled and removed her reading glasses when she saw me. "So you decided to stop by and say hello before you left?"

Millie was at least a foot shorter than Arkady and about half as big. The two of them usually garnered a few smiles when they appeared together in the Agency cafeteria.

Millie's feistiness more than made up for any height issues.

I said, "I couldn't leave without consulting my favorite expert on Korean politics, could I?"

She gave me an exaggerated look of disbelief. "Yeah, right. I know you didn't come in here to talk politics with me, Korean or otherwise."

"Your perceptiveness is only exceeded by your culinary skills."

"Statements like that make you sound like a nerd."

"We both know that's not true."

Millie hopped off the kitchen barstool and walked over to the refrigerator, removing a large pitcher of lemonade. "I used up all my lemons making this for you."

"But surely you did it out of the goodness of your heart."

She smiled. "Well, there's that, of course. But mainly, it was because Douglas asked me to do it when he called and said you were coming out to The Meadows with a guest."

I sat down on one of the barstools. "Does Douglas often entertain guests like the one I brought out here today?"

Millie frowned. "I can't believe you're asking me that."

"Why? Because I shouldn't be asking you the question or because you don't want to answer the question?"

She shook her head. "I'm not giving you a fish, Titus."

"What's that supposed to mean?"

Before giving me an answer, she poured a glass of lemonade and set it in front of me. "There's an old Korean proverb that says 'Don't trust a cat with a fish.'"

"I was just curious, Millie. You know I'm not trying to dig up any dirt on Douglas. I wouldn't do that."

She sat down next to me and picked up her reading glasses. After putting them back on, she peered at me over the dark green frames. "Gladys once described you as one of the good bad guys, so that's probably true. Still, I'm not answering your question."

"Fair enough. Here's another one. Did Arkady give you a bag of potato chips to hold for me?"

She leaned over and opened a drawer on the island. Pushing aside a couple of potholders, she pulled out Felipe's yellow bag of potato chips and laid it down on the counter between us.

She said, "Like you, I'm the curious type. But, unlike you, I'm won't be asking questions about matters that don't concern me."

She pushed the bag of chips toward me and went back to studying her cookbook. "How do you feel about turtle soup for dinner?"

I grabbed the bag of chips and headed out the door, taking my lemonade with me. "I'm not staying for dinner, Millie. But, if I were, I think I'd prefer fish."

♦♦♦♦

When I opened the door to Carlton's study, I found him staring at his bookshelves. He didn't turn around as I closed the door behind me.

"Someone moved a couple of my books," he said.

"That alone could bring down civilization as we know it."

I watched as he gave one of the books a light tap on its spine, bringing it into perfect alignment with the one standing next to it.

After making a few other adjustments—so the world would continue spinning in the right direction—he turned around and faced me.

I held the bag of potato chips out to him.

"No, thanks," he said, sitting down at his desk. "Millie's fixing dinner for me."

I sat down on the other side of the desk and pushed the bag of chips toward him. "This was in Felipe's backpack. The feds are gonna come looking for it sooner rather than later."

He glared at me for a couple of seconds.

Finally, he picked up the yellow package and looked it over. He treated it gingerly, almost as if it were an ancient document and it might easily disintegrate in his hands.

"Let me guess. The phone number on the back of this bag is the reason the feds will be showing up here again."

"Correct."

He quickly jotted down the number on his legal pad, and then he picked up his cell phone and snapped several photos of it from different angles.

Once that was done, he laid his phone down, pressed his hands together to form a steeple, and pointed them in my direction.

"Talk," he ordered.

I filled in the parts of Felipe's story I'd left out before, ending with how insistent Felipe had been about the phone number.

"Felipe was convinced that number belonged to the guy interested in buying the heroin they were transporting."

"And you're not?"

I shrugged. "I'm not sure. We'll know more after you've had the analysts run the phone number through the system. But for now, here's what I think. I believe the drugs were given to Reyes to serve as a diversionary tactic, to disguise the fact he was at the Navy Yard this morning to martyr himself."

"The drugs were a smoke screen then?"

I nodded. "We know the drug cartels and Hezbollah are cooperating with each other, so acquiring the heroin certainly wouldn't have been a problem for them. Making the incident this morning appear as if it were a drug deal gone bad was an easy way to cover up what they were really doing, which I believe was observing the city's response to an emergency."

Carlton said, "If Reyes really killed those people in the name of Allah, as Felipe claimed, then I agree Hezbollah was just testing the waters before initiating a much bigger terrorist event."

"We're on the same page then."

Carlton shook his head. "You and I may be on the same page, but I'm not so sure the feds will see it that way. They'll take one look at the heroin in Felipe's backpack and dismiss the killings as some sort of drug war. Those conclusions will only be reinforced when they question Felipe and discover he's been dealing drugs on campus."

"I believe that's why Reyes brought Felipe along with him to Washington in the first place. When he found out Alejandro wasn't able to make the trip, he thought Felipe would make a great stand-in. He was already acquainted with Felipe as a small-time drug dealer, so he probably figured the guy would jump at the chance to be involved in some of the big league stuff."

Carlton picked up the bag of potato chips again. "How could Felipe resist the prospect of making a million dollars?"

I said, "Of course, that wasn't ever going to happen. I'm certain Reyes planned to kill him just like he killed those hostages."

Carlton placed the bag in the center of his desk and carefully straightened out the corners. Once that was done, he looked up at me and asked, "I know you probably just wanted to jerk the FBI's chain by withholding this phone number, but was there some other reason you didn't turn this evidence over to them?"

I shook my head. "Nothing more than just information hoarding, a concept I believe you're familiar with."

I waited a second to see if Carlton might want to acknowledge he'd done the same thing by failing to let me know he was aware of my relationship with Nikki.

He just stared at me.

I continued, "It's knowing certain facts, but keeping those facts a secret until it proves beneficial to use that knowledge to further one's goals."

The semblance of a smile played across Carlton's face. "I'm familiar with that practice, Titus. I learned it from you."

# Chapter 11

Carlton sent Katherine's office the phone number from Felipe's bag of chips, along with the photos he'd taken. Since she already had the initial information at her fingertips, I knew she'd be getting back to him in record time.

Seconds later, a high-pitched *beep-beep* from Carlton's computer alerted him to an incoming top-priority message from the Ops Center.

He scowled as he read the flash traffic. "They've located Alejandro."

"Is he still in the hospital?"

"No, he's dead."

"From an appendectomy?"

Carlton kept reading. "His death is under investigation. Apparently, he was about to be discharged from the hospital when a nurse found him unresponsive."

"Hezbollah must have killed him. They were afraid he'd talk when the feds started investigating Reyes."

Carlton nodded. "Arnie said the Bureau is already in Fayetteville looking into his background."

Suddenly, he leaned across the desk and pointed down at the floor, close to the chair where Felipe had been restrained.

"You need to pick those up," he said, indicating the zip ties I'd removed from Felipe's wrists.

I walked over and picked up the zip ties, depositing them on

Carlton's desk. "Make sure the feds thoroughly question Felipe. I'm convinced he knows more about Reyes and Alejandro than he told me. If I'd had a little more time with him, I could have—"

"Forget about Felipe. You're finished here."

"What? Why?"

"Sit down, and I'll tell you why."

I took a seat in front of his desk.

"Tomorrow morning, you and Ben will be briefed into a new operation. The DDO has labeled it Operation Citadel Protection, and, as the name suggests, its aim is to protect our nation's capital from a chemical weapons' attack. The first phase of the operation will be initiated in a couple of days when you and Ben board a plane for Buenos Aires."

Although I was relieved to hear I'd been tasked with a new operation, I wasn't happy about being sent to Argentina. "Does this trip have anything to do with Roberto Montilla?"

"Yes, but what I'm about to tell you is strictly off the record. When you receive the official briefing in the morning, your reaction should be that of an operative hearing this information for the very first time."

I wasn't surprised Carlton was about to give me an unofficial briefing before I sat down for the official one. Whenever Carlton was forced to share leadership with another division head—such as what had occurred with C.J. Salazar during the Clear Signal operation—he seemed to enjoy knowing his operative was already aware of the facts before the DDO's briefer presented them.

I wasn't certain why this pleased him so much, but I suspected it was the sense of control it afforded him, control he was forced to give up whenever he had to share the reins of power with someone else.

In my mind, Carlton and control were synonymous terms.

♦♦♦♦

For the next twenty minutes, Carlton outlined the logistics of our mission into Buenos Aires.

Although he left out the cover identities Mitchell and I would be using in country, that didn't bother me. I knew Support Services would send someone from their Legends division to give us those important details during the official briefing.

At the moment, all I cared about were the mission's objectives and protocols.

After Carlton spent what seemed like an inordinate amount of time on the logistics, he finally explained why the DDO had called me back to Langley and why Mitchell and I were being sent to Buenos Aires.

"After the voice techs examined the audio tapes of your interrogation of Roberto, they concluded he'd been lying to you about certain aspects of his conversations with Rehman Zaidi."

I nodded. "The details he gave us were pretty sketchy. That's one of the reasons I asked him to give us his written account. I thought he might trip himself up, perhaps not remember what he'd said the first time."

"That appears to be exactly what happened. Once the analysts compared Roberto's written account with the stress points observed in his voice analysis, they came to the conclusion he didn't tell you everything about Hezbollah's plans for initiating terrorists' attacks in the U.S."

"Does this mean Ben and I are flying down to Buenos Aires to find out what Roberto wasn't willing to tell us before? Is that our objective?"

Carlton rubbed his right temple. "Yes and no. If a simple interrogation of Roberto yields some verifiable information, then, yes, you will have achieved your objective. But, if Roberto isn't forthcoming, then your objective will be to extract him from Buenos Aires and transfer him to a location where he'll receive some extra incentives to start talking."

I was disappointed to learn my assignment was only an interrogation—possibly an extraction—and had nothing whatsoever to do with locating chemical weapons or penetrating Hezbollah's network in Syria.

I tried to change Carlton's mind about that. "What about the ships carrying the chemical weapons from Syria? Have they been located yet?"

"Yes, we've tagged three cargo ships, and it appears all three of them are headed for Cuba and not Venezuela as we'd originally thought."

"Roberto mentioned Cuba was their backup plan, so that's not too surprising. Is there any indication Hezbollah rerouted the ships because of Ahmed's death?"

"That's a big possibility. Once Rehman Zaidi heard about Ahmed's death and discovered Roberto had disappeared with his family, he left Caracas and returned to Syria. We have an ongoing operation tracking his movements in Damascus now, and we already know he's been in contact with the head of Hezbollah's leadership council since arriving back in the city."

"Who's heading up the operation in Damascus?"

"That's none of your concern." Carlton picked up a nearby trash can and swept the zip ties into it. "And don't think I'm unaware of why you're asking me that question. I know you'd rather be running assets in Syria instead of heading down to Argentina to interrogate Roberto. But that's why the DDO brought you back to active status, so don't try changing my mind about your assignment."

"I wouldn't think of it."

Moments later, Carlton received a phone call. It sounded like Katherine had called him back about the phone number.

"By all means," he said, "do a full data probe on him. We need to know everything about this man and his business."

After he hung up, he said, "That was Katherine."

"Already?"

He smiled. "She always expedites my requests."

He picked up Felipe's bag of chips. "This number belongs to WK Photography. The WK stands for Walid Khouri, a Jordanian who appears to be a legitimate businessman."

"But you're having her run a full analysis on him anyway?"

He nodded. "She noticed some red flags on the initial data dig. I told her to find out everything she could about the man."

"Of course."

Carlton stared at me for a moment, and, for a split second, I thought he might ask me if I'd already contacted Katherine about the number. Instead, he said, "It might be appropriate for me to take some pre-emptive action now."

Before I had a chance to ask him what he meant, he keyed in some numbers on his cell phone.

"Hi, Arnie," he said. "Yes, I understand, but I'm not calling you for another favor. In fact, I'm about to do you a favor. When I was straightening up around here, I discovered an item had been left out of the backpack Felipe was carrying. I'll have someone drop it by your office later today."

After he hung up, he said, "That may keep us out of hot water with the feds, and by the time Felipe tells them about the phone number, we'll know everything there is to know about Walid Khouri."

Carlton turned out to be wrong on both counts.

♦♦♦♦

I asked Carlton to clarify who was going to be running Mitchell and me on the ground in Buenos Aires, and his answer surprised me.

"Since this is a straightforward interrogation and doesn't involve hostiles, no one will be in country with you. If Roberto should prove difficult, then the DDO will provide you with a field officer. He might even send Olivia McConnell down there to serve as the FO again. In that case, she'll work with you on the ground to facilitate Roberto's extraction."

"I don't believe there'll be a need for an FO. Most likely, Roberto will cooperate with us."

"That wasn't what happened when you spent two days in Caracas with Roberto."

"The circumstances are much different now."

When Carlton glanced away for a second, I thought he was about to bring up Ahmed's murder, but when he turned and faced me again, he said, "I assure you, Titus, I'll be in the driver's seat at the Ops Center when you're on the ground in Buenos Aires. If you should hear any differently at the briefing tomorrow, don't be alarmed."

"Thanks for letting me know."

Carlton picked up his briefcase and placed the bag of potato chips inside. After adding the notes he'd jotted down on his yellow legal pad, he snapped the briefcase shut and said, "When Arkady drives me back to Langley tonight, I'll have him deliver Felipe's bag of potato chips to Arnie."

"I'd be happy to drive you back to Langley."

"No, I have a better idea. Why don't you stay out here tonight? In fact, just leave your things out here until you get back from Buenos Aires. That way, when Detective Saxon arrives in the area, you'll have a place to entertain her."

His suggestion left me speechless, but before I could find my voice, he had already walked over to the door.

I called out after him. "While I appreciate your invitation, Douglas, I could never impose on you like that."

"It's not an imposition. Consider it done."

As he opened the door, he pointed over to the game table. "Before you leave the room, put those chess pieces back the way I had them. I was in the middle of a chess tournament with a world-class player from my CCLA group, and he was about to lose the game."

He didn't wait for me to respond before leaving the room.

I walked over to the game table and stared down at the empty board. A few seconds later, I jerked open the drawers and removed the chess pieces.

After recalling the last mental snapshot I'd made of the game before tossing Felipe's backpack on the table, I carefully repositioned the pieces on the board.

The moment I did, I realized Carlton was an excellent chess player.

I wasn't surprised.

He'd always been able to outmaneuver me.

# Chapter 12

*Tuesday, June 23*

I woke up the next morning in one of the guest rooms at The Meadows, and it took me a few seconds to decide whether the dog I heard barking outside my window was real or whether it was a leftover figment of the dream I'd been having.

Once I was fully awake, I recognized it was no dream.

I rolled out of bed and walked over to my second-floor window and took a look outside.

The window overlooked the backyard. The moment I arrived, the sun was just beginning to make its appearance across the horizon.

The sight was spectacular.

Shafts of golden sunshine pierced through the forest of trees and displayed themselves across Gladys' flower garden. The iridescent beams made the water on the surface of the swimming pool shimmer in the early morning haze, and the gentle breeze moved the leaves back and forth in a kind of slow dance.

I stood there completely mesmerized for several seconds.

Suddenly, the dog barked again, and I spotted him down by the swimming pool, next to the diving board. Like the water on the surface of the swimming pool, the golden retriever's fur coat shimmered in the bright morning sun.

Arkady was cleaning the pool, and he appeared to be having a serious conversation with the dog. The animal kept trying to hold up his side of the conversation by barking occasionally—or maybe the dog was a her; it was hard to tell from this distance.

I slipped on a jogging suit and went downstairs in search of some coffee.

Although there was no sign of Millie in the spotless kitchen, there was a coffeemaker with a carafe full of hot coffee and a note that said, "You're on your own for breakfast. If you decide to cook, be sure and clean up after yourself."

I rummaged around in the kitchen cabinets until I found a mug, and once I filled it to the brim, I walked out on the patio.

Arkady waved at me. "Good morning. I hope Frisco didn't wake you up."

Frisco trotted over to greet me.

"Not a chance," I said, reaching over and scratching the dog's ears.

Frisco appeared to be enjoying the attention, even smiling if that were possible, and I knew I'd made a friend for life.

After taking a seat in one of the cushioned lounge chairs, I said, "I know Frisco doesn't belong to Douglas. He hates animals."

Arkady laughed. "You're right about that. Frisco belongs to me. When Millie and I moved out here, I brought him with me."

"Douglas didn't object?"

"No. I usually keep him in the dog run on the other side of the house, so he never sees him when he's out here. You like dogs?"

I hesitated. "I haven't been around dogs very much, but I recently adopted a stray, and he's beginning to grow on me."

"Frisco loves other dogs. You should bring him out to The Meadows for a visit sometime."

I said, "I'd love to do that, but Stormy lives in Oklahoma."

While I drank my coffee, Arkady and I engaged in a few minutes of conversation about Russia, and I asked him what he thought of Vladimir Putin. He reverted to his native tongue to describe the Russian president, and, although I wasn't fluent in Russian, I was able to pick up enough to know he wasn't impressed by the man.

Once I'd finished my coffee, I excused myself and went back upstairs. Before getting dressed, I read some chapters from the Bible, a habit I'd adopted shortly after arriving back in the States from Iran.

I had just closed my Bible when Carlton called me.

"How soon can you get here? There's been some developments overnight, and we should talk about them before the briefing."

"I'm on my way."

♦♦♦♦

For breakfast, I went through the drive-thru at McDonalds in Fairfax. As soon as I got on the freeway again, I got another call.

"Where are you?" Mitchell asked.

"On my way to Langley."

"Our briefing doesn't start 'til ten."

"Douglas wanted to see me before the briefing. He mentioned something about overnight developments."

"He was probably talking about Olivia."

"What about Olivia?"

"She's in the hospital. The Senator got the call this morning. She tried to commit suicide last night."

For a moment I was stunned and couldn't think of anything to say.

Perhaps I shouldn't have been surprised; this wasn't the first time Olivia had tried to take her life.

Her first attempt had taken place not long after we'd met at Camp Peary. Then, I'd found her asleep in her car with an empty bottle of sleeping pills beside her. I'd immediately rushed her over to a nearby hospital and stayed with her until the doctors had notified me she was out of the woods.

Once she was back at work, I assured her I wasn't going to tell anyone at the Agency about the incident, and from that moment on, Olivia had considered me her friend.

It wasn't easy being Olivia's friend, and, as far as I knew, I was the only one willing to claim that title. I wasn't sure whether this was due to her abrasive personality, her social ineptitude, or one of her other personality quirks.

I asked Mitchell, "Why would someone call your father about Olivia?"

"Lucy Fulton, one of the secretaries in his office, called him. She and Olivia live in the same building, and she was there when the ambulance came and got her last night. Since Olivia used to be the DDO's liaison with the Senate Intelligence Committee, Lucy thought the Senator might be interested. Lucy is more or less the office gossip."

"Was your father interested?"

"Not really. He told Lucy to send some flowers to the hospital, but then he immediately told her about some corrections he wanted to make on a speech he's giving on the floor of the Senate this afternoon."

Mitchell paused and I heard him take a deep breath. "Why would Olivia do something like this?"

"She's the only person who can answer that question, Ben."

"She's as hard as nails and doesn't seem to be the type of person to take her own life."

"I'm not sure there is a *type* for this sort of behavior."

"It's just that she—"

"Was Olivia the only reason you called?" I asked, cutting Mitchell off before he could start speculating about her again.

I found it hard enough dealing with my own emotions about the woman without listening to his sentiments as well.

"No, I wanted to know if the feds had contacted you about the phone number Felipe gave us."

"After you left, I gave the number to Douglas, and he immediately sent it over to DHS. That number could be a dead end, though. It belongs to a photography business, and the guy who runs it looks legitimate."

"What about the lecture you gave me about saving that information for a rainy day?"

That was a good question. One I'd asked myself.

After a bit of self-analysis, I'd come to the conclusion I'd turned the information over because I felt I owed Carlton something for securing Nikki a spot at Quantico.

However, I wasn't about to start explaining myself to Mitchell.

"Let's just say I thought it was pointless saving up for a rainy day, when I had bills I needed to pay right now."

Mitchell muttered something I couldn't understand and moved on to his next topic.

"C.J. wouldn't tell me anything about our mission. Did Douglas give you any hints? Are we headed back to Caracas?"

Although I briefly questioned whether I should share the details of the operation with him before our official briefing, I decided to treat him the same way Carlton had treated me, and I went over what he'd told me about Operation Citadel Protection.

His reaction surprised me.

"I can't believe this. It makes no sense for him to send the two of us to Buenos Aires. Why doesn't the DDO send someone Roberto doesn't know?"

"It makes perfect sense. You and I followed through on our promise to get Roberto out of Venezuela, so we've already earned his trust. I'm certain he'll be more than willing to talk to us now."

"But he's lied to us once already."

"All prisoners lie to their captors, Ben. It's their means of telling themselves they have control over their destiny."

"I'd say Roberto took control of his own destiny by killing Ahmed."

"No, by killing Ahmed, he gave us control. Now, we can leverage that control to get the truth from him."

Mitchell was quiet for a few seconds, and I thought he might be trying to readjust his thinking about the mission. I felt sure once we left Caracas, he never expected to see Roberto Montilla again.

He asked, "Who's our handler in country?"

"No one. Carlton will be running us from the Ops Center."

"Without Salazar?"

"That's what he said."

"At least our handler won't be Olivia."

Before I had a chance to respond, he said, "Oh, wait . . . I didn't mean it that way. I'm sorry for what happened to Olivia. Or rather for what she did . . . and . . .uh . . . and . . . I really hope Olivia's okay."

"That makes two of us."

I was tempted to ask Mitchell if he knew which hospital Olivia was in, but I decided I should end the conversation before I did something foolish.

"I'm on the outskirts of McLean now; I'll see you at the briefing."

"See you there."

"Wait a second, Ben. Did Lucy say where the ambulance took Olivia?"

"I heard the Senator tell her to send the flowers to McLean Medical. Why? Are you—"

I hung up before I heard his question.

I wasn't going to answer it anyway.

♦♦♦♦

After arguing with myself for several minutes, I called Carlton's secretary, Sally Jo Hartford, and told her to tell the boss I might be a few minutes late.

When I entered the lobby of McLean Medical, I realized Olivia probably wasn't registered under her own name, and I tried to remember the name the Agency used when a female covert officer was admitted to a civilian hospital.

It was either Pam Black or Pat Brown.

However, I quickly discovered Olivia was registered under her own name, which meant no one from the Agency's seventh floor had bothered to keep Olivia McConnell's identity a secret.

That was probably because Olivia had never been a covert operative.

From the moment she'd graduated from training school at Camp Peary, she'd been groomed for upper echelon work, and they'd put her in a variety of positions to make her look as qualified as possible for any type of managerial post.

Olivia was brilliant when it came to risk assessment, particularly defining the appropriate controls to reduce or eliminate those risks, and she was also very good at pattern analysis. Thus, for the past two years, Olivia had been the Director of the RTM Centers or Real Time Management Centers at the Agency, where the day-to-day operations of the CIA took place.

Olivia was seldom sent to the field, and, even though she'd been the field officer for Operation Clear Signal, being the FO hadn't been her choice.

The DDO had given her the FO assignment at the behest of Senator Elijah Mitchell, who wasn't pleased his son was a member of the Agency's covert operations unit. The Senator had told the DDO he wanted Olivia to make his son's life as difficult as possible during the mission, and by doing so, he thought the younger Mitchell might be willing to take a desk job instead of being assigned to the more dangerous field work.

Now, I wondered if the pressure the Senator had put on Olivia, plus the stress caused by her own health issues, had pushed her over the edge.

If Olivia had been successful in taking her own life, I knew it might be difficult for me not to hold the Senator personally responsible for her death.

# Chapter 13

I got off the elevator on the fifth floor of the medical center and followed the signs to Room 5641. When I arrived, I noticed the door was slightly ajar, and, after hesitating a moment, I pushed it open and walked inside.

The room was full of medical personnel—a couple of nurses in floral uniforms and two guys in long white coats, plus a slender young girl in a green uniform emptying a trash can.

Everyone, except for the young girl, had their eyes on Olivia, who was sitting up in the hospital bed in the middle of the room.

As soon as Olivia spotted me, she swatted the air as if she were trying to rid herself of a pesky fly.

"No. No. You shouldn't be here. Leave me alone."

Although she was hooked up to an IV, I thought Olivia looked remarkably well. She wasn't wearing any makeup, but her skin appeared flawless, and her short black hair looked no different than the last time I'd seen her a couple of weeks ago.

I moved away from the door and stood against the wall, ignoring her wishes. When a nurse politely asked me to leave, Olivia said she'd changed her mind and I could stay.

Five minutes later, after everyone had left the room, I walked over and stood beside her bed.

In an apparent attempt to ignore me, she stared over at the IV machine. It was pumping a colorless liquid into her arm, and she was giving it her full attention.

I waited her out.

"How did you know I was here?" she finally asked. "Was it Lucy? I bet it was Lucy. She's always been such a busybody."

I leaned over and took her hand.

She immediately took her eyes off the machine and looked up at me. I was surprised to see tears in her eyes.

Seconds later, she was weeping.

I was at a loss.

I'd never seen her cry before, and since I couldn't think of anything else to do, I stood there and held her hand. A few minutes later, she pulled away from me.

"Give me a Kleenex. I know I must look a mess."

I handed her a mini box of tissues from the nightstand, and while she dabbed at her face, I pulled up a chair.

"You look fine, Olivia. Much better than I expected."

"I can always tell when you're lying."

"No, you can't."

"Yes, I can. Most of the time, I can."

Having a conversation with Olivia always meant having an argument with Olivia, and I was convinced she drew energy from an argument the way I drew energy from silence.

"Tell me what happened, Olivia. How did you end up here?"

"Ending up here wasn't my intention. Ending my miserable life was my intention."

"I don't believe that."

She raised her voice in protest. "I swallowed a whole bottle of sleeping pills, Titus. You can ask the doctors in the ER. I should be dead by now."

"So what happened? Who called the ambulance? Why are you still around?"

Once again, Olivia refused to look at me. Instead, she stared across the room at the windows overlooking the parking lot.

"I was told the pizza delivery kid showed up, and when I didn't open the door, he knocked on Lucy's door. Maybe he thought he could get his money from her; I don't know. For some reason, though, the two of them called 911."

"So you ordered a pizza, and then you swallowed the pills?"

She nodded. "I hadn't made up my mind to do it when I ordered the pizza. When I did, I just emptied the bottle down my throat. By the time I did it, I'd forgotten all about the pizza."

"Okay, now I get the picture," I said. "You have a pizza delivery kid who insists on being paid, and a nosy neighbor who lives right across the hall, and both of them are available to you at the very moment you need them. How convenient."

Olivia gazed up at me, pointing her manicured finger in my face. "Are you accusing me of timing the whole thing just so someone would find me before it was too late?"

"That's exactly what I'm saying. But don't get me wrong, I believe you thought you might die by swallowing those pills, but you also evaluated the risks—something you're very good at—and you knew there was a high probability someone would find you before the pills completely kicked in."

Olivia sighed and leaned her head against the pillows, staring off into space for a few minutes.

"Maybe I did. I don't know. All I could think about was being all alone up here dying of breast cancer. It just seemed easier to end my life by taking the sleeping pills, instead of enduring what my mother and sister went through with this disease."

"I don't suppose you thought about calling me before you unscrewed the lid on those sleeping pills?"

"Yes and no. It briefly crossed my mind, but then I remembered the conversation we'd had about your new faith, and I knew if I called you, you would just get all religious on me. And, for your information, the lid wasn't the screw-on type, it was a snap-top lid."

I wasn't sure what to say to Olivia, so I tried breathing a prayer. It went something like, *"Help, Lord. What do I say to Olivia?"*

In an effort to buy myself some time, I walked across the room and looked out the window. A large basket of yellow flowers had been placed in the middle of the extra wide windowsill, and, since the bouquet was the only one in the room, I presumed the Senator had sent it.

After a minute or so, I walked back over to Olivia's bed. "If you *had* called me, Olivia, I would have told you to go ahead. I would have told you to take your own life."

She looked at me in disbelief.

I hurried on, "But I also would have told you what to expect as a result of that decision."

"Is this where you—"

"If you were to end your life without accepting God's gift of eternal life, then you'd be confronted with the very thing you were trying to avoid, because an eternity without Christ means being alone forever. And, as I understand it, that loneliness is far greater than anything you'll ever experience on this earth."

Olivia glanced down at the twisted bed sheet in her hands. When she finally looked up at me, there were tears in her eyes again.

"How can I make sure that doesn't' happen to me?"

For the next few minutes, I explained how I'd come to the realization I was living my life without God, and I needed to repent and ask His forgiveness. I told her by accepting Christ's death as the payment for my sins and committing my life to follow His teachings, God had given me eternal life. I told her He would do the same for her. All she had to do was to ask Him for forgiveness and commit her life to Him.

I waited for Olivia to respond, but for several seconds she just sat there and massaged her temple. When she finally spoke, her voice was so soft I could barely hear her.

"That sounds beautiful, Titus."

"I'm not very good at this prayer thing yet, Olivia, but I believe I could help you pray a prayer right now."

She looked alarmed at my suggestion and shook her head. "No. No. Absolutely not. I couldn't do that right now. Maybe someday, but right now I have to get out of this place."

I knew I couldn't push Olivia on this question—or any other question—so I dropped the subject.

♦♦♦♦

A few minutes later, when a nurse arrived with some papers for her to sign, I excused myself and went down to the gift shop, where I made several purchases.

When I returned to Olivia's room, I was surprised to see her IV drip was gone, and she'd changed into her street clothes.

I walked across the room and handed her a vase of pink roses with a balloon attached. For one brief moment, I thought I saw a smile on her face.

"What's this?" she asked.

"Those were the only ones left in the gift shop. Sorry about the balloon."

She pulled the "It's A Girl!" balloon from the vase of roses and stuck it in the trash. "You did that on purpose."

"I told you I—"

"The buds look wilted," she said, touching one of the long-stemmed roses.

"You're welcome, Olivia. I hope you enjoy the flowers."

She set the vase down on the nightstand and said. "At least I'm not allergic to roses."

"I also brought you this."

I pulled a small, white New Testament from a gift bag and handed it to her. When she took it from me, I thought it was about to end up in the trash can along with the balloon.

Instead, she carefully placed the Bible next to the roses. Then she asked, "Any more surprises?"

"No, except I'm surprised to see you in your street clothes. Does your doctor know you're about to break out of here?"

Olivia sat down on the edge of the bed. "When I agreed to a psychiatric consult, the doc agreed to sign my release papers. I can go home now."

"Then what?"

"Then, I'll have to convince the DDO to let me come back to work."

"You know the Agency's medical policy, Olivia. That's not going to happen."

"Don't be so sure about that. I know where all the bodies are buried, and if they refuse to give me a MED clearance, I'll threaten to dig up a few of those corpses. After I'm done, I may not be able to return to my old job, but at least I'll still be an Agency employee."

"I have another suggestion, Olivia, and if you follow my advice, I'm pretty sure you'll retain your present position at the Agency."

"What's your advice? Murder? A kidnapping? I could go for either one, but I don't think they'd let me keep my job if I got caught."

"Call your surgeon. Schedule your mastectomy. Once you do that, they'll have to reinstate you. They won't have a choice."

Olivia chewed on her fingernail as she considered this, and the look on her face was one I'd seen several times. It meant she was weighing the options, constructing all the possible scenarios, and assessing the risks before arriving at a decision.

When she got up from the bed and walked across the room to a wardrobe cabinet, I was pretty sure she 'd already decided what to do. After jerking open the cabinet door, she pulled out a pair of sneakers.

"Okay, as much as I hate to admit it, you're right. If I'm scheduled to start receiving cancer treatments, they'll have to hold my job for me. In the end, the seventh floor will probably overlook this . . . episode."

"I'm sure of it."

"Don't look so smug. Yes, I'm going to do what you're asking me to do, but that doesn't mean a thing. I still believe I'm going to die of this disease. Having the mastectomy doesn't change that."

"I still believe having the mastectomy will prevent that from happening."

"Why does that not surprise me?"

She reached over and plucked the acknowledgement card from the bouquet of flowers on the windowsill. "Did you see this? He sent these flowers before they even gave me a room assignment."

In her own way, she seemed genuinely pleased by his attention.

"No one's ever accused him of being inefficient."

I stole a look at my watch. "I'm on my way to my briefing now, but I still have time to give you a ride home."

That wasn't really true, but I couldn't leave her alone to call a cab.

"No, I'm due for my little chat with the crazy doc in thirty minutes. Once that's over, I'll have them call me a cab—unless they think I'm too nuts to be left alone."

She walked over and sat down on the bed once again.

"Let's talk about your briefing today. Be sure and question Nolan about the new intel from Syria."

It took me a second to make the contextual jump over to my upcoming operation, and, when I did, I motioned for her to keep quiet while I walked over and shut the door to the hallway.

Once that was done, I asked, "Are you sure you're up to talking about this?"

"You think my brain function has been affected just because I got a little emotional? Of course I'm up to discussing this."

"Okay. What about the new intel from Syria?"

"First of all, you need to know what happened when Rehman Zaidi returned to Damascus after leaving Caracas, because I believe it could affect your run into Buenos Aires. Quiz Nolan about it, because otherwise, I don't think he'll mention it at the briefing today."

Nolan Wilson was the highest ranking team leader under Olivia's command, and, like Olivia, he had his own way of approaching an operation. Not surprisingly, he and Olivia had often clashed over the seemingly inconsequential tidbits of intel arriving in the Ops Center daily.

I said, "If you're talking about Zaidi making contact with the head of Hezbollah when he arrived back in Damascus, Douglas already told me about that."

She looked surprised. "He told you that before the briefing today?"

I nodded.

"Did he also tell you Marwan Farage was at that meeting with Zaidi?"

I had a momentary brain freeze, but, seconds later, the name clicked with me. "You mean Ahmed's cousin? That Marwan?"

She nodded. "He was Roberto's translator when Roberto was in Damascus negotiating the trade deal between Venezuela and Syria."

"I remember that now; but to answer your question. Douglas didn't mention they had made contact."

"That's probably because Nolan didn't include that information in his briefing notes."

"So why is Marwan Farage on your radar?"

"Because we heard from an asset inside Hezbollah that Marwan was angry when he heard Ahmed had been killed. He and Ahmed grew up together, and they were more like brothers than cousins, so he may consider it his duty to locate Roberto Montilla and avenge his cousin's death."

"I guess that's a possibility, but since only a few people at the Agency know where Roberto is right now, Marwan would have a difficult time locating him."

"Even so, you should have Nolan put a tracker on Marwan's travels."

"I'll request it, but let's hope you're wrong about that."

"I'm seldom wrong about such things."

She was right about that.

# Chapter 14

Traffic was heavy as I made my way over to Langley. I was concerned about getting there in time to meet with Carlton before my ten o'clock briefing.

FIve minutes out from Langley, my iPhone rang, and I forgot all about Carlton.

The call was from my nephew, and since he'd never called me before, as soon as I saw the caller ID, I was suddenly worried he might be calling to tell me something was wrong with my sister Carla.

"Hey, Titus, it's Brian."

"Hi, Brian. Is everything okay?"

"Yeah, no worries. My mom gave me your number because she thought you might be able to help me."

I relaxed. "Sure. What's up?"

"When you were here for Grandma's funeral, I mentioned I was looking for an internship in Washington for the summer."

Brian was a political science major in his senior year at the University of Michigan, and I vaguely remembered he had talked about doing an internship in Washington.

"I remember. Did you find something?"

"I hope so. Senator Conrad's office called me yesterday. He's the junior Senator from Michigan, and he wanted to let me know an opening had come up in his office. In order to be considered, I have to have three recommendations, and one of them has to be from someone who holds a position in government. Since you've been living in the D.C. area for several years now, I thought you might know someone who could help me."

Brian sounded nervous, but I realized he might have been anxious about talking to me because the two of us hardly knew each other.

He was the oldest of Carla's two children. His sister, Kayla, was sixteen, and I thought Brian must be around twenty-one. Despite his age, we'd never had more than a five-minute conversation with each other before.

"I'd be happy to help you, Brian. Is there a form to fill out or would you prefer a letter of recommendation?"

"What I'd really prefer is for you to have the person call Senator Conrad's office. The opening just came up, and there are two other candidates for the position. His assistant told me he'll be making his decision tomorrow."

I pulled up to the front gate of the CIA compound behind a line of cars waiting to be cleared through security. Since I no longer had any kind of Agency ID on me, I knew I'd have to speak to the guard personally, and, in order to do that, I needed to get Brian off the phone as quickly as possible.

"Sure, Brian, I think I know someone who might be able to help you."

"Really? Are you serious?"

"I'll get in touch with him today."

"Well, thanks. When Mom said I should call you, I was a little nervous."

"I realize we haven't had much of a chance to talk before."

The car ahead of me was quickly waved through the gate, and my car was next in line at the guard house. The security officer held out his hand for my ID, but I signaled I needed a minute more on my phone.

He wasn't happy about that.

Brian said, "No, that's not it. I think it's because you've always seemed so secretive about your job, I was beginning to believe you weren't really employed at a think tank and were working at Walmart or something."

Brian laughed when he said this, and I tried to sound amused at his observation. "I'm sure my job's not half as interesting as that would be."

The guard stepped out of the security hut and came over to my car. "Could you hurry up, sir? There are people waiting in line behind you."

Brian laughed. "Sounds like you might be at work right now."

"Sorry, Brian, I have to go now, but I'll get you that recommendation by tomorrow."

I quickly disconnected the call, and, once the officer found my name on his computer, I was cleared through to the Old Headquarters Building.

However, the moment I parked my car, it suddenly occurred to me what I'd promised Brian.

I realized getting Carlton to change his mind about something might be a whole lot easier than getting that recommendation for Brian.

♦♦♦♦

At two o'clock, after Mitchell and I had finished up our initial briefing with the Citadel Protection operations teams, I pulled out of the parking lot at Agency headquarters and drove over to the Russell Senate Office Building on Constitution Avenue in D.C.

During our lunch break, I'd quizzed Mitchell about his father's schedule, but I'd tried to do it in such a way it would be impossible for him to know I was gathering intel—intel I needed in order to get in to see the Senator about recommending my nephew for a job.

I probably could have asked Mitchell's help in having a face-to-face meeting with his father, but, as things turned out, it was better he wasn't involved in the process.

Mitchell said the Senator was due to speak on the Senate floor around one o'clock, and, after that, he expected him to honor his long-standing policy of hosting an open house for his constituents, something Senator Mitchell usually did after delivering a major speech.

The open-house always took place in his suite of offices in the Russell Building, and anyone who resided in his home state of Ohio was welcomed to attend the event.

Although I was from Michigan and not from Ohio, I decided to take the Senator up on his invitation. I didn't think he'd throw me out if I didn't meet the criteria. The two states shared a common border, and if he decided to confront me, I'd just say I was being neighborly.

Being neighborly might count for something, but I'd heard what the Senator valued more than anything else was loyalty; specifically, loyalty to him.

Mitchell didn't know it, but I'd made his father's acquaintance once, although I wasn't expecting the man to remember the occasion.

It had taken place several years ago when Carlton and I had attended a classified briefing at the White House. After Carlton had introduced me as a covert intelligence officer, the Senator had referred to me as an agent. Later, when I'd corrected him about his terminology and explained I should be addressed as an officer instead of an agent, he'd let me know he didn't appreciate being corrected.

Now, as I walked down the hallowed halls of the prestigious Russell Building, I went through some options on how to approach the Senator.

Since I had to leave my weapon in the Range Rover to get through the building's metal detectors, firepower wasn't one of those options.

In the end, that turned out to be a good thing.

♦♦♦♦

As a ranking member of the U.S. Senate, Senator Mitchell was afforded certain privileges. Among those privileges was a suite of offices on the second floor of the Russell Senate Office Building, complete with opulent furnishings, expensive carpeting, and a magnificent view of the Capitol Building.

As I walked through the door of SR214, I couldn't help but be impressed by the décor in the Senator's office. However, what immediately drew my attention was the Senator himself.

He was standing in the middle of a large reception area surrounded by a room full of average-looking Americans.

I planted myself in the middle of the group and listened as the Senator held everyone spellbound by his colorful description of a recent surprise visit he'd made to a small contingent of American troops still left in Afghanistan. He invoked patriotic phrases and paid homage to the sacrifices made by the men and women of our military. He ended his rhetoric by pointing out several of his own achievements in the U. S. Congress.

Once he'd finished charming the group, he invited everyone to enjoy the refreshments he'd provided for them. He also told them to make sure they viewed the artifacts of American history—most of them related to Ohio—on display throughout his office suite.

As the Senator moved among the people, he appeared taller than anyone else in the room. Whether that was true or simply an illusion brought on by the man's presence, I wasn't sure. However, with his coal black hair, graying temples, and sharp, aquiline nose, no one could deny he cut an impressive figure.

Before long, he made his way over to where I was standing in front of a portrait of James Findlay. According to a small plaque next to the painting, Findlay had been the mayor of Cincinnati in the early 1800's before becoming a member of Congress.

The Senator gestured toward the portrait. "Now there's someone I greatly admire."

"Is that because Findlay was a Congressman who exposed a conspiracy, or do you admire him because he was a man who never failed to turn a tragedy to his own advantage?"

Elijah Mitchell turned away from the portrait and stared at me for several seconds.

"Well, well," he finally said. "What have we here? Are you a student of history," the Senator paused a moment and added, "Officer?"

I tried not to look too surprised he'd recognized me.

"Only as it relates to keeping our country safe. I know Findlay helped thwart the Burr Conspiracy, which would have been disastrous for our country, but, at the same time, his actions also made him so well-known he was able to get himself elected to public office. It's easy to see why you admire the man, Senator. His story is much like your own."

He smiled a politician's smile. "You seem to know Ohio's history pretty well. I didn't realize you were one of my constituents, Officer."

"Oh, I'm not. I'm from Michigan. I hope you won't hold that against me."

His smile faded a bit, and, after a quick glance around the room, he leaned in toward me and asked, "Am I to assume your visit here is *not* a social call?"

"That's correct, Senator. To be honest, it's not exactly a professional visit either. Is it possible for us to speak somewhere in private? I promise I won't take up too much of your valuable time."

After a moment's hesitation, the Senator crooked his finger and said, "Follow me."

Before leaving the room, I saw him gesture at one of his staffers. I didn't know whether this gesture was some sort of secret signal telling the staffer to contact the Capitol police, or whether he was telling the staffer to do the meet and greet without him.

I knew the DDO wouldn't be pleased if it were the former.

Seconds later, the Senator led me through an unmarked door, down a narrow passageway, and through a second door into his private office. He gestured over at two high-backed chairs positioned across from each other and invited me to have a seat.

As soon as we sat down, he immediately took charge of the conversation. "Now, tell me, Officer, what can I do for you?"

"First of all, Senator, my real name is Titus Ray. Since I know you have the nation's highest security clearance, and you already know I work for the CIA, I don't believe I'm breaking any rules by giving you my real name." I handed him my CIS business card. "My Career Legend identifies me as a Senior Fellow with CIS in Maryland."

He glanced at the card and then he offered me his hand. "I'm happy to put a name with that face. Does your presence here have anything to do with my son Ben? He's also an intelligence operative, but, to be truthful, I've been trying to get him to reconsider that decision."

"No, sir, my visit has nothing to do with your son. But, just out of curiosity, why would you want him to quit the Agency?"

He shook his head. "No, I don't necessarily want him to quit the Agency. He can stay on at the CIA, but I believe he's better suited to a desk job. I know my son, and he's like his old man. He knows how to manage a crisis and solve problems. Running a desk at the Agency makes more sense for him."

"You don't believe those skills are necessary to manage an asset or penetrate a terrorist cell?"

He chuckled. "Now don't take what I said personally. I'm sure you're very good at what you do. If you weren't, the DDO wouldn't have allowed you to be in the Situation Room during the Mumbai crisis. But, like I said, I know my son. I'm aware of his weaknesses as well as his strengths."

"Would you consider his inability to hold his emotions in check a weakness?"

He smiled. "I see you do know my son."

"I'm well acquainted with Ben."

"You've worked with him?"

I nodded. "I specifically requested he be assigned as one of the principals on Operation Clear Signal. I was the primary on that mission."

While the rest of the Senator's face remained impassive, his eyes widened. "Is that so? Well, congratulations on a job well done. This world's a whole lot safer without that terrorist in it."

"The skills your son brought to the table during that mission helped put Ahmed Al-Amin in his grave."

The Senator's features suddenly hardened, and I could hear the anger in his voice. "So you're contradicting my assessment of my own son?"

"No. What I'm saying is that I believe Ben has all the necessary skills to develop into an excellent covert operative, despite his weaknesses. Don't discount your son because of those weaknesses, Senator. No one's perfect, not even you."

The Senator tensed up immediately, and I realized I'd allowed the meeting to get off track. To make matters worse, I wasn't sure how to get it back on course again.

However, the Senator had no such difficulty.

"What are you doing here, Titus? I trust you didn't come here just to insult me."

"No, sir. I came here to ask you for a favor. Insulting you was never my intention."

He appeared amused at my answer. "So, what's the favor? How can I help you?"

I had the feeling he didn't mind granting favors, and, even though I thought I knew why, I asked him anyway.

"My nephew, Brian Simpson, is a political science major at the University of Michigan, and he's applied for an internship in Senator Conrad's office. He needs a recommendation from someone in government service, and I was wondering if you'd mind putting in a good word for him. I can vouch for the guy."

The Senator got up and walked over to his desk. "What kind of student is he? What's his grade point average?"

I had no idea, but I took a stab at it. "Uh . . . he's a straight A student."

"What's his name again?"

He scribbled Brian's name down on a notepad and asked some more questions about him.

I made up some more answers.

Finally, he walked back over to his chair and sat down.

He smiled at me. "I'll call Pete Conrad tonight. He owes me a few favors, so you can tell your nephew he'll be offered the position."

"Thanks, Senator. I really appreciate your help."

He nodded. "I'm glad I could help out, Titus, but I've always believed one good turn deserves another, and I'm asking you to remember that if you're paired up with my son on any future operations. I think all Ben needs is a little encouragement, and he'd be willing to ask for a transfer to an analyst position. If that encouragement were to come from another operative, say someone like yourself, I'm sure it would carry a lot of weight with him."

After underscoring the fact he expected a little quid pro quo from me for his efforts to get my nephew the internship, he immediately got out of his chair and headed for the door.

The meeting was over.

"No, sir, I won't do that."

The Senator stopped at the edge of his desk.

When he turned around and looked at me, the scowl on his face was one I'd seen on the evening news when the Senator was grilling a hostile witness during a Senate committee hearing.

He walked back over to where I was seated. "Is that right?"

I stood up. "That's right, sir. Like I said, Ben is going to make an excellent covert officer, and I'm committed to helping him achieve that goal. I believe our country will be better off with him in that position than if he were sitting behind a desk at headquarters. And Senator, I'm sure you want what's best for your son, as well as what's best for this country.

"That goes without saying, but—"

"Here's what I *will* do for you, because, as you said, one good turn deserves another. Actually, this is what I won't do. I won't tell Ben you've been working behind the scenes at the Agency to have him transferred out of Operations. I won't tell him you conspired with the DDO to force Olivia McConnell to be the FO on a mission hoping she'd give him a bad report."

We stood there for a few minutes, toe to toe, staring at each other. Finally, he broke eye contact with me and walked over to a window overlooking the Capitol. The glass extended from the floor to the ceiling, and I was sure he'd been photographed there dozens of times for publicity purposes.

His voice was subdued when he spoke again."I just wanted Ben to be safe," he said, gazing outside. "I didn't want to lose him."

"There's no place on earth that's safe today, Senator, but, if you're willing to let him go, you won't lose him."

He didn't reply.

I took that as my cue to leave.

As I opened the door, he said, "If you want to see me again, make an appointment."

# Chapter 15

I slipped into a conference room on the ground floor of the Old Headquarters Building at six o'clock, precisely on time for my final briefing before Citadel Protection went operational.

There were four other people in the room, and I was the last person to arrive. I didn't apologize for being late.

I wasn't.

Despite that, Carlton, who always arrived at a meeting thirty minutes before it began, made it sound as if I were.

"Titus is here now, so we can get started," he said.

I sat down next to Mitchell.

"Where have you been?" he whispered.

"Family matter."

"Better you than me."

Carlton, who was seated in the center seat on the right hand side of the table, nodded over at Wilson, who was at the head of the table. "Initiate the call to Vasco," he said. "I'm sure he's tired of waiting."

Nolan hit a few keystrokes, and Ken Vasco, the CIA's chief of station in Buenos Aires, appeared on the screen at the far end of the room. At first, his head seemed to be taking up at least two-thirds of the video display, but then, someone adjusted the zoom function on the camera, and the rest of the room came into view.

I could tell Vasco was in The Bubble at our embassy in Buenos Aires, a soundproof room designed for secure communications with government entities back in the U.S. Anyone employed by the CIA was required to use either The Bubble or an encrypted satellite phone when communicating with the Agency back at Langley.

I always preferred to use my Agency phone when I was in the field, and, unless I needed to have a video conference with the Ops Center, I seldom went inside The Bubble.

The room's smaller dimensions, along with the weird acoustics, always reminded me of a prison cell—something I never wanted to be reminded of again—so I avoided it as much as possible.

Vasco didn't appear to be the least bit affected by his environment. He smiled and gave Carlton a big wave."Douglas, how are you?"

"Katherine, is that you?" he said, cupping his hand over his eyes as if the lights in the conference room were bothering his eyesight.

Katherine looked up from her computer briefly and gave him a weak smile. "Hi, Ken. Nice to see you again."

Vasco shifted his attention to Wilson. "Nolan, I can't believe they let you out of the Bat Caves for this."

The RTM Centers were sometimes referred to as the Bat Caves because they were made up of a labyrinth of underground rooms, and all the sophisticated electronics cast a bluish glow over everything.

Carlton had never seen the humor in referring to the RTM Centers as Bat Caves. And, since he didn't tolerate other jokes about Agency matters, I thought he might want to explain such things to Vasco, but before he had a chance to do that, Vasco continued his conversation with Wilson.

"Seriously, what are you doing here, Nolan? Was this operation too small for Olivia's attention, or did she finally get promoted to the seventh floor?"

Wilson, who had an impressive looking goatee and wore a pair of half glasses perched over his nose, was not a quick-witted kind of guy. Before he could formulate a response, Carlton spoke up.

"Olivia's not feeling well today, and Nolan's been appointed acting director until she returns. Now, Ken, let me introduce you to the principals of the mission."

I wasn't sure how Carlton knew I'd never met Vasco before, but when he told him I was the primary for the operation, Vasco said, "I'm happy to finally make your acquaintance, Titus."

I muttered something equally inane, and once Carlton had introduced Mitchell, we got down to business.

Vasco had been the point man for the Agency when Roberto Montilla and his family were relocated to Buenos Aires. He'd helped them rent a house, locate a school for Emma, and now, he was in the process of finding employment for Roberto.

When Mitchell and I arrived in Buenos Aires, Vasco would be responsible for providing us with logistical support while we were in country conducting our mission.

In the earlier briefing, Carlton had told us Ken Vasco was listed as a General Services Officer on the personnel roster of our embassy in Buenos Aires. This position encompassed a wide variety of duties, involving both procurement and trade, and enabled him to easily move around the city, managing his own stable of CIA operatives and assets.

Carlton asked, "What arrangements have you made for the meeting with Roberto?"

When Vasco replied, his demeanor reflected a more somber tone than his initial jocularity, and I suspected this change in mood was caused by the sobering effect Carlton often had on people.

Vasco said, "I've rented office space in one of the upscale business districts. Three days from now, I'll pick Roberto up and drive him over to the office suite so he can discuss his dream of owning a sandwich franchise with the executives of Bub's Subs."

Vasco pointed over to Mitchell and me. "The rest is up to you guys."

When the Ops Center team had mapped out the Citadel Protection operation, they'd made the decision not to inform Roberto he was about to be interrogated a second time. Instead, Vasco had told him he'd be meeting with representatives from Bub's Subs about setting up a sandwich franchise in Buenos Aires, capitalizing on his desire to own one of the fast-food enterprises.

"We'll take it from there," I said.

When Mitchell and I got off the plane in Buenos Aires, I'd be carrying a passport identifying me as Geraldo Lucia, while Mitchell would be entering Argentina as Ignacio Rubio. Both of us would be posing as executives of Bub's Subs out of Orlando, Florida.

Carlton asked Vasco a few more questions, and the call ended when Vasco said he had already arranged for a driver to meet the Bub's Subs executives at Ezeiza International Airport in Buenos Aires two days from now.

I'd never eaten a sub from Bub's, but I decided if our flight had a layover in Miami, I ought to try one.

♦♦♦♦

When the conference call ended, Carlton asked Katherine for an update on the location of the cargo ships carrying the chemical weapons from Syria to Cuba.

"There are three vessels, and they should arrive at the port in Santiago de Cuba in six days."

"The ships aren't headed for Havana?" I asked.

Carlton said. "Apparently, the Castro brothers are trying to distance themselves from their Hezbollah friends—at least while our government is normalizing relations with them—and they've banished them to the other side of the island. We know there's a Hezbollah cell containing at least twelve operatives in Santiago de Cuba, and their fingerprints are all over a warehouse there. Satellite surveillance shows it's recently been refurbished. Since it meets all the criteria for housing the gas canisters, we believe that's where Hezbollah has set up shop now that the warehouses in Venezuela are out of the picture."

Wilson removed his half glasses and spoke up for the first time. His voice reflected his Boston upbringing.

"Those canisters are completely useless to Hezbollah without a delivery system. Our analysts believe The Caracas Document hints at the possibility Roberto knows what that delivery system is and where it's located."

Carlton nodded at Mitchell and me. "Your interrogation of Roberto should focused not only on discovering how Hezbollah plans to deliver the sarin gas, but also on what their timetable may be."

I said, "Roberto was pretty insistent he didn't know anything about the delivery system when we questioned him before, and, although I saw the same inconsistencies in The Caracas Document as you did, I'm not as optimistic he'll be able to give us any more information other than what he's already given us. I think those answers will have to come from the intel we get out of Syria or Cuba."

Wilson smiled and looked over at Carlton. "I think Titus is trying to tell us he'd rather be traveling to Cuba or flying to Syria instead of making the trip down to Buenos Aires."

Carlton said, "Subtlety has never been his strong suit."

Mitchell said, "I also believe interrogating Roberto is a waste of time."

I said, "No, I'm not saying it's a waste of time. In fact, I'm sure we'll pick up some extra intel by having another go at Roberto. What I *am* saying is that we may not get the necessary intel in time to stop Hezbollah from dropping a rocket load of sarin gas on Washington, especially if those canisters arrive in Cuba in a few days."

Carlton said, "We'll be sending Agency personnel to Cuba, and we already have operatives monitoring Rehman Zaidi in Damascus. The team in Damascus also has a solid asset in Hezbollah's camp, and this asset may be our best chance of learning the timetable for the event."

I remembered Olivia's advice about Marwan Farage, and, since the briefing appeared to be almost over and Wilson hadn't brought up the man's name once, I decided it was time to toss it out there.

"Have our people in Damascus mentioned anything about Marwan Farage?"

If Carlton was surprised to hear Marwan's name, he didn't show it. "I'm not aware of any reports about him." He pointed over at Wilson. "Marwan Farage? Is there any new intel on him? He was one of Ahmed Al-Amin's relatives."

Katherine spoke up, "His cousin. Marwan was his cousin."

Katherine had uncovered the connection between Ahmed and Marwan, and, unlike most counterintelligence analysts, she never minded receiving attention for her efforts.

Wilson typed in a few keystrokes on his laptop.

Seconds later, he sat back in his chair and nodded. "Here it is. His name was mentioned in a report about the meeting Zaidi had with Hassan Naballah, the head of Hezbollah in Damascus. There's nothing there, though. The report just mentions Marwan's name."

I asked, "Just his name? Nothing else?"

"See for yourself."

Wilson projected the document on the screen in front of everyone.

It was a typical Field Report Summary (FRS). This one described a meeting between an asset and his handler.

The body of the document was the printed transcript of the audio recording from the meeting, and, as soon as I saw the handler's initials were KP, I knew Keever Pike had to be one of the principals working Operation Citadel Protection in Syria. I wasn't able to figure out the asset's name, because, as per Agency policy, an asset's initials were only listed as UA for unnamed asset.

The transcript read:

*KP:* Who was at the meeting between Naballah and Rehman Zaidi when he returned to Damascus?

*UA:* Marwan Farage and Abdul Latif were present, and, of course, I was also there.

*KP:* Did Naballah tell you why he'd called the meeting?

*UA:* He wanted a full report on Zaidi's role in Ahmed Al-Amin's death.

*KP*: Why did he want the report? Did Naballah blame Zaidi for his death?

*UA:* Maybe. I don't know. He just wanted to know how Ahmed had died.

*KP:* Did Zaidi take responsibility for Ahmed getting killed?"

*UA:* No, he placed the blame on Roberto Montilla. He said he was sure Montilla was working for the CIA, and he even gave Naballah one of the bullets from Ahmed's body to prove it. He said the bullet had come from a Glock.

KP: What does that prove?

UA: He said most CIA people use a Glock.

*KP:* Some do. Some don't. Okay, so what was Naballah's reaction?

*UA:* He didn't have a reaction. The only person in the room who showed any emotion was Marwan. He got so angry Naballah had to calm him down.

*KP:* Did Naballah discuss the chemical weapons at the meeting?

*UA:* Naballah said the ships carrying the canisters were being diverted to Cuba because the warehouses in Venezuela had been compromised by Montilla's betrayal.

*KP*: And the target? Has that changed?

*UA:* No. It remains Washington, D.C.

*KP*: Did he talk about how he plans to disperse the gas or say anything about the timing of the attack?

*UA*: All he said was the Cuban location wasn't going to change the schedule. He said nothing about how he plans to use the gas.

*KP:* And you still don't know when the attack will take place?

*UA:* No. Naballah said only General Suleiman knows the schedule.

*KP*: You mean the Iranian general?

*UA*: Yes. General Suleiman, the head of Al Quds. He's the one who has the final say.

♦♦♦♦

Wilson stayed quiet until it was obvious everyone in the room had finished skimming the FRS.

"See what I mean?" Wilson said. "There's nothing there."

I said, "The UA said Marwan was upset when he heard about Ahmed's murder. He thought it was significant enough to mention it to his handler. "

Wilson said, "You sound like Olivia. She said the same thing."

Carlton gave me a curious look. "What are your concerns about Marwan Farage?"

"Revenge is my concern. Jihadists feed on anger. All the 9/11 hijackers were fueled by anger at the Americans for some reason or another. We should be proactive and start monitoring Marwan's travels before he shows up over here to exact his revenge."

Whether he agreed with my reasoning or not, Carlton instructed

Wilson to put a tracker on Marwan. Once that was done, he said he wanted to wrap things up by taking care of some housekeeping details.

"The DDO has decided to split Citadel Protection into two separate components. Everyone here in this room is a member of Component One. Component Two will be led by C.J. Salazar, who'll be investigating yesterday's incident at the Washington Navy Yard. His team will ascertain if the shootings had anything to do with the threat posed by Hezbollah to use chemical weapons on the capital."

Now I understood why Carlton has assured me he would be the handler for my run into Buenos Aires. As soon as he saw the drugs in Felipe's backpack, he must have realized Salazar would ask the DDO to allow him to explore the drug cartel's role in the Navy Yard incident.

I had no doubt Carlton had also encouraged the DDO to give Cartel Carlos that assignment—moving the pieces on the board in such a way as to protect his territory and remain in control.

Carlton pointed over to Katherine. "Ms. Broward's team will continue to do a deep background check on Walid Khouri, whose phone number was found in the second shooter's backpack. If she finds a Hezbollah connection, I'll let you know."

At the mention of her name, Katherine smiled and glanced across the table at me. I was tempted to give her a wink, but I didn't want her to interpret it as anything other than signaling we were co-conspirators when it came to Walid Khouri.

I gave her a brief smile instead.

She returned my smile with a wink.

♦♦♦♦

Our flight to Buenos Aires didn't leave until four o'clock the next day, so, after leaving Langley, I headed back out to The Meadows to spend the night.

The moment I pulled in the driveway, I got a call from Nikki.

"Your timing's perfect. I was just about to call you," I said.

"Does that mean you're still in Virginia?"

"I'll be leaving tomorrow."

"I'm glad I caught you before you left."

"Is something wrong?"

"Yes, in a way. My captain was involved in a pretty bad car accident today."

"I'm sorry to hear that. He's not—"

"No, no. Other than having two broken legs, he's okay. His doctor said he'll be fine in a couple of months, but I'm afraid this means Stormy will have to stay in a kennel after all. I couldn't ask the captain's wife to take care of an extra dog while she's busy taking care of the captain."

"No, of course not."

"I'm sorry it worked out like this. I know he won't like being confined. I'm talking about Stormy, not the captain." She laughed. "The captain won't like it much either."

"His wife might not be happy about it herself." I got out of the Range Rover and headed toward the front door. "What are the kennel options for Stormy?"

The moment she started explaining them, another thought popped in my mind.

"Forget the kennel," I said. "Bring Stormy with you. I have the perfect place for him here."

"Really? Are you kidding?"

I told her I wasn't kidding, and I gave her the address.

Once we said goodbye, I went inside and told Arkady to expect a companion for Frisco to arrive at The Meadows by the end of the week. I said he'd be in the company of a beautiful woman.

I assured him Carlton wouldn't mind having Stormy around—once he'd met the beautiful woman.

Of course, that was sheer fantasy on my part.

♦♦♦♦

The next morning, around ten o'clock, I received a phone call from Brian. As soon as I saw the caller ID, I tried to figure out the best way to explain my failure to get the recommendation I'd promised him.

Since he didn't hold me in very high esteem anyway, I knew he probably wouldn't be too surprised when I told him I hadn't come through for him.

"Did I catch you at work?" he asked.

"Just heading in."

"Late start, huh? Well, I won't keep you, but I wanted to let you know I didn't get the internship with Senator Conrad."

"I'm sorry about that. I did try to—"

"Don't be sorry. As soon as I got off the phone with Senator Conrad's office, I got a call from Senator Mitchell. I go to work for him on Monday."

"Senator Mitchell called you?"

He sounded breathless. "Yes, can you believe it? He's the highest-ranking senator on two intelligence committees. Anyone who interns with him gets paid really well and is pretty much assured of employment in Washington after they're done."

"He's a powerful man."

"From what I understand, Senator Conrad was so impressed with my application, he forwarded it to Senator Mitchell, and that's how I got the position."

"I bet it was your grade point average that won him over."

Brian laughed. "That's the funny part. My grades this semester haven't been all that great. It's been a rough year."

"I'm happy for you, Brian. It sounds like a wonderful opportunity."

"I'll probably be stuck at a desk all day, but, according to the Senator, that's how he got his start. He emphasized how he had managed to work his way up from the bottom."

"Sounds like he was sending you a message."

"He also said he plans to take a special interest in me."

"I'd definitely say he was sending a message."

"Well, I heard the message loud and clear."

I also heard the Senator's message—my nephew's future was in his hands.

# PART TWO

## Chapter 16

*Thursday, June 25*

The freckled-face driver the American Embassy sent to Ezeiza International Airport to pick up the two executives from Bub's Subs was a loquacious kind of guy.

As soon as Mitchell and I were settled into the back seat of his car, he told us he was born in Brooklyn, New York. Along with giving us the highlights of his life, including a story about his engagement to an Argentinean actress, he also pointed out some of the city's attractions on our way into downtown Buenos Aires.

I did my best to feign an interest in the Art Museum, the Planetarium, and the Botanical Gardens, but I was happy when we finally pulled up in front of the Park Hyatt Hotel. The Brooklyn Guy checked us in and took care of our luggage. Then, a short time later, he drove us over to the American Embassy, about six blocks away.

After the Marine security guard waved us through the gate at the embassy compound, Brooklyn Guy drove the car around to the back entrance, where there was an underground parking facility. From there, Mitchell and I rode the elevator up to the second floor. When the doors opened, Vasco was waiting for us with a big smile on his face.

"Hey, guys. Nice to see you again." He gestured toward a hallway. "Come this way."

Mitchell and I followed him down a short corridor.

After using his key card on an unmarked door, Vasco entered The Bubble, the same room we'd seen him occupying during the video conference call two days earlier.

The moment Vasco turned to face us, he began rubbing his hands together vigorously, as if he were anticipating the pleasures of an all-you-can-eat buffet. "I can't tell you how delighted I am to be working with the two of you."

Extending his hand toward Mitchell, he said, "Ben Mitchell. You're Elijah Mitchell's son, right?"

Mitchell pulled away from him. "That's right, but I don't see how that's relevant to this operation."

Vasco laughed. "Oh, it's not, but I did meet the Senator once, and I just thought I'd let you know that. Not to worry, though. Outside of this room, I'll address you as Ignacio Rubio."

Vasco turned away from Mitchell and shook hands with me. "Titus Ray. You probably don't know this, but I took over your operation when the Agency pulled you out of Colombia."

"I had no idea."

During my early days at the Agency, I'd been assigned to the Latin American desk, and, as a newbie, I'd gotten my feet wet in Nicaragua. After my handler was almost killed in Managua because of my failure to follow orders, I was transferred to Barranquilla, Colombia.

I hadn't made the request for a transfer (TR); that request had come directly from my handler.

My new assignment in Colombia had been to recruit assets inside the two big drug cartels, which turned out to be a nearly impossible task. By the end of three years, when I heard the Agency was offering an intense language course in Arabic, along with a transfer to the Middle East, I'd jumped at the chance to fill out the TR for a new assignment.

The Arabic language course meant living in Pakistan with a non-English-speaking tutor for six months. Learning a language had never been that difficult for me, and by the end of my six months, I could speak Arabic fluently. I could also communicate in Farsi, after having spent a lot of time with an Iranian neighbor who lived across the hall from me.

Vasco nodded. "Yeah, the Agency assigned me to Colombia after you left. I finally recruited a couple of assets inside the Medellin cartel, and then I got really lucky when three brothers inside the Cali cartel agreed to work with us. They helped our guys bring down one of the major drug families in the cartel."

Mitchell said, "Are you talking about Miguel Rodriguez? One of my instructors at Camp Peary lectured us on that operation. He said it was a textbook case."

Vasco nodded. "It was pretty sweet."

"Congratulations," I said. "I wasn't as successful in penetrating the cartels."

"Yeah, but look at what you've done since. You're a Level 1 intelligence officer now, and from what I hear, your operation in Afghanistan pulled in some pretty big fish a few years ago."

Before I had a chance to respond, Mitchell asked him a question about Miguel Rodriguez, and that launched him into a colorful story about the drug lord's nefarious ways. The moment he wrapped up that story, Mitchell peppered him with even more questions.

It was clear Ken Vasco had made a big impression on my partner.

I couldn't say the same.

Something about the man irritated me.

As I listened to him answering Mitchell's questions, I realized the station chief reminded me of Sal Westerfield, a police detective who'd lived down the street from us in Flint, Michigan.

I figured that resemblance was why Vasco was hitting the wrong notes with me.

Like Vasco, Sal was also a big man with an overlapping gut—courtesy of one too many donuts—and, like Vasco, he was also a slap-you-on-the-back, gregarious kind of guy.

As a teenager, I hadn't liked Sal very much.

In fact, I'd found him loud and overbearing. If my parents had allowed me to use the word, I probably would have described him as stupid, maybe even a little dense, certainly laughable.

However, during breakfast one morning—I was probably sixteen at the time—I'd changed my mind about Detective Westerfield's personality. It was right after my mother had shown me an article in the morning newspaper.

"You should read this," she said, indicating a front-page article describing how Detective Sal Westerfield had disarmed a suicidal young man bent on killing his family and taking his own life.

She pointed to the picture of Sal with his arm around the young kid. "That's Sal for you. People underestimate him because he acts dumb. Personally, I think he's learn to use that to his advantage."

Now, as Vasco sat down at the head of the conference table and pulled a computer keyboard toward him, I wondered if the same could be said about the station chief.

Vasco said, "Let me see if I can manage this uplink with Langley without calling in one of our tech guys."

His fingers moved rapidly over the keyboard.

A few seconds later, Carlton, along with Nolan Wilson, could be seen on the wide-screen monitor at the other end of the room. The two of them were seated in Carlton's small conference room next to his office.

Vasco looked up at the screen and gave Carlton a snappy salute, along with a big smile. "All present and accounted for, sir."

Carlton wasn't smiling.

"We've had some disturbing news."

♦♦♦♦

Before giving us the details, Carlton asked Vasco about the surveillance he was running on the Jihadist groups in Buenos Aires.

The Agency, along with Mossad, had kept a close eye on all the Hezbollah militant groups operating out of Argentina, especially after a car bomb had destroyed a Jewish community center a few years ago.

A group calling itself *Islamic Jihad* had claimed responsibility for the Jewish center attack, but, even so, none of its members had ever been prosecuted.

Like Venezuela, the government in Argentina appeared reluctant to move against the militant arm of the Muslim community for fear of upsetting the societal structure they'd built, including a couple of hospitals and several schools. More importantly, Argentina had tied itself economically to Iran in the form of trade agreements, exchanging their agricultural products for Iranian oil, and they seemed reluctant to see this balance of trade upset in any way.

As a result of this cozy relationship, the Islamic militant elements in Hezbollah had flourished in Argentina, and, according to Carlton's briefing a couple of days ago, they were even sending operatives abroad now.

Vasco quickly answered Carlton's inquires by giving him a surprisingly thorough rundown on several players in the militant groups in Argentina.

Carlton asked, "So you've discovered nothing to connect Roberto Montilla to *Islamic Jihad* or any of the Hezbollah groups there in Buenos Aires? There's been no chatter about Montilla at all?"

Vasco shook his head, "Absolutely none. He's not on their radar."

I asked, "What's your disturbing news, Douglas? Have you received new intel on Roberto?"

Carlton gave me a sharp look, but, while I knew he abhorred impatience, he immediately answered my question.

"No, there's nothing new on Roberto." He gestured toward Nolan Wilson. "Nolan will give you the update."

Wilson looked up from his computer and said, "The tracker we placed on Marwan Farage shows him on the move. Around dawn yesterday morning, he left Damascus and traveled by car, actually a mini-van, to Beirut, Lebanon, where he caught an early morning flight to Madrid on Turkish Air. That flight landed around noon, and we can confirm Marwan disembarked from the plane."

I had a sinking feeling in the pit of my stomach, but I waited for Wilson to confirm my suspicions.

"Unfortunately, he disappeared after that."

Wilson glanced down at his computer for a second. "If he boarded another plane, there were three possible flights he could have taken during that time frame. On the other hand, if he rented a car, or if he got picked up by someone, he could be anywhere by now."

Vasco asked, "Should we be on the lookout for him here? Is

Buenos Aires one of those possibilities?"

"No. Assuming he got on another plane, we've narrowed it down to Mexico City, Caracas, and Houston. Buenos Aires wasn't on the list."

"He won't fly into Houston," I said. "You can scratch that one."

After discussing all the different scenarios for several minutes, Wilson said, "We've alerted everyone in the intelligence community to be on the lookout for him, but, in the meantime, the Ops Center has added extra personnel here to monitor the chatter coming out of all the known Jihadist groups south of the border."

Carlton addressed Vasco. "Is everything in place for Roberto's meeting tomorrow?"

Vasco gave him a thumbs up. "Everything's all set. We'll be ready to party at ten o'clock in the morning, and a good time will be had by all."

While Vasco may have been excellent at recruiting assets inside a Colombian drug ring, he was lousy at predicting the future, and a good time was not had by all.

## Chapter 17

Once the conference call had ended, Vasco began making plans for the three of us to visit the office suite where Mitchell and I would be interrogating Roberto Montilla. Carlton had requested video of the layout, and Vasco made it sound like making the video would be great fun.

I suggested he and Mitchell go shoot the video, while I stayed behind and had a talk with some of the Level 2 operatives conducting the surveillance on Roberto.

As we got up from the table, Vasco slapped me on the back and said, "You're not getting all squirrely on me, are you? I have three teams of watchers and all of them are top-notch people."

I gave him my best smile. "Well, Ken, if by squirrely you mean I'm nervous about the job they've been doing, then no, I'm not squirrely. On the other hand, if you're asking me whether this job has made me a little nutty, then the answer is definitely yes. I *am* a little squirrely."

Vasco guffawed like a late-night talk show host who'd just heard his guest tell an awful joke but was pretending otherwise.

I wasn't sure what the motive behind his laughter was, but I had a feeling it was in the category of having another agenda.

"Now that's a good one," Vasco said, chuckling some more. "I've heard people say you were a pretty serious guy, but it's nice to know they were wrong."

They weren't wrong.

♦♦♦♦

Vasco and I rode the elevator up to the third floor of the embassy together. When we got off, he turned left and entered a door marked Communications.

Inside the room, there were dozens of computers, a mass of electronic equipment, and racks of telephony and network servers. Lining the wall on one side were data storage units and, on the opposite wall, were two large consoles with video monitors in front of them.

Seated in front of the consoles were two Level 3 operatives, a man and a woman. Each one was wearing a headset, and both nodded at Vasco and me as we passed by.

Vasco led me over to a door tucked in a corner of the room by some filing cabinets. When he opened it, we entered a room with a couple of desks, a dark colored couch, a small refrigerator, and a table with four chairs.

I'd spent a lifetime in such rooms.

Most operatives referred to them as waiting rooms.

There were two Agency personnel inside, and I figured both of them were waiting for something—waiting for their shift, waiting to hear from a source, waiting to go home, waiting for an assignment.

Vasco introduced the woman first, "Titus Ray meet Juliana Lamar. You'll fall in love with her. Everybody does. Juliana meet Titus. Yes, he's that Titus Ray."

Juliana rolled her eyes and smiled at me.

Vasco said, "And that big guy over there, the one who's too lazy to get off the couch, we call him Otis. As you can see, he loves to eat as much as I do."

Otis was devouring a sandwich, but he stopped chewing long enough to gesture around the room and say, "Welcome to our humble abode."

Vasco said, "Juliana manages our surveillance teams, and she'll be able to answer any questions you have about the stakeouts at the Montilla location." He turned and headed for the door. "Have fun, kids. I'm off to make a dirty movie."

Once he was gone, Juliana got up from her chair and walked over to me. She had an amused look on her face. "I hope you don't embarrass easily. Otherwise, you'll never survive here."

"I don't embarrass easily."

She looked me in the eye and nodded. "I would have guessed that."

She held my gaze for several seconds and didn't flinch when I stared back at her.

Although her narrow face was dominated by her large blue eyes, what drew my attention was a small, black beauty mark at the corner of her mouth.

She finally looked away and grabbed a ball cap with the letters SF printed in orange on the front. After pulling her blond ponytail through the back opening, she asked, "What questions do you have for me?"

"Were you headed somewhere?"

She slung a small rectangular purse over her shoulder. "Yeah, Otis and I are due at the Montilla location in a few minutes."

"Let Otis stay here and finish his sandwich. I'll ask you my questions when we ride over to the Montilla location together."

Otis waved and said, "Hey, thanks, man."

Juliana hesitated a second, and I thought she was about to nix the whole idea of the ride along.

In the Agency's chain of command, I outranked her, so she really couldn't refuse to let me go with her. But, I'd seen some fire in those big blue eyes of hers, so she might not be all that big on the whole chain of command sort of thing.

I'd also seen some sadness in those eyes.

"Let's do it," she said. She gave Otis a wave. "Catch you later."

"Call me if you get bored."

We called him, but not because we got bored.

♦♦♦♦

Juliana and I headed west out of the embassy compound in the direction of the Palermo district. She drove an older model Jeep

Cherokee, and I sat beside her and rode shotgun.

Once we'd cleared the compound, I pointed to her ball cap. "Does that mean you're a San Francisco Giants fan?"

"I grew up in San Francisco, and my dad was an avid Giants fan. He gave me this cap the day I told him I'd taken an overseas assignment with the State Department."

She touched the cap's logo. "An hour after he gave it to me, he had a massive heart attack. He died in the ER a few hours later."

Her matter-of-fact way of telling me this caught me off guard for a minute, and I quickly mumbled, "I'm sorry."

"No, it's okay. While he was in the ER, the doctors discovered he had lung cancer. If he'd been given the choice, I believe he would have preferred a quick end to his life rather than a slow one."

"That ball cap looks new. You must not have been with the Agency very long."

She glanced over at me and smiled.

"I'm not unacquainted with indirect interrogation techniques, Titus. But let me spare you the trouble. The short version of my bio is that I've been with the Agency for seven years now. The reason the cap looks new is because I don't wear it very often. For some reason, I was thinking about him today and grabbed it."

"I wasn't trolling for information, I just wanted—"

She didn't let me finish. "Before I joined the CIA, I was a detective in the narcotics division of the San Francisco Police Department. I'd been with them for less than three years when my husband, who was also a cop, got killed by some gang members. After he died . . ."

She paused when her voice broke, but she quickly recovered and finished her thought.

" . . . I found it impossible to go to work every day. That's when I decided to do something completely different. Now, seven years later, here I am."

"Have you been stuck in surveillance the whole seven years?"

"Yeah, pretty much. I'm not complaining, though. The routine's been good for me."

We drove along in silence for a few minutes, and, while I wanted to change the subject and ask her what she'd noticed at the Montilla house, I wasn't sure if I'd given her enough time to compose herself. I didn't know how long I was supposed to wait after hearing about a dead husband before I got back to the business at hand.

Social niceties had always been a mystery to me. Even when I thought I had them figured out, someone was always changing the rules on me.

She said, "By the way, Titus, now would be a good time for you to tell me something about your own career. Despite what Ken said, I'm not really acquainted with Titus Ray, and, if I'm not mistaken, a give and take is what's supposed to happen in polite conversation."

Case in point.

I gave her my best smile. "There's not that much to tell. I grew up in Flint, Michigan and graduated from the University of Michigan. I joined the Agency right after my graduation, and I was a Level 2 operative on the Latin American desk until I was transferred over to the Middle East. That was back when the Agency put out a call for operatives who were willing to learn Arabic right after the first Gulf war. I've spent most of my career as a Level 1 covert operative assigned to the Middle East, but, as you probably know, special circumstances have brought me to Buenos Aires today."

She glanced over at me. "The facts you've just recited told me nothing except you're really good at making your life sound as dull as possible. If all that's true, then why did Ken imply you're some kind of CIA legend, and I should swoon over you?"

"For the same reason he said I'd fall in love with you."

She laughed. "I think you've got Ken figured out."

♦♦♦♦

After Juliana made a left turn onto a residential street, she brought the Jeep to a stop in front of a row of houses.

She pointed down the block. "The third house. The one with the ash tree out in front. That's Roberto Montilla's new address."

It was a modest-looking house on a quiet residential street. I wasn't sure how much the Agency had spent on relocating Roberto and his family to Buenos Aires, but at least it didn't look as if the U.S.

taxpayer had been stuck with an extravagant bill to pay for his housing needs.

Within seconds of Juliana maneuvering her way into a parking space, a Nissan Pathfinder, parked a little further down the block, pulled into traffic and disappeared around a corner.

"Was that one of ours?" I asked.

"Pretty obvious, huh?"

"He could have waited a few more minutes before leaving."

She shifted in the driver's seat so she was facing me. "Why not ask me those questions now? If Montilla keeps to his schedule, he'll be on the move soon, and I might get distracted."

"What's his schedule?"

"Today, he usually drives over to the cemetery to visit his son's grave."

I nodded. "That doesn't surprise me. He and Ernesto were very close."

"He gets extremely emotional when he goes over there. It's hard not to be moved by his tears."

"That's the kind of information I need when I question him tomorrow. I also need to know if anyone has shown any interest in him. Have you noticed anyone following Roberto or his family? Even someone just cruising around his neighborhood?"

She shook her head. "I haven't spotted anyone, and no one's reported anything. Why? What makes you think someone might take an interest in Roberto or his family?"

"I'm assuming you're aware Roberto was a Venezuelan government official who helped the Agency take out a Hezbollah assassin?"

She nodded. "That would be Ahmed Al-Amin. Ken briefed us on Montilla's background. He said Ahmed also targeted Montilla after he refused to help Hezbollah build some warehouses in Venezuela. At least the guy didn't want anything to do with storing Syria's chemical weapons."

I looked across the street at Roberto's new residence. "Before Ahmed went after Roberto, Ahmed tortured and killed Roberto's son, Ernesto. When we informed Roberto what Ahmed had done, he was willing to help us take him out. Now, it seems Roberto has information on how the Iranians are planning to use those chemical weapons on us. That will be the main topic of conversation when I meet with him tomorrow."

"Are you afraid Hezbollah will send someone else to assassinate Roberto to keep him from talking? Is that why you're worried about his safety?"

I shook my head. "It's hard to say. Roberto may be completely off their radar by now, and we've certainly taken precautions to keep his whereabouts a secret. But since I'm about to interrogate him again, I want to make certain I won't have any company when I do that. And, although I think it's unlikely, I'd also like to be sure Roberto hasn't had any contact with any of the Hezbollah groups in Argentina."

Juliana nodded her head at Roberto's house. "Here he comes."

Roberto walked out of his house and headed over to his driveway. He was dressed in casual clothes and running shoes, like the last time I'd seen him, but now, his moustache was gone, and he was sporting a different hairstyle.

Even though he'd changed his appearance—which I had to assume he'd done for security reasons—he didn't bother looking around his environment before getting inside a Honda Accord.

When he was about halfway down the block, Juliana pulled away from the curb and followed him.

She was extremely proficient at tailing a target, but even so, when we pulled up at a stoplight, several cars in front of us decided to change lanes at the same time, and we suddenly found ourselves directly behind Roberto's car.

I immediately lowered my head and slid down in the passenger seat.

Juliana said, "If you're afraid Montilla might recognize you, there's a hat in the console."

I opened the console and pulled out a slightly crushed, brown fedora. When I put it on, the soft felt regained its shape.

Juliana smiled. "I can't say that style does much for you."

"You think anyone at the cemetery will notice my style?"

She laughed. "Dead men tell no tales."

Once we arrived at the cemetery, the dead men weren't my concern, it was the live ones carrying guns who worried me.

## Chapter 18

The cemetery was located one block south *of Camino Delgado* about twenty minutes from Roberto's house. When Roberto turned in at the gate at *Cementerio de Flores*, Juliana drove on past the entrance and circled back around, entering the cemetery a few minutes later.

Conducting surveillance at a cemetery was difficult because two people sitting in a car at a graveyard tended to draw unwanted attention, especially from the cemetery's caretakers.

Since very little activity seemed to be taking place around the grounds, I wondered how Juliana was going to handle keeping an eye on Roberto without drawing attention to us.

It turned out she had that covered.

As she pulled into the driveway of a small chapel in the center of the cemetery, she pointed off to the east, where I could see Roberto just getting out of his car.

"Ernesto is buried next to that *quebracho* tree," she said, opening the glove compartment and removing a pair of binoculars. "We'll be able to observe him from inside the chapel."

The small stone chapel was situated beside a much larger mausoleum, and the two buildings were connected to each other by a covered walkway.

As we crossed the threshold of the chapel, our footsteps echoed off the walls and high ceiling, and since the stained glass windows made it almost impossible for any sunlight to get through, we lingered at the doorway a moment to let our eyes readjust themselves to the darkened conditions. Even though I could smell the lingering odor of flowers, the air inside the chapel was oppressive.

A few seconds later, I followed Juliana down the aisle and over to an unmarked door next to an organ. The door provided access to an odd-shaped storage room where extra chairs and a few flower stands were stacked in rows against the interior wall. Numerous boxes of candles were sitting in the middle of the floor, along with two containers of old hymnbooks.

Juliana walked past the containers over to the only window in the room. It faced the east side of the cemetery, and once she'd taken a quick look outside, she handed me the binoculars.

I immediately trained the glasses on Roberto. He was kneeling in front of a gravestone next to a *quebracho* tree.

He was weeping.

♦♦♦♦

We took turns watching him. When I had the binoculars trained on him, Juliana monitored the doorway, making sure no one popped in on us, and I did the same thing while she was scanning the area.

Twenty minutes after our arrival, a funeral procession entered the cemetery and wound its way around the network of roadways. I watched as they drove past Ernesto's grave, where Roberto continued his vigil.

The hearse finally pulled up to a stop at a funeral tent some three hundred yards away from Roberto's location, but the line of cars following the hearse continued to roll past him.

Roberto didn't appear to be disturbed by this, and he never glanced up to observe the procession.

A few minutes later, at least two dozen people piled out of the cars parked alongside the roadway and began walking toward the funeral tent, which had been placed over a freshly dug grave.

As I watched the mourners heading toward the burial site, I noticed a Ford sedan slowly cruising passed them.

The driver's face was partially hidden by a pair of dark sunglasses, but, as he passed by the *quebracho* tree, I saw him crane his head around, as if he wanted to get a better look at Roberto's kneeling form.

Seconds later, the car disappeared from sight.

Keeping the binoculars trained on the *quebracho* tree, I asked Juliana, "Have you ever seen a green Ford sedan sniffing around Roberto?"

"What part of I haven't spotted anyone did you not understand?"

"No need to get huffy on me."

"I don't do huffy. That was me being miffed."

"If that was miffed then . . ."

I paused and readjusted the focus on the binoculars.

When the scene came into view, I quickly turned away from the window and handed the glasses to Juliana. "I want to check on something. Keep those trained on Roberto."

She shook her head. "No, I'm coming with you."

"Stay here." I removed the Glock from my holster, "I'll signal you if I need backup."

She lifted the glasses to her eyes. "It's the green Ford, isn't it?"

I chambered a round in my gun and headed for the door.

"Yeah, it's the green Ford."

♦♦♦♦

I walked across the chapel and slipped out a side door. The door led onto the walkway between the chapel and the mausoleum. Once I reached the mausoleum, I skirted around the building and headed across the parking lot.

There was a slight slope down to the roadway, and, as I hurried down the embankment, I momentarily lost my footing. When I regained my balance, I suddenly realized I'd lost the fedora, but, at that moment, it hardly seemed to matter.

I raced across the cemetery, weaving in and out of the tombstones, while at the same time trying to be as inconspicuous as possible to the mourners across the street burying their dead.

Seconds later, I arrived in the clearing by the *quebracho* tree.

From there, I could see Roberto on his knees in front of Ernesto's tombstone. Now, though, standing over him was Marwan Farage.

He was holding a pistol to Roberto's head.

It was a 9mm Ruger with a silencer attached.

♦♦♦♦

Both men had their backs to me, so I quietly eased my way forward, praying I could get to Marwan before he ended his conversation with Roberto and shot him in the head.

Marwan, who'd been Roberto's translator in Damascus, was speaking to him in Spanish. "Why do you mourn for your son? It was your betrayal that killed him. You killed your only son."

Roberto murmured something I couldn't understand, and Marwan pushed the pistol further into his skull. "And Ahmed? Did you also kill him?"

"No," I said, pointing the Glock at him, "that was me. I killed Ahmed."

At the sound of my voice, Marwan quickly spun around and leveled the Ruger at me.

I stepped toward him. "Drop your weapon."

He ignored me and centered the Ruger on Roberto once again. "Lay your weapon on the ground or I'll blow his head off."

As I considered my next move, Juliana suddenly walked up behind Marwan and placed her gun directly above his right ear.

"Not before I shoot you first," she said quietly.

For a few seconds, there was a tense standoff, but with two guns pointed at him, Marwan finally admitted defeat and dropped his weapon.

Roberto, who'd been watching this drama play out while on his knees, now got to his feet. As he did so, he picked up Marwan's gun.

For a brief second, I had a flashback of him standing in the living room in the safe house in Caracas and shooting Ahmed.

This time, though, he handed the gun over to me and said, "Thank you. You've saved my life once again."

I nodded at Juliana. "Thank her instead."

♦♦♦♦

A few minutes later, I contacted Ken Vasco. After briefing him on our encounter with Marwan, he agreed to dispatch Otis and two other operatives to *Cementerio de Flores.*

Once they were headed our way, I told him I wanted to take Marwan and Roberto over to *Edificio Catalina*, the office park where the Bub's Subs executives were supposed to meet with Roberto the following day.

Vasco said, "I like the way you think, my friend. Everything's already in place over there for Roberto's interrogation."

"Send the Ops Center an alert about what went down here, and let them know I plan to do an initial interrogation of Marwan immediately."

"Should you need an extra body when you question him, let me know. People have been known to open up to me."

"Will do."

By the time Otis and his crew arrived, the graveside services across the roadway from us were just finishing up, and the mourners were going their separate ways. Their departure made it easy for those of us gathered around the *quebracho* tree to pile into our own vehicles and leave the cemetery with them.

One of Vasco's guys drove Marwan's green Ford, while Otis and Roberto went off in Roberto's Honda Accord.

After placing a set of zip ties on Marwan's wrists, I shoved him in the backseat of Juliana's Jeep.

Once again, I rode shotgun.

This time, though, I did so figuratively as well as literally; although, since I had a semi-automatic pistol aimed at Marwan, maybe it wasn't so literal after all.

I refused to let Marwan speak until we arrive at our destination, and, since I couldn't think of anything I wanted to say to Juliana in front of Marwan, the forty-minute trip turned out to be a quiet one.

I rather enjoyed it.

# Chapter 19

The office park, *Edificio Catalina,* was located a block west of *Avenida Libertador* and provided parking for its customers in an underground facility.

When we arrived, Juliana parked the Jeep well away from any other vehicles, which made it easier for the two of us to usher Marwan into the parking garage's elevator and up to the third floor without anyone noticing he was entering the building at gunpoint.

There were two suites on the third floor and Bub's Subs—a.k.a. the Agency—had leased Suite 301. The franchise's logo, a shiny red and gold BS, was prominently displayed by the doorway, just above the nameplate identifying the offices as Suite 301.

Inside the suite was a reception area, where large photographs of sandwiches were prominently displayed on the muted green walls. A woman from Vasco's embassy staff was seated behind the reception desk. As soon as we entered the room, she pointed over to an unmarked door on her right.

Once she'd hit a buzzer, which released the security lock on the door, I directed Marwan to open it. The moment he hesitated, I prodded him with the barrel of the Glock, and he promptly jerked it opened.

We entered a hallway with two doors on the right and one on the left. Even though I was expecting it, the contrast with the décor in the reception room was mind-jarring.

There was no artwork covering the walls and no colorful BS logo in evidence anywhere. The façade of Bub's Subs business enterprise was no more. What remained were bare white walls and thin beige carpeting.

Ken Vasco leaned his head out of the room on my left and motioned us inside.

The signage indicated it was 301-C.

The room contained a sturdy rectangular table and two chairs. The table, along with the chairs, had been bolted to the floor, and, other than the two cameras mounted on the walls, there was nothing else in the room.

I shoved Marwan into one of the empty chairs.

Ben Mitchell was standing behind the table, and he looked extremely pleased the instant he saw Marwan. For one brief moment, I thought he was about to give me a high five.

Instead, he grabbed a set of restraints and attached them to Marwan's legs. After that, Vasco cut the zip ties from his wrists and snapped on a set of metal handcuffs, fastening the cuffs to an anchor in the center of the table.

Once that was done, we left Marwan alone in the room and walked across the hall to 301-B.

♦♦♦♦

This room was similar in size but contained more furnishings than 301-C. One of those furnishings was a table full of electronics, including two video monitors.

As soon as the four of us entered the room, Vasco turned to Juliana and said, "Nice work out there today."

She gave him a big smile.

He glanced over at me. "I should have told you she was more than just a pretty face."

Mitchell walked over and introduced himself to Juliana, and the two of them migrated over to the coffee machine. Vasco and I stood around in front of the video monitors watching Marwan Farage stare at the walls.

We were also waiting to hear back from Langley about how they wanted us to proceed with our prisoner.

Earlier, Vasco had sent the Ops Center a flash bulletin about Marwan's capture, along with my request to do an initial interrogation on site. I wasn't sure how Vasco had worded my request, but I found myself hoping he hadn't asked for permission to be one of Marwan's interrogators.

That might not matter, though, since I usually conducted my interrogations in the native tongue of the one being interrogated, and I was pretty sure Vasco couldn't speak a word of Arabic.

Otis suddenly appeared in the doorway and inclined his head in the direction of the reception area. "I just brought Roberto up, and he seems pretty rattled."

Vasco pointed over at me. "You're up to bat now, slugger. Hit one out of the park for us."

I glanced over to the other side of the room where Mitchell seemed to be enjoying Juliana's attention. "Ben, let's go reintroduce ourselves to Roberto Montilla."

Mitchell reluctantly left Juliana's side and joined me.

Before leaving the room, I told Vasco, "Don't switch on the recording devices until I send Ben back in here to grab us some water. Once he heads back to our location, do a five-minute countdown, and then start the recording on that mark."

Vasco grinned and nodded. "Gotcha. I'm good with that."

Mitchell and I headed down the hallway.

Before entering the reception area again, I paused outside Room 301-A and looked inside.

Along with 301-C, this room had the look and feel of a prison. The only items inside the room were a single bed, a straight-back chair, and a toilet.

"Is this where we'll be questioning Roberto?" Mitchell asked.

"No, after what happened at the cemetery, I've had second thoughts about the best way to deal with Roberto."

"Does Douglas know about the change in plans?"

"Not yet."

♦♦♦♦

When Mitchell and I entered the reception area, we found Roberto looking at a colorful Bub's Subs display. Two of Vasco's men were watching him.

In Roberto's hand was a Bub's Subs promotional brochure. The moment he saw me, he waved the pamphlet in my face. "Is this for real or was Mr. Vasco lying to me?"

"We'll explain everything, Roberto. But first—"

"Will you also explain how Marwan Farage was able to find me in the first place? I could have . . ."

When Roberto glanced behind me and saw Mitchell standing there, he hesitated. Now, his voice seemed to soften, as if he thought he'd found a more sympathetic audience.

". . . I could have died at the cemetery today. I could have been killed as I knelt there beside my dead son's grave."

"But you weren't," Mitchell said, stepping forward and grabbing the brochure from his hand. "Your life was spared."

Next to the receptionist's desk was a frosted glass door with the words, Bub's Subs Executive Offices, etched in gold lettering across the front.

I pushed it open. "If you want answers, Roberto, you'll need to come with me."

He immediately turned and followed me down the hallway.

♦♦♦♦

The floor plan for Bub's Subs Executive Offices mirrored the floor plan on the opposite side of the suite. However, the layout was the only thing the two wings had in common.

In this wing, the walls were painted a shade of warm beige and the floors were covered in plush, off-white carpeting. Lining the corridor were photographs of happy, heel-kicking young people, and everyone was smiling as they enjoyed a delicious sub from Bub's.

I walked down the corridor to Room 301-D, where the nameplate on the wall identified it as the senior manager's office.

According to my legend, that was me, so I opened the door and walked inside.

It was obvious Vasco hadn't spared the taxpayer's money in decorating the executive's office. All the furnishings looked expensive, including the paintings on the wall, and I suspected Vasco might be planning to use the DDO's outlay of money for Operation Citadel Protection to keep the offices of Bub's Subs on the books long after the operation was over.

Doing so violated a whole bunch of Agency rules, but keeping station chiefs from breaking rules wasn't on my radar at the moment.

All I cared about was finding out what Roberto knew about some sarin gas canisters being exploded over Washington, D.C.

I motioned for Roberto to take a seat in one of the guest chairs. There were three of them positioned in front of the leather-topped mahogany desk.

I sat down in the chair next to him, angling it slightly so I could face him. By doing so, I hoped to create an I-want-to-be-your-friend-and-share-secrets-with-you kind of atmosphere. I wasn't sure my efforts would do away with the antagonistic relationship Roberto and I had experienced during our last get-together in a safe house in Caracas, but I thought I would give it a try.

Mitchell didn't seem to pick up on what I was doing or maybe he simply wasn't interested in making Roberto feel at ease. A few seconds after I sat down, he walked over and plopped himself down in the executive chair behind the oversized desk.

When he looked over at Roberto, he glared at him, as if Roberto were some kind of errant employee, and he, Mitchell, was the boss intent on firing him.

At that moment, I knew I was never going to achieve any kind of rapport with Roberto until Mitchell confronted him about what had happened in Caracas when his gun had suddenly ended up in Roberto's hands.

As I was considering how to force Mitchell to bring up the issue, Roberto made it easy for me.

"What have you done with Marwan Farage?" he asked. "He was my interpreter in Syria. Did you know that?"

"Yes, Roberto, I knew that."

"I need to talk to him. I want to know how he found me."

"We'll ask—"

Mitchell interrupted. "Really? You just want to talk to him? Don't you mean kill him like you did Ahmed?"

Suddenly, Mitchell pulled his Glock out and placed it on the desk. "Here's your chance Roberto. This time, there's no need for you to give me some bogus story about your intentions."

Roberto's eyes twitched as he looked down at the gun. "Ahmed killed my son. He deserved to die. I thought you understood that."

"I understood you wanted to confront him. I agreed to let you do that. I trusted you to do that. Nothing else. You violated that trust when you took my gun and left me there in that alleyway."

Roberto dropped his head. "It's true, I lied to you. But I thought killing Ahmed would help me get over Ernesto's death." He shook his head. "It hasn't helped at all."

After a few seconds, Roberto lifted his head and pointed over to the gun. "I don't want to shoot Marwan. I just want to know how he found me, so I can keep my wife and daughter safe. You said you understood how I felt about Ernesto. Can't you also understand how I feel about them?"

Mitchell picked up his gun and put it back in his holster. "I understand I won't be manipulated again."

"Believe me, all I care about right now is keeping my family safe."

Mitchell didn't reply, and the silence hung in the air between them for a few seconds.

Finally, Roberto looked over at me and said, "I've already thanked the woman for saving my life today, but you deserve my thanks as well."

I nodded. "I accept your gratitude, Roberto, but if you're serious about protecting your family from another Hezbollah hit man, then you better start filling in the missing blanks about those chemical weapons."

He looked surprised at my statement. At the same time, he started rubbing the palms of his hands against his thighs, as if they were covered in sweat. "You don't believe I already told you everything I know?"

"I believe you may not know what you know."

He leaned across the desk and picked up a Bub's Subs business card. "Is that why Mr. Vasco arranged for me to meet the franchise people? Was it all just a hoax so you could question me again?"

He glanced over at Mitchell. "Was Mr. Vasco manipulating me?"

Mitchell nodded, "Yes he was." He extended his hand toward Roberto. "I'm Ignacio Rubio, and this is our senior manager, Geraldo Lucia. We're your Bub's Subs franchise team, and we're very pleased to make your acquaintance, Mr. Montilla."

Roberto ignored Mitchell's outstretched hand. "There wasn't any need for you to go to all this trouble. Why didn't you just kidnap me again?"

He replaced the business card in the desk holder. "Or instead, you could have asked me to come over to the American embassy for a conversation. I would have been happy to do that. Why bother with this circus?"

I focused on his body language when I answered him.

"Well, Roberto, after reading the written statement you prepared for me in Caracas, I wasn't exactly sure where your loyalties were. I was afraid if I called you up and invited you down to the embassy for a little chat, you might be on the next flight to Damascus. On the other hand, since you told Ken Vasco you were interested in owning a Bub's Subs' franchise, I was sure you wouldn't refuse to meet with some of their executives."

He looked genuinely perplexed at my answer. "Why would you think I'd be on the next flight to Syria? Didn't I give you a detailed account of Hezbollah's plans to attack your country? After what Hezbollah did to Ernesto, why would I want anything to do with them?"

Mitchell said, "You told us they were planning to use chemical weapons on some of our cities. When you put that in writing, you changed your statement to say they were only interested in attacking Washington. Why would you lie about that if you weren't trying to protect them?"

Roberto sighed. "Yes, I did say the chemical weapons were destined for several cities, but when I told you that, I was afraid I might need some leverage later on. You hadn't agreed to help me relocate my family here to Buenos Aires, so I told you Hezbollah had targeted several cities. If you hadn't approved my request, I would have negotiated with you to reveal which city it was. Once you signed the agreement, though, I decided to reveal the truth in my written account."

As I sat there listening to Mitchell argue with Roberto over several other discrepancies in his statement, I realized what Roberto had said made sense. As a trade minister, he was used to negotiating deals, and that's what he'd done to keep his family safe from Ahmed.

At the same time, his answer didn't account for the verbal stress points the analysts had heard when he was talking about the conversations he'd had with Zaidi, nor did it explain the gaps in his own written record of those conversations.

I decided getting Roberto to fill in those gaps might require I tell him something I seldom told detainees—the truth.

As a method of extracting intel from a subject, being truthful was considered too risky. Also, the DDO explicitly discouraged it.

Now, I considered giving it a try.

# Chapter 20

I knew it didn't mattered to anyone in the Ops Center which method of interrogation I used in order to get Roberto to talk. All they really cared about—other than having the intel he possessed—was acquiring a recording of his answers for the official record.

Nevertheless, if I opted to use the truth to get some answers from Roberto, I didn't want what I revealed to him to be on the official record—not when there was a good possibility someone on the seventh floor might use it against me later.

I thought about how I could prevent that from happening, and I finally decided I needed some time alone with Roberto before Vasco started recording the session. I figured having Mitchell distracted when I sent him back to Suite 301-B might do the trick.

I felt sure Juliana would be the perfect person to do the distracting.

When Mitchell started goading Roberto again, I said, "Give Roberto a break and go grab us some water. While you're at it, ask Juliana to give you a description of the black van she saw cruising around Roberto's neighborhood yesterday. Roberto might be able to give her some more information about it."

As soon as Mitchell heard our pre-arranged signal about the water, he nodded and said. "I'll be right back."

I resisted the temptation to tell him he didn't need to hurry.

Once he was gone, Roberto said, "Someone's been following me?"

I lowered my voice, "Look, Roberto, forget about the black van. It doesn't exist. I just made that up so I could have a few minutes alone with you."

He looked intrigued—maybe a little frightened—by my admission.

"Why?"

"Because I wanted to tell you some things my superiors wouldn't want me to tell you, and I wanted to do it before they started recording our conversation."

He laughed. "Your superiors? Look, Mr. Lucia, or whatever you name is, if you're about to tell me you work for the CIA, don't bother. I figured that out a long time ago."

"What I'm about to tell you doesn't concern my employer. It concerns you."

He shook his head. "You'd have to be pretty convincing before I'd ever believe anything you had to say."

"And that's my point, Roberto. You've been honest with me, and now it's time for me to be honest with you."

He stared at me for a second or two. "Honest about what?"

"Honest about what was going on behind the scenes in Caracas when we were questioning you."

"Okay, so tell me what was going on."

"To begin with, everything you said to us in the safe house was being recorded. After you left, those recordings were thoroughly analyzed and compared with what you wrote down in your written statement."

He shrugged. "I'm not surprised."

I went on. "When I say those recordings were thoroughly analyzed, I don't just mean someone compared the tape of what you said with what you wrote down. Someone did that, of course, but what I'm talking about is the use of highly sophisticated software with the capacity to measure how much tension you were feeling and to gauge your anxiety level when you were saying it."

He shrugged again. "It probably showed I was under a lot of stress when you were questioning me."

"Your physical circumstances were factored into those final results."

Now, he looked concerned.

"Those results showed you weren't being truthful about your conversations with Rehman Zaidi. They indicated you were concealing something about him, maybe even concealing the true nature of your relationship with him."

Roberto shifted his gaze over to one of the abstract paintings on the wall and didn't say anything.

I waited a second to see if he would respond. When he didn't, I said, "This time, Roberto, if you decide you're not going to answer my questions about Zaidi, you won't be returning home to your wife and daughter."

He finally looked me in the eye.

I continued. "Despite the fact Marwan tried to kill you today, my government will assume you're working with the terrorists and treat you accordingly. That means you and Marwan will be shipped off to a detention facility, and the two of you could end up at Camp Justice together. And, just in case you didn't know it, that's the Jihadi prison camp at Guantanamo Bay, Cuba."

"No, that can't happen." He shook his head back and forth. "You've got things all wrong."

"Then you need to tell me exactly what I've got wrong."

Before Roberto had a chance to reply, Mitchell walked in the room carrying several bottles of water.

Juliana walked in right behind him.

♦♦♦♦

Seeing Mitchell enter the room with Juliana was definitely a surprise. On the other hand, since I'd deliberately used her to delay Mitchell's return, perhaps I should have expected her to show up.

As a rule, women rarely appreciated being used, and I had the feeling Juliana was the rule and not the exception.

Mitchell handed Roberto and me each a bottle of water. "When I told Juliana what you said about the black van, she offered to come back and tell Roberto about it herself."

I immediately got up and offered Juliana my chair.

It was hard to decipher the look she gave me. "What I have to say won't take that long. I don't need to sit down."

Juliana looked over at Roberto. "The black van I saw in your neighborhood yesterday turned out to be a delivery truck. We checked it out, and, apparently, the driver just couldn't find the address he was looking for. That's why he kept circling around."

I waited to see how Roberto would respond to her story because I felt certain what he said next would indicate whether he'd decided to cooperate with me or not.

Since I'd just told him I'd invented the story of the black van in order to get rid of Mitchell, he might decide to call Juliana a liar and create all kinds of havoc for me.

Or, he could play along, accept her story, and work with me.

Roberto pointed his finger at me. "When you said I might be able to identify the black van, I knew that couldn't be true." He looked over at Juliana. "Since I only moved in the neighborhood a few weeks ago, I have no idea who belongs there and who doesn't."

Although this was the kind of answer I'd hoped for, I tried not to show it.

I looked over at Juliana, "Thanks for clearing up any confusion about that vehicle."

She gave me a half-hearted smile. "I hate it when things get confusing."

♦♦♦♦

After Juliana had left, I began my official interrogation of Roberto. Even though I had a pretty good idea he'd decided to be forthcoming with me, I still spent several minutes warning him about the consequences of refusing to answer my questions.

Now that I knew I was being recorded, I was vague about what those consequences would be, and I definitely didn't mentioned shipping him off to Gitmo. Still, the picture I painted for him was pretty dire.

When I finished, Roberto said, "There's no need to threaten me. I'll tell you everything you want to know."

"We want to know more about the conversations you had with Rehman Zaidi," I said. "In your written statement, you said he talked about his meetings with the security council in Damascus, but you never gave us any details about who attended those meetings. Was there some reason you didn't tell us who was in attendance?"

He nodded. "I knew you'd want me to give you some specific names, but I was afraid if I identified them, they might know I was the person providing you with that information, and they'd come after me."

Mitchell asked, "How would they be able to know who'd given us that information?"

Roberto uncrossed his legs and leaned forward, jabbing the air with his finger as he tried to make his point.

"Because I knew Rehman Zaidi couldn't keep quiet. He talked to me about things he shouldn't have. That made me afraid he might talk to someone about me. If your military targeted anyone in that group with a drone strike, then the others might be able to figure out I was the one giving out that information."

I assured Roberto once he told us what we wanted to know, I'd make sure he was protected. I emphasized those assurances by pointing out I'd just saved his life in the cemetery.

Finally, he relented and identified four people Zaidi had told him were responsible for planning the attack against the U.S., including Marwan Farage.

I asked, "How well do you know Marwan?"

He shook his head. "Not well at all. I met him when I was sent to Syria to negotiate a trade agreement between our two countries. Since Marwan was fluent in both Arabic and Spanish, he acted as my translator during the negotiations."

I urged Roberto to try and remember any personal details about Marwan, especially something I could use as leverage against him. He mentioned Marwan loved Turkish coffee and talked a lot about soccer, but he couldn't remember anything of significance about the man.

When I quizzed him about Marwan's family, he said, "I met a few of his family members the summer I brought Ernesto to Syria with me. That was when he introduced me to Ahmed."

"Did you meet his immediate family?"

Roberto described meeting Marwan's wife, a daughter named Samira, and a son who was serving in the Syrian army. He thought the son's name was Arshad, but he wasn't sure.

After I'd exhausted his knowledge of Marwan's family, I grilled him about Hezbollah's timetable for the attack on Washington.

Once again, he insisted Zaidi had never given him an exact date. "Zaidi didn't know what the timetable was. He told me it was up to the Iranian general."

Although Wilson had identified the Iranian general during my briefing, I asked Roberto, "What's the general's name?"

"Suleiman. General Alizadeh Suleiman."

"When Zaidi told you about the attack on Washington, did he say how they planned to disperse the chemicals? Did he give you any details about the delivery system they were planning to use?"

"Like I told you before, I remember Zaidi saying he couldn't wait to see the video of the gas canisters being dropped on Washington, so I just assumed they'd be using an airplane."

Mitchell asked, "He didn't mention firing off some kind of rocket?"

Roberto shook his head. "No, Zaidi said nothing like that." He put his empty water bottle on the desk and said, "Look, I've told you everything I know. Why don't you ask Marwan these questions?"

"Trust me," I said, as I got to my feet, "Marwan will get his share of questions in the weeks ahead. In the meantime, you'll need to be patience and remain here a little longer."

"Do I have a choice?"

"Not really."

I went out to the reception area and returned with the two guys in charge of babysitting Roberto. Then, Mitchell and I headed back down to 301-B.

The moment we walked in the door, Vasco winked at me and said, "I can't say much for your style, but you certainly got the guy to talk."

"I was absent the day they taught style at The Farm."

Juliana laughed.

♦♦♦♦

I asked Vasco if he'd heard back from the Ops Center, and he handed over the reply he'd received. Although I'd been given permission to interrogate Marwan, it was only a PIA, a Preliminary Interrogation Authorization.

The PIA was temporary and would only remain in effect until Carlton had finished making arrangements for Marwan to be transferred to Gitmo, where his interrogation would begin in earnest.

Before that happened, I wanted to pull enough intel out of Marwan to convince Carlton he needed to send me over to Syria to see what I could turn up on Hezbollah's plans to use the chemical weapons.

I'd just finished digesting the reply from the Ops Center when my sat phone started vibrating. I excused myself and went out in the hallway to answer it.

"Are you clear?" Carlton asked.

I opened the door to 301-A and went inside. The prison-like room made me feel claustrophobic, but I tried ignoring it.

"Clear," I said.

"I was in the Ops Center when the feed came in and their initial assessment was that Roberto was finally telling you the truth. Do you agree?"

I was surprised to hear Carlton say the Ops Center had been receiving a real-time feed of Roberto's interrogation. Usually, an interrogation was recorded first, and then, after being reviewed by the primary, was uploaded to the Ops Center.

Of course, should events warrant, the primary could always request a real-time feed back to headquarters, but, in this case, I hadn't done so.

"I agree with your assessment. I don't believe Roberto knows any details about the attack, but Marwan may be a different story."

There was a note of warning in Carlton's voice. "The DDO only issued a PIA on Marwan. Nothing more. He wants you to leave the heavy lifting to our people at Gitmo."

I ignored his cautionary tone and asked, "Did you request the real-time feed of my session with Roberto?"

There was silence on the other end of the line.

After a few seconds, Carlton said, "No, I didn't request the feed. Since you're asking me that question, I have to assume you didn't request it either. Did you and Ken have a misunderstanding?"

"Maybe."

"Don't get distracted by Ken Vasco. I've heard he's into the political side of this business a little too much. You need to be careful. Don't let his agenda get in the way of your main objective."

"That won't happen."

Carlton briefed me on the latest signals intelligence from the Middle East and gave me a situational report on Salazar's investigation of the shooting at the Navy Yard, which the DDO had labeled Component Two of Operation Citadel Protection. Carlton said Salazar had traced the heroin in Felipe's backpack to Los Zetas, one of several Mexican drug cartels with known ties to Hezbollah in Syria.

Once Carlton had finished updating me, I asked him if the names Roberto had spouted off were known to the Ops Center. He told me Katherine was still probing the databases on one of the men, but our operatives in Syria already knew about the other two, as well as the Iranian general, Alizadeh Suleiman.

"Has she uncovered anything about Marwan's family yet? Did she find anything I could use as leverage when I question him?"

"She said the preliminary data showed Marwan shipped his wife and daughter off to Beirut when the Syrian rebels first started taking over some of the outlying neighborhoods in Damascus. When Katherine accessed Syria's military records, she discovered his son, Arshad Farage, had been killed in Al-Hadar when his unit tried to take out a rebel stronghold there."

"Tell Katherine to keep turning over those rocks. If I'm able to get Marwan to talk, he might be able to give us the timing of the attack, as well as how Hezbollah plans to execute it."

"I agree," Carlton said. "I believe Marwan's capture will yield a treasure trove of intelligence for us. We were lucky he showed up in

Buenos Aires when he did."

Was that true?

Was the capture of Marwan just pure luck?

Maybe so, but I was beginning to believe it might be the answer to the prayer I'd prayed before leaving Washington, D.C., the one asking God to look on me with favor and grant me success in Buenos Aires.

I said, "Marwan's presence here was definitely a gift."

"Be careful how you unwrap this gift, Titus. I wouldn't want it to get broken."

In the end, Marwan didn't get broken.

He didn't even get bent.

## Chapter 21

I wasn't ready to question Marwan yet. There was someone else I needed to question first. I went back inside 301-B and found him over in the corner by the coffee machine.

"Hey," Vasco said, "how about a cup of Joe? I'm buying."

After I said yes, I waved off the creamer he offered me, and then I nodded over at the video monitors across the room.

"What's our prisoner doing?"

"Mostly rocking in place and talking to himself. Are you ready to have a go at him?"

"Just about."

I lowered my voice and looked Vasco in the eye. "Let's get something straight before I go in there. I'm the primary on this operation, and unless I tell you to send the Ops Center the real-time feed of the audio, don't send it."

Even though the smile on his face remained fixed, his eyes didn't look happy. "Sure thing. Did I get that wrong before? I sure thought you said to wait five minutes and then send the feed to Langley."

"I didn't say that."

"Well then, sorry about the miscommunication. I'll get it right next time."

"Get what right?" Mitchell asked, walking up behind him.

Vasco seemed startled to hear Mitchell's voice and almost spilled his coffee. "Oh, hey, Ben, I didn't see you there. Titus and I were just discussing procedures. I sent Langley the real-time feed when you were questioning Roberto before, and, evidently, I wasn't supposed to do that."

Mitchell looked over at me and said, "No harm done, right?" He laughed, "It's not like we laid a hand on him."

Vasco laughed along with him. "Exactly."

My aversion to doing a real-time feed while interrogating a subject stemmed from a bad experience I'd had in Kandahar, Afghanistan when I hadn't been able to alert the Ops Center I wanted to pursue an unusual line of questioning with a Taliban fighter. After the Ops Center had listened to the audio for a few minutes, they'd notified my handler to pull me out of there. Consequently, we'd never gotten the answers we needed from the guy.

Now, I preferred to delay the feed and inform the Ops Center later about what I was trying to accomplish with my line of questioning.

I was tempted to explain this to Vasco and Mitchell, but instead, I turned to Mitchell and said, "When you're the primary on an operation, you'll discover it's less about appearance and more about context."

I wasn't sure Mitchell got my meaning, but I was sure Vasco did.

♦♦♦♦

A few minutes later, as Vasco began telling Mitchell about a sting operation he'd run in Colombia—one he claimed was all about context—I excused myself and walked across the room to where Juliana was manning the computers and monitoring the surveillance cameras.

I nodded toward the screen showing Marwan rocking back and forth in his chair. "Any thoughts about our prisoner?"

"He continues running through the gamut of self-comforting techniques, so I'd say he's pretty afraid right now. If you played around with that fear, he might be willing to tell you what you want to know."

"Tell me again why you're still in surveillance after seven years."

She laughed. "Routine. I like the routine."

"Now I remember."

"Then you probably remember my surveillance crew never spotted any suspicious vehicles, especially black vans, within a mile of Montilla's residence."

"I do remember that. You were excellent in there, by the way."

"Would you mind telling me what was happening in that room before I interrupted you?"

"I'd rather not, but I'll give you a hint."

Before saying anything, I glanced over and made sure Mitchell and Vasco were still engaged in conversation.

They were.

I said, "When you were a detective, and you wanted a suspect to spill his guts before he started screaming for his lawyer, what would you do?"

She thought about it for a second. "Get him to trust me."

I nodded. "And now you know what was happening in the Bub's Subs senior manager's office before you and Ben showed up."

I heard a *ping-ping-ping* from the computer in front of Juliana, and, at the same time, a blue box popped up in the lower right hand corner of her screen.

We both glanced down at it.

It was a red-flagged message addressed to *Principals, Operation Citadel Protection, Component One, Buenos Aires.*

Juliana said, "It's a priority one message from the ASA office for you."

The office of Analysis and Strategic Assessment (ASA) was Katherine's department, and her counterintelligence analysis teams were some of the best at the Agency. Even so, I was surprised to be hearing from her so soon after Carlton's update.

After Juliana printed off Katherine's five-page report, I took the document over to a small conference table in a corner of the room. Once I'd read the first page, I got Mitchell's attention and told him to join me.

I didn't invite Vasco over.

When Mitchell sat down, I laid the first page in front of him and continued to feed him the rest of the pages as I finished reading them.

The first three pages of the Strategic Analysis Report (SAR) provided the biographical data on Marwan and his family. Although it was just the raw data—listed chronologically without analysis—Katherine pulled all the threads together in the final two pages. Here, she noted the areas where her team had been unsuccessful in digging up information or exact dates. Notably absent from Marwan's biography was anything about his parents, his growing up years, and the time he'd spent in Hezbollah's militia unit.

She summarized her findings in the final three paragraphs at the end of the report.

*Although Marwan was born in Beirut, Lebanon, he was living in Barcelona, Spain by the time he was a teenager. He met his wife, Yamina, when he went to work at her father's restaurant in Barcelona, and they continued living there until their daughter, Samira, was three years old. At that time, he moved his family back to Beirut, and that's where their son, Arshad, was born.*

*Around that same time, probably 1992, Marwan joined a Hezbollah-funded militia fighting the Israelis in southern Lebanon. After Marwan distinguished himself in that action, he rose rapidly in the ranks of Hezbollah's militant wing, and, several years later, he came to the attention of Hezbollah's leadership when they needed a Spanish translator to deal with the Zeta drug cartel.*

*As more of the drug cartels in Mexico and Colombia joined forces with Hezbollah to expand their drug trade, Marwan took on the role of an advisor to Hezbollah instead of just a translator, Now, Marwan is a member of Hezbollah's security council in Syria and represents their Latin American interests.*

At the very end of the summary, Katherine had added a notation: *"Trying to ascertain the location of Yamina and Samira Farage. At the present time, whereabouts unknown."*

After I handed Mitchell the last page, I sat there and thought about Katherine's report. Something in the data gnawed at me. It was on the very edges of my gray matter, and I waited for the synapses to fire and send me my own red alert.

Or a blue one.

I wasn't picky. Even a yellow one would do.

♦♦♦♦

Once Mitchell had finished reading the report, we both agreed there wasn't much in the document I could use as leverage. Marwan Farage was a dedicated Hezbollah fighter, probably trained to withstand interrogation, and he wasn't going to give up his secrets easily.

I gestured toward the video screens. "He's exhibiting coping behavior, so he's obviously afraid of something."

"He knows he blew his mission; he failed to kill Roberto."

"I'm not sure about that. This could have been a lone operation; something he decided to do on his own to avenge Ahmed's death."

"If that's the case, then maybe he's afraid Hezbollah will send someone after him for disobeying orders and getting caught in the process."

I stood up. "Let's go find out."

Mitchell looked surprised. "You want me in there? I thought you'd want to conduct your interrogation in Arabic."

"For all we know, Spanish could be his native tongue. Besides, I might end up needing your bad cop routine."

"I don't have a bad cop routine."

♦♦♦♦

Before heading across the hall to question Marwan, I asked Vasco if he'd heard from any of his Hezbollah contacts about Marwan's arrival in Buenos Aires.

"I checked in with them as soon as you called me from the cemetery. One of my assets said he'd never heard of him, and the other one said he'd heard of Marwan Farage, but he wasn't aware he was here in the city. That guy is also connected with the cartel, so he may not be playing straight with me."

"That sounds about right."

I handed the ASA report off to Juliana. "You can put this in the burn bag now."

Vasco said, "Would you mind if I took a look at it first?"

As chief of station, Vasco was well within his rights to request access to a document relevant to an operation for which he was providing support. At the same time, as the primary for the operation, I had the right to refuse him permission to view such a document.

Vasco seemed less bombastic since I'd confronted him about the audio recording issue, and, while I was slightly suspicious of his change of attitude, I considered it to be a positive thing.

"Sure. Have a look," I said, handing him the document. "There's a summary statement on the last page."

He flipped through the pages and quickly read through Katherine's synopsis.

"So Marwan is connected to the drug trade? Maybe my asset was telling the truth after all."

"I don't believe Marwan came to Buenos Aires with an official sanction. My guess is that he flew in here with the intention of making the hit on Roberto, and then he planned on getting out of here without making any contact with the other Hezbollah brothers."

Juliana, who was still in front of her computer screen, said, "I just heard back from Otis about Marwan's car. It's an airport rental, and Marwan picked it up after arriving here on a flight from Caracas. There's video of him deplaning from Flight 363."

Mitchell said, "So Marwan left Beirut yesterday and flew to Caracas and then caught another flight to Buenos Aires last night. At least we know he's jet-lagged. That should make our job a whole lot easier."

The moment Mitchell mentioned Beirut, the synapses fired, and I immediately grabbed the elusive thought gnawing away at me since reading Katherine's report. I looked at my brainchild from every angle, and then I made a quick decision.

Vasco said, "Yeah, I'd say go in there and hit Marwan with both barrels right now."

"No," I said. "We won't be questioning Marwan right now."

Mitchell looked surprised. "But I thought—"

I addressed Vasco. "Put Marwan in 301-A. Give him something to eat and make sure he's not disturbed during the night. I don't want him sleep-deprived when Ben and I question him in the morning."

Vasco nodded. "Okay, if that's what you want. What about Roberto?"

"You can release Roberto but continue your surveillance on him."

Vasco looked over at Juliana. "You heard the man. Continue the surveillance on Roberto."

I said, "If it's all the same to you, I'd like for Juliana to go back to the embassy with Ben and me. Let someone else run the surveillance on Roberto."

Vasco said, "You're headed back to the embassy? You two are Bub's Subs executives. You might blow your cover if you don't go out and party tonight. Never pass up a perfectly good excuse to party."

I ignored Vasco and addressed Juliana. "I'll need a secure hookup with Sam Wylie, our head of station in Caracas. Can you set that up for me?"

She nodded. "Of course."

"You're contacting Sam?" Mitchell asked. "Is this about Roberto?"

"No, it's about Marwan, and who was on that flight from Beirut to Caracas with him yesterday."

## Chapter 22

Mitchell and I rode over to the embassy in Juliana's Jeep Cherokee. This time, I rode in the back seat and Mitchell rode shotgun—but only figuratively.

While they were talking sports in the front seat, I was having an argument with myself in the back seat, debating whether I should contact Carlton before initiating the call to Sam Wylie.

Since Carlton was running me, there probably shouldn't have been a debate. As a field officer, I had a lot of leeway in calling the shots, making quick decisions, and acting on my instincts, but sitting high above the maze was Carlton, and, if I didn't keep him informed about what I was planning for my next move, I might get boxed in and never find my way out.

Still, I hesitated to pick up my phone and tell him I was on my way into The Bubble to conference with Wylie.

Sam Wylie was the chief of station (COS) in Venezuela, and he'd played a major role in the Clear Signal operation by helping Mitchell and me locate Ahmed Al-Amin. He'd also been instrumental in the cover-up of who had really pulled the trigger on Ahmed, but I didn't intend to rehash that ill-conceived conspiracy with him.

My hesitancy about phoning Carlton stemmed from my uncertainty about Wylie's status in Operation Citadel Protection. Although Wylie had been thoroughly briefed into Clear Signal, there was no reason for me to believe he'd been briefed into Citadel Protection, and the Agency had certain rules about a field operative contacting a COS who hadn't been briefed into a operation.

If I told Carlton I was planning to call Wylie, and he thought I was violating Agency regulations, he'd be obligated to forbid the action.

No matter what he said, I planned to contact Wylie, but if Carlton was against it, I'd probably have to do some groveling later.

Groveling wasn't my strong suit.

♦♦♦♦

As Juliana pulled into the embassy's underground parking garage, I remembered Carlton saying Reyes Valario had attended a Hezbollah training camp in Venezuela.

Wylie had briefed me on Hezbollah's use of this so-called "youth camp" when I'd been with him in Venezuela, and, in my mind, this connection tied Citadel Protection to Clear Signal.

Could this connection justify my contacting Wylie? At the very least, I could easily make the case I was simply doing a follow-up to Clear Signal, and I wasn't in direct violation of the rules.

When Juliana parked the car, she glanced up and saw me staring at her in the rearview mirror. "You haven't said a word. Is something wrong?"

Mitchell said, "In case you haven't noticed, Titus isn't much of a talker."

I said, "It's hard to talk and scheme at the same time."

Juliana nodded. "I can see how that might tax you."

Mitchell laughed—a little longer than necessary—and I joined in to show it didn't bother me.

After the three of us got off the elevator on the second floor, I gestured down the hallway. "You two go ahead. I'll meet you in The Bubble in thirty minutes."

"Skipping out on us?" Mitchell asked.

"I need to make a phone call. Now that I've finished scheming, I'm ready to talk."

♦♦♦♦

I headed in the opposite direction of The Bubble and entered an office suite. The nameplate on the door identified it as General Services, Procurement and Trade Division.

A receptionist was seated at a desk in the middle of the room and looked up from her computer when I walked in. I pointed to the door behind her, which had Ken Vasco's name on it.

"Ken said I could use his office to make a phone call."

When she hesitated, I pulled out the temporary security badge I'd been issued earlier in the day and waved it in front of her.

She glanced at it and said, "Oh, sure. Go ahead. It's not locked."

When I walked into Vasco's office, I fully expecting it to be a reflection of the man himself—disordered and untidy—but instead, I found it neat and uncluttered.

His bookshelves were full of photographs of Ken Vasco shaking hands with politicians and government officials. One of those photographs was with the President. However, Vasco was one of about fifty other people in the frame.

Still, he'd managed to be standing next to the President when the picture was taken.

He also appeared to be an aficionado of biographies of past presidents, as well as those of present-day politicians.

I removed one of the newer books from the shelf.

The thick tome was the biography of a man everyone assumed would run for president someday. On the flyleaf was the signature of the man himself, along with an inscription.

*"To Ken,"* it read, *"a man who's never met a stranger and tells a great story."*

I slid the book back on the shelf, resisting the temptation to add a few words of my own. Finally, I sat down in Vasco's cushy executive desk chair and pulled out my sat phone.

Carlton didn't sound surprise to hear from me, but he immediately jumped to the conclusion I was calling to complain about the ASA report on Marwan.

He said, "I'm aware there's not much there you can use as leverage, but I've seen you make do with a lot less before."

I suddenly realized he'd just provided me with the opening I needed, and, if I played it right, he might actual be the one to suggest I contact Sam Wylie.

I said, "I plan to use his family as a touchstone and see where that takes me."

"His family? You realize there's only a wife and daughter now. His son was killed in Al-Hadar."

"You told me that earlier."

I heard him shuffling papers. "I believe I also told you Marwan moved his wife and daughter to Beirut last year when the civil war broke out in Damascus. They're not living with him now, so they may not be that important to him."

"I disagree. I believe moving them to Beirut shows Marwan is concerned about their safety. I plan to capitalize on that concern by implying we've picked up his wife and daughter. I could even show Marwan some doctored photographs of them."

"That could work . . ." Carlton paused, and I could hear him flipping pages now. "but Katherine noted she didn't have confirmation of their location in Beirut. Here it is, on the last page of the SAR, she has 'whereabouts unknown.' If Marwan knows where they are, that tactic could backfire on you."

"I wonder . . ."

I let the thought hang in the air, and when I didn't say anything for several seconds, Carlton asked, "You wonder what?"

"Nolan said Marwan drove from Damascus to Beirut and took a flight from there. Is that right?"

Carlton said, "That's right. He flew from Beirut to Madrid, and we lost him at the airport in Madrid. At this point, we know he flew from Madrid to Caracas and from there on to Buenos Aires."

"I was wondering why—"

"Why he didn't fly a shorter route to Buenos Aires?"

"That's right. Why didn't he fly here directly from Damascus?"

"That's a good question."

I prompted him. "Why did he drive to Beirut? He could have caught a flight from Damascus just as easily."

I waited, hoping I'd drawn the target large enough.

Carlton said, "Yamina and Samira could have met Marwan at the airport in Beirut, or perhaps even met him in Madrid, and then flown with him to Caracas."

Dead center. Bulls eye.

"You know, Douglas, I think that makes sense. Marwan seems upset right now, like he's afraid of something. Maybe he's not only concerned about his own life, maybe he's also worried about his wife and daughter. If I could locate them and document I have access to them, I could use that leverage to force Marwan to talk about Hezbollah's plans for the attack."

Carlton's tone was upbeat as he explored this idea. "You should contact Sam Wylie. Tell him to tap into the security cameras at the airport in Caracas, view the tapes, and see if Yamina and Samira arrived in Caracas with Marwan. I'll check if the Ops Center has any photographs of his family. If so, I'll have them sent to Sam immediately."

"Has he been briefed on Citadel Protection or should I do that?"

"Salazar already briefed him because of Valario's connection with the training camp in Venezuela."

"Right. I'll initiate the call to Sam once we're done here."

"I'll alert the DDO on my end. One other thing before you go. The Ops Center just learned our principal asset in Damascus went dark. At this point, Marwan may be our only source of intel on what Hezbollah is planning."

"Is this the asset Keever Pike was running? The guy who gave us the intel on the meeting between Naballah and Zaidi?"

I'd never told Carlton I'd already figured out Pike was one of the principals running our operation in Syria, but he didn't comment on this.

"That's right," he said. "Keever's asset hasn't responded to his request for an update for several days now."

"That means when General Suleiman meets with Naballah to discuss the details of the attack, we won't have any ears in that meeting."

"That's the situation as it stands right now. You know Keever, though; he won't give up. He's working 24/7 to locate the guy. Unfortunately, Mossad recently informed us there's some chatter indicating Hezbollah recently beheaded a traitor. Keever may be less optimistic when he hears that news."

After saying goodbye to Carlton, I realized I still had a few minutes left before meeting Juliana and Mitchell in The Bubble.

I decided to remain at Vasco's desk a little longer and enjoy the solitude. I needed time to recharge my batteries.

Nikki once told me being alone drained her. She said when she was around people, she always felt energized. I told her I was just the opposite. Being alone reinvigorated me.

Did that mean Nikki and I weren't really compatible or was it just the opposite?

Did it count if I laughed a lot more when I was with her?

♦♦♦♦

When I entered The Bubble, I discovered Juliana had already informed Wylie's office in Caracas I'd requested a conference call with him.

She said, "He sent word he'd be available in fifteen minutes."

Mitchell spoke up. "What he probably said was, 'Hold your horses, partner. I'll be there as soon as I've lassoed this steer.'"

Juliana laughed. "Why would he say that?"

I said, "Because Sam Wylie's a Texan who's never gotten over it."

Ben nodded. "Yeah, when I met him, he immediately let me know his parents had named him after Sam Houston."

Juliana said, "I probably should know this, but who exactly is Sam Houston?"

Mitchell said, "Don't feel bad. I didn't know who he was either. I ended up Googling him."

Mitchell told her some facts about the now deceased Texan, including some of his funnier quotes, and, as I watched the two of them laughing together, I came to the conclusion they were definitely compatible.

Before Wylie came on the line, I told Mitchell what I'd discussed with Carlton about Marwan's family.

He said, "When I saw Katherine's note about not being able to locate Marwan's wife and daughter, I wondered if that was relevant, but then I didn't give it a second thought."

"Always give those little seedlings room to grow, Ben. You might be surprised at what comes out of the ground."

"Should I write that down?" he asked. "It's not quite up to one of Sam Houston's quotes, but it's close."

Wylie's face suddenly appeared on the screen in front of us. "Did someone just mention the great Sam Houston?"

## Chapter 23

*Friday, June 26*

At six o'clock the next morning, Mitchell and I were sitting inside The Bubble, waiting to hear back from Sam Wylie.

When we'd talked to him around midnight, he'd assured us he wouldn't have any trouble getting access to the security cameras at the airport in Caracas, and he was confident he could do it in less than six hours.

If anyone else had made that promise, I might have been skeptical. However, when we'd worked together in Caracas, I could tell he ran a very competent team of operatives, so I hadn't doubted him.

After Mitchell and I had signed off with Wylie, Juliana had dropped us off at our hotel so we could grab a few hours sleep. Even though I'd offered to call a cab for our return trip to the embassy, she'd insisted on picking us up herself.

When we'd climbed inside her Jeep a few hours later, she'd smiled and handed each of us a large cup of black coffee.

The coffee alone might have been enough for me to fall in love with her, but, for Mitchell, it had sealed the deal.

He carried on a non-stop conversation with her all the way over to the embassy, pelting her with embarrassing personal questions and sharing equally personal stuff with her about his own life.

The moment Juliana had left us alone in The Bubble, Mitchell had clammed up.

I was fine with that, because I needed a few minutes to gather my thoughts before Wylie checked in with us.

Around 6:05, Mitchell broke the silence.

"How old do you think Juliana is?"

"Too old for you."

"No, she's not."

"Probably late thirties."

"I'm thirty."

"She could be forty."

"I doubt that. She—"

Wylie's image pixilated across the video monitor.

"Are you boys saddled up and ready to ride?" he asked.

Mitchell responded with a passable Texas drawl. "Shoot, I reckon."

Wylie formed a six-shooter with his hand and aimed it at Mitchell, whispering "POW" after making the shot. Afterward, he blew away wisps of imaginary smoke.

Wylie said, "This kid's a quick learner, Titus. Have you noticed that?"

"Hard to miss."

Wylie smiled. "Okay, here's what I've got."

After spending a few minutes explaining how he'd been able to access the data at the airport, he said, "You called it right. In the security cam's video, Marwan's wife and daughter were seen getting off the flight from Madrid with him."

Mitchell executed a fist pump. "Yes!"

Wiley said, "I've also retrieved a still shot which shows the ladies going through customs."

Yesterday, after briefing Wylie on Marwan Farage and his attempted murder of Roberto, I'd explained my theory about Marwan meeting up with his wife and daughter and the three of them flying into Caracas together. Besides asking Wylie to verify this, I'd also asked him to make certain the wife and daughter hadn't flown to Buenos Aires with Marwan and weren't somewhere here in the city right now.

I asked, "Marwan wasn't in that still photo, right?"

"That's right. He didn't go through customs with them. His flight to Buenos Aires took off at the same time they were clearing customs here in Caracas."

Mitchell asked, "Any luck locating an address for them?"

"Hold on," he said, taking a sip of his coffee, "I'm getting to that."

He put his "Don't Mess With Texas" mug down and continued. "Truth be told, I didn't need much luck. The Ops Center sent me the list of Rehman Zaidi's contacts they'd lifted from his phone when they'd bugged his apartment a few weeks back. That made it easy for me to track the ladies to an apartment leased to Nassir Ibrahim. It's located in the *Bello Campo* district, and it turns out he's a teacher at that same Muslim school where Zaidi was employed."

"I like what I'm hearing," I said. "Any chance you've already managed to get some pictures of Yamina and her daughter?"

"No, it was too late last night. Buck and his crew are outside the apartment right now, and as soon as the ladies show their faces, he'll capture it all on camera. I'm sure at least one of the women will mosey out later in the day."

"Make sure the photographs clearly show their location in Caracas and what day it is," I said. "I want Marwan to realize we have access to his wife and daughter right now."

"Yeah," Wylie said, "my boys know what the objective is here, but if the ladies don't show their faces in a couple of hours, you may have to go to Plan B."

Mitchell glanced over at me. "We have a Plan B?"

Wylie laughed. "I figured Plan B is a snatch and grab of Mrs. Farage and Ms. Samira. If that happens, I can guarantee you this cowboy will be able to stage some photographs sure to strike fear in the heart of Mr. Farage."

I said, "I hope it doesn't come to that. Right now, I have no reason to believe his wife and daughter are involved with Hezbollah or with any of Marwan's activities. If I discover that's not true, I won't hesitate to use Plan B."

Wylie said, "Here's my question. Why would Marwan bring his wife and daughter along on a revenge killing?"

I said, "I've been asking myself that same question since

yesterday, and I haven't come up with a satisfactory answer yet. In a few hours, I plan to put that question to Marwan himself."

Mitchell said, "His wife and daughter provide him with a good cover story. To any interested party, it looks as if the whole family is vacationing together in Venezuela; except, of course, Marwan took a little side trip to Argentina."

Wylie picked up his cell phone. "Buck just texted me."

He tapped out a quick answer. "He says both women have just exited the apartment, and they're heading down the street. They're on foot."

I asked, "What's on that street? Any restaurants? Businesses?"

Mitchell added, "What about internet cafes? Samira might want to go online, message her friends back home, maybe check out her social media contacts."

Wylie said, "Don't worry. My boys and I have this covered. By the time you get Marwan under the lights, I'll have the photos you need, and I'll make sure they're enough to convince Marwan the two of you are despicable human beings who are about to kidnap his wife and daughter and do unspeakable things to them."

Mitchell said, "I find it hard to believe he's going to care about two people being hurt when he's willing to have thousands killed."

I said, "Marwan plans to kill the infidels, that's us, the *kafir,* and Yamina and Samira are *usra*, family. To a Muslim, nothing is more important than *usra*."

Wylie said, "As soon as we get the photos, I'll have them uploaded to the Ops Center."

I immediately started to protest, but Wylie held up his hand. "Don't be a nervous Nellie, buckaroo. I'll be sending you everything I'm sending them."

"I'm not sure about that Nellie part, Sam. But, yeah, I'm probably a little anxious. I'm afraid I won't have enough time to question Marwan before he's shipped off to Gitmo. Did I mention I'm only authorized to do a preliminary assessment on the guy?"

"I heard about the PIA. Olivia told me about it this morning."

Mitchell said, "Olivia? I thought she—"

I cut him off. "We heard she was sick."

"Well, she's back at work now. That's how I was able to locate Yamina and her daughter so quickly. Once I uploaded the airport video to the Ops Center, Olivia contacted me directly. She said she was sending me the list of Zaidi's contacts."

I found it strange Carlton hadn't mentioned Olivia was back at work, but then, seconds later, I realized what that probably meant.

"Has Olivia been assigned to Salazar?" I asked. "Is she running the second component of Citadel Protection?"

"Yeah, that's right, but that's only temporary because she said she was scheduled for some kind of surgery in a few days. I don't think she was too happy about being assigned to Salazar, even temporarily."

"I can relate to that."

"Then you'll appreciate what she had to say about him."

"Don't be so sure."

Wylie grinned. "She said, 'Being told you have to work with Salazar is like being told you have cancer. At first, you think you might fight it, but later on, you realize it's not worth the fight.'"

I couldn't decide whether I appreciated what Olivia had to say or not, but I knew I was happy she was still around to say it.

♦♦♦♦

When Juliana, Mitchell, and I arrived back at the offices of Bub's Subs, the only person we found in 301-B was Otis. He told us Vasco had gone home around midnight, and he hadn't heard from him since.

I glanced over at the security monitor.

Marwan was sitting on the edge of the bed in 301-A. He was bent over, with his head cradled in his hands.

I asked, "Has he slept at all?"

Otis popped the last morsel of some kind of pastry in his mouth. "Oh, yeah, he slept through the night. I woke him up and gave him a Danish and some coffee around six this morning."

"Has he said anything? Asked for anything?"

"He's been demanding to speak to *el jefe*."

I considered it a good sign Marwan was asking to speak to

someone in authority, and I told Otis to transfer him to 301-C and tell him *el jefe* was ready to speak to him now.

A few minutes later, I sat in front of the monitor and watched as Otis and another operative moved Marwan over to 301-C and secured his hands to the table once again. He appeared calmer than the day before, and I figured it was probably due to the rest he'd gotten the night before.

For a brief moment, I wondered if I'd made a mistake by not questioning Marwan when he'd been exhausted, as Vasco had suggested. However, after Otis had left the room, I saw the same look of fear I'd seen in his eyes the day before, and I knew I'd made the right decision to shut things down for a few hours.

I told Mitchell I wanted to give Marwan thirty minutes alone in the room before we showed up, and I used the time to grab another cup of coffee and a couple of sweet rolls. Meanwhile, Juliana was setting up an encrypted iPad for me, programming it to receive the photos Wylie had promised to send us.

As soon as she'd finished with the iPad, I handed it off to Mitchell, and then I explained how I wanted to conduct the interrogation.

"This isn't going to be anything like the time we questioned Roberto at the safe house in Caracas. I want Marwan to see me as a threat. I want him to believe I'm holding his life in my hands. We're not going to coddle him, feed his ego, or say pretty please. You got that?"

"Loud and clear."

A few minutes later, Vasco entered the room.

He apologized for being late and excused himself by saying he'd been with a Congressional delegation from Washington. After throwing out the names of some Senators who were in the city to discuss economic issues with the new Argentinean president, he paused, as if he thought one of us might like to comment on the company he was keeping.

I murmured, "No problem" and told him we were on our way across the hall to interrogate Marwan.

He grinned and handed me the paper bag he was carrying.

"Don't worry. I didn't forget about our prisoner. In fact, I remembered what Roberto said about Marwan liking Turkish coffee. I couldn't get any Turkish coffee, but I got him a cup of some really strong stuff, and I was thinking you could use this little gift to soften him up, get him to trust you, before you start interrogating him."

I realized, as much as anything else, this gesture proved Vasco and I were living on two entirely different planets.

## Chapter 24

As per my instructions, as soon as we entered 301-C, Mitchell took a seat in a corner of the room with the iPad in full view, and I sat down at the rectangular table across from Marwan.

The moment I sat down, he lifted his handcuffed wrists off the table and asked, "Will you remove these?"

"That depends on how willing you are to answer my questions."

Although he didn't respond, he inclined his head toward me, and I proceeded with my first question.

"How did you locate Roberto Montilla?"

He held my gaze for a few seconds before answering me, and I noticed, despite what Otis had said about Marwan getting some sleep the night before, there were dark circles under the man's eyes.

"It wasn't that difficult," he said. "When I heard Ahmed had killed Roberto's son in San José, I contacted some acquaintances in the city and asked them to find out where the body had been taken. They discovered it had been flown here to Buenos Aires and buried at *Cementerio de Flores.* After that, the rest was easy."

"Define easy."

"My plans were to scout out the cemetery first and look for Roberto's address later. I never expected to encounter him at the cemetery the moment I landed."

"You came to the cemetery straight from the airport?"

He nodded. "When I saw Roberto kneeling there at Ernesto's grave, I knew it was a gift from Allah."

"Did Allah also send me there to stop you?"

He ignored my question. "Do you have a name?"

"I'm Geraldo Lucia, a friend of Roberto Montilla."

His eyes narrowed as he stared at me. "No, Señor Lucia," he said, "I don't believe you're his friend. I believe he works for you."

"In what capacity?"

"What shall I call it? Intelligence gathering? I believe you're a member of America's intelligence community, and you recruited Roberto to spy for you. Despite what you said at the cemetery, I know it was Roberto who killed Ahmed. I knew that as soon as I saw the way he looked at me. I'm convinced he killed Ahmed. It wasn't you."

Instead of trying to refute his statement, I went on the attack.

"Hezbollah sent Ahmed to kill Roberto Montilla. Do you deny this?"

There might have been a flicker of surprise at my question, but I wasn't sure.

"No, I don't deny it. Roberto betrayed Hezbollah, even though he took our money. If you're familiar with the Quran, you know all betrayers must be slaughtered."

I stared at Marwan for a moment, trying to get a read on the man. What I sensed was a mixture of guilt and discontentment. I imagined his days were full of anxiety, exacerbated by the radical elements of his Muslim faith.

I said, "If anyone betrayed Hezbollah, it was Rehman Zaidi. He was the one who revealed Hezbollah's plans to use Syria's chemical weapons. Roberto was just trying to save innocent American lives."

At the mention of the weapons, I noticed Marwan's right thumb twitched. Even though he was able to conceal his emotions, he wasn't able to conceal how his body reacted to stress.

Marwan said, "Roberto was only concerned about what might happen to his son. He didn't care about American lives. By refusing to work with us, he was just trying to prevent his son from becoming a martyr."

I realized I'd reached a crossroads with Marwan and needed to make a decision.

Was it time to introduce his own family into the conversation? He'd given me an opportunity with the mention of Roberto's son. But it might be too early for that, especially since Mitchell hadn't given me any indication Wylie's promised photos of Yamina and Samira were on their way.

On the other hand, up to this point, Marwan had been surprisingly forthcoming with his answers. Was this just to get his handcuffs removed or did he have a different agenda? Did it have anything to do with the fear I'd seen on his face earlier?

I decided to ask him.

"Roberto was worried about his son. You're right about that. What are you worried about, Marwan?"

He sat up straighter in the chair. "Nothing worries me. Even if you torture me, I know I'll survive. If you abuse me like you did those prisoners at Abu Ghraib, I might be humiliated, but I won't be broken. And don't make the mistake of thinking I'm afraid of being a martyr, because I'm not."

I had my answer.

The man was afraid of being tortured.

In his mind, I was about to subject him to some horrific ill treatment and demean him in some way. It wasn't the first time I'd come across the psychological aftereffects of the scandal brought on by the aberrant behavior of the private contractors running the Abu Ghraib prison in Iraq.

I usually tried to dispel such thoughts. However, it seemed to be working in my favor now, so I decided to run with it for awhile.

"We *will* break you, Marwan; you can be sure of that. You can resist for awhile, but everyone breaks eventually. There's an alternative, but it's contingent on your willingness to answer all my questions."

His eyes widened slightly. "What's the alternative?"

"I'll explain that option when you've provided me with a few more answers. In the meantime, here's a little taste of what's ahead."

I stood to my feet and immediately Marwan flinched, as if I might be about to strike him. He relaxed only when he saw me remove a key from my pocket and unlock his handcuffs.

Once the cuffs were off, he began massaging his wrists. I knew the restraints hadn't been tight enough to cut off his circulation, but his actions gave me a brief glimpse into the way his mind worked, and I decided it wasn't too early to start laying the groundwork for the photos I was expecting from Wylie.

I looked over at Mitchell, "Start the timer now. Set it for ten minutes."

He nodded and touched the iPad screen several times.

Marwan looked puzzled and a little apprehensive at these instructions.

"Here's the way this works, Marwan. You have ten minutes to give me your background or the cuffs go back on. Don't lie to me, because while I don't know everything about you, I do know some things. And, if I discover you're lying, I assure you, there *will* be consequences."

"I . . . ah . . ." He looked up at the ceiling a minute. "What do you want to know? My birthplace? Something about my family?"

"You're wasting time. Start talking."

He nervously clasped and unclasped his hands. "My father was from Spain, but my mother was Lebanese. I was born in Beirut, because that's where my parents met, but, when I was seven, my mother died, and my father returned to Barcelona. I was raised by my grandmother."

Marwan went on to sketch out his education, which was sparse because he'd quit school at the age of fifteen. He told me about marrying Yamina, whose father owned the restaurant where he worked. As he began telling me about the birth of his daughter, Mitchell gave him a two-minute warning.

The pressure of a deadline, plus not knowing exactly what I wanted from him, clearly made him nervous, and, by the time a chime sounded on the iPad, drops of sweat had broken out across his forehead.

Although his recitation had filled in some missing blanks and explained his ability to speak both Spanish and Arabic, he hadn't told me anything about his Jihadist background.

I dangled the handcuffs in front of him. "I'll leave the cuffs off for now. Let's move on to—"

"Is it too cold in here for you?" Mitchell asked. He walked over to a thermostat on the wall and adjusted the temperature. "That should warm things up."

After delivering the pre-arranged signal telling me Wylie had sent him the photographs of Marwan's wife and daughter, Mitchell returned to his seat.

"Let's move on to another topic," I said. "Tell me about Hezbollah's plans to use chemical weapons on Washington, D.C."

Marwan shook his head. "I don't know anything about that."

I nodded at Mitchell, who walked over and handed me the iPad.

Marwan tried to get a look at the tablet, but, for the moment, I kept the display hidden from him.

When I glanced down at the screen, I decided Wylie deserved a great big Texas-sized star for the photos he'd sent me.

♦♦♦♦

There were five photographs in all. Three of them had been taken from inside some kind of pastry shop, or maybe, as Mitchell had suggested, it was an internet café.

The shots had been cleverly staged so there could be little doubt as to what day it was or where the pictures were taken, because, in one corner of the café, someone was reading *El Universal*, the most widely read daily newspaper in Caracas.

The front page of the paper was clearly displayed, and the headline screamed about a strike by postal workers and the president's decision to intervene.

In all three of the indoor shots, Yamina and Samira Farage were seated at the table next to the person holding the newspaper.

In the first photograph, Samira was looking at her cell phone, while Yamina was staring off in the distance. The second shot showed two men standing next to them. While the ladies appeared to be oblivious to anyone around them, one of the men was looking down at Samira with a smarmy grin on his face, while the other one was staring straight at the camera.

The next shot was of a waiter bringing the ladies their order. The camera had caught him at the moment he was about to set a plate of food in front of Yamina. She was looking at the plate, but he was looking at the camera. The smile on his face was enough to make any husband uncomfortable.

The last two photos were taken outside. The photographer, who I presumed was Buck, had snapped a photo showing the back of Yamina and Samira as they walked down the street. It appeared Buck was walking directly behind them. The last picture showed the ladies entering a building. Opening the door for them was one of the men from the pastry shop, the one with the smarmy grin.

♦♦♦♦

I closed the iPad and looked up at Marwan.

"I'll ask you the question again. This time I expect an answer. Tell me how Hezbollah plans to use the chemical weapons on Washington."

Marwan nervously rubbed his hand across his forehead. "I don't know about the chemical weapons, and I can't tell you what I don't know."

"Tell me something you do know then. Tell me about your family."

He told me about his son who'd been a soldier in the Syrian army, but who'd recently been killed in the battle for Al-Hadar.

After explaining what a good solider Arshad was, Marwan went on to describe his daughter in equally glowing terms. He ended his description by saying, "My wife and daughter are living in Beirut now."

"If that's true," I said, pushing the iPad toward him, "then how do you explain these photographs?"

## Chapter 25

Marwan went through the five photographs quickly, clenching and unclenching his jaw as he swiped through them from side to side. Once that was done, he returned to the first one and lingered over it, studying it for several seconds. He did the same with the other four.

Finally, he pushed the iPad away and bowed his head.

"Don't harm them," he murmured. "They don't know anything."

When I handed the iPad back to Mitchell, I said, "Tell our friends in Caracas to hold off for now . . ." I waited a beat and then I added, "But keep them on standby."

Marwan raised his head and watched Mitchell silently pecking away on the screen's keyboard, pretending to send a message to the photographer and his friends.

When Mitchell stopped typing, Marwan looked over at me.

There was no mistaking the anger in his voice. "Ask me your questions."

Instead of beginning with the important stuff, I started off by questioning him about his wife and daughter. My intention was to dissipate some of that anger with inconsequential matters before bringing up what I really cared about, namely, Hezbollah's secrets.

"Why are your wife and daughter in Caracas?"

He stared at me defiantly for a second or two, but then he said, "They're waiting for me to return from Buenos Aires. I told them I had some business to take care of here, and I'd return in two days."

"You're not answering my question, Marwan. Why are they in Caracas in the first place? What is the purpose of your trip to Venezuela?"

When he didn't answer me immediately, I glanced over at Mitchell as if I were about to give him some instructions.

Marwan quickly spoke up, "I wanted to keep them safe. I didn't want them to die like Arshad."

"Your son was killed in battle."

He nodded. "Yes, but ISIS is bringing the battlefield to the whole Middle East now. Damascus may fall to ISIS soon, and when that happens, Lebanon will be next. Just last week an ISIS suicide bomber killed over forty people in southern Beirut. There's no doubt my wife and daughter are safer on this side of the world."

"Why Caracas?"

"On the same day I learned Roberto was living in Buenos Aires, Rehman Zaidi told me about a teacher at the Islamic school in Caracas who wanted to sublease his apartment. I saw that as a sign from Allah I should take them to Caracas."

"Does anyone besides your wife and daughter know you're in Buenos Aires?"

He shook his head. "No, I didn't tell anyone I was coming after Roberto."

"When were you planning to return to Damascus?"

"When?" He hesitated and looked away. "In . . . ah . . . one week. I'm due back in Damascus next week."

His faltering answer, plus the return of his twitching thumb, made me wonder. "What's happening next week?"

He ignored me and looked over at Mitchell for a moment.

"I'm a member of Naballah's security council. He's called a meeting for next week."

"Will General Suleiman be attending that meeting?"

He quickly jerked his head around. "Why are you asking me all these questions if you already know the answers?"

"Answer me. Will the general be attending that meeting?"

He nodded. "Yes, that's when the security council meets with General Suleiman. Naballah has announced the meeting for July 4th."

That date gave me pause.

"I'm assuming you know the significance of that date?"

He gave a short laugh. "Of course. July 4th is America's independence day."

"Is that when the general will give Naballah the schedule for the attack on Washington?"

"That's correct."

"Tell me about the delivery system for the chemicals. What method will be used to disperse the gas?"

"I told you before. I don't know. Only Naballah knows that information."

He'd denied it twice now, so I was beginning to believe him.

I veered off in another direction.

"What's your role on the council?"

"I'm an adviser for Hezbollah's interests in Latin America."

"You'll have to do better than that, Marwan."

He wiped the moisture from off his upper lip. "Hezbollah has certain agreements with the cartels in Mexico and with the FARC organization in Colombia. I advise Hezbollah on those agreements."

"By agreements do you mean weapons? Are these arms agreements?"

He nodded. "We supply them with weapons and training."

That information wasn't new. The Agency was aware of such agreements, and the Israelis had a meticulous method in place for tracking all of Hezbollah's weapons deliveries. More often than not, they shared that information with their American counterpart.

His explanation, though, sparked across the synapses in my brain and triggered my next question.

"Do you always attend the council meetings called by Naballah?"

"Not all of them. I'm only invited when Naballah wants advice on how to deal with the cartels or when he's negotiating a weapons package."

"What advice does Naballah need from you when he meets with General Suleiman?"

"I wasn't given that information . . ." he paused and glanced at his surroundings, ". . . but since it's obvious I won't be at that meeting now, it hardly matters, does it?"

Was that true? Did it matter?

I suddenly realized it mattered a great deal.

♦♦♦♦

I paraphrased some previous questions and dug further into Marwan's background. When I returned to the question of the chemical weapons, Vasco stuck his head in the door and said he needed to see me.

I called Otis into the room to keep an eye on Marwan, and Mitchell and I followed Vasco across the hall to 301-B. Once inside, he waved a document in my face.

"I've just received a directive from the DDO telling me to arrange transport for Marwan to Gitmo."

"You pulled me out of the interrogation session to tell me this?"

"I needed to—"

"Look, Ken, you can drag your feet, wait a couple of days, and then—"

"The DDO alerted me about the transfer yesterday, so I went ahead and chartered a flight. It leaves in two hours."

He gestured over at Juliana, who was still seated in front of the monitoring equipment. "I've already had Juliana inform the DDO to expect Marwan at Gitmo by five o'clock this evening, and I'm not about to tell him I've decided to change those plans."

Mitchell grinned. "It's never a good idea to break your word to Robert Ira. Your career may never be the same if you do."

Vasco slapped him on the back. "Exactly. He appreciates a man who keeps his word."

Although I was angry at the way Vasco had maneuvered things around just to make himself look good in the DDO's eyes, I was determined not to let his behavior get to me. A few months ago, I would have lost my temper and lashed out at him, but, ever since Tehran, I'd found it a little easier to control myself.

I turned my back on Vasco and walked across the room to speak to Juliana. "Send the audio feed of Marwan's interrogation to the Ops

Center immediately and then alert Douglas Carlton about the transfer of Marwan to Gitmo."

"The audio's almost ready to go. As soon as I get it downloaded, I'll inform Mr. Carlton."

I leaned down, as if I were trying to get a closer look at the monitor, and whispered in her ear. "I'm going back inside the interrogation room now, but don't record my final conversation with Marwan. I'd prefer it be kept off the record."

She nodded. "Understood."

When I straightened up again, I waved at Vasco and said, "I'm going across the hall to tell Marwan he's about to take a little trip."

Mitchell motioned toward the door. "You want me in there?"

"No, this won't take but a minute."

♦♦♦♦

Marwan was staring down at his hands when I entered the room, and, when he looked up, I actually thought he seemed relieved to see me. Once I'd dismissed Otis, he appeared to relax even more.

I decided to speak to him in Arabic, just in case Vasco or Mitchell were monitoring my conversation.

"Do you trust me, Marwan?"

He looked amused.

I wasn't sure if it was because I'd switched over to Arabic, or if it was because of my question.

"Not really, but what choice do I have?"

"You actually have two choices. You can choose to believe me when I say I'm going to make it possible for you to see your family again, or you can choose to believe everyone else who will tell you you'll never see your family again."

He stared at me. "Is this some kind of test?"

"No, it's not a test. You remember earlier when I mentioned an alternative? Instead of being subjected to the kind of treatment that went on at Abu Ghraib, in a few hours, you'll be transferred to our military prison at Guantanamo Bay, Cuba. We call the place Gitmo. I assume you've heard of it."

"Yes, of course."

"If you agree to cooperate with me, then your stay there will be very short."

"By cooperate do you mean answer your questions?"

"No, I won't be asking the questions at Gitmo. However, within a few days, a Mr. Chessman will show up to interrogate you. When he does, you should tell him you're willing to go to work for us. In exchange, we'll—"

"You mean go to work for the CIA?"

"In exchange, we'll agree not to harm your wife and daughter. But, even more than that, we'll promise to do everything we can to keep them safe."

He was silent for a few seconds. When he spoke again, he sounded subdued. "Are you saying if I act as your spy, my family will be safe, and you'll let me go?"

I nodded. "It's a little more complicated than that, but, yes, that's what I'm saying."

He closed his eyes as if he might be praying. I doubted that was the case. More than likely, he was thinking about how to use my proposal to his advantage.

A few seconds later, he opened his eyes and said, "Traitors are beheaded in Syria. I'm sure you know that."

"I'll be around to make sure that won't happen to you."

"How soon will I be able to talk to my wife and daughter?"

"Once you've agreed to return to Damascus as my asset, then I'll see what I can work out about your wife and daughter."

"You want me to attend the meeting with General Suleiman, don't you?"

"That's right. But don't worry. We'll work out all the details, and your risk will be minimal."

He folded his arms across his chest. "I want to know those details before I make such a commitment."

"You're in no position to negotiate with me, Marwan. If you want to see your wife and daughter again, then you'll agree to cooperate with us. That's the deal. Take it or leave it."

In the end, he took the deal.

Now, all I had to do was convince Carlton and the DDO to make the deal and let me go to Damascus and run Marwan as my asset.

How hard could that be?

♦♦♦♦

Vasco left the Bub's Subs executive office suite with Marwan an hour later, and Mitchell and I rode with Juliana back over to our hotel.

As she pulled up to the front of the hotel, Mitchell asked her if she'd have dinner with us in The Red Room, one of the hotel's restaurants.

She accepted his invitation immediately, but, since I was waiting for a phone call from Carlton, I told the two of them to go ahead without me.

Mitchell didn't try to convince me to join them.

The moment he walked over to the concierge's desk to see about getting them a table, I pulled Juliana aside.

"Mitchell and I will be heading out of here in a few hours, so this may be my last chance to say thanks for all your help."

"I should be thanking you instead."

"Why? Because I gave Ken a reason to fire you today or because Ben educated you on Sam Houston?"

She laughed, "Because you made me realize I've been missing the rush. I'm sure you know what I mean. It's that feeling you get when you're playing a game of cat and mouse with the bad guys."

I nodded. "Or in some cases, the good guys."

"Unfortunately, that's also true."

"Does this mean you've been reconsidering your love affair with having a routine?"

She nodded. "I think it might be time for me to apply for a change in status."

Mitchell walked up and announced the maître d' had a table ready for them.

Before they left, I said to Juliana, "You should do it. You'll regret it if you don't."

"Regret what?" Mitchell asked.

"Regret not asking you to recite more of Sam Houston's funny sayings. Juliana was just asking me if I thought you'd mind telling her more about the great man."

Mitchell smiled, "Are you kidding me? I'd love to do that."

I ignored Juliana's dirty look and headed for the elevator.

♦♦♦♦

A few minutes after I entered my suite on the fifth floor, Carlton called me.

"Are you clear?"

"Clear."

"Preliminary voice analysis of the interrogation tape indicates Marwan was telling the truth."

"Even when he talked about the delivery system for the chemicals?"

"Yes, even then. I'm convinced he doesn't know how they're planning to disperse the sarin."

I asked, "Has Keever been able to locate his asset in Damascus yet?"

"Unfortunately, we've just received confirmation the asset's been killed. We're flying blind now, but at least Marwan gave us a date when General Suleiman will meet with Naballah to go over the details of the operation."

"I have a proposal, Douglas. It's a bit risky, but—"

"Once you get back to Langley, we'll discuss where we go from here. Right now, I'm about to walk into a briefing with C.J. Salazar about the arrival of those ships in Santiago de Cuba in a few days. C.J. is running the show, but since those ships are carrying some of Syria's chemical weapons, the DDO wants me to sit in on the meeting."

"Who's been assigned to work surveillance on the warehouse?"

"You know I'm not about to tell you that."

"I just thought if you needed an extra body, you might consider one of Ken Vasco's operatives. Her name is Juliana Lamar, and she's been running surveillance for Ken. Before she came to the Agency, she worked Narcotics in the San Francisco Police Department. That is sure to impress Cartel Carlos."

"Sounds like she impressed you."

"I've been impressed by how well she and Ben have worked together down here. The two of them would be an excellent addition to the team tracking those canisters once they arrive in Santiago."

"I'll see what C.J. thinks. Does that mean you're not willing to work with Ben anymore?"

"No, it means it's about time for him to be the primary on an operation. Running surveillance would be a good start, and if Rehman Zaidi shows up to supervise the weapons, there's the added bonus Mitchell would be able to recognize him."

"Did I miss something? Did Marwan tell you Zaidi is on his way to Cuba?"

"No, I've just been thinking about some possibilities, and I believe one of them is that Zaidi will show up in Santiago."

"We'll talk about all the possibilities when you get back to Langley."

Once he hung up, I thought about the possibilities.

One of them included Nikki again.

# PART THREE

## Chapter 26

*Sunday, June 28*

When Mitchell and I arrived back at Langley, we were immediately debriefed by Douglas Carlton and Nolan Wilson. Our session included a replaying of the audio tapes from our interrogation of both Roberto and Marwan, plus a quick video call from Ken Vasco about his continuing surveillance of Roberto.

When the debrief was over, C.J. Salazar sent word for Mitchell to join him in the RTM Center next door to the conference room, and I followed Carlton up to his office on the fourth floor.

Once he'd shut the door, Carlton said, "C.J. plans to give Ben his first solo assignment today. He'll be leaving for Cuba this afternoon and heading up the surveillance team monitoring the arrival of those vessels at the port in Santiago tomorrow."

"Was this Salazar's idea?"

Carlton shrugged. "I nudged him a bit."

"And Juliana Lamar?"

"He's also agreed to have her assigned to Ben's team. This is strictly a non-engagement mission. They'll only be there to observe the offloading of the ships and to verify whether their cargo contains the gas canisters. After the weapons have arrived, Ben's team will monitor how they're handled and warehoused in Santiago. Once we've determined how Hezbollah plans to get the canisters to the

States, the DDO will decide how to proceed."

"Ben may not like the non-engagement part, but he should be happy about having his own assignment, and I'm sure he'll enjoy working with Juliana again."

Carlton walked over and sat down behind his desk, while I took a seat in one of his guest chairs. After straightening the stack of yellow legal pads in front of him, he looked up and said, "I'm ready now."

"Ready for what?"

"To hear your risky proposal, the one you mentioned a couple of days ago when you were down in Buenos Aires."

"Did I say it was risky? Maybe you misunderstood me. The way I see it, the risks are minimal compared to the reward."

"If the reward consists of preventing an attack on Washington, then I'm ready to hear it."

I gave him my spiel. "The best chance we have of stopping Hezbollah from using those weapons is for us to know what happens in that meeting between General Suleiman and Hassan Naballah in Damascus on July 4th. What I'm proposing is that we send Marwan Farage back to Damascus to serve as our ears in that meeting."

Carlton nodded. "While I agree with your assessment, from what I heard, Marwan wasn't offering the CIA his services when you were questioning him."

"That's true, but later on, when I told him he was being shipped off to Gitmo, he agreed to make the deal."

"I don't believe I heard that conversation."

I smiled. "It was strictly off the record."

He wasn't smiling.

"Look, Douglas, he's worried about his wife and daughter. That's our leverage. I promised him I'd keep his family safe in exchange for his help, and he agreed to return to Damascus and attend the meeting with Suleiman."

"And then what?"

"Once we get the intel, we'll get him out of there and back into the loving arms of his wife and daughter in Caracas."

Carlton shook his head. "I talked with Al Johnson at Gitmo this morning. He said Marwan isn't being cooperative with our people there."

"That doesn't surprise me. Marwan is afraid of two things. He's afraid of being tortured, and he's afraid of losing his family. He knows he's not going to be tortured at Gitmo, and I've already assured him I'll keep his family safe if he returns to Damascus as my asset. Right now, he has no reason to cooperate with anyone at Gitmo."

"So you've painted yourself into this picture now."

"I know that doesn't surprise you. Since Marwan trusts me, I'm the best person to run him in Damascus."

Carlton looked skeptical.

"Okay," I said. "Maybe trust is too strong a word. He tolerates me. But, believe me, the feeling is mutual, and we both know it."

Carlton immediately pulled out his Cross pen and scribbled something down on his legal pad.

I couldn't make out the words.

Once he put his pen aside, he said, "I'll go upstairs and run this by the DDO. At this point, your proposal appears to be our most viable option, but, as usual, he may have a different idea. If it's a go, you can expect a briefing tomorrow, and, after that, I'll fly down to Gitmo and make Marwan the official offer."

The fact that Carlton himself would fly down to Gitmo was standard operating procedure. Senior Agency officials were the only persons authorized to make agreements with known terrorists.

I'd already prepared Marwan for this eventuality.

I said, "I told Marwan a new interrogator would show up at Gitmo and offer him a job."

"He gets a new interrogator every four hours. By the time I get there, he may have already told the Defense Intelligence Agency he's willing to be their man in Damascus."

"No, he won't talk to anyone but you."

"How'd you manage that?"

"I told him a new interrogator by the name of Mr. Chessman would arrive in a few days, and he should only offer his services to him."

Carlton actually looked pleased at the name I'd chosen for him, but other than clearing his throat, he didn't comment on it.

We talked for a few minutes about how we might handle getting some photos of Marwan's wife and daughter to dangle over Marwan's head, and, after that, Carlton suggested I go down to the cafeteria and get a cup of coffee while he went upstairs and pitched my proposal to the DDO and his staff.

I decided to go find Olivia instead of hanging out at the cafeteria.

♦♦♦♦

If Olivia was in the building, I knew she'd be in the basement level of the Old Headquarters Building where the Ops Center was located.

The maze of corridors, conference rooms, and RTM Centers was the hub of Agency's operations, the place where America's covert intelligence from around the world was assimilated, analyzed, and implemented. Briefings and planning sessions were held in the conference rooms, while ongoing operations were coordinated and monitored in the RTM Centers.

I found Olivia in Corridor C, outside RTM Center C. She was wearing a headset with a wraparound mike, and, as I walked up, I could hear her talking to someone, "We just got the video. You can stand down now."

The moment she saw me, she pulled her headset down around her neck.

"What are you doing here?" she demanded.

"I just stopped by to say hello. I heard you were back at work."

"You're such a lousy liar. You came down here to check up on me."

"Guilty as charged." I pointed down the hallway toward the employee lounge. "Let's get some coffee."

She shrugged. "Whatever."

Corridor C's employee lounge was occupied by two other people. However, both of them left a few minutes after Olivia and I arrived. I attributed their quick exit to Olivia's pointed stare.

Once I'd poured us some black coffee, I brought the cups over to the small round table where Olivia was seated.

I immediately broached the subject I knew she didn't want to talk about.

"What's happening with your surgery?"

She took a sip of her coffee before answering me. "It's tomorrow."

"What time?"

Her eyes narrowed. "Why?"

I shrugged. "Just a question."

She shook her head. "You never ask *just* a question, Titus."

I grinned at her. "If I'm around tomorrow, I thought I might drop in on you."

"Don't bother. I'll be so out of it, I won't even know you're there."

I dropped the subject, and we drank our coffee in silence for a moment.

I said, "I've heard Cartel Carlos is sending Ben Mitchell to Cuba to keep an eye on those canisters."

She nodded. "He's briefing him now. I'm surprised you didn't get the assignment. You must be losing your touch with Douglas."

"It's a non-engagement surveillance op. Not my thing."

She placed her cup down on the table, placed her chin in her hand, and proceeded to study my face as if I were a new species of animal and she were a biologist.

Finally, she said, "Douglas is sending you somewhere, isn't he?"

"What makes you say that?"

"Aside from the fact you just implied you might not be around tomorrow, you would jump at the chance to run surveillance on those canisters. That is, unless you were headed somewhere else."

I nodded. "Carlton's working on it, but nothing's been settled yet."

"I know you're not going to Cuba, so you must be headed to the Middle East, and, if I had to guess, I'd say it was Damascus."

I just looked at her, refusing to confirm or deny her theory. When it became apparent I wasn't about to talk about any upcoming op, she quickly snatched up our empty coffee cups and headed over to a trashcan. After she'd taken a few steps, she suddenly stopped and turned around.

The look on her face was one of triumph.

"You're taking Marwan Farage back into Syria, aren't you? You going to run him as our asset in Damascus."

I smiled at her.

She stood there for a moment with a look of disgust on her face and said nothing. After tossing the cups in the garbage can, she walked back over to the table and gave me a lecture.

"I'm sure you know the risk assessment on that kind of operation is off the charts. Marwan is committed to Jihad. No matter what you've promised him, you'll never be able to trust him."

"We're facing a much bigger risk if we don't know the timing of the hit on Washington."

She didn't respond.

"If Marwan can get us that information, any risk will be worth it."

She rubbed her arms as if she'd suddenly gotten a chill.

"I know it's useless to try and talk you out of it, but before I leave tonight, I'll speak to Nolan about positioning another surveillance satellite over Damascus. There's also the possibility he could free up one of the smaller drones to do some recon for you."

"While I appreciate your concern, Olivia, I'm confident Nolan can handle this. You should go take care of yourself and not give the Agency another thought."

"What makes you think I'm concerned about you?"

"Don't be such a—"

"Even if I was concerned about you, you'd probably just say you were relying on your faith and there was nothing to worry about."

"You're right, I might say that, but it's only because I really do believe God is ultimately in control of everything."

She nodded. "That's all well and good, but I'm repositioning a surveillance satellite over Damascus tonight."

"The DDO hasn't signed off on the mission yet."

"He'll sign off on it. After the way you embarrassed him in that debrief, I'm sure the DDO considers you expendable. Rest assured of that."

Olivia put the headset back on her head and repositioned her wraparound mike. "It's time for me to get back to work. Good luck on the mission. You're definitely going to need it."

She gave me a little wave and headed for the door.

I immediately got up and followed her. "Wait a second, Olivia."

She turned around.

"When you go into your surgery tomorrow, remember I'll be praying for you."

She drew a deep breath and lowered her head. When she looked up at me a few seconds later, she looked sadder than normal.

"Why bother, Titus? I'm not worth it."

"That's where you're wrong, Olivia. The God of the universe considered you so valuable He came to earth 2,000 years ago and willingly gave His life for you. That's how much you're worth."

"You really think that's true?"

"Absolutely."

She walked out the door without saying goodbye.

♦♦♦♦

I stayed behind in the break room and had a second cup of coffee. After a sip or two, I pulled out my iPhone and called Nikki.

I thought she sounded excited to hear from me.

"Are you back at Langley?" she asked.

"I just got here this morning. Where are you?"

"I'm at Quantico. I arrived on Friday, but we weren't allowed to check in and get our room assignments until yesterday."

"Which dorm are you in?"

"The Jefferson. All the trainees are being housed in the same dorm, but at least I'm able to have my own room. Are you familiar with the facilities at Quantico?"

"Oh, yeah," I said, and then I quickly changed the subject before the detective started asking me a follow-up question. "When do you start your classes?"

"Tomorrow morning. Our orientation was yesterday. That's when we met our instructors and got a tour of the facilities. I have to admit, Titus, this place is pretty awesome."

"What's happening now?"

"Nothing's on the schedule for today, so I'm using my time to unpack my suitcase."

"As exciting as that sounds, would you be willing to drop

everything and meet me somewhere for dinner?"

"Let's see. You're offering me a choice between putting away my toothbrush and spending the evening with you. Give me a moment to think about that."

"I know it's a tough decision."

There was silence on the line for a few seconds.

She laughed."Okay, you win. Where shall we meet?"

We settled on a restaurant in Fairfax, about halfway between Quantico and Langley, and after we decided on a time, she asked me what I knew about the incident at the Navy Yard on Monday.

"I arrived here just as the crisis broke. Why?"

"The incident came up at our orientation yesterday. One of our instructors said we'd be studying the crisis as part of our training. He cited it as a good example of how local law enforcement was joining with the FBI to solve the crime. In fact, several of our instructors had worked the shooting."

"They're calling it a crime instead of an act of terrorism?"

"They said the shooting appeared to be drug-related, which is why I brought it up. One of the instructors implied there's a ongoing feud with the CIA about whether this incident was related to terrorism or not. I was just wondering if you'd heard anything about it."

"I've been out of town for a few days."

She was quiet for a moment—probably biting her tongue because she knew I wasn't going to discuss my travel itinerary with her—but then she changed the subject and told me about spending two days on the road with Stormy.

When she got to the part about arriving at The Meadows, she said, "I was told you were out of town when I took Stormy to the address you gave me. I love that house, by the way. The grounds are just gorgeous, and I'm sure the inside of the house is just as beautiful."

"So you met Arkady?"

"Yes. Stormy and I were both a little intimidated by him at first, but then Stormy seemed to warm up to him right before I left. He wasn't so sure about Frisco, but Arkady kept insisting the two dogs just needed some time together."

"I'm sure he's right."

"I'm curious about Arkady. Does he own the house?"

I started to explain about The Meadows, but just then my Agency phone vibrated, and Carlton's name appeared on the screen. "No, Arkady's not the homeowner. I know you're curious, Detective, but your questions will just have to wait. I have to go."

"I'll bet the owner is some beneficent fatherly type who loves dogs and took a liking to you."

"Not even close."

## Chapter 27

After I heard Carlton's voice mail, I left the break room and rode the elevator up to his office on the fourth floor.

His voice message, "I'm back, and we need to talk," was short, but I was betting its brevity meant the DDO had signed off on allowing Marwan to return to Syria.

When Carlton was focused on a task, he didn't spend time on long explanations, and if the mission had been approved, I suspected he was already considering the protocols and assembling the ops team.

As expected, when Sally Jo ushered me into Carlton's office, she refused to give me a clue as to what I should anticipate from her boss. However, the moment Carlton pointed me over to the right side of the room, where a sofa and two matching armchairs were arranged around a small coffee table, I took that as yet another clue my mission was a go.

Carlton seldom used the cozy seating arrangement for anything other than announcing something favorable, like giving me the results of a polygraph screening or presenting me with a commendation.

In fact, I could only recall one exception to this good news rule, and that had been when Carlton, in his own quiet, indomitable way, had positioned himself in front of the sofa and lectured me about controlling my temper.

That episode had taken place after a mission to rescue some hostages in Yemen, when Frank Benson, the primary on the operation, had refused to act decisively when confronted with more armed resistance than the Ops Center had anticipated. As a result of Benson's ineptitude, all the hostages had been killed, plus our team had barely gotten out of there alive.

During our debrief back at Langley, I'd delivered a long, angry rant about Benson's leadership to the debriefing committee. Afterward, Carlton had indicated he wanted to see me—see me as in, "Meet me in my office, right *now*."

The moment I'd entered his office, I'd veered off to the right and plopped myself down on the sofa, while Carlton had ignored me and strolled over to his desk without uttering a word. About the time I'd decided he was waiting for me to calm down, he'd gotten up from his desk and come over to the sofa to confront me.

His lecture about self-control was one I'll never forget.

A few months after the Yemeni debacle, the Agency had given Frank Benson his walking papers.

Not long after that, Benson had been hired by the FBI.

♦♦♦♦

Now, as I sat down in one of the armchairs, Carlton came around from behind his desk and sat down on the sofa.

He nodded. "You're on, Titus. Deputy Ira has approved your proposal to play Marwan back into Syria as our asset. He did, however, make some adjustments to the protocols you and I had discussed."

"Such as?"

Carlton held up his fingers and ticked off the DDO's requirements.

"First, Keever Pike will remain the primary for the mission. You'll be his second."

Before I could utter a word of protest, he stopped me and said, "I know you recruited Marwan and for that reason alone, you should have been named as the primary, but Keever has been in country for over a year now, and the DDO felt he deserved the primary slot."

I shrugged. "I can live with that. What else?"

"His second stipulation is that you and Keever have a handler in country. He'll be assigning a field officer to direct the operation in Damascus and maintain contact with the Ops Center 24/7."

Earlier, when we'd discussed the logistics of the operation, I'd been ambivalent about having a field officer (FO) in country. However, since our embassy in Syria had closed back in 2012, Agency personnel had been required to operate out of safe houses and communicate with the Ops Center through encrypted satellite linkups, and that could prove problematic during an active operation.

I nodded. "With the embassy closed, I guess that makes sense. Any idea who the FO will be?"

"I volunteered."

I tried not to look too surprised. "And the deputy agreed?"

"Without hesitation."

Carlton had always been a hands-on operations officer, and he sometimes took on the FO's responsibilities as well. However, this usually occurred when the mission was anticipated to be a massive undertaking or when the operatives in the field had demonstrated a tendency to go off on their own.

In this case, the mission was pretty straightforward, so I had to believe he considered Pike a wild card. Although Pike was an exceptional operative, if a mission started going sideways, he had a tendency to go a little sideways himself.

I didn't think Carlton was worried about me, but, just in case, I decided to ask him anyway. "Any special reason you made the decision to tag along on this one?"

"No special reason. You and Keever will have your hands full trying to manage Marwan, and I'm familiar with the city. That's all there is to it."

Maybe he *was* worried about me.

"Any other changes to the protocol?"

"Just one. The DDO wants Marwan's wife and daughter to be taken to a safe house in Caracas until Marwan provides us with the intel on the attack."

Previously, Carlton and I had agreed not to grab Yamina and Samira. Simply from an operational standpoint, we had decided it would be much easier for Wylie to supply me with occasional photographs—doctored up if necessary—in order to convince Marwan we had his wife and daughter in custody.

Kidnapping innocent civilians usually created more problems than the enterprise was worth. At least, that had always been my experience. Evidently, the DDO hadn't learned this lesson, or perhaps, he'd decided to ignore it in order to stop a chemical weapons attack.

"Has Sam Wylie been notified?"

"C.J. has contacted Sam about locating a safe house and doing a snatch and grab of the ladies."

"You know I don't agree with the DDO's decision about Marwan's family."

He nodded. "For what it's worth, I voiced my concern to the deputy, but, in the end, this maneuver may turn out for the best. Marwan has demanded to speak to his wife directly. As things stand right now, we can't let that happen. Having the ladies in our custody means he can talk to them now."

I wasn't happy about it, but I agreed with him. "You're probably right. It's possible we'll need that leverage to keep Marwan in line."

Carlton looked pleased at my response and stood to his feet. "Nolan and I will brief you in the morning at ten o'clock. We'll have Keever on a video feed at that time, and, more than likely, you'll be on an overseas flight tomorrow evening or the day after that."

I asked, "How's the investigation at the Navy Yard going? Did the feds get anything new out of Felipe?"

He shook his head. "They're treating the whole thing as a drug-related shooting, and Arnie said the lawyer assigned to represent Felipe wasn't letting him answer any questions."

"What about Katherine's probe into that photographer, Walid Khouri? Has she figured out why Reyes Valario had his phone number or why Felipe thought he was their drug connection?"

Carlton walked over to his desk and rifled through a stack of papers. After pulling out a single sheet, he looked it over and said, "She's still searching for any anomalies in the man's business or personal life, but all she's come up with so far is that he's made a trip to the Middle East recently."

"Did she say where?"

He looked down at Katherine's report and read off a list of names. "Pakistan, Turkey, and Dubai."

"Syria isn't on that list?"

"She doesn't mention Syria here, but she'll be at your briefing in the morning and you can ask her about that yourself."

I decided his reference to the next day's briefing was his way of dismissing me, so I got up and headed for the doorway.

"I'll see you in the morning at ten."

"Wait a second, Titus."

He walked out from behind his desk. "Before you leave, I think you should know Arnie told me some members of the FBI were pushing to have a formal complaint filed against you for helping Felipe escape the compound. You probably won't be surprised to learn Frank Benson was one of those leading the charge. So far, I've been able to quash those attempts, but I wanted you to keep that in mind just in case you're tempted to wander over to Walid Khouri's photography studio and do some snooping around on your own."

I feigned shock at his suggestion. "That's the last thing on my mind, Douglas. Right now, I'm on my way to Fairfax to meet Nikki Saxon for dinner, and, after that, I plan to head out to The Meadows for some shuteye."

He smiled. "Good. That's good. Take your detective out to The Meadows and show her around Gladys' garden. All women love flowers."

"I just might do that."

He wagged his finger at me. "Make sure Arkady keeps his dog penned up. That animal could spoil the moment."

I wasn't exactly sure which "moment" Carlton was referring to, but, in the end, it wasn't a dog—at least not the four-footed variety—who ended up spoiling my evening with Nikki.

♦♦♦♦

After closing the door to Carlton's office—doing so gently, as he had instructed—I stopped by Sally Jo's desk on my way out.

"That's a lovely cameo you're wearing," I said, complimenting her on the brooch pinned to the left side of her navy blue suit.

She smiled as she touched the piece of antique-looking jewelry. "It was my grandmother's."

"Is that gold filling around the edges?"

She looked up at me. "What's the sudden interest in my jewelry?"

"It was just a comment."

"Don't try to scam me, Titus Ray. It never works when my grandchildren try it, and it's certainly not going to work for you. Just tell me what you want."

Sally Jo had been Carlton's personal assistant for as long as I could remember, and even though she was a soft-spoken Southerner from Alabama and looked as if she might cringe if she had to squash a bug, she was, in reality, a tough old bird.

However, I was sure there was a soft spot in her heart for me.

I put my hands in the air as a sign of surrender. "You're definitely on to me, Sally Jo. There *is* something I want from you."

Her eyes twinkled. "Let's hear it."

"I'd like for you to find Ben Mitchell for me. I know he's in the building somewhere, but he's not answering his phone."

A little known feature of the temporary security badges issued to visitors and short-term occupants entering the headquarters of the CIA was an embedded tracking device. Any administrative employee with a high enough clearance could easily access the Security Tracking System (STS) on the Agency's main computer server and find the location of anyone wearing one of the ID badges.

However, the STS wasn't supposed to be used for convenience purposes. According to The Blue Book—the in-house employee manual—use of the STS software was strictly for emergencies only.

Not surprisingly, everyone ignored this rule.

Mitchell was wearing such a badge, and Sally Jo had one of the highest security classifications in the building, so I knew she'd have no trouble finding him on the grid.

"Hmmm," she said, pressing her forefinger to her lips, "I might be willing to access the STS screen, but, in return, you'd have to do something for me."

"Whatever you want, Sally Jo."

She smiled sweetly and pulled up the STS screen. In less than a minute, she was able to show me where I could find Mitchell.

I said, "Thanks so much. You're a jewel in your own right. Now, what can I do for you?"

She looked over at Carlton's door as if she thought her boss might be listening in on our conversation.

She whispered, "Tell me what's going on with Olivia McConnell. I heard she was taking some time off."

Sally Jo's request shouldn't have surprised me. Although I'd never heard her gossip about other people, I knew she loved knowing about the lives of her co-workers.

In that respect, she was like everyone else at the Agency.

From the first floor to the seventh floor, from assistants to division heads, knowledge was the currency that kept the power flowing at the Agency.

I gave Sally Jo some of that currency by telling her about Olivia's upcoming mastectomy.

She said, "Well, I'm so sorry to hear that. Bless her heart."

"You could have ask Douglas about this. Olivia isn't keeping her surgery a secret."

She shrank back in her chair as if I'd just brought up something repugnant. "Oh, no. That wouldn't be proper. He's my boss. Ours is a very professional relationship."

Even though I wasn't exactly able to follow her line of reasoning, I said, "I understand."

"No, no," she said, continuing to shake her head, "I just asked because I was concerned about the type of flowers I should send her. This is the second time Mr. Carlton has asked me to send her some flowers. The first time, she was just ill, but now that I know she's having surgery, I'll need to send her something different."

I wasn't aware there was a protocol for ordering flowers for the sick, but even so, this was something I knew I'd consign to the deep abyss of my consciousness and never think about again.

On the other hand, Sally Jo's statement brought up something that definitely required further exploration.

"I'd also like to send Olivia some flowers," I said, "but I wouldn't want her to have the same ones again. Do you remember what Carlton sent Olivia the first time?"

She nodded. "It was a big bouquet of yellow daffodils in a woven basket. I'm sure she loved it. She called Mr. Carlton later and thanked him for it."

I thought back to the big bouquet of yellow flowers on the windowsill in Olivia's hospital room, the ones I assumed Senator Mitchell had sent her. Now that I knew Carlton had sent her the flowers, I realized their relationship was a lot closer than I realized, and the smile on her face when she'd read the card would certainly seem to suggest such a possibility.

This tidbit of information was *not* something I would be consigning to the deep abyss of my consciousness and never thinking about again.

♦♦♦♦

Mitchell was in the NHB or New Headquarters Building where Support Services was located. I found him in a section of the building known as The Library, where volumes of books on military systems, hardware, and weapons were housed.

He was sitting all alone, pouring over stacks of photographs of chemical weapons canisters. I took a seat across from him.

"Doing your homework?" I asked.

He looked startled. "Why did you sneak up on me like that?"

"It's normal to be jumpy before your first run as a primary. Don't let it bother you."

"I'm not jumpy. I just didn't hear you come in."

"Maybe you should have your hearing checked before you leave."

Mitchell's shoulders were all hunched up around his ears. He was wound up pretty tight.

"So how'd you find me?" he asked.

"Cartel Carlos told me you were over here."

"I never told him where I was going."

"I guess he didn't tell me then."

Mitchell shook his head at me and glanced down at the photographs.

He said, "I saw plenty of slides during the briefing, but I wanted something I could hold in my hands."

He paused for a few seconds, and then he said, "I guess that sounds pretty dumb."

"No, it doesn't. It's always smart to go with your instincts, and the more information you have going into an operation, the better off you'll be."

"Yeah, right."

Mitchell seemed a little out of sorts with me. His ill-temper could be the result of his first primary operation being classified as a non-engagement op.

He might also suspect my assignment didn't have that stipulation attached to it.

I took a look at one of the photographs. "When the containers are offloaded from the ship, you probably won't get a look at the canisters themselves. They'll be in crates packed inside shipping containers."

He nodded. "I was told that at the briefing. Our Special Ops team on the ground in Santiago has already installed cameras inside the warehouse. The moment Hezbollah unpacks the shipping containers, it should be fairly easy to determine if the contents are the actual sarin gas canisters from Syria's stockpile."

I said, "Once the Ops Center has made that determination, you'll just have to hunker down and keep an eye on the place. With any luck, we'll know Hezbollah's timetable before those canisters show up in Washington."

He busied himself making a pile of the photographs.

"Is discovering Hezbollah's timetable your assignment?"

"Pretty much."

"I guess that means you're headed to Syria, while I'm stuck in Cuba babysitting the warehouse."

"That's right, Ben, but don't discount your role in preventing this attack. If you were fluent in Arabic, you'd be going to Syria with me, but since you're not, I recommended you for the warehouse assignment instead. I did that because it's crucial to this operation."

He appeared to relax a little. At least, the frown lines around his eyes disappeared.

"I didn't know that." He sat back in his chair. "You recommended me for the primary slot?"

I nodded. "I also told Douglas they should pull Juliana Lamar out of Argentina and have her run the surveillance with you."

He looked puzzled. "Juliana has been assigned to this operation?"

"Didn't C.J. tell you who was on your surveillance team?"

"He gave me a list of names, but I haven't looked at it yet."

"You missed an opportunity there. Once a briefing is over, the DDO's office isn't likely to make changes. The next time you're given a list, you should immediately make sure they haven't assigned you some incompetent. If there's someone on the list you don't want, you should protest. However, always have someone else in mind as a replacement before you say anything."

Mitchell had a faraway look in his eyes, and he responded to my sage advice by saying, "This means I'll be seeing Juliana in a few hours."

I immediately began to second guess myself about the wisdom of putting Mitchell and Juliana together. The reason I'd done so was to take advantage of Juliana's expertise in surveillance, but I also felt sure her level-headedness would be a good counterpoint to Mitchell's youthful passion. What I hadn't counted on was Mitchell's romantic notions.

When I looked across the table at him, I experienced a momentary flashback of Senator Mitchell standing in front of the window in his office and voicing his concerns about his son's safety.

My stomach churned and I started getting a very bad feeling about sending Mitchell out on his own. Then, I remembered the advice I'd given the Senator about his son.

*If you're willing to let him go, you won't lose him.*

Suddenly, I decided it was time for me to go.

Mitchell and I both got to our feet at the same time. As we shook hands with each other, he said, "I hope I'm able to live up to the confidence you've shown me. Thanks for the recommendation."

"You have good instincts, Ben. Use those instincts, set aside your emotions, and always have a contingency plan. If you do, you'll be just fine."

Several months later, Mitchell told me he wished he'd followed my advice. If he had, things would have turned out much differently.

# Chapter 28

I picked up my wallet and some personal items from Support Services, along with the keys to my Range Rover, and pulled out of Agency headquarters around four-thirty. Since it was Sunday, the traffic on the Beltway around Washington was light, and I realized I'd probably be arriving early for my six o'clock dinner engagement.

Because I had the extra time, I thought about taking a slight detour in order to check out WK Photography, owned by Mr. Walid Khouri. At the last minute, I took note of Carlton's warning and headed west on Interstate 66 instead.

After making a lane change about a mile down the freeway, I considered the possibility I was being followed.

What alerted me wasn't anything specific.

The feeling was more a vague sense of unease, much like the sensation I used to get before taking the field in a losing football game.

I told myself it was nothing, just a little pre-operations paranoia.

That was understandable, because I was about to embark on a dangerous mission in a volatile country. To make matters worse, the success of the entire operation depended on a Jihadi terrorist who hated Americans. If that wasn't enough, the primary intelligence officer, Keever Pike, who'd been assigned to lead the operation, carried around a lot of baggage. Unfortunately, he wasn't shy about unpacking it at the most inopportune times.

As I got near Fairfax, just in case my feelings weren't simply preop paranoia, I executed a few counter-surveillance tactics.

After doing so, the only vehicle that kept reappearing in my rearview mirror was an older model silver Ford Mustang. Since it had fancy chrome wheels and didn't exactly fit the profile of a standard surveillance vehicle, I gave it low marks for viability.

After I made three right-handed turns, and the Mustang didn't follow me, I blamed my uneasiness on mission jitters and forced myself to ignore the yellow caution lights dancing around the outer perimeter of my cerebral cortex.

♦♦♦♦

It was five-thirty when I pulled up to The Waterwheel, a restaurant overlooking an old gristmill on the outskirts of Fairfax. Since Nikki's car wasn't in the parking lot, I decided I'd wait for her in the Range Rover.

Also, I wanted to see if the occupant of a certain Ford Mustang had chosen to dine near the old gristmill on a summer's eve.

Five minutes later, my iPhone rang.

"Hi, Titus, it's Carla. I can't believe you actually picked up."

This wasn't the first time my sister had expressed frustration at the difficulty of getting in touch with me.

More often than not, whenever she called my personal number, she was rerouted to the Agency's communications hub—although she didn't know that. From there, she heard my own voice telling her to leave a message on my voice mail. Depending on my circumstances, it might be several days before Communication Services could actually deliver the message she'd left me.

"You caught me at a good time. I'm not working tonight."

"I should hope not. It's Sunday evening."

"Well, my employer can be a slave driver at times. How's everybody there? Did Brian tell you I talked to him a few days ago?"

"We're all fine. Kayla has a new boyfriend, so she's on cloud nine right now, and Eddie just wrapped up a successful two-day training conference with his marketing team. Yes, Brian mentioned he'd talked to you. That's why I'm calling. I wanted to thank you for trying to help him with his internship."

I watched as two cars pulled into The Waterwheel parking lot. Neither one of them was a silver Mustang.

"I wish I could have gotten him the recommendation he needed."

"I'm sure you tried your best. He didn't think you'd be able to help him in the first place, but now that he's been given the chance to work with Senator Mitchell, none of that matters. I can't tell you how excited he is to be in the same office as such a great man."

When Carla launched into a long explanation of how the Senator's assistant had paired Brian up with another intern who was looking for a roommate, my eyes wandered over to the access road off to my left, the one leading from the highway over to the restaurant's parking lot. What caught my attention was the line of cars waiting at the traffic light, particularly one vehicle, a silver Ford Mustang with chrome wheels.

Even though the Mustang wasn't in the turn lane for the access road leading to The Waterwheel, its reappearance bothered me.

I made a quick decision and decided to get back on the highway and follow it.

However, as soon as I inserted my key in the ignition, I saw Nikki's SUV pull up to the restaurant, and, at the same time, I suddenly realized Carla had asked me a question.

"Do you think we could see you then?"

"See me when?"

"When we come to D.C. to visit with Brian. Weren't you listening to me?"

"Of course, I was."

"It doesn't sound that way."

"Okay, I got a little distracted because I'm meeting Nikki Saxon for dinner, and I just saw her car pull in the parking lot here at the restaurant."

"Now that's exciting. Is she in town for a visit?"

Carla remained in a perpetual state of distress about my marital status, and now, having recently met Nikki at my mother's funeral, she was certain wedding bells were in my future.

"No, she's in the area for some training with the FBI. What were you telling me about coming to D.C.?"

"I said Eddie has some time off in July, and we thought we'd come to Washington and see Brian then. I was also thinking we could see you at the same time."

"You're coming to Washington?"

My mind suddenly conjured up a scene from an old Agency training video showing the effects of a chemical weapons attack. This time, though, instead of seeing the horrifying faces of a bunch of strangers, I saw my sister's family staring back at me. Then, as I watched Nikki emerge from her Buick Enclave, I suddenly realized that scene could include her as well.

"Yes, Titus, I'm talking about coming to Washington, D.C. Are you okay?"

"I'm fine," I said, trying to refocus. "You'll love Washington, and if I'm in town, I'd be happy to show you the sights."

"We'll enjoy that. If Nikki's still there, you could ask her to join us."

"We'll discuss that later. I need to go now."

"Okay. I'll call you back when Eddie and I have firmed up the date. Give Nikki a hug for me."

"I promise I will."

I had no problem keeping that promise.

I met Nikki at the front door of The Waterwheel, and, while I was delivering the promised hug from Carla, I took one last look around the parking lot.

Nothing.

No Ford Mustang on the access road either.

Nikki said, "What a lovely setting for a restaurant." She pointed over to a wooden building on her right. "Is that the original gristmill?"

"According to the restaurant's website it is."

She laughed. "You've never been here before, have you?"

I held the door opened for her. "No, but the other day, when I was driving out to The Meadows, I saw a billboard advertising this place as one of the area's most romantic dining establishments. For some reason, that made me think of you."

Nikki smiled, but before she had a chance to respond, the hostess said, "Welcome to The Waterwheel. There's a thirty-minute wait this evening, but if you'll give me your name, I'll get you seated as soon as possible."

I said, "I called ahead and made a reservation. It should be listed under the name of Douglas Carlton."

The hostess quickly found my reservation, and a few seconds later, she led us over to a secluded table in a corner of the room.

Once we were seated, Nikki leaned across the table and whispered, "Should I call you Douglas while we're here?"

"Only if you want to irritate me."

She picked up her menu. "I'll keep that in mind."

I quickly picked out an entrée, and then I gave Nikki my full attention.

She was wearing a sleeveless black and white dress with a pair of black sandals, and her dark brown hair was pulled away from her face, revealing a pair of black and silver earrings.

"Did I pass your inspection?" she asked, laying aside her menu.

"Forgive me for staring, but you are an incredibly beautiful woman."

She looked surprised by my words—I was a little surprised by them myself.

"Thank you, Titus," she said, reaching across the table and squeezing my hand.

I held onto her hand until the waitress came to take our orders. Once she'd left, Nikki asked, "Okay, seriously. Who's Douglas Carlton?"

"You asked me earlier about the owner of The Meadows. That would be Douglas. He's more or less an absentee owner."

"Does he know you're boarding your dog at his house and impersonating him around town?"

"Douglas doesn't know about Stormy yet, but I suspect he's aware I sometimes use his name when making a reservation. He's never appreciated his name being bandied about, and that's the reason I do it."

She nodded, and I could tell by the look on her face she was trying to work through my scant details about Carlton to reach some kind of conclusion about him.

I said, "Look, Detective, don't tax that pretty brain of yours tonight. Save that for your classes at Quantico tomorrow."

She sighed and sat back in her chair. "If those classes turn out to be anything like the instruction manuals they gave us at orientation yesterday, I'll need every bit of this gray matter just to pass this course."

"You'll do fine. You were probably a straight A student in college."

"Hardly."

For a brief moment, I thought about telling her my future at the Agency might depend on her passing the Quantico training, but then I quickly reconsidered.

When our entrées arrived, she started quizzing me about Arkady Orlov and his relationship to the owner of The Meadows, so I told her how the Russian weightlifter had fallen in love with Millie Durkin, the embassy employee in Seoul, South Korea. I also mentioned that Millie had been friends with Carlton's wife, Gladys.

The way in which Arkady and Millie had become Carlton's housekeepers appeared to intrigue her, even though I had to give her a sanitized version of the truth and refused to answer her questions about Carlton. What seemed to fascinate her more than anything else was my description of Millie.

Whether this was a woman thing or not, I couldn't tell.

As we were finishing up our meal, I started racking my brain for some way I could spend a few more hours with her, preferably alone.

An easy solution presented itself.

"What would you think about leaving your car here at the restaurant and driving out to The Meadows with me?"

"That's very tempting.".

"I'm sure Stormy would love to see you."

"Could I also have a tour of the house?"

"I'll show you every nook and cranny of the place myself."

"And what would Mr. Douglas Carlton think if he knew you were playing the tour guide at his house?"

"I'm sure he'd suggest I show you around the gardens as well."

"This Carlton guy sounds like an interesting character."

"That all depends on how you define interesting."

♦♦♦♦

For some reason, the drive out to The Meadows took on a whole new dimension with Nikki in the seat beside me.

First, she pointed out a faded barn with a old mural painted on the side of it, and I had to admit I'd never noticed it before. And then, strangely enough, she was able to name the architectural style of the country church a few miles from the turnoff to Carlton's house.

"You've never lived anywhere but Oklahoma. How do you know about country churches in Virginia?"

She sounded amused at my question."There's this wonderful invention called a book. It can take you anywhere you want to go; it can teach you anything you want to know; and it's guaranteed to transform the most ignorant soul into the most annoying expert."

"Isn't that what the internet is for?"

"Without books, there wouldn't be an internet in the first place."

I nodded. "I suppose you're right, Detective, but I have to say I'm surprised at your choice of reading materials. Architectural styles of Virginia sounds like pretty heavy reading to me."

She laughed. "The truth is, I read a lot of historical fiction, and gothic buttresses and gabled roofs show up in almost every one of them."

I suddenly realized I couldn't remember the last time I'd read a fiction book, and I knew I'd never read a historical novel before.

If my cover story required me to grab a paperback book off the rack in an airport gift shop, I always picked up a spy novel, if only for the sheer irony of it.

♦♦♦♦

I parked my Range Rover in the circle drive of Gladys' magnificent house, and seconds after closing my car door, an enthusiastic yellow lab ran out from behind the garage and pounced on me.

"Stormy, how's it going, boy?"

He answered with a couple of short barks and then dashed over to see Nikki. After she'd scratched his ears sufficiently, he raced around to see me again, putting his paws on my chest and licking my face.

"I'd say he was happy to see you."

"My boss treats me the same way every time I get back in town."

A few minutes later, Frisco appeared in the driveway, and following close behind him was Arkady, whose excitement at seeing me again was muted in comparison to the delight he expressed at seeing Nikki.

Arkady immediately assured her that Stormy and Frisco had already become good friends, and then, in an obvious attempt to impress the lady with his dog training expertise, the Russian began demonstrating how Stormy had learned to obey some simple commands. For some reason, he used his native Russian tongue when telling Stormy to sit, come, and stay.

I decided not to mention I'd taught Stormy these same commands—albeit in English—when I'd first adopted him.

Despite Arkady's training, when a squirrel suddenly ran across the driveway, both dogs abandoned their stance and took off after it. A disheartened Arkady threw his hands up in the air and began yelling Russian curses at them.

When it became apparent the dogs were more interested in pursuing the squirrel than in obeying Russian commands, Arkady looked over at Nikki and shrugged. I could tell she was having a hard time not laughing at him, so I tried diverting his attention by telling him I was here to give Nikki a tour of the house and introduce her to Millie.

He grinned. "Yes, yes. Of course, you must do this. She should meet my Millie."

As soon as Arkady ushered us in the front door, he went in search of Millie, and, immediately afterward, I took Nikki's hand and led her across the foyer and into Gladys' great room.

I stopped in the middle of the room and put my arms around her. "I've been wanting to do this all evening."

I leaned over and kissed her gently on the lips.

She smiled up at me. "What happened to the tour you promised me?"

I kissed her again. "Do you think the tour could wait?"

"Hmmm," she said, as I caressed her neck. "Maybe so."

When I cradled her face in my hand and gave her a long, lingering kiss, she wrapped her arms around me, pulling me even closer. My pulse quicken, and I suddenly found myself lost in the smell of her skin and the tantalizing sweetness of her mouth.

"Oh, sorry. We didn't mean to interrupt," Millie said, breaking through my passionate reverie.

I pulled away from Nikki like a teenager caught on the front porch by a worried dad.

I heard Arkady snickering.

Nikki, however, didn't seem fazed by the couple's sudden appearance and immediately stepped forward and introduced herself to Millie.

"Hi, I'm Nikki Saxon. You must be Millie."

Millie shook Nikki's hand, and then pointed her finger at me. "I've never seen this guy speechless before."

"I was giving Nikki a tour of the house," I said, although the minute it came out of my mouth, I knew how incredibly ridiculous it sounded.

Millie laughed. "Oh, anyone could see that."

She took Arkady's arm. "We'll let the two of you get on with the . . . tour. Stop by the kitchen when you're finished . . . touring."

As they left the room, Millie looked up at Arkady and shook her head.

## Chapter 29

At the end of the house tour, Nikki and I ended up in the kitchen, where we found Millie preparing a pot of coffee. After placing the carafe back on the warmer, she gestured out the window and informed us we were having dessert out by the pool.

When I started to protest, Nikki spoke up and said we'd love to have dessert, but only if Millie and Arkady would join us. Millie agreed, and then she immediately shooed me out the kitchen door and told me to go find Arkady.

I decided it might be best to follow her instructions and left the room.

I found Arkady down by the pool giving the dogs a lecture. Even though I couldn't fully understand his Russian, I figured his scolding had something to do with both dogs getting water all over him every time they shook themselves dry.

Apparently, they'd just taken a forbidden dip in Carlton's pool.

"Sorry, Arkady, I guess I should have told you Stormy loves the water."

After explaining how Stormy swam regularly at the lake on my property in Norman, Arkady responded by telling me about a dog he had when he was growing up in Tbilisi. In the middle of describing how he'd taught the dog to catch fish, the ladies arrived with mugs of hot coffee and four dessert plates piled high with strawberry shortcake.

I urged Arkady to finish telling the story, and in a move that surprised us all, he immediately got out of his chair and grabbed Frisco, using him to demonstrate how he used to wrestle his childhood dog to the ground in order to force him to give up the fish he'd just caught.

Naturally, Stormy thought the sight of Arkady wrestling with Frisco looked like great fun, and he immediately jumped right in the middle of the twosome.

In the end, Arkady managed to extricate himself from the pile of wet fur without any help from the rest of us, which was a good thing, because I seriously doubted whether we would have been able to help him in the first place, since the three of us were laughing so hard.

As our laughter died down, I glanced over at Nikki.

By the look on her face, I could tell she was enjoying herself, and, at that moment, I realized how important her happiness meant to me.

Such a realization caused a wealth of emotions to well up inside of me, including a kind of happiness of my own, yet my predominate feeling wasn't one of joy, but of fear.

Moments later, my fear was justified.

Before Arkady sat back down at the table, he ordered both dogs away from the pool, and they reluctantly obeyed him. Stormy trotted over and sat down beside me, while Frisco made his way over to the big oak tree close to the garage.

About thirty minutes later, after the ladies had cleared off the table and gone inside, I saw Stormy's ears perk up. The next thing I knew he was making a beeline for the front of the house with Frisco right behind him.

Arkady quickly looked down at a screen on his mobile phone and said, "There's a car in the driveway."

"Were you expecting someone?" I asked.

"No," he said, "but sometimes people get lost out here."

I pointed at his cell phone. "Mind if I take a look?"

After he handed me his phone, I saw him pull his weapon from the gun holster at his back.

I took a quick look at the screen, which displayed a video feed from the home's security camera, and handed it back to him.

"I'll coming with you," I said, removing my Glock.

He nodded and pointed over to his right. "I'll approach the vehicle from front. You bring up rear."

I immediately headed off toward the gate on the other side of the property, the one opposite the garage, while Arkady moved out in the direction of the garage.

As I made my way forward, I realized the dogs had ceased their continual barking and were just yapping intermittently now. I knew that probably meant the driver was trying to reason with them, perhaps attempting to gauge their intentions, before exiting his vehicle.

The vehicle appeared to be a silver Ford Mustang with chrome wheels.

♦♦♦♦

Although it was after nine o'clock, the sun had just fallen below the horizon, and, consequently, just as I rounded the corner of the house, the automatic security lights in front of the house suddenly switched on.

This turned out to be both good and bad.

It was good because I could clearly see the target as he emerged from the vehicle. It was bad because the target could also clearly see me.

Fortunately, the driver was so focused on Arkady, who was standing directly in front of him, and on the two large dogs, who were circling around him, he wasn't even aware of my presence a few feet behind him.

"How can I help you?" Arkady asked, keeping his pistol out of sight.

"I'm looking for the owner of that Range Rover," the driver said, nodding his head in the direction of my vehicle.

"That would be me, Frank."

At the sound of my voice, Frank Benson wheeled around, took one look at my Glock, and raised his hands.

"You can put away the firepower, Titus. You won't be needing it."

"You'll have to convince me of that."

Suddenly, Stormy bared his teeth and snarled at Frank Benson—something I'd never seen him do before—and Benson immediately took a step back and said, "I'm just here to have a conversation with you, that's all."

I walked around to where Benson was standing in front of the Mustang. After ordering Stormy to sit—which he immediately did—I looked over and nodded at Arkady, who holstered his weapon.

I lowered my Glock and said, "Start talking, Frank."

"Some of what I have to say is classified," he said, glancing over at the big Russian. "We should have this discussion in private."

I was spared the embarrassment of asking Arkady to give us some privacy when he suggested, "You could use the study to entertain your guest."

Although I found it difficult to think of Benson as my guest, I did as Arkady suggested."You heard the man," I said, nodding toward the front door. "Let's go inside."

The moment we entered the foyer, I realized I should have asked Arkady to let Nikki know where I was, but, as soon as we started down the hallway toward the study, she came around the corner.

"There you are," she said. "I was just . . ."

She paused when she noticed Benson standing beside me.

"Well, hi," she said, giving him a smile.

Benson returned the smile and said, "It's Nikki, isn't it? I believe we met at the orientation yesterday at Quantico."

"That's right," she said. "What are you—"

"Frank just dropped by for a chat," I said, anticipating her question. "This shouldn't take long."

"Not long at all," he said, stepping over to Carlton's study and opening the door.

The moment he moved away from me, Nikki was able to see the Glock I was carrying at my side, which I'm certain was his intention all along.

She looked down at the gun and then glanced over at Benson.

"I'll wait for you in the living room," she said, heading down the hallway.

To say she looked disconcerted when she realized I was holding an FBI agent at gunpoint would be an understatement.

♦♦♦♦

Benson entered Carlton's study as if he owned the place, and I suspected he'd visited The Meadows before. As one of Carlton's former operatives, he might have even attended a couple of Gladys' dinner parties, perhaps even a Thanksgiving dinner at the house.

"Nikki's a beautiful woman," Benson said, running his finger over a row of books on Carlton's orderly bookshelves. "How do you know her?"

"None of your business," I said, putting away my gun. "Why were you following me?"

Benson sat down in the same armchair Felipe Arcos had occupied just a few days earlier. As he did so, I found myself thinking about those implements from the basement dungeon Mitchell had wanted to use on Felipe.

Not that I would have used them on Benson—not at all.

He nodded. "So you knew I was tailing you? I borrowed my son's car thinking it might throw you off."

"Surveillance was never your strong suit, Frank."

He gave a short laugh. "I'm here, aren't I?" He pointed over to the other armchair and said, "Have a seat, Titus."

At the moment, I was standing in front of Carlton's desk, and I chose to remain there.

"I know I burned you right after mile marker 61," I said. "That means you must have spent the last couple of hours trying to figure out where I could have gone after you lost me. Coming here to The Meadows wasn't anything more than just a wild guess on your part."

He didn't dispute my conclusion. "Douglas has always treated you differently than the rest of his operatives. Personally, I think it's because he feels sorry for you. Finding you here, entertaining your lady friend inside his house, just proves my point."

I bristled at his reference to Nikki. "You have one minute to tell me why you're here before I throw you out."

"You know why I'm here. That stunt you pulled at the Navy Yard on Monday morning almost got me fired. I received an official reprimand because I allowed you to enter the compound without checking your creds. Now, the incident's been noted on my record as a misconduct infraction. One more violation, and I'll be getting my discharge papers from the Bureau."

I was tempted to point out if the feds fired him, at least it wouldn't be because his actions caused a bunch of hostages to lose their lives.

But, to save time, I decided not to bring up his past and deal only with the present.

As I thought about what he'd said, though, I suddenly felt guilty about the heartless way I'd used him at the Navy Yard. The feeling was like a weight pushing down on me in every direction, and I realized what I had to do.

"I apologize, Frank. I had my reasons for needing to check things out at the Yard, but I didn't stop to think I might be putting your career in danger when I did so."

He folded his arms across his chest and stared at me. "What's that supposed to mean?"

"It means what it means. I'm apologizing for my behavior."

"If you think I'm about to do you another favor, then you're—"

"Look, Frank. I just apologized. Take it or leave it, and then get out. We're done."

He settled back in his chair. "We're not finished here until you've given me some answers. If that was a real apology, then you'll have to prove it, because the Titus I knew would never have apologized to anyone for anything at anytime."

"You want proof I'm apologizing? How would that work?"

"Tell me what you know about the shooting at the Navy Yard."

"I thought the Bureau had already decided it was a drug deal gone bad."

"You and I both know it wasn't."

Even though Benson's past actions proved he was incapable of making spur-of-the-moment decisions, he was extremely adept at drilling down below the surface of a knotty problem and extracting critical information.

I'd seen this on more than one occasion.

Once, when the two of us were tracking a Palestinian terrorist across Europe and were faced with an inconsistency in his movements, Benson had stayed up all night charting out a minute-by-minute timeline of the man's activities. In the end, the only reason we'd been able to grab the guy was because of Benson's dogged determination to ferret out some minor detail.

I asked, "What makes you think the shooting wasn't drug-related?"

"Because that scenario doesn't fit the facts."

He reached in his jeans' pocket and dug out a folded sheet of paper, bringing it over to Carlton's desk.

"Take a look at this," he said, unfolding the paper and laying it out on the desk in front of me.

The drawings on the sheet of paper turned out to be a synopsis of his research on the shooter, Reyes Valario. One look at it, and I quickly came to the conclusion he'd done his homework.

Benson had outlined what he'd discovered about Valario in a series of arrows and boxes, with each detail in the man's life written in a rectangular box and each box used as a signpost leading over to the next event. Then, he'd tried to connect each of the signposts with an arrow pointing to Valario's final destination—the Navy Yard.

Benson was still missing a few key details, though, and I suspected it was the absence of those details, and not primarily his anger at me for putting his job in jeopardy, which had caused him to follow me out to The Meadows.

Benson pointed to one of the rectangular boxes on his outline and said, "Let's start here with WK Photography. Valario had his first contact with the studio three months ago."

He moved his finger over to another box.

"One week later, he joined a hobby club, the Razorback Century Club in Fayetteville. Immediately after showing up at the club,

Valario called the studio's owner and chatted for a few minutes."

"The owner? You mean Walid Khouri, the owner of the photography studio?"

Benson nodded. "That's right, and that brings me to this question. What does the Agency have on Khouri?"

"Why ask me?" I said. "You know the Bureau has channels for acquiring information from the Agency."

"I've submitted a request to the Agency but it's taking too long, and I suspect it's being stonewalled by Douglas or someone further up the chain of command. I'm still persona non grata over there, thanks to you."

I knew he was baiting me, but I refused to bite. Instead I said, "Since you've asked me that question, I have to assume you have something to offer me in kind?"

He nodded. "Oh, yeah. You give me the intel on Khouri, and I'll tell you what Valario was doing on his visits to the Century Club."

I shook my head. "Cartel Carlos is heading up the investigation into the Valario connection. If there's anything new there, I would have heard of it by now."

"Seriously? Are you kidding me? The only thing Cartel Carlos cares about is tracing that heroin back to the cartels. I just got back from Fayetteville, and I didn't stumble across any of Salazar's spooks anywhere near that hobby club."

"You've been down to Fayetteville?"

"I just got back on Friday. This morning, when I heard you were also back in town, I headed over to Langley and—"

"Yeah, I know. That's when you followed me out here."

For the first time since seeing him in the driveway, I took a really good look at Benson.

He looked pretty haggard. I was guessing he hadn't had much sleep, and his beard was more than just a five o'clock shadow. Whether it was a style choice on his part, or the result of not having enough time to shave, I wasn't sure. At any rate, his square jar seemed less prominent now, which made me wonder if Clarice Duncan would still find him so appealing.

Benson tapped the spot on the paper where he'd written

Razorback Century Club. “Do you want to know why Reyes Valario joined the hobby club or not?”

“I’m sure Douglas has that information by now. He’s pretty tight with some of your colleagues over there at the Bureau.”

He shook his head. “The Director doesn’t know about these details yet. You’d be the first to hear what I’ve learned about Valario.”

Benson was hitting me in my soft spot. He knew exactly what he was offering me.

Fresh intel.

Newly minted.

Never touched by human hands.

I grabbed the bait. “It’s a deal.”

# Chapter 30

I walked away from Carlton's desk and sat down in the armchair by the fireplace. Benson immediately grabbed his outline off the desk and took the chair opposite me.

I said, "The details I have about Walid Khouri are pretty sketchy right now, but after tomorrow's briefing, I could learn a lot more."

Once I'd told Benson what Katherine had turned up on Khouri and what I'd learned from Carlton earlier in the day, he said, "That's it? Khouri recently traveled to the Middle East, and he's not connected to the drug trade. That's all the intel you've got on him?"

"Yeah, that's it. Your turn now. Tell me about the hobby club. Was Valario interested in photography? Was that his connection to Khouri?"

For a few seconds, he looked at me without saying a word, and I thought he was about to refuse to share his intel on Valario with me because of the limited details I'd given him on Khouri.

Finally, he shook his head and said, "Not exactly. Razorback Century Club is a conglomerate of hobbies housed under one roof. Besides photography, they offer classes in a bunch of crafty stuff like painting and quilting, but those are just their indoor activities. They also sponsor outdoor hobbies, and that's what he was interested in."

"Bird watching? Archery? What?"

"Reyes Valario was there to learn about model airplanes, specifically how to fly them."

When I heard this, I experienced an immediate letdown. "You

mean those remote-controlled airplanes made out of Styrofoam?"

"I guess that's what they were made of when you were a kid, but, in these modern times, they've improved them quite a bit."

"I'm not that much older than you."

"Have you looked in a mirror lately?"

I tapped my watch. "Wrap this up, Frank. Nikki's waiting for me."

He smiled, and I thought he was about to make another smart remark, but then he turned serious. "I interviewed the president of the club and also the guy who'd been giving Valario lessons. Both of them told me Valario had already mastered the rudiments of flying the larger models. What he really wanted to do was to learn how to fly the new stuff, like drones, especially the commercial ones. He said he'd been offered a summer intern position requiring him to take aerial photographs for a real estate agent who owned a drone, and he needed to get up to speed quickly."

I considered this new intel a moment. "Were you able figure out why Valario kept calling Khouri after every lesson? Did you find out if those conversations were ever overheard by anyone?"

"That's a negative. The Agency should contact the National Security Agency and get a transcript of those actual conversations. I was only able to access the phone number Valario called. When I did, I realized he was making calls to Khouri after almost every session."

"While this is interesting, Frank, for all we know, Reyes could have been telling the truth. Maybe he *did* have a summer job lined up with a realtor. Maybe he was just consulting a professional photographer about how to take aerial photographs."

"I also did some research on his intern story, and I came up with nothing. It was a big fat zero."

"What's the bottom line on Reyes Valario then? What's your assessment?"

Benson leaned forward in his chair. "Reyes had no connection with buying or selling drugs, except for the time he bought some weed. Yeah, I know he had over a million dollars worth of heroin with him at the Navy Yard last Monday, but I believe the heroin was a diversion."

"To what end?"

"I don't know the answer to that, but I'm betting you do."

Carlton had told me the Agency had briefed the Bureau on the possibility of a chemical weapons attack on Washington, so I decided to share my theory about the Navy Yard shooter with Benson. I also told him I believed the whole episode had been a suicide mission for Valario from the very start.

He wasn't totally convinced.

"If that's true, why was Valario intent on learning to fly a UAV? Why would he have spent the money for lessons only to martyr himself a few weeks later?"

"You'll have to get those answers yourself, Frank. I have other fish to fry."

"I *will* figure this out. You can bet on that."

"I suspect the key player is Walid Khouri."

He nodded. "I totally agree."

I stood up and headed for the door, but then, after taking a few steps, I turned and faced Benson again.

"As I said, there's a possibility I'll pick up some new intel on Khouri at my briefing tomorrow. Of course, you'll probably get that same information . . . eventually."

He stared at me until my pointed remark clicked with him. "Let's suppose I wanted access to that intel earlier. Is there something I could do to expedite that process?"

I looked up at the ceiling a minute. "Ummm, let's see, Frank. I can't really think of anything. Oh, wait," I gave him my best smile, "there is *one* thing."

"Just name it."

"I know how difficult that Quantico training course can be. If I have your assurance Detective Saxon will get all the help she needs to pass that course, then I might give you a call after my briefing tomorrow and tell you what I've learned about Khouri."

He smiled. "Oh, you bet. I'll take good care of her." He pulled a business card out of his pocket. "Here's my number. Call me anytime."

I pocketed the card and said, "Let's be clear about one thing, Frank. The detective doesn't need to know we've had this conversation."

"You have nothing to worry about."

If only that were true.

♦♦♦♦

As I drove Nikki back to The Waterwheel to pick up her car, I tried keeping the conversation light by bringing up Arkady's stories about growing up in Tbilisi.

She changed the subject immediately.

"What was really going on with Frank Benson tonight?"

Her voice sounded flat, but the darkened interior of the car made it nearly impossible for me to read the expression on her face.

"Like I told you earlier, he just wanted to talk. He and I go way back. We've known each other for years."

"That doesn't explain why you drew your gun on him."

"I can't talk about that."

She didn't say anything.

After a few minutes, I said, "I'm sorry if that bothers you."

"Look, Titus. I can certainly understand why I'm not supposed to question you about what you do and where you go. I get that. I really do. But maybe keeping secrets has become such a part of who you are, you're no longer able to share your life with anyone."

I thought about arguing that point with her, but I reconsidered.

For one thing, she might be right.

"Maybe that's true, Nikki, but my personality has nothing to do with my refusal to tell you why I drew my weapon on Frank."

She turned away from me and stared out the side window as if the countryside had suddenly gotten very interesting.

It was pitch black outside; she couldn't see a thing.

A few minutes later, she shifted her attention back to me. "Are you saying Frank presented some kind of threat to you tonight?"

"Don't press me on the details, Detective, but, yes, that's exactly what I'm saying."

"Did it have anything to do with the shooting at the Navy Yard?"

"We must have a different definition of what 'don't press me on the details' means. I can't—"

"I was just wondering, because when the subject of the Navy Yard incident came up at our orientation, I got the feeling Frank was upset with someone over at the CIA. Was that you?"

"I'm done with this subject, Nikki."

She grew quiet once again, and I realized my response had come out sounding harsher than I'd intended.

Several minutes passed without either of us saying a word. Even so, the tension between us only seemed to increase.

I decided I had to break the silence, so I turned on the radio.

Ordinarily, my car radio was tuned to an all news station, so I was surprised to hear music coming from one of those Oldies But Goodies stations when I switched it on. Seconds later, I realized Carlton must have changed the dial when he'd driven my Range Rover out to The Meadows.

I wasn't bothered by him changing the channel. What bothered me were the lyrics blaring out of the speakers.

The song, "You Always Hurt The One You Love," was all about hurt, heartache, and disappointing the one you love.

I immediately turned it off.

♦♦♦♦

A few minutes later, we arrived at The Waterwheel, and I pulled up next to Nikki's car. We sat there a minute, and then I placed my hand on her shoulder and pointed down the lighted path toward the old gristmill.

"Before you leave, would you take a walk with me?"

She nodded, and we got out of the SUV and strolled down the brick walkway leading to the original gristmill, which had been built on the bank of Little Doe Creek.

The owners of the restaurant had remodeled the structure to accommodate a small gift shop and an ice cream store. Both establishments had kept the old-fashioned theme, complete with gas lighting, sales clerks in period clothing, and wrought iron benches on the sidewalk outside.

The gift shop was already closed for the day, and the ice cream store looked as if it were about to close. However, there were still a few patrons sitting around outside.

I took Nikki further down the pathway, into the shadows beyond the gift shop, where we could have some privacy. As we sat down next to each other on a park bench, it was easy to understand why the owners had chosen to advertise their establishment as a romantic spot. The ambient lighting, plus the relaxing sound of water from the nearby creek flowing down the rungs of the restaurant's signature waterwheel, made for a intimate setting.

I put my arm around Nikki and held her close for a few minutes.

Then, because I wanted to gauge her reaction to what I had to say, I pulled away and looked into her eyes.

After pushing a lock of hair away from her face, I said, "I'm leaving tomorrow, and I'm not sure when I'll be back."

She bit down on her lip. "I'm sorry, Titus, I shouldn't have—"

I gently placed my hand over her mouth. "No, let me finish."

She nodded, and I took my hand away.

"I won't lie to you, Nikki. This is a risky assignment, and it's happening in a very dangerous country. If the mission doesn't succeed, the consequences are enormous. That's the reason I can't leave tonight without telling you how I feel about you."

Suddenly, her face looked flushed.

I was afraid she was about to say something, so I hurried on. "I'm pretty sure I'm falling in love with you."

It was the first time I'd seen her smile since we'd driven away from The Meadows.

"I know for sure I'm in like with you," I said.

She laughed. "In like?"

I smiled. "I'm sure you'd appreciate those sentiments if you knew me better. Liking people isn't my strong suit."

She leaned over and kissed me. "I'm in like with you too, Titus."

"I know this isn't easy for you, not just because of the work I do, but also because I'm not used to being open with people. I agree with what you said earlier. I'm not used to sharing my life with anyone."

"I'm sorry I said that. I was just frustrated because there's this barrier between us, and I keep wanting to knock it down."

"I assure you, Nikki, if you pass your Quantico course, some of those walls will come tumbling down."

"Like the walls of Jericho?"

"Exactly."

"I believe the Bible says God had to perform a miracle to bring those walls down."

I smiled. "You're right, but if I recall the story correctly, he had the people do something every day. After that, he performed the miracle. So, Detective, here's what I'm thinking. You do your part in class every day, and God will take care of the rest."

"I promise I'll do my best."

"I know you will."

"You'll have to promise me something as well."

"I don't make many promises."

"Promise me when you're away, especially during those times you're required to take risks, you'll remember I'm praying for you."

I made her that promise, and then we sealed it with a kiss.

Actually, we sealed it with several kisses.

## Chapter 31

*Monday, June 29*

My briefing on Operation Citadel Protection was scheduled to begin at ten o'clock, but I arrived in Conference Room A across the hall from RTM Center A at around nine-fifteen.

When I walked in, Duncan Fredrick, the scheduler from the DDO's office, was in the process of setting up the conference room, and, after I joked with him for a few minutes about his son's Little League team, he allowed me to read through the overnight cable traffic on his computer. Mainly, I was looking for any flash traffic from Santiago de Cuba.

Nothing came up. There were no messages from Mitchell.

Ten minutes before the meeting was due to begin, Carlton arrived. I was expecting him to comment on my early arrival, but he only nodded at me and didn't say anything. Seconds later, when Robert Ira walked in the door, I immediately understood why.

The Deputy Director of Operations seldom left his office, and, when he did, the occasion was never a happy one.

The DDO was a heavyset man with a chubby face and longish gray hair. He was not a well-liked person, and while he may have believed his lack of popularity was due to the nature of his job, in reality, most people were simply turned off by his Machiavellian attitude.

He governed his office with a results-oriented philosophy based on "the ends justify the means" and appeared willing to do anything to accomplish his goals. Using the same duplicitous skills he'd perfected as a covert intelligence officer, he tended to manipulate both co-workers and politicians alike.

On the flip side, he had an uncanny ability to exploit the weaknesses of America's enemies, a feat which continually earned him the respect of the intelligence community, both here and abroad.

Although I knew Ira and Carlton had gone through several rough patches in their relationship, I had the distinct impression the DDO admired Carlton. I suspected this was because Carlton refused to act as the DDO's lapdog and also because Carlton knew a thing or two about manipulating people.

The last time I'd seen Robert Ira had been a few months ago when he'd shown up at my debrief following my failed mission in Tehran. After learning of his role in the deaths of my assets, I'd accused him of being responsible for bringing down my network in Iran.

After that, he'd put me on medical leave.

Now that he'd restored me to active duty status, I was hoping for a more amicable relationship with him.

Or, at the very least, a less hostile one.

♦♦♦♦

Carlton began the briefing by noting the presence of the DDO, who bobbed his head a couple of times and acknowledged the introduction.

Afterward, the deputy gave his attention to the open laptop in front of him and didn't say a word until we were more than halfway through the proceedings.

Deputy Ira and Carlton were seated across the table from me. At the end of the table was Nolan Wilson and next to him was Katherine Broward, plus several other counterintelligence analysts. Dispersed along the outer perimeter of the conference room were various Agency employees. Most of them represented Support Services, but I also saw a couple of people from Legal there as well.

After Carlton mentioned C.J. Salazar would not be joining us due to his own ongoing operation, he instructed Wilson to initiate the video call to Keever Pike in Damascus.

Pike had obviously been waiting for the call and immediately came on the screen. He was sitting in what appeared to be a loft, and I was guessing he was inside an Agency safe house in Damascus. The satellite feed was excellent, and he could have been sitting in the room next to us and no one would have been able to tell the difference in the quality of the transmission.

Pike was operating in Damascus as a freelance journalist, a career he'd had before coming to work for the Agency. For almost a year now, he'd been covering the war in Syria for several newspapers who could no longer afford to send out their own correspondents. Pike's work was high quality stuff, and he'd once been given a SCROLL award in recognition for his excellence in journalism. However, none of the newspapers who paid him for his stories had the slightest inkling he was a covert intelligence operative employed by the CIA.

Pike's cover made it possible for him to travel throughout the area without being questioned and to scout out potential assets and conduct interviews with known terrorists. His cover story wouldn't have held up, though, had he not been able to tell the difference between a verb and a noun, which was why I was a little worried about the cover story Legends had fashioned for me as Pike's friend and fellow journalist.

Unfortunately, posing as an executive from Bub's Subs wouldn't have been appropriate in war-torn Syria, so I needed to brush up on my grammar before arriving in Damascus.

Carlton made reference to the seven-hour time difference between Langley and Damascus when he greeted Pike.

"Good afternoon, Keever," he said. "We're about to get started here."

"Ready on this end as well."

Pike, who was dressed in a loose-fitting brown shirt, with a pair of sunglasses dangling from his front pocket, had an angular face, sandy colored hair, and blue eyes. I'd always found him to be an easy man to read, but as I studied his reaction when he recognized the DDO was present in the room, he hardly showed any emotion at all.

Once the preliminaries were out of the way, Carlton asked Wilson to explain how the Agency planned to get Marwan Farage out of Gitmo and back to Damascus.

Wilson pushed his glasses further up the bridge of his nose and looked over at Carlton.

"If Marwan agrees to be played back into Syria when he meets with you tonight, then the two of you will be flown by military transport to our air base in Morón, Spain. From there, you'll both be on a commercial flight out of Seville to Damascus. After that, you'll part ways with Marwan at the airport until Titus contacts him the next day."

Wilson gestured at me. "You'll be leaving tonight and taking a commercial flight into Damascus from Washington, with a layover in London. Your arrival in Damascus is scheduled for Wednesday morning and Douglas and Marwan will arrive a few hours later."

Pike spoke up. "I plan to pick Titus up at the airport myself so we can maintain our cover story of being best friends."

I said, "Please don't refer to me as your BFF, at least not in public."

My remark barely got a smile from the DDO, but it got a laugh from Pike, who was a humorous kind of guy.

Wilson turned and looked over at Carlton. "Douglas, when you arrive at the airport, a group of EAI workers will pick you up and take you across town to the EAI compound."

Carlton's legend in Damascus would be a familiar one for him. Whenever he was running his operatives in country, more often than not, he posed as one of the directors of Emergency Aid International (EAI), a not-for-profit relief agency, providing food and other aid for countries whose citizens were living in chaos.

Although EAI was a Agency-funded organization, it was a legitimate non-profit whose workers were committed to helping people. However, no more than a handful of EAI employees knew the organization they worked for was a CIA-run entity.

After Carlton discussed a few more of the logistical aspects of the operation, he turned the meeting over to Katherine for her input.

Katherine stood up and hit a few keys on her laptop, projecting a slide of General Suleiman on a screen opposite the one displaying Pike's satellite feed.

"We've confirmed General Suleiman will be traveling from Tehran to Damascus on July 3rd. He's booked into the Sheraton, along with a small staff."

Her next slides showed transcripts of the chatter taking place among Hezbollah's inner circle in Damascus.

Katherine continued, "While there's been no official confirmation yet, as you can see in these transcripts, Naballah and Suleiman have set up a meeting for July 4th. That meeting will take place at Naballah's compound in Damascus."

She wrapped up her report by emphasizing the volatile nature of the civil war in Syria brought on by the rebel groups fighting the Assad regime on the outskirts of Damascus. She also cited new evidence indicating ISIS fighters were seeking to penetrate the hierarchy of some of these groups, particularly, the al-Nusra group affiliated with al-Qaeda.

"These rebel groups are operating outside the city and shouldn't pose a threat to you, but we'll continue to keep an eye on their activities throughout the mission."

As she sat back down, she looked over at the side of the table where Carlton and the DDO were seated and gave them her best smile. "That's all I have for now, but I'll be more than happy to answer any questions you may have."

The DDO returned her smile, but Carlton simply acknowledged her offer and noted he would reserved time for questions later.

Turning his attention to Pike, Carlton asked, "Do you agree with this assessment, Keever?"

As if the question were a difficult one, Pike pressed two fingers to his forehead and closed his eyes for a moment.

"Yes and no. Even though the Free Syrian Army continues to fight Assad's forces in the outlying areas, only a few neighborhoods in Damascus have been affected. So, yes, I agree our mission shouldn't be endangered by the fighting."

He paused and shook his head. "But I disagree with Katherine if she believes the civil war in Syria was brought on by the rebel fighters. This war is a direct result of the atrocities Assad has continually inflicted on his own people, including the use of chemical weapons."

Katherine immediately spoke up. "I don't believe I said that, and I certainly didn't mean to imply it. I am more than aware of Assad's vicious attacks on the civilian population. If anyone is to blame for this war, it's Assad himself."

Pike said, "It's not just Assad. His whole power structure is—"

"Let's save that topic for another day," Carlton said.

Carlton seldom tolerated superfluous talk during a briefing, so it didn't surprise me to hear him refuse to allow Pike to pontificate on the subject.

Pike was a big pontificator.

After Carlton consulted his notes, he instructed Wilson to explain the status of Marwan's wife and daughter, Yamina and Samira.

Wilson said, "The two ladies have now been taken to a secure location. If Marwan needs some extra incentive to cooperate with us, Sam Wylie is offering to supply us with the photographs necessary to do that."

Carlton nodded. "Tell him I'll need several of those for my meeting with Marwan later this evening."

For the next thirty minutes, we discussed the nuts and bolts of the operation and viewed aerial satellite photographs of Naballah's headquarters. We were also shown photographs of Rehman Zaidi and Abdul Latif, members of Naballah's security council who would be attending the meeting with General Suleiman. Most of the photographs were either taken by Pike or by the asset he'd been running, the man Hezbollah had recently beheaded for being a traitor.

I suspected this man's death was on Pike's mind when he brought up the subject of Marwan. "These Jihadists are always on the lookout for suspicious behavior, and they don't tolerate betrayal. If Marwan gets skittish about attending the meeting with Suleiman, what happens then?"

The DDO spoke up for the first time. "If that happens, then I'll issue an order for his removal."

# Chapter 32

Whether it was the DDO's statement, or the fact he hadn't said anything prior to uttering the words, there was a brief lull in the proceedings after his pronouncement. During those few seconds of silence, I was battling a loud voice telling me to keep quiet.

However, I lost that battle.

"Look," I said, "Marwan is aware of what's at stake here. If he doesn't get us the intel we need, he knows he'll never see his family again. That motivation alone will be enough to calm his nerves and execute the plan. It isn't necessary to issue a call for removal."

The DDO didn't bother to mask his displeasure at my remark.

"I'm trying to prevent an attack on our nation's capital. That means I'm keeping all my options on the table. Convince your man to deliver the goods and there won't be a problem."

I didn't like the sound of Marwan Farage being "my man," but common sense finally prevailed, and I didn't respond.

I'd noticed Carlton's eyes were glued to his legal pad during my exchange with the DDO, and although he'd appeared disinterested in my conversation, I seriously doubted his lack of concern.

Once it was obvious I had nothing else to say, Carlton immediately turned his attention to Pike. "I want at least two surveillance teams assigned to Hassan Naballah for the next several days."

"I may need extra personnel to do that, and, if you can spare it, a surveillance drone wouldn't hurt my feelings."

Carlton said, "I'll check on the drone, and once I arrive in country, I'll also look at putting some additional watchers on the members of Naballah's council. What's happening with Rehman Zaidi?"

"My surveillance on him is continuing, and I'd suggest we keep that up. According to my asset, Rehman knew more about the chemical weapons than anyone else on the council."

I nodded. "I agree with Keever. If Naballah sends someone to Cuba to oversee those weapons, more than likely, it will be Rehman."

Pike asked, "What about the gas canisters? Have they arrived in Cuba yet?"

"No, they—"

Robert Ira interrupted Carlton, never missing an opportunity to demonstrate he was a hands-on administrator.

"There was a tropical storm off the coast of Cuba yesterday. The ships weren't able to dock at the port in Santiago last night, but they should arrive sometime tomorrow. C.J. has Agency personnel covering the docks and warehouse, and he's also ordered UAV coverage for the entire area."

The DDO's update made me wonder how Mitchell was handling the delay in the ships' arrival, but since Juliana was with him, I was betting he was handling it pretty well.

"That's all I have for now," Carlton said, looking first at Pike and then at me. "Do either of you have any questions?"

"I have one for Ms. Broward," I said.

After Carlton gestured for me to go ahead, I asked Katherine, "Have you come up with anything new on Walid Khouri?"

I was surprised to see her glance over at the DDO before saying anything. Once he'd nodded at her, she said, "Deputy Ira has the update on Khouri."

The DDO eased his considerable bulk out of his chair and stood to his feet. With his wide girth and short stature, he didn't cut a very impressive figure, but when he spoke, his authoritative voice garnered everyone's attention.

"After receiving the analysis report from Ms. Broward's ASA team last night, I made the decision to deliver the results of the background check on Walid Khouri myself."

I could only recall one other instance when the DDO had attended a briefing in order to present the findings from an ASA report himself. That had been several years ago when a full data probe had been executed on an U.S. ambassador suspected of sharing intel with the Saudis. Everyone in that meeting had been required to sign a separate confidentiality agreement following the DDO's presentation, and I had been the person assigned to deliver the Director's message to the ambassador.

Ira lifted a sheet of paper from his briefcase. "Here's a bio Walid Khouri's public relations office released on him for a recent newspaper story."

*"In 2005, when Walid Khouri arrived in the Washington, D.C. area from Amman, Jordan, he opened up a studio in Brentwood, where he specialized in portraits and headshots. In 2009, after expanding his portfolio to include commercial advertising, he moved his studio to its present facility in the Dover district to accommodate his growing reputation. Today, he employs several photographers, and his client base includes commercial establishments, celebrities, government agencies, as well as several Congressional leaders. Just recently, he broke ground on a new studio facility, which includes a photography showroom, plus outdoor landscapes for accommodating creative wedding photos and family portraits."*

The DDO put down his notes and picked up a remote mouse from the table. He clicked it once and a man's image appeared on the screen.

"Here's a photograph of Walid Khouri as seen on his website."

The photograph was of a Middle Eastern man in his late forties with thick, heavily gelled black hair and a sparse beard. His dark eyes held a look of surprise, almost as if he hadn't been expecting the camera's flash. Since I knew he was in the business of taking photographs for a living, I had to believe his startled look was totally staged, perhaps intending to show his vulnerable side.

Khouri was wearing a light colored, open-collared shirt under a navy blue blazer, and his left hand was hooked around a leather camera bag slung over his shoulder. If Khouri had chosen this particular shot because it portrayed a sophisticated, yet approachable photographer, he had definitely accomplished his purpose.

The DDO said, "The background information Khouri gives out on himself is short on details. Here's what it says on his professional website."

He picked up his notes and read from them again. *"Following the death of his father, Walid Khouri arrived in the United States from Jordan and decided to invest his inheritance in a photography studio, fulfilling his lifelong dream of living in America and pursuing his love affair with photography."*

The DDO laid aside his notes. "While there's evidence Khouri spent his early years in Jordan, Ms. Broward's team of analysts have determined Khouri's father worked in a bicycle shop in Amman for most of his life and barely eked out a living for his family."

This discrepancy didn't surprise me.

I suspected it was one of the red flags Katherine had spotted as soon as she'd run a preliminary data scan on him. The DDO said as much when he clicked on the next slide.

"This red flag is one of many inconsistencies in Khouri's background, inconsistencies which were only revealed when our analysts initiated a full investigation on him. I've asked Ms. Broward to present those findings for you now."

The DDO sat back down, and, for the next hour, Katherine laid out what she and her team of analysts had turned up on Walid Khouri, including his source of revenue.

As much as I appreciated the analysts' work, some of the stuff was mind-numbing—especially the explanation of the money trail—and I was getting really bored by the time Katherine made her summary statement.

"I'll try to pull all these threads together for you now," she said, displaying a slide with several bullet points.

Circling the first one with her laser pointer, she said, "First, we discovered Walid Khouri left Amman, Jordan in the late 1990's and moved to Iran where he attended Tehran University. There, for reasons unclear at this time, he drew the attention of the Iranian Revolutionary Guard Corps (IRGC), who ended up paying for his education and directing his studies. Second, following his graduation, the records show he joined the IRGC, where he received further training in photography."

Katherine turned away from the screen and said, "Although we couldn't find any definitive evidence of this, we believe it's safe to assume Khouri also received tutoring in English and American business practices during his time with the IRGC."

She pointed her laser at the screen again. "Third, a few days after Khouri arrived back in Amman in 2005, several million dollars was transferred from an IRGC account in Tehran to a private bank in Zurich under Khouri's name. Two months after that, Khouri arrived in Washington, D.C., where he invested some of that money in WK Photography."

Katherine clicked off her summary slide and projected a collage of photographs showing Khouri with a bunch of beautiful people. I found it easy to identify the Washington bureaucrats in the shots, but I had no clue who the rest of them were.

"As you can see from this collage from his Facebook page, Khouri fosters his reputation of being a first-class photographer with ties to both Hollywood celebrities and Washington insiders."

Her next slide showed Khouri aiming his camera at some fashion models on a white sandy beach. I immediately recognized a famous landmark in Dubai in the background.

"Since arriving here in 2005, Khouri has seldom traveled outside of the United States. However, last month, he booked a photo shoot for an Arabic fashion magazine and traveled to Pakistan, Turkey, and Dubai. We haven't been able to determine if he met with any IRGC or Hezbollah members in those countries yet, but we're still shifting through that metadata, so we may yet come up with something."

At this point in her presentation, Katherine displayed a photograph of the yellow bag of potato chips found in Felipe's backpack. A close-up shot showed the phone number Reyes Valario had contacted before entering the Navy Yard and killing a bunch of innocent people.

She said, "The second suspect in the Navy Yard massacre wrote down this phone number, which he believed belonged to a drug dealer willing to buy several kilos of heroin he was carrying. In reality, this is the personal phone number of Walid Khouri, who, as far as we have been able to tell, has never had any kind of connection to the drug trade."

Katherine concluded by showing the passport photo of Reyes Valario and explaining his connection to Hezbollah. "According to Valario's cell phone records, he was in regular contact with Khouri. He even called his number just hours before arriving at the entrance to the Navy Yard. Of course, we've filed the necessary forms requesting the NSA supply us with the transcripts of those conversations. As soon as they become available, I'm sure many of our questions will be answered."

Katherine ended her presentation, and the DDO started speaking again. When he began cautioning everyone about reading too much into the data, I tuned him out for a few seconds, because I was trying to decide whether or not I should say something about Frank Benson's trip down to Arkansas and his discovery about Valario's connection to the Razorback Century Club.

I realized it would be difficult to mention this information without getting Benson in some hot water, and since I'd already done that earlier in the week, I decided to keep my mouth shut—at least for now.

When I tuned the DDO back in, he was saying, "So I suggest we all take a deep breath before jumping to any conclusions. While there's every reason to believe Walid Khouri is a deep cover operative sent here by the Iranian regime, there's no reason to believe he's connected to the threat we're facing right now from a chemical weapons attack on Washington. That's why I believe, before contacting our friends over at the Bureau, we should give our analysts more time to explore Khouri's background."

He began gathering up his notes while delivering his final remarks. "Whether Khouri is a lone wolf or part of a larger sleeper cell, it's imperative we gather all the facts before exposing him. Everyone should keep in mind, during the past ten years, Khouri has been given unequaled access to photograph Congressional leaders and high-level government officials alike. Not only that, he's become close friends with some of them."

Ira appeared to be looking directly at me when he made his concluding statement. "I'm sure everyone will agree with my decision."

Most people in the room probably agreed with the DDO's decision. I wasn't one of them.

♦♦♦♦

When my briefing ended, I stayed behind in order to meet with Legal and put my signature on the if-you-die-during-this-mission-we-can't-be-sued document, which was required of all covert operatives before heading out on a mission.

After finishing with them, Josh Kellerman, who directed the Legends arm of Support Services, went through the intricacies of the cover story I'd be using while in Syria.

"You'll be operating in country as Donovan Bartlett, a freelance journalist from Chicago."

"You know how much I hate to write, Josh. Couldn't you think of a better cover for me? And Donovan? What kind of name is that?"

Kellerman, who was used to hearing such protests, ignored me. "You and Keever Pike have been friends for years and, just in case anyone gets curious about you, an internet search will pull up several stories you've filed with newspapers here in the States."

After Kellerman had walked me through my travel documents and the contents of my wallet, he handed me a well-worn duffel bag containing some scruffy-looking clothes, a Kevlar jacket, laptop, toiletry kit, camera, cell phone, sat phone, backpack, and first-aid kit.

All the tangible items Legends issued to an intelligence officer were collectively referred to as The Kit, and when Kellerman had finished going over these items with me, he said, "Of course, since you're flying commercial, your Kit doesn't contain a weapons package. However, once you're in country, Keever will get you whatever you need. If he doesn't have it, I'm sure we'll hear about it."

I didn't doubt that.

Pike never went anywhere without a small arsenal.

And, of course, his attitude.

♦♦♦♦

The moment Josh Kellerman finished up with me, a driver from Transport arrived to take me over to Dulles, where I was scheduled to catch a flight to London. After a brief layover there, I'd be on a flight to Damascus.

When the driver pulled away from CIA headquarters, I asked him to take a short detour over to McLean Medical before dropping me off at the airport.

The driver—who said his name was Jefferson, but who insisted I not call him Jeff—was responsible for making sure I arrived at the airport on time, so when I asked him to take me by the hospital, he pulled an electronic tablet out of his front pocket and consulted it before agreeing to my request.

"My dispatcher always builds an extra fifteen minutes into the schedule. As long as this stop doesn't take too long, we're good."

"Fifteen minutes and I'm outta there."

"Let's do it."

Jefferson ran into some traffic on our way over to the medical center, so I called ahead and got Olivia's room number, which meant I was able to bypass the main reception desk and head straight to the elevators.

When I arrived at the nurse's station on the sixth floor, a flirty charge nurse there asked me what I was doing on her floor. After I told her I was a close friend of Olivia McConnell, she personally volunteered to escort me down to her room.

On our way down the corridor, I used the opportunity to quiz her about Olivia's condition. "Can you tell me how Olivia's surgery went today?"

She stopped in the hallway outside her room. "She had a double mastectomy with no complications, but depending on her lab results, she may be required to have some radiation treatments. Her surgeon was just here looking for her family. I'm sure he would have been happy to answer your questions."

"Olivia asked me not to come."

She smiled. "Are you Titus Ray?"

I nodded.

She pointed toward Olivia's room. "She may be too drowsy to talk to you right now, but on the table next to her bed is a note with your name on it."

After giving me a little Ta-Ta wave, she headed back down to the nurse's station, but I waited until she'd turned the corner before entering Olivia's room.

Compared to the bright lights of the hallway, the lighting inside Olivia's room was subdued, and it took my eyes a few minutes to make the adjustment. Once that happened, I walked over and stood beside her bed.

She appeared to be sleeping, and I decided not to disturb her.

Just to make sure she wasn't faking it, though, I stood there for a few minutes and watched her.

When I'd entered the room, I'd noticed a cellophane wrapped flower pot on the windowsill with some kind of dark green tropical plant inside. As soon as I determined Olivia was fast asleep, I walked over and took a look at the card sticking out of it.

Even though the card was tucked inside a thin envelope, it was impossible to read the handwritten message inside.

After glancing back over at Olivia, I pulled the envelope out of the plastic card holder and opened it.

The message read, *"Get well soon. Call you later, DC."*

I put the card back inside the envelope and stuck it back on the plastic holder, precisely where I'd found it.

I'm a spy. It's what I do.

I walked back over to Olivia's bed and glanced down at the table next to her. At first, I didn't see the note the nurse had mentioned, but a few seconds later, I spotted a green envelope tucked inside the little white New Testament I'd given her.

I picked up the Bible and pulled out the envelope. It had Titus Ray written in Olivia's big bold script across the front of it.

Earlier in the day, I hadn't made up my mind about whether or not I would stop by the hospital and check up on her.

Apparently, Olivia knew I would.

I wasn't sure what that said about me, or, for that matter, what that said about my relationship with Olivia, but I decided not to think about it.

My time was running out, so I removed Donovan Bartlett's wallet from my back pocket and pulled a Syrian bank note out of it. Flipping through the New Testament, I placed the bill in the book of Acts, next to chapter nine, knowing, when Olivia woke up, it wouldn't take her long to realize I'd stopped by the hospital to see her.

I also felt certain she'd be able to guess where I was headed, because the ninth chapter of Acts told the story of the apostle Paul and his trip to Damascus, Syria. What happened there had been a life-changing experience for him.

I waited until I was on the plane before reading Olivia's note.

# Chapter 33

After checking in at Dulles International, I still had an hour's wait before my flight to London began boarding, so I strolled down to an unmarked door near Concourse C and punched in a numbered code on the keypad above the doorknob.

Once inside the tiny room, I secured the door's locking mechanism and greeted the person seated at the table.

In Agency jargon, the space was known as The Closet and served as a private place to make a phone call, to have a chat with another operative, or to check classified email while stuck at the airport.

Such cubicles were available to high-level Agency personnel and could be found in some of the major airports across the country and in a couple of NATO countries as well.

Because Agency employees used Dulles more often than any other airport, there was a hideaway located within walking distance of every concourse. Thus, if I were meeting someone near Concourse C at Dulles, I would need to designate my location as TC-C-DU, which is exactly what I'd done when I'd texted Frank Benson before leaving Langley.

"You're late," he said, as soon as I came through the door.

"I had to take a short detour."

The room wasn't much bigger than a cheap motel room and was furnished just as lavishly. It contained a grungy old couch, a couple of plastic chairs, and a small wooden table. To my right was a door leading to a tiny bathroom.

I wasn't sure how often the two rooms in The Closet were cleaned, but if smell were any indication, it wasn't often enough.

Benson used the tip of one of his shoes to push a plastic chair away from the table. "I thought this place might have been upgraded since I left the Agency, but nothing's changed."

"Budget cutbacks, Frank. You know the Agency can't afford to upgrade these hidey holes when Congress keeps cutting back our operating budget every year."

"You sound like the DDO."

"Don't insult me."

"Sorry," he said, "I shouldn't have gone that far."

I sat down. "Speaking of the DDO, he attended my briefing this morning and delivered the report on Walid Khouri himself."

Frank raised his eyebrows at this disclosure. "That's not good. I bet that means Walid Khouri's background has some political ramifications to it, and now, he's probably telling everyone to proceed with caution."

I nodded. "He doesn't want us to share the intel we have on Khouri until he's had time to assess how much it could hurt the Agency or, more importantly, how an intelligence failure could endanger *his* job. He doesn't believe Khouri has anything to do with the present threat on Washington, so he's content to wait and see what else turns up on the man before he gets the Bureau involved."

Benson looked surprised. "The deputy actually said he wouldn't be sharing Khouri's background with the Bureau?"

"Well, not exactly. He qualified his statement by saying the nondisclosure was only temporary, and he'd eventually get around to giving the feds the goods on Khouri."

Benson didn't sound very happy. "If you can't tell me anything, then what am I doing here?"

"You didn't expected me to follow the DDO's directive, did you?"

♦♦♦♦

Once I'd summarized Katherine's findings on Walid Khouri, Benson pulled out the diagram he'd been making on Valario and made several new notations, including the addition of a few more boxes.

The sheet of paper was beginning to look a lot like Egyptian hieroglyphics to me, but Benson seemed pleased with the results.

He pointed to a rectangle with Valario's name on it. "Here's Reyes Valario, a converted Muslim, who attended a militant Hezbollah training camp in Venezuela."

He moved his finger over to another box that had The University of Arkansas written across it. "Here's Valario being educated at an American university, while, at the same time, taking lessons on how to use a drone for aerial photography."

He tapped on a new box he'd drawn with Walid Khouri's name on it. "And now, here's Khouri, an Iranian deep cover operative, who's been communicating with Valario on a regular basis."

He pointed to the word Washington written in bold letters inside a coffin-like figure. "And here's the city where Valario committed suicide, or I guess I should say death-by-cop. This also happens to be the city where Khouri resides, a man who may or may not have anything to do with an upcoming attack on the city, but who's recently taken a trip to the Middle East."

He focused on his diagram a minute and didn't say anything.

Finally, he drew another box with nothing in it.

"Here's the missing piece of the puzzle. I don't know whether it's a person or a city. All I know for sure is whatever goes in that box will solve the equation."

"Maybe it's not a person or a city, Frank. Maybe it's a reason. Maybe it's the reason why the Iranians sent Walid Khouri here in the first place. That's your missing piece."

"You could be right, but I can't exactly call someone up in the IRGC and ask them to give me their rationale for placing Khouri here, can I?"

"No, but I'm betting there's a certain Iranian general named Suleiman who has some of those answers. And, as it turns out, a few days from now, the general and I will both be in Damascus at the same time."

Benson looked surprised. "That's where you're headed? To Damascus?"

I nodded. "My flight leaves in less than an hour."

He shook his head. "Watch your back, Titus. I hear there's some pretty nasty stuff happening over there right now."

"I won't be going in solo. Keever Pike is the primary, and Carlton will be in country running the operation."

"Since Keever's there, you won't need to worry about someone covering your back," he said. "He always carries enough firepower to supply a small army. On the other hand, you might need to worry about whether or not you have the patience to put up with him."

"I'm a man of infinite patience."

Benson burst out laughing. "Yeah, since when?"

He grabbed his diagram off the table. "But seriously, Titus, after I heard your apology last night, I realized you've changed. Does getting older do that for you? Does it soften you up around the edges? Make you a kinder, gentler soul?"

"You keep bringing up *my* age, Frank. While I may be crossing that half-century mark soon, I happen to know you're only a few months behind me."

"See, I knew you were older than me."

"I haven't changed my attitude because of a few gray hairs," I said, getting to my feet, "and if I had more time, I'd tell you what happened to me one night in Tehran, because that's what changed my life forever. Getting older didn't do it."

Benson slipped his diagram inside his jacket pocket and stood to his feet. "I can't wait to hear *that* story."

I glanced down at my watch. "Maybe we can talk about it when I get back."

"Thanks for the info on Khouri," he said. "I plan to continue investigating him, and, if the Director allows it, I'll put him under surveillance." He gave me a knowing smile. "But don't worry. While you're away, I'll also set aside plenty of time to keep an eye on Ms. Nikki Saxon for you."

Before I knew it, I was right up in his face.

"I may have changed in some respects, Frank, but I'm still the jealous type. While I'm away, you should also keep that in mind."

I left the room without saying goodbye.

♦♦♦♦

Once my flight was airborne and over the Atlantic, I pulled out the green envelope Olivia had left me and read the note inside.

*Dear Titus,*

*If you're reading this, I guess that means you came by to see me, even though I explicitly told you not to bother. Of course, this is so typical of you. You're such an infuriating man. Typical and infuriating, like most men.*

*I'm leaving you this note just in case I don't make it through my surgery. I know that's unlikely, but there's always a certain amount of risk in any surgery. However, I'm willing to admit—because I can hear you arguing this point—the risk assessment on this one is fairly low.*

*Here's my point: I wanted to let you know I realized last night I was ready to pray that prayer, the one you wanted me to pray the other day. I couldn't think of any reason to wait until you were around to do it, though.*

*I'm perfectly capable of saying a prayer without you.*

*I hope I did it right. I think I did. I just told God I knew I wasn't a very good person, that I'd ignored him all my life, and that I wanted him to be in my life now.*

*Of course, I haven't been living in a godless bubble all my life. I've heard about Jesus dying for my sins, but, until I started reading that Bible you gave me, I never really understood what that meant. His death paid for my sins—my own personal sins. I accept that now.*

*That's mostly what I said in my prayer.*

*I have to say I didn't feel much different after praying that prayer. But, I guess that's what faith is all about, just believing, even when you don't have any special feelings.*

*Okay, maybe I ought to correct that. I wasn't as anxious about facing this disease by myself after talking to God. And, okay, I have to admit, since praying that prayer, I'm looking forward to reading my Bible, or at least those sections about Jesus' teachings.*

*All that other stuff looks pretty boring to me.*

*So, just in case I don't make it through my surgery, I wanted to assure you, I won't be alone for eternity after all.*

*If I do make it, though, I might be willing to talk with you about my decision, but, then again, if you act like a know-it-all, the way you usually do, I might not.*

*Olivia*

I folded up the note and put it back inside the envelope. Then, I immediately made my way down the aisle to the nearest restroom. After locking myself inside, I leaned back against the wall and, for the next few minutes, I let the torrent of tears I'd been holding back flow freely down my cheeks.

At first, I wasn't sure why my emotions had managed to get the best of me, but then I suddenly realized Olivia had decided to take this step of faith because I'd shared my own commitment with her.

What if I hadn't done that? What if I hadn't been willing to say anything?

After a few seconds, I took Olivia's note, along with the envelope, and tore it up in several little pieces, Then, I flushed them down the toilet.

The moment I returned to my seat, I set my face toward Damascus and a general named Suleiman.

# PART FOUR

## Chapter 34

*Wednesday, July 1*

There were so few passengers aboard my flight to Damascus, I moved over and sat next to a window. I usually opted for an aisle seat because it afforded me a much better view of the plane's interior, and it gave me the ability to act quickly, should events prove necessary.

However, since I hadn't been in Damascus for awhile, I thought it might be useful to have a bird's eye view of the city. I wanted to see firsthand how the civil war had changed the landscape.

Despite having read Nolan Wilson's operational brief on what to expect, the moment the plane began its descent into Damascus International Airport, I wasn't prepared for the apocalyptic scenes of the bombed-out neighborhoods on the outskirts of the city.

It was evident the civil war had especially taken its toll on the Jobar suburb, home to several thousand Sunni Arabs. The neighborhoods had been the focus of heavy aerial bombardment by the military forces of Assad's Shia government, and it looked as if the whole area was one big pile of rubble.

However, parts of the city appeared untouched by the rebellion. In fact, traffic seemed to be moving normally on the roadways, even though I saw several army checkpoints around the outer loop.

From the air, it was easy to spot Yarmouk, a large refugee camp in the northern part of Damascus. It was filled with thousands of tents and makeshift shelters and went on for miles.

The airport terminal itself was teeming with refugees. Most were young parents with small children, but scattered among the families were able-bodied men as well. Perhaps some of them were simply trying to escape being forced to put on a government uniform, but I knew at least a few of them had to be ISIS recruits, along with other undesirables.

In an effort to establish my cover as a war-time journalist, I took out the expensive camera Kellerman had included in my Kit—a Nikon no less—and snapped some pictures of crying babies.

A few seconds later, someone walked up behind me, grabbed me by the arm, and began yelling at me in Arabic, "No photographs allowed."

I immediately pivoted to my right and came face-to-face with Keever Pike.

He had a silly grin on his face. "Admit it, for a second there, you were shaking in your boots."

"I'm not wearing boots. Support Services has me wearing these stupid loafers."

He laughed. "Let's get out of here."

The air outside the terminal was stifling, and I figured the temperature had to be at least a hundred degrees on the sidewalk.

Damascus had never been an ideal spot for a vacation, especially in July.

I followed Pike over to a black SUV parked at the curb. It was a newer model Renault, and, as we approached the vehicle, I saw a female driver inside. She used a remote fob to flip open the trunk lid.

Pike said, "Throw your gear in there and hop in the backseat."

By the time I got inside the SUV, Pike was already in the front passenger seat buckling up his seatbelt.

When Pike introduced the woman behind the wheel, she turned and smiled at me.

"Trudy Rose, meet Titus Ray, henceforth known only as Donovan Bartlett."

As Trudy pulled the Renault away from the curb, Pike said, "Since you're my BFF, can I call you Donnie?"

"Why not?" I said, knowing it didn't matter what I said, Pike would call me whatever he wanted to call me.

He looked over at Trudy. "Sometimes, I call her sweetheart."

She gave him a forced smile, and he laughed at her. "Trudy's embedded at EAI as a nurse, but she's also our tech specialist. Douglas told her to spread the word around the compound we're dating, so it won't seem strange for us to be seen together."

"But," Trudy said, cutting her eyes over at Pike, "just to be clear, our relationship is pure fiction."

"Yeah," he said, "it's pure fiction, just like the concept of peace in the Middle East."

From Pike's tone of voice, it was clear he wished both of these concepts weren't fiction, pure or otherwise.

I could see why Pike might be attracted to Trudy. She had curly black hair, dark, animated eyes, and an engaging smile. There was a vibrant effervescence about her, as well as a bit of mischievousness.

The moment we pulled away from the airport, Pike began lecturing her on how to avoid certain neighborhoods on the ride into Damascus. Watching the way he ignored her protests, reminded me of an incident, a few years ago, when Pike and I had flown into Baghdad together.

I'd been posing as a photojournalist then, and Pike and I had supposedly just met on the plane and were sharing a taxi into the green zone. From an operational standpoint, our mission was to ferret out some assets among the Sunni opposition groups in Iraq.

The taxi driver had immediately recognized Pike as a journalist, and he'd tried to engage him in conversation. However, Pike wasn't interested. He was more concerned about where the driver was taking us—like right into a red zone, a strict no-go area where Sunni opposition forces weren't friendly to journalists, especially American journalists.

Pike began shouting commands at the man. "Turn here. No, don't go there. It's this way."

The driver kept yelling back at him, but Pike was so intent on making his own opinions heard, he wasn't listening to anything the taxi driver was saying.

I'd heard the driver say his cousin was a tribal leader who wanted to talk to a journalist, and when I'd had enough of their nonsense, I grabbed Pike's arm and said, "Shut up, Keever. He's offering you a story."

Pike stopped yelling long enough to ask, "Will I get a chance to write it before I'm shot?"

The driver shrugged and said, "You'll have to negotiate those terms with Hussein."

Hussein turned out to be Hussein Ibrahim, the leader of an Islamist Sunni group, a person the State Department had hoped would serve as a buffer between the Iraqi Shiite forces and a new group of radicals calling themselves ISIS.

The Agency had been trying to locate the charismatic leader for several months, and when the taxi driver brought us right up to the house where he was staying, it was obvious Pike could barely contain his excitement.

But, to be honest, I was pretty stoked about it myself, and I would have given anything if Carlton had been with us.

Pike had an easy time interviewing Hussein Ibrahim. The Sunni leader was eager to give us his opinions on how to stop the infighting among the tribal leaders in Iraq. In fact, Pike ended up writing an extensive piece on Ibrahim, and all the major papers had picked it up.

After the story ran, Ibrahim agreed to meet with us occasionally, but he always insisted on meeting in a different location every time. Even though we were usually forced to listen to his views on a variety of topics, we were still able to pick up some tidbits of useful intel at the same time.

During one of those get-togethers, we convinced Ibrahim to talk with some of our "friends" from the State Department. During that meeting—after receiving a promise of unlimited financial support—he had agreed to work with U.S. officials on the ground in Iraq to bring together a hodgepodge of other militant groups who would serve as a bulwark against ISIS.

Unfortunately, ISIS had prevailed, and now, Ibrahim had faded into the Iraqi countryside. The last I'd heard of him, he was living in some obscure village near Fallujah, trying to escape the creeping onslaught of a black death squad.

Now, as I observed Pike giving Trudy his opinion on the best route into the city, I suddenly remembered how Pike had described Hussein Ibrahim in his article.

*"This is a man so passionate about his own opinions, he fails to listen to the opinions of others."*

At the time, I'd been struck by how well Pike had managed to capture the essence of Ibrahim, while characterizing himself at the same time.

From all indications, Pike hadn't changed all that much in the last four years.

♦♦♦♦

The airport was located just east of Damascus, about thirty miles from the heart of the city, and the Agency's safe house was twenty miles further north, near the Anaser Mosque in the Al Tal suburb.

Due to several checkpoints and heavy traffic along the way, a trip that should have taken us less than an hour to complete took us almost two.

Pike used the time to quiz me about how I saw the operation playing out.

In true journalistic style, he questioned me about everything—from what I thought about Marwan Farage to the intel I expected to gain from General Suleiman's visit.

"I see Marwan a little differently than you do," he said, after we'd talked for awhile. "The asset I was running inside Naballah's inner circle described him as being sure of himself. He never said anything about him being nervous or afraid of anything."

"That may have been true when Marwan was around Naballah, but when he was in our custody, he was definitely distressed, especially when he thought his wife and daughter were in danger. That's when he started sweating buckets and agreed to cooperate with us."

"But will he be able to handle himself in the company of General Suleiman?"

"After I meet with him tomorrow, you'll have to make that determination. I'm the second chair in this operation."

Pike shook his head. "Being designated the primary wasn't my idea. That was strictly the DDO's choice. I never—"

Trudy suddenly brought the Renault to a complete stop.

"We've got trouble," she said.

♦♦♦♦

On the road in front of us were several men dressed in military gear. They appeared to be members of the Syrian Army.

The men had surrounded a battered old BMW and were forcing its passengers to exit the vehicle. There were four young males inside, and when they were told to get out of their vehicle, they immediately put their hands on top of their heads.

"Do you have a—"

"There's a loaded revolver underneath your seat," Pike said, anticipating my question.

He'd already removed a weapon from his side holster, and, as I reached underneath the seat, I saw Trudy remove her own handgun from her purse.

After locating the revolver, I left it on the floorboard within easy reach. Then, I glanced out the back window. "We're boxed in here. We have cars on both side of us."

"They're just kids," Trudy said, watching the scene unfold.

Pike said, "They're probably conscripts who've refused to fight their fellow citizens. They'll be arrested, and after a couple of beatings, they'll be more than happy to put on a uniform."

A few minutes later, the ranking officer lifted something out of the trunk of the BMW and nodded at one of the soldiers. The four males were immediately forced to their knees, and one of the soldiers put a gun to the head of the youngest kid.

I said, "This doesn't look promising, Keever. It might be a good time for us to start acting like journalists."

"My thoughts exactly," he said, putting away his gun and pulling a PRESS placard out of the glove box. After placing it on the windshield, we waited to see if it drew any attention.

However, as the officer walked over to the kneeling men, he seemed oblivious to the parked cars and the crowd gathering to watch the drama play out on the street in front of them.

The officer went over and stood behind the oldest boy, leaning over and whispering something in his ear. The kid immediately began shaking his head back and forth.

The officer straightened up and hit him with the back of his hand. Afterward, he nodded at the soldier standing over the young boy.

The soldier pushed the kid's head down with one hand while pressing his pistol against the back of his head with the other.

I immediately grabbed the Nikon, swung open the car door, and began shooting multiple frames.

Pike came out of the Renault right behind me, his press ID swinging from a lanyard around his neck. I suddenly realized I hadn't dug mine out of my duffel bag at the airport.

Now, I wished I had.

Pike began firing questions at the officer, which caused the soldiers guarding the four boys to abandon their positions and move toward him.

I shouted at them in Arabic, "Press. Press. We're journalists."

The officer glanced over at the sign on the SUV, then back at the camera I was holding, and finally at Pike, who said, "Could I ask you a few questions?"

The officer ignored Pike and motioned at one of the soldiers, who walked over and grabbed the Nikon out of my hands.

"No pictures," he shouted at me.

The officer turned and said something to the four boys, and the four of them took off running for their car.

Pike and I did the same.

Well, we didn't actually run.

Both of us took very long strides, though.

As we piled back in the car, Trudy said, "That went well."

Seconds later, as the cars ahead of us started moving again, Pike turned around and grinned at me.

"Support Services will want a four-page document explaining how you let some two-bit soldier take that expensive Nikon out of your hands. Remember to add a notation clarifying I explicitly told you not to take any pictures."

"Since when have I ever listened to you?"

# Chapter 35

The Agency safe house in the Al Tal suburb of Damascus was a two-story concrete building with a long narrow footprint and a satellite dish perched atop its low flat roof.

It didn't look all that different from the other houses in the neighborhood. However, I had to believe some of the furnishings inside the house were substantially different from any of those found in the other residences.

Like most Agency safe houses, this one came equipped with a number of security devices, including a video surveillance system in every room, a backup generator, and a vast array of electronic equipment used to communicate with both intelligence officers on the ground and the Ops Center back at Langley.

As soon as we arrived at the safe house, Trudy told us she needed to get back to the EAI compound, and Pike walked her over to the mini-van parked at the curb, putting his arm around her for the benefit of any nosy neighbors who might be wondering why there was an EAI van parked in front of his house.

The vehicle had the relief agency's familiar black and gold lettering on the side, and below the words, Emergency Aid International, was the EAI logo. It depicted a small child receiving a bowl of rice from a kneeling figure. A graphic artist had designed the EAI letters to form an umbrella over the two darken silhouettes.

Underneath the logo was the relief agency's motto written in both Arabic and English. The motto, *"Kneeling In Service, Standing In*

*Hope,"* had come straight from the CIA's Disinformation and Propaganda Department. Carlton said their director, Nora Kaylor, had come up with the slogan herself.

After Trudy drove off, Pike and I entered the safe house. Once he'd given me a quick tour of the layout, and I'd deposited my duffel bag in one of the bedrooms, we ended up in the kitchen.

It wasn't a modern-looking kitchen by American standards, but it appeared to have all the basics, plus a well-stocked pantry. When I grabbed a bottle of water out of the refrigerator, I noticed it was also crammed with food supplies.

"Are you planning a dinner party? There's enough food in here for an army."

"I remembered your cooking fetish, so I had Trudy go by the market and grab some stuff."

"I don't have a cooking fetish, but if that's your way of asking me to make you some of my world-class chili, then the answer is yes."

He grinned. "I've always loved your chili. And your barbeque brisket. I even sorta like that chicken and spaghetti stuff you made one time."

"You mean chicken tetrazzini?"

"Yeah . . . that."

Suddenly, his smile disappeared.

I thought I knew why.

♦♦♦♦

The night I'd added some chicken to some leftover spaghetti and called it chicken tetrazzini had been the night he'd gone off the wagon.

That night, the two of us were stuck in an apartment in Mosul doing surveillance on a couple of Iraqis across the street. The two men were suspected of being responsible for an attack on a resupply convoy in which four Americans had been killed.

Since Pike had only recently joined the Agency, it was the first time we'd worked together.

Around midnight, a call had come in from Communication

Services informing Pike he needed to call his mother-in-law. After making the call, he'd come out of the bedroom, mumbled something about needing some air, and left the apartment.

When he'd staggered back in almost three hours later, he was plastered.

The next morning, fully sober now, he told me his ex-wife had been killed in a freak accident. He said his mother-in-law had been a nervous wreck when she'd told him.

I thought he still looked pretty shaken up by the news himself.

He said, "I'd appreciate it if you wouldn't tell anyone I got drunk last night."

"I can't think of any reason I'd tell anyone. Even if I did, why would they care?"

He looked surprised. "My employment at the Agency is contingent upon my ability to stay sober. Didn't you know that?"

"Why would I know that?"

"I thought everyone at the Agency knew."

"Not me."

I didn't bother explaining I wasn't all that sociable and seldom spent any time in the cafeteria listening to the latest gossip.

After Pike took a couple of aspirin, followed by several gulps of strong coffee, he explained the circumstances surrounding his CIA employment.

He began by telling me about his illustrious newspaper career. Even though I knew he'd been a respected journalist for a number of years and had won several awards for his writing before joining the CIA, I wasn't aware he'd been fired by the last three newspapers he'd worked for. He said it was because of his drinking.

"The last time I was fired, I'd hit rock bottom. That's when one of the suits from the Agency's seventh floor found me. I can't say who it was, because I've been sworn to secrecy, but you can probably guess his identity. Anyway, he came to me with a proposition, and I accepted."

"He propositioned you and you accepted?"

He laughed. "That's about it. He said he'd read all my stuff; he knew I was an expert on the Middle East and could speak Arabic. He told me if I would sign on the bottom line, I'd be able to file stories under my own byline again. He promised to send me to places where news was happening on every corner, and he assured me the stories I wrote would be picked up by all the major news organizations."

"But there was a caveat?"

He nodded. "I had to stay sober. Before the Agency sent me to their spook training camp at The Farm, I had to spend twelve weeks in a recovery treatment facility, courtesy of Uncle Sam. Believe me, the latter was harder than the former."

"So what happened last night?"

He shook his head. "I'm not sure, but I swear it'll never happen again. I live in the best of both worlds now. Not only am I reporting the news, I'm trying to make a difference in the news I'm reporting. If you could keep last night's slipup just between the two of us, I'd really appreciate it."

"As far as I'm concerned, it never happened."

That was the end of it.

I had never mentioned Pike's failure to anyone.

However, colleagues who share embarrassing secrets are sometimes reminded of them, and I felt certain Pike's mention of my chicken tetrazzini had triggered both our memories of that night.

Now, an awkward silence hung in the air between us.

♦♦♦♦

I quickly changed the conversation from food to one of Pike's favorite topics, one he could talk about for hours.

"How about my weapon's package, Keever? Is it ready?"

"You bet. Come this way."

I followed Pike down the hall to a back bedroom where he opened the closet and took out several aluminum cases. Each case contained a handgun.

Pike spent the next hour describing the pros and cons of each gun in much the same way a professional chef might describe the minute subtleties in a variety of cheeses.

Pike was a gun guy.

He loved guns; he collected guns; he told me once he even loved the smell of guns.

Okay, fine. I understood that.

Different strokes for different folks.

But, I wasn't a gun guy.

I wasn't all that interested in where, when, or how a gun was manufactured, and I especially didn't care about the smell of a gun. What I cared about was a gun's reliability.

If a gun fired when I pulled the trigger, and it was able to deliver the bullet reasonably close to its intended target, then that was the gun I loved.

Pike and I had discussed guns before—endlessly.

Now, after telling me more than I wanted to know about each of the four handguns he'd laid out for me, he asked, "See anything that suits you?"

"You know I'm not picky," I said, taking the sub-compact Sig out of its case. "This is fine."

He nodded. "That's a good choice. Very reliable."

He picked up the Beretta. "You don't like the Beretta Px4?"

"It's not a question of not liking it. I just chose the Sig instead."

"The ergonomics on this Beretta make it a good choice."

"Okay, fine. I'll take the Beretta."

He took the Sig out of my hands and handed me the Beretta, observing me closely as I checked it out.

"You're right," I said. "A Beretta's an easy gun to handle, and this one feels well balanced."

"If it's balance you're looking for, then a better choice might be the Browning Hi Power." He lifted the HP out of its case and said, "It's famous for its perfect balance."

"I like the HP. I carried one in Iraq, but this Beretta's fine."

"No, if you're more familiar with the HP, then you should probably take it instead. Give me back the Beretta."

I handed over the Beretta and picked up the Browning HP.

"It looks brand new," I said, examining the weapon. "Has it been fired before?"

"You'd prefer a used gun?"

"Not necessarily."

"Here's a 9mm Makarov I bought off another journalist," he said, picking it up. "The Makarov is standard issue in the Syrian military. If our mission goes sideways, you can always wave this around and blend right in. I've carried one ever since I got here."

I laid the HP back in its silver case and said, "I'll take the Makarov then."

"You may not be picky, but you certainly have a hard time making up your mind."

I raised my voice. "I thought I *had* made up my mind when I first told you I'd take the Sig."

"So you want the Sig now?"

I remembered telling Frank Benson I was a man of infinite patience, and I'd be able to handle Pike and his contentious nature.

I was beginning to doubt that.

♦♦♦♦

Carlton and Trudy arrived at the safe house around five o'clock. They weren't alone. As per Agency regulations, Carlton had two Level 3 security guys with him, something the CIA required whenever a division head operated in country.

Once they'd gone through the safe house and verified it wasn't occupied by someone who might pose a threat to Carlton—evidently, Pike and his closet full of guns didn't count—they went back outside and hung around the mini-van.

Trudy, who was the tech specialist for the mission, immediately went upstairs to the loft where the communications equipment was located. Carlton told her to notify him the minute an uplink with the Ops Center at Langley had been established.

Even though Carlton had been in transit for the last couple of days, his sports shirt and Khakis still looked crisp and wrinkle free. Despite that, I saw sweat glistening on his baldhead, and there were bags under his eyes.

He walked over and put his briefcase down on the dining table. "Do I smell chili?" he asked.

I detected a note of irritation in his voice.

Pike said, "Titus insisted on making us dinner."

Carlton looked over at me. "Chili? In this weather?"

I shrugged. "Forget the chili. Tell me about Marwan. Was he cooperative when you met up with him at Gitmo?"

Carlton dabbed at the sweat on his brow with a white handkerchief. "More or less. But I've never met a guy who acted paranoid because his prison cell was too comfortable. Evidently, he was expecting something far less accommodating than the facilities he found at Gitmo."

Pike said, "That place is a luxury hotel compared to how the detainees were living in their own country. At Gitmo, they get free food, free medical care, and an unlimited supply of entertainment."

"Marwan wasn't complaining."

Pike said, "I bet neither one of you can guess the most popular author in the prison library."

Carlton and I just looked at him and didn't say a word.

"And the winner is," he said, pretending to consult an imaginary card in his hand, "Danielle Steel."

"And how would you know *that*?" I asked.

Pike looked over at Carlton. "You remember last year when you sent me to Gitmo to interrogate Ismail Abedni?"

Carlton nodded.

"While I was there, I did a piece for one of the news magazine. The article was entitled *Surprising Finds at Gitmo.* It ran last August. Didn't either one of you see it?"

I shook my head. "No, last year I was out of the country. Otherwise, I'm sure I would have been the first in line to buy a copy."

Pike barely cracked a smile. "It wasn't all fluff, you know. I wrote a lot about—"

Carlton cut him off. "Could we just get back to Marwan?"

Pike shrugged. "Sure, I just thought it was a terrific article."

Carlton said, "Marwan refused to honor the deal you made with him in Buenos Aires until he knew his wife and daughter were safe. He still wasn't satisfied after I showed him the photos Sam sent me, so I—"

"You didn't allow him to call his wife, did you?"

Carlton frowned. "Of course not. I told Sam to send me a video feed of the two women watching a live news program on television. When he sent the feed, I had Marwan watch the same program. After that, he seemed satisfied. At least he ended up signing the agreement."

I said, "Allowing Marwan to talk to his family is an enticement I want to hold in reserve. If he gets twitchy about attending the meeting with the general, I'll dangle it in front of him."

Carlton said, "While he said he'd cooperate with us, he demanded we get him out of Damascus as soon as possible after the meeting."

Pike said, "I can understand that. His lifespan will be considerably shorter if Naballah finds out he betrayed him."

I asked, "Were you able to observe Marwan's actions at the airport when he got off the plane?"

"No, it was the other way around. He kept his eye on me when we landed. I'd told him I'd be boarding a flight to Beirut shortly after we landed in Damascus, and when we deplaned, he followed me over to the next terminal."

"Did he wait around until your flight was called?"

Carlton nodded. "I played out the whole scenario for him. I'm sure he assumes you have backup here in Damascus, but I doubt if he believes there's any high-level CIA personnel here on the ground with you. The DDO was insistent we keep him in the dark about that."

Pike said, "The surveillance team I have on Marwan reported he went straight to his apartment after he left the airport. They wired the whole place and put cameras everywhere, so we'll be able to keep an eye on him. I'm betting he won't leave there until he hears from Titus tomorrow."

Carlton and I agreed with Pike, and then Carlton asked him about the surveillance protocols he'd put in place for General Suleiman's arrival in the city. Although he seemed pleased with Pike's plans to install listening devices inside the general's hotel suite at the Sheraton, he made a few minor changes.

For the next thirty minutes, the three of us discussed the logistics of the operation, along with the procedures the Ops Center had developed for monitoring Marwan's movements inside Naballah's headquarters, and the arrangements they'd made for Marwan's extraction from Syria.

Once Carlton had finished outlining these details, he turned to Pike and said, "I'll need a weapon before I leave today."

"Sure thing," he said, gesturing toward the back bedroom. "Follow me, and you can choose whatever you want."

Carlton shook his head. "That's not necessary. Just make sure I have a sidearm before I leave today."

"I'll get it for you right now."

Once Pike was out of the room, Carlton leaned over and said, "Don't ever let him talk you into choosing your own weapon. Whatever you choose, it's sure to be the wrong one."

"I could have used that information earlier."

I hoped this didn't mean Carlton had lost his sense of timing when it came to getting me viable intel.

# Chapter 36

Before Pike returned with the handgun, Trudy came downstairs and told Carlton the DDO had scheduled a video call with him in five minutes. She said the Ops Center would be updating everyone after that.

Once she and Carlton had gone back upstairs to the loft, I went outside to the EAI van and invited Carlton's security detail inside for a bowl of chili.

The older guy had thick black hair and a dark moustache and said his name was Dave. Although he insisted we'd met at our forward operating base in eastern Afghanistan in the spring of 2009, I couldn't place him. Around that time, a suicide bomber had entered the compound and blown himself up, so my memories of that time were understandably sketchy.

As we walked inside the house, Dave introduced his red-headed partner as Finn. With his fair skin and freckled face, I figured Finn had some ancestors from Ireland somewhere in his background.

After I handed each of them a bowl of chili, Finn said, "I hope this stuff tastes as good as it smells."

"You won't be disappointed," Pike said, entering the kitchen and dishing up a bowl for himself.

I put a plate of cheese on the table, along with some Syrian bread—*Khubz* in Arabic—and Pike grabbed some locally bottled fruit juices out of the refrigerator for us to drink.

The four of us sat around the table together—not exactly like a family but close enough. Once we'd finished eating, we started telling exaggerated stories about our harrowing exploits while serving our country.

It was Pike's anecdotes that won the day.

Although he had a knack for remembering details, it was his ability to describe people and places that captivated everyone, making it easy for me to understand how he'd been able to turn his creative talents into a successful journalism career.

His observation skills also made him an appealing recruit for the Agency, and I could see why the DDO had gone after him—not to mention the kudos the deputy had received from the suits on the seventh floor by snagging a member of the media and enlisting him as a covert intelligence officer.

From what he'd told me, Pike had also managed to put together a workable surveillance operation in Damascus and hadn't blown his cover doing it.

I knew from experience that wasn't an easy thing to do.

Once Pike had exhausted himself—and everyone else—with his colorful stories, I quizzed Dave and Finn about their schedule for the following day.

"We might need your help transporting an asset to the safe house tomorrow," I said. "Would you be available?"

Dave said, "Mr. Carlton's not leaving the compound tomorrow, so, as far as I know, I'm available."

Finn raised his hand. "Count me in."

I nodded. "Okay, I'll use both of you, but we'll need the EAI's full-size van, and make sure there aren't any relief supplies inside the vehicle. I don't want my asset making a connection between us and the EAI organization.

Dave said, "Not a problem."

"Be here at ten o'clock tomorrow morning. and I'll brief you then." I looked over at Pike. "Anything you'd like to add to that?"

"We'll be heading into a hot zone. Dress accordingly."

They both smiled. They knew Pike wasn't talking about the weather.

♦♦♦♦

After Dave and Finn went back outside, Pike asked me how I wanted to handle my upcoming meeting with Marwan. Although he wasn't enthusiastic about my plan, he didn't nix the idea.

About fifteen minutes later, Trudy came downstairs and said the Ops Center was ready to give us an update on the mission. After making this announcement, she walked over to the stove and sampled a spoonful of chili.

"It needs more salt."

Pike laughed. "Here's a woman who's never cooked a day in her life telling the master chef how to cook."

Trudy gave Pike a shove as she walked past him. "I may not be able to cook, but I can certainly tell when something's not salty enough."

"Take a bowl upstairs with you," I said, "It won't hurt my feelings if you want to add more salt."

She shook her head. "No, that's probably not a good idea. I don't think Mr. Carlton particularly likes chili. The whole time he's been upstairs, he's been complaining about the odor coming from the kitchen."

Her statement surprised me because I knew Carlton loved chili.

Then, as we climbed the stairs to the loft, I suddenly realized why he was upset about the smell.

It had nothing to do with the chili.

It had everything to do with Gladys.

♦♦♦♦

A few months before Gladys passed away, Carlton had called me up and asked me to drop by his townhouse in McLean. I'd been surprised to hear from him, because the two of us had just been through an exhausting all-day debriefing session following my run into Peshawar, Pakistan to rescue an American businessman.

When the call had come in, I was staying in an Agency safe house near Langley—identified by Support Services as The Red—and I was looking forward to spending the evening alone. I immediately abandoned those plans and called a taxi, thinking Carlton had some urgent intel to share with me, or that he wanted to alert me about my upcoming operation.

However, the minute I walked in the front door of his townhouse, he pointed at the dining table and told me to have a seat. On the table were two formal place settings with steaming bowls of chili at each of them.

He said, "Gladys made up a batch of chili this weekend. Believe me, there's nothing like it. I tell her it's the nectar of the gods."

After eating just one bowlful, there was little doubt in my mind Gladys' chili was a winner. When I told him so, his face lit up, and he said he'd tell Gladys I agreed with him about her culinary expertise.

"Don't bother asking her for her recipe, though. It's one of her closely guarded *secrets*."

He'd laughed when he'd said *secrets*, as if Gladys having secrets was particularly amusing.

That's when I realized he had no urgent intel to share with me, nor did he want to talk about my upcoming operation.

Apparently, he simply didn't want to spend the evening alone.

Unlike me.

A few days later, inside my Agency mail box, I found a pink envelope. It contained a note from Gladys written on a single sheet of rose-scented paper.

The note read, "*Thanks for being a friend to him.*"

The only other item inside the envelope was a recipe card with Gladys' chili recipe on it.

Like any good spy, after memorizing the secret formula, I immediately destroyed the evidence.

A couple of months after Gladys' death, while I was living in an apartment in Beirut with two other operatives, I decided to make Gladys' recipe for the very first time. Although I had to substitute a couple of ingredients, the guys said they loved it and asked for seconds.

Since then, I'd made batches of the stuff on numerous occasions, but I'd never made it when Carlton was around, and I had never made it on the anniversary of her death.

Until today.

♦♦♦♦

The loft at the safe house was a large undivided room with a set of narrow stairs leading up to the roof. Having used a similar set of stairs to make a quick escape from a house in Baghdad once, I immediately noted the stairs availability.

Although the room was filled with communications equipment, along with a couple of sound masking devices, it held little in the way of furnishings, except for a few chairs and a long wooden conference table with a wide screen monitor mounted at the end of it.

Most of the electronic equipment was easily transportable. If all went as planned, a few days from now, Pike and I would place the devices inside a van and drive over to a site near Hassan Naballah's compound where we'd monitor General Suleiman's conversation with Naballah and his security council.

Carlton was seated at the end of the conference table, and, as soon as we stepped inside the loft, he motioned for us to join him there.

"The DDO has just briefed me on a new development with Citadel Protection," he said, as we sat down. "The Ops Center is ready to update you on that now."

He looked over and nodded at Trudy, who keyed in a five-digit code on her computer. A few seconds later, a view of one of the Real Time Management Centers back at Langley immediately appeared on the screen.

The feed looked as if it were coming from Center C, the RTM unit monitoring Component Two of Citadel Protection. This was confirmed a few seconds later when I noticed C.J. Salazar, the chief of the Latin American desk, sitting at a console with his back to the screen.

As soon as someone tapped him on the shoulder, he faced the camera, adjusted the headset wrapped around his head, and entered the identification tag of the operation for the official recording of the update.

*"C.J. Salazar, RTM Center C, Component Two, Operation Citadel Protection, OFU, Code 21698."*

The Operational Field Update (OFU) usually followed a certain pattern. At the beginning, the officer was required to establish a timeline. Then, a short narrative of events was given, and finally, a recommendation was offered.

Depending on the personalities of those involved in the process, there might also be some extended discussion of the recommendation, along with some very loud arguments and some very angry disagreements. However, those comments weren't ever recorded for the official record.

Salazar initiated the OFU by reciting the timeline.

"The three vessels transporting the sarin gas canisters from Syria were due to arrive at the port in Santiago de Cuba on June 28, but, due to a storm in the area, they were delayed until yesterday, June 30. When the ships arrived, there was heavy fog in the area and visibility was poor. That situation changed around mid-morning, and that's the point at which the primary officer begins his narrative on this video."

Salazar walked over to a nearby console and gestured toward a computer screen. "I'm about to play the operational update from Ben Mitchell, the Primary for Component Two of Citadel Protection. He's narrating events on the ground in Santiago, and you'll also be able to view a clip from the video he took of the offloading of the containers."

Salazar signaled the RTM operator seated at the console next to him, and the moment he hit the play button, the video started streaming across the screen.

The first image was of Mitchell's face, which wasn't all that interesting, but the video he sent, along with what he had to say, definitely got everyone's attention.

Mitchell began the narrative by describing where his surveillance teams were located around the dock, and the technical specifications of the zoom features on the three cameras he'd used to film the shipping containers being offloaded from the cargo ships.

Finally, he got around to the specifics of the narrative; namely, what his surveillance teams had observed when the ships were unloading their deadly cargo at the port in Santiago.

His demeanor changed when he began this section of the report, and I thought I could detect some frustration in his voice the moment he started speaking.

"Because of the heavy fog, it was impossible for any of my surveillance teams to observe the entire unloading process. Once the fog began to lift around nine o'clock, we were able to get a better view of the shipping containers being removed from the ship's hold. As you can tell from this video, the containers were placed onto flatbed trucks and immediately driven away."

The video appearing on the left side of the screen was hazy at first, and I could barely make out the outline of the cargo ship in the distance. Within a short time, though, the thick clouds had dissipated, and I spotted a crane moving an orange-colored shipping container marked Hazardous Material from the main deck of the ship onto a waiting truck. There were three other containers already positioned on the truck, and, once the fourth one was added, the truck pulled away from the dock.

As a second truck arrived to receive the next containers, Mitchell continued, "There were a total of eighteen containers on this ship, the *Sea Star*, and there were another twenty on each of the other two ships, the *Sea Lady* and the *Sea Master*. In all, we counted fifty-eight containers."

Mitchell looked directly at the screen and shook his head. "I know the math I've given you isn't good news."

I immediately glanced over at Carlton, who had no reaction to Mitchell's numbers. I had no doubt he'd already heard the bad news from the DDO while we were downstairs eating.

In our earlier briefing, Carlton had told us the three ships were transporting twenty shipping containers apiece. This information had come from Mossad, the Israeli intelligence agency, who had verified the intel as extremely reliable.

Mossad seldom got their intel wrong, and I didn't doubt their numbers. If sixty containers had been onboard the ships when they left Syria, and Mitchell had only counted fifty-eight containers being offloaded in Santiago de Cuba, then this wasn't just bad news; this was devastating news.

This was the worst possible news.

Two shipping containers were missing. Each container had two pallets inside; each pallet held fifty canisters full of sarin gas.

Now, some unknown party was in possession of two hundred canisters of sarin gas, and the Agency had no idea where they were or who had them.

Mitchell said, "Once the shipping containers arrived at the warehouse, we double checked the accuracy of that number. Unfortunately, that was the correct count. The trucks delivered only fifty-eight containers to the warehouse."

Mitchell not only sounded frustrated, I detected a note of desperation in his voice as well.

"When the ships first arrived at the port, the entire area was covered in fog, so I believe there's a possibility the other two containers were offloaded during that time frame and taken elsewhere. I've started making inquiries around the dock, and I'm also trying to locate any additional video surveillance of the area."

*Proceed with caution, Ben. Don't let your emotions get the best of you. Think outside the box. Consider the possibilities.*

I realized my telepathic advice was futile, and, even if I'd been there to deliver the advice in person, Mitchell might have ignored my sagely wisdom.

In the end, I did the one thing I knew for sure would make a difference, and I breathed a quick prayer for Mitchell and his success in locating the canisters. Granted, it was hard for me not to suggest some things the God of the Universe might do to help Mitchell achieve that goal, but I decided he probably had a few ideas of his own, so I kept my opinions to myself.

I couldn't say the same for C.J. Salazar.

# Chapter 37

When Mitchell began asking for any satellite images of the port at Santiago to be downloaded to his computer, Salazar immediately stopped the video.

"The rest of Ben's narrative is taken up with housekeeping items," Salazar said. "You may have heard him ask for any available signals intelligence, but the heavy cloud cover prohibited the acquisition of any workable images."

Salazar left the main console and walked over to a cubicle where a UAV specialist was seated. She was manning the controls of an aerial surveillance drone, and there, on the screen in front of her, was a bird's eye view of a container vessel in the middle of the ocean.

Salazar said, "As soon as the weather cleared yesterday, I ordered satellite reconnaissance of the entire Caribbean Basin. In addition," he pointed over to the UAV operator, "we have our own surveillance drone monitoring the shipping lanes along the eastern seaboard of the United States."

The UAV operator, whose left hand was on a joystick, was piloting one of the Agency's surveillance drones above the unidentified container ship. The cameras, mounted on the wings and underbelly of the drone, were taking multiple sets of pictures while hovering over the vessel.

I knew reconnaissance specialists would later spend hours scrutinizing the photographs for any evidence there were two orange-colored shipping containers marked Hazardous Materials strapped to her deck.

Salazar returned to the main console located at the front of the RTM Center and faced the camera. "I've also notified our station chiefs in Latin America about the missing canisters, and I'm requisitioning extra personnel from those areas to be sent to Santiago to help with the search."

At this point, Salazar should have signed off on the official recording of the OFU without voicing an opinion, but instead, he added, "The Mexican drug cartels would like nothing better than to have their hands on those gas canisters, so it wouldn't surprise me if that's exactly what's happened to them."

Salazar ended the OFU in the same way he began it: *"C.J. Salazar, RTM Center C, Component Two, Operation Citadel Protection, OFU, Code 21698."*

Although I knew Salazar's ending remarks could be seen as merely reflective of his ongoing paranoia about the cartels, I didn't dismiss the possibility Hezbollah could have joined forces with one of the drug cartels to carry out their plan to attack Washington.

At the very least, I felt Katherine's ASA office should be instructed to start data mining any connection between the cartels and the missing containers, especially since Marwan Farage was Hezbollah's liaison with the drug cartels.

However, I seriously doubted Katherine would ever receive a call from Salazar. When it came to analysis, Salazar seldom saw the need for anything beyond his own studied opinion.

I decided I needed to change his mind about that, and, as soon as he signed off on the OFU, I laid the groundwork to make that happen.

I said, "I agree with your recommendation, C.J. The asset I'm running here in Damascus has ties to the cartel, and he's known about Hezbollah's plans for the chemical weapons from the very beginning."

He looked surprised to hear me say I was in agreement with him.

I rarely was.

"Yeah? Well, what's the catch?" he asked.

"There's no catch. I agree with you. Offloading those containers onto a truck or another ship would have been a complicated task, especially with the heavy fog in the area. I believe it would have taken an organization as competent as Los Zetas to pull it off."

"Exactly," he said, nodding his head vigorously at my suggestion, "Los Zetas could have orchestrated this whole thing. They have both the expertise and the manpower, and for years now, they've used the port in Santiago as their transfer point between their cocaine suppliers in Colombia and their distributors in Mexico."

"No, I'm not buying it," Pike said, leaning forward in his chair the way he usually did when he wanted to be argumentative. "There's a big difference between knowing how to stuff some cocaine bundles in the hold of a fishing boat and having the ability to offload a couple of heavy-duty shipping containers."

Salazar said, "Los Zetas interests are far more extensive than just heroin and cocaine. In the last ten years they've expanded into automobile engines, appliances, machine parts; you name it, they want to control it. Just recently, they've acquired their own fleet of container ships, so being able to handle a couple of shipping containers wouldn't have been a problem for them."

Although Salazar's counterpoint made sense, and I knew he was far more qualified than Pike to assess the cartel's ability to remove the canisters from the ship, Pike continued to disagree with him.

Carlton and I both kept quiet as the two men went back and forth for several minutes. Finally, when it became apparent neither one of the men would be backing down any time soon, Carlton said, "Could I offer a suggestion on this matter?"

Pike immediately said, "Please do."

A few seconds later, Salazar shrugged and nodded his head.

Carlton said, "One way to know for certain whether or not the Zetas or any of the other drug cartels have their hands on the missing containers is to have our ASA office look at the electronic trails they've left behind. My advice is to have our analysts run an data probe on their banking, electronic communications, shipping interests, or anything else they can dig up on them during the last forty-eight hours. By doing so, we'll have a better handle on what we're dealing with here."

I immediately voiced my agreement with Carlton' suggestion, and

Pike chimed in with his own approval. In the face of such overwhelming odds, Salazar couldn't help but acquiesce.

"Sure, why not?" he said. "I'll contact the ASA office. But I already know what we're dealing with here. It's one of the drug cartels."

In what appeared to be an effort to change the subject, Carlton asked, "What's the latest update from Caracas? Have you heard anything about how Marwan's wife and daughter are handling their confinement?"

"Sam Wylie's last update indicated the ladies were being very vocal about their kidnapping, but they weren't giving him any real trouble. If that should change, I'll let you know. Any other questions?"

I spoke up.

"Before you go, C.J., I'd like to ask Buddy a question."

Salazar looked surprised at my request to speak with one of the Agency's maritime specialist, but he motioned for Buddy, whose cubicle was at the far end of the room, to join him over at the main console.

Buddy was a muscled up guy with reddish-brown hair. I noticed he had a slightly bemused look on his face when he ambled over and faced the camera.

"How's it going, Titus?"

"Things could be a lot better, Buddy, but I'm sure you know that."

He nodded. "That's for sure."

"You've been tracking the ships carrying Syria's chemical weapons?"

"That would be me, yes."

"I have a few questions for you."

He nodded.

"Were you surprised the ships were delayed because of the storms in the area? Did that seem unusual to you?"

He laughed. "Yeah, it was a little unusual. Those storms were just tropical in nature; they certainly weren't of the hurricane variety. Of course, the dockworkers wouldn't have been able to unload any cargo during a thunderstorm, so maybe the person in charge just preferred to wait out the storm at sea."

"Tell me about the heavy fog in the area yesterday. Was it forecast ahead of time?"

"Oh, sure. The harbormaster had alerted all the ships in the area in advance. When it rolled in during the early morning hours, it didn't take anyone by surprise."

"That's all I have. Thanks, Buddy."

He started to walk away, but then, after a quick glance over at Salazar, he stopped and said, "The fog was particularly dense yesterday morning. Unless you were right there on the dock, you wouldn't have been able to see a thing. In fact, those conditions were just about perfect for offloading some containers without being observed. If you want my opinion, I'd say someone knew the docks were under surveillance, and that's the reason the ships remained at sea. They were waiting for the heavy fog to roll in before they made port. That's just my opinion, though. You can take it or leave it."

Since it was also my opinion, I took it.

♦♦♦♦

As soon as Buddy walked back over to his cubicle, Salazar said he would keep Carlton informed about the missing containers, and then he abruptly ended the transmission.

I had planned to ask Salazar about the likelihood Mitchell's surveillance teams were themselves under surveillance, either by Hezbollah or some other interested party. Before I could question him further, the screen went blank.

I had the feeling Salazar knew that question was coming, and he'd chosen to make a quick exit before it was asked.

Such actions were typical of him.

He wasn't necessarily incompetent, but he *did* have a tendency to have tunnel vision, and, if someone pointed out he'd missed some critical aspect of the operation, it tended to unnerve him.

I told myself to concentrate on my own mission and not worry about Mitchell and his activities, but that didn't stop me from considering how I could help him in some way, nor did it make the gnawing feeling in my gut go away.

"The transmission from the Ops Center was shut down on their end," Trudy said, trying to explain the blank video screen we were viewing.

"I'm aware of that," Carlton said, rubbing his temple.

"Shall I try the call again?" she asked.

Carlton shook his head. "No, Trudy. I think we're done here. If you'd like to go downstairs and get something to eat before we leave, you should probably do that now."

Trudy nodded and headed downstairs.

Pike, who'd been unusually quiet during the last few minutes, suddenly slapped his hand down on the table. "I've got it now. Ben Mitchell is Senator Elijah Mitchell's son. When I first saw him on that video, I knew I'd seen him somewhere before."

Carlton and I both kept quiet.

Pike asked, "When did he come to work for the Agency?"

Carlton never talked about another operative, so I knew he wasn't about to answer Pike's question.

"I believe it was about five years ago," I said.

"Are you kidding me? Didn't C.J. say he was a Level 1 operative?"

"He got bumped up from Level 2 status a few months ago."

"I can't believe C.J. named him as the primary for the mission."

"He seems competent."

"Two hundred canisters of sarin gas just disappeared on his watch. You call that competent?"

"No one could have seen that coming," I said, defending Mitchell. "Even if he'd been able to observe the whole thing, his assignment was a non-engagement surveillance op. He wasn't allowed to interfere with the transfer."

"Whose idea was that?"

Carlton spoke up, "I believe the DDO made that decision."

Pike decided not to respond to that statement—which was definitely a wise move on his part.

Instead, he said, "I interviewed the Senator at his home about eight years ago for an article I was doing on national security. When Ben entered the room, the Senator stopped the interview and proceeded to tell me about the plans he'd made for his son's future.

As I recall, none of those plans included being employed by the CIA."

"I don't imagine they did," I said.

I immediately regretted making that comment, because I figured Pike wouldn't let it pass without asking me a follow-up question.

Evidently though, he didn't hear me or he chose to ignore it, because after relating the anecdote, he stood to his feet and said he was headed downstairs for another bowl of chili.

He tapped Carlton on the shoulder. "You should come downstairs and have a bowl."

Carlton pushed his chair away from the table and said, "Maybe I should."

I decided it was time to address a certain personal issue. "Douglas, could I have a word with you before you go?"

He nodded and remained seated.

When Pike heard this, he stopped at the landing on the stairs and looked at me. "If you're about to discuss trading the Makarov for the Sig I picked out for him, I don't recommend it."

I assured him I was keeping the Makarov.

He nodded. "You made a good choice."

Once he was gone, I turned to Carlton and said, "Let's talk about Gladys."

♦♦♦♦

As Carlton gave me his full attention, his eyes appeared to be twice their normal size.

"What about Gladys?" he asked.

"Was she an equestrian? In one of the guest rooms at The Meadows, I saw several photographs of her standing next to a horse. I don't believe I've ever heard you talk about her riding."

Carlton actually smiled.

"She loved horses. She grew up on a horse farm in Kentucky, and when we met, she'd already won several national competitions in dressage."

He told me about the circumstances of their meeting and about how he felt when he saw Gladys for the first time.

"She had on this short riding coat, jodhpurs, and black boots." He shook his head. "From that moment on she had me."

"That's the way she was dressed in the photograph."

He nodded. "That picture was taken a couple of years after our wedding. I believe she'd just won a national championship then."

He described watching her compete, comparing her moves on a horse to a well choreographed ballet.

"I really believe she could have made the Olympic dressage team, but then, her father was injured by a horse, and after that, she gave it up. When he died a few years later, I thought she might take it up again, but she never did."

"The Meadows looks like a great place to raise horses. Is that why you bought the property?"

"That was partly it, but mainly it was because Gladys loved to entertain, and she thought the house would be perfect for that."

That seemed like a good opening for my confession.

"I realize I haven't ever told you this, Douglas, but just before Gladys passed away, she sent me her chili recipe. It was right after the two of us ate together at your townhouse following Operation Business Enterprise. The chili I made today was her recipe."

He bowed his head. For a brief moment, I wasn't sure how he felt about my revelation.

Seconds later, I heard him laughing, something he seldom did.

"Oh, my," he said, raising his head. "No, I never knew that. She gave you that recipe?" He shook his head. "She was always able to amaze me."

"Gladys was an incredible woman."

His face turned somber. "Today's the anniversary of her death."

I didn't say anything, and for a minute or so, we both remained quiet. It wasn't an awkward kind of quiet. It was more like a brief interlude of silence in honor of her memory.

Finally, I looked over at Carlton and said, "I wouldn't have made the chili today, if I'd remembered this was the anniversary of her death."

He shook his head. "No, it's okay. Gladys would have thought that was very appropriate. For some reason, she really liked you. The fact that she gave you the recipe just proves that."

He picked up his legal pad, tore off the top sheet where he'd scribbled down a few notes, and said, "I might go downstairs and try some of your chili now; see how it compares with hers."

I watched him as he walked over to the paper shredder.

"I hope you won't be disappointed."

He stood there a moment, watching the shredder do its work.

When the grinding stopped, he said, "Gladys wasn't afraid of dying. She believed her soul would just leave her body—she always called it her earth suit—and she'd arrived in heaven with a new body. I told her she would need a lot of faith to believe that, but she said she only needed a small amount of faith, as long as it was in the right person."

"That sounds about right. My faith is pretty small, but I know it's in the right person."

He walked back over to the table. "Until you lived in Tehran with those Christians, you never talked about your faith. Since then, it's become a big deal to you."

"That's because it *is* a big deal. People usually like to talk about what affects them. That's why I talk about my faith now, and that's why you talked about Gladys tonight. She was a big deal to you. She was an important part of your life."

"You were the one who brought her up."

"Aren't you glad I did? When I asked you about that photograph, it gave you an opportunity to remember the good times you had with her."

"I knew that's what you were doing all along."

"Of course you did."

Later, when Carlton went downstairs and sampled a bowl of the chili, he said, "It's a close second to the chili Gladys used to make, but next time, you should add more salt."

## Chapter 38

*Thursday, July 2*

After spending a restless night, I woke up around five o'clock and made myself a pot of coffee.

Since Pike had gone back to his apartment to spend the night, I was able to enjoy my morning coffee without having to speak with anyone—making someone engage in conversation before they've had their morning coffee is a form of cruel and unusual punishment and should be illegal.

Although I had several things to do before Pike showed up, I poured myself a second cup of coffee and read a couple of chapters from the Bible.

While my Donovan Bartlett persona didn't pack a Bible in his duffle bag, my Titus Ray persona was able to log onto the encrypted laptop in the upstairs loft and access an online Bible from the Agency's library.

Once I'd finished reading, I said a prayer for Nikki. Due to the time difference, it was only ten o'clock Wednesday evening at Quantico, and I knew she was probably exhausted after having completed her third day of training.

The third day at Quantico was always the worst, and right now, she might be asking herself why she'd signed up for the course in the first place. I could picture her sitting on the edge of her bed in the cramped quarters of the dorm and massaging her feet. Her hair was probably still wet from her shower and her . . .

I suddenly realized my prayer for Nikki had turned into something else altogether, and I immediately returned to reality.

The reality was that I would be bringing Marwan Farage to the safe house in a few hours, and I needed to prepare for his visit.

Since there wasn't much furniture in the loft, it didn't take me long to arrange the room the way I wanted it. Once everything was in position, I logged into the Latin American desk at the Agency and took a look at the overnight cable traffic.

There was nothing of interest there; no bulletins about finding missing gas canisters.

I switched over to the Latin American feed and scrolled down to the Cuban link. Nothing there either; most notably, no update from Mitchell.

I scrolled further down the page to Venezuela.

I noticed Sam Wylie had just sent Salazar his daily bulletin from Caracas, so I pinged him to see if he had time to chat with me. A few seconds later, his face appeared on the computer screen.

"Hey, what's up cowboy? Is the sun up there yet?"

"Just barely."

"I'm about to hit the sack here, unless you're about to tell me there's been a change in plans."

"No, we're right on schedule. I'll give you a call about eight hours from now. You haven't said anything to Yamina and Samira about the possibility of speaking with Marwan, have you?"

"Not a word. They're not happy campers, though, so Marwan may get an earful."

"That's perfect. I want the ladies to give him plenty of incentive to cooperate with us."

"If you're not calling about a change in plans, what's on your mind?"

"I'm assuming you saw Salazar's bulletin about the missing canisters?"

Wylie nodded. "Oh, yeah, if you ask me, assigning Ben as the primary for that mission wasn't very smart. In my book, that kid's still a greenhorn."

Although I was beginning to question whether I'd made the right decision when I'd recommended Mitchell to Carlton, I still felt the need to defend him.

"The surveillance schematic Ben described on the OFU yesterday sounded more than adequate. However, he probably needs additional personnel on the ground to help him locate those canisters now."

"Cartel Carlos has already assigned some of my boys to the search. They're leaving for Santiago tonight."

"That's what C.J. told us yesterday. Would you mind having one of them deliver a message to Ben for me?"

"Okay, now I get it," he said, slapping his forehead, "this call isn't about Marwan; it's about Ben. You've already taken the blame for killing Ahmed Al-Amin because of his mistakes. Why are you still trying to help that kid?"

"Let's don't go there."

"Yeah, not a good idea. What's the message?"

"It won't make any sense to you, but it will to Ben."

Wylie picked up his cell phone and tapped the screen once. "Should I write this down?"

"That probably won't be necessary. Just tell him, 'Give your little seedlings room to grow. You might be surprised at what comes out of the ground.'"

"Seriously?"

"Just give him the message."

"It's some kind of code, isn't it?"

"Yeah, Sam, it's a code."

"Let me guess. You're telling him to find someone else to blame for losing track of those canisters."

"Thanks, partner. We'll be in touch."

*Follow your instincts, Ben. Think about the possibilities.*

♦♦♦♦

Pike showed up at the safe house at nine o'clock, and Dave and Finn arrived forty-five minutes later. When I briefed them on my plans for Marwan, I said I was planning to call Marwan at eleven o'clock and tell him to meet me at a bookstore a few blocks away from his apartment.

However, that meeting wasn't going to take place.

Instead of meeting him at the bookstore, I was going to grab Marwan off the street as soon as he left his apartment. After that, I planned to take him to a remote location, a place Pike had specifically chosen for what I had in mind.

This type of disorientation technique was one I'd used before to gauge an asset's state of mind. In Marwan's case, I wanted to assess his willingness to go through with his betrayal of Naballah and General Suleiman. Not only that, I wanted to probe a little further into what he knew about Naballah's reason for having him at the meeting with the general.

When I finished briefing the two guys, I went outside and examined the interior of the EAI vehicle they'd driven over to the safe house. It was one of the relief agency's full-size cargo vans, ordinarily used to distribute emergency food packages to refugees flooding into Damascus from the outlying areas. There was nothing inside the van except for a stack of blankets piled up in a corner.

"Looks good," I said, closing the cargo doors. "Don't make the ride too easy on him, though. Try and find a few potholes along the way."

"Are you kidding?" Finn said. "I won't have any trouble finding potholes. Avoiding them is the problem. Every time the military orders an air strike on a rebel neighborhood, they destroy a few more roads."

"I understand they're bombing east of Damascus. Is that right?"

Dave nodded, "In the Ghouta district, There's a major rebel stronghold there, and the Syrian Air Force is hitting the area almost daily now. EAI has been assisting a lot of refugees from that area."

Finn said, "Dave and I almost got caught up in a bombing raid ourselves a couple of days ago."

"This run today won't be nearly as exciting as that," I said.

Pike, who'd been sitting inside his SUV talking on the phone, suddenly rushed over to the van.

As he tossed Dave the keys to the Renault, he said, "Marwan's on the move and headed toward Tekkiye Mosque for noonday prayers.

Carlton wants you and Dave to go ahead and pick him up before he gets there. He'll brief you on the way. We've now gone to Plan B."

When Pike got inside the EAI van with Finn, he said, "Finn and I will head over to the rendezvous site. Text me when you've picked Marwan up and then again when you're five minutes out."

"Roger that," I said.

Dave and I headed west in the Renault, and Pike and Finn drove off in the opposite direction in the EAI van.

A few seconds later, we heard Carlton's voice on the Agency sat phone I'd mounted on the dash of the Renault. "Trudy and I are tracking you on the Grid," he said. "Dave, turn left at the next intersection. Traffic is heavy on Hareth. Take Al Khouri instead. You need to push it but don't exceed the speed limit."

The Schematic Tracking Grid (STG), better known as the Grid, was the tracking system used by the Agency to monitor and locate the movements of its operatives in the field during an operation. The STG depended on the GPS devices in Agency phones, but there were also several backup systems, including reconnaissance satellites and drones.

"What's up with Marwan?" I asked. "Why did we have to go to Plan B?"

"The guy's been pacing his apartment all morning long. It made me nervous just watching him on the video. A few minutes ago, he—"

"He's probably anxious to hear from me. I consider that a good sign."

"That may be true, but a few minutes ago, he got a call from Rehman Zaidi. Zaidi asked Marwan to meet him at Tekkiye Mosque for noonday prayers, and Marwan immediately agreed."

"Zaidi has a lot of influence on Marwan. I don't like the sound of that."

"All the more reason to pick Marwan up before they have a chance to talk."

"We're still fifteen minutes out. I'm not sure that's possible."

"I'm confident you'll make it. The mosque is six blocks from Marwan's apartment, but he didn't take a taxi; he's on foot. I'm sending his coordinates to your phone right now. Pike's surveillance crew says he looks clean; no one's tailing him."

I glanced down at the map on my phone. A small blue dot appeared. It was slowly moving east.

"He's three blocks from the mosque now. We'll be cutting it close."

"Get it done."

With those encouraging words, Carlton disconnected the call.

♦♦♦♦

Five minutes later, Dave and I spotted Marwan a block away from the mosque. He was making his way along the crowded sidewalk on Al Nawfara Street, a narrow two-lane avenue lined with outdoor stalls and small shops.

Although Carlton had mentioned no one was following Marwan, I took a few extra seconds to make sure of that.

Then, as traffic slowed to a stop, I told Dave, "Let me out here. Circle the block and meet me at the corner. If I'm not there when you get there, leave the area and wait for my call."

When I got out of the SUV, I quickly punched in the numbers for the cell phone Carlton had given Marwan before they left Gitmo.

As I stood in the doorway across the street, I watched Marwan pull the phone from his pocket and glance down at the screen.

For a second, I thought he might ignore my call.

Instead, he answered with a tentative, "Hello?"

"It's me. I'm in the coffee shop on your left. Walk up to the intersection and head east. I'll meet you at the corner."

When Marwan hung up, he immediately looked over to his left, and I used the opportunity to slip out of the doorway and make my way down the opposite side of the street toward the corner. There was no sign of the Renault yet, but I still had a few minutes before going to my alternate plan.

I watched as Marwan walked past the coffee shop and paused at the corner, waiting for the light to turn green.

I saw him searching the crowd, as if he might be looking for a familiar face.

When the light turned green, he hurried across the street.

At the same time, Dave brought the Renault to a stop at the crosswalk, and I quickly opened the back door. As soon as Marwan stepped on the sidewalk, he spotted me standing beside the SUV.

Although he appeared surprised at my sudden appearance, he didn't balk when I motioned him inside the vehicle.

The moment I slid in the backseat beside him, Dave pulled away from the intersection.

Unfortunately, the rest of Operation Citadel Protection didn't go quite as smoothly as this textbook maneuver did.

# Chapter 39

After making sure Marwan didn't have a weapon on him, I leaned over the front seat and grabbed a bottle of water out of the cup holder.

He refused to take it when I offered it to him. "I was told you would call me today. No one said anything about any of this." He flapped his hand back and forth, indicating he meant the car, the situation, Dave, me, whatever.

"Plans change."

"Where are we going?"

I ignored his question and asked one of my own.

"Why did Zaidi want you to meet him at the mosque?"

He stared at me and didn't say anything.

I noticed his appearance had changed since the last time I'd seen him in Buenos Aires.

He looked drawn, almost gaunt, as if he'd recently lost a lot of weight. The dark circles underneath his eyes appeared even darker now, and his beard looked shabby, as if he hadn't trimmed it in several days.

I suspected the changes were due to a combination of jet lag and worry, or maybe it was something else entirely.

"How did you know Zaidi called me?" he finally asked.

It was my turn not to answer.

He bobbed his head up and down and said, "Oh, now I get it. You've wired my apartment. You're watching me."

"Answer the question, Marwan. Why did Zaidi insist on meeting you?"

He shrugged. "He said he wanted to talk to me before the general arrived. He's probably afraid Suleiman will blame him for Ahmed's death, and he wants my support. I plan to tell him it was Roberto Montilla who killed Ahmed."

"Send Zaidi a text and tell him you've changed your mind about meeting him. Say you're not feeling well."

Although I expected an argument from him, he pulled his cell phone from his pocket and typed out a brief message. I made him show it to me before allowing him to push the send button.

A few seconds later, Zaidi replied with the standard Islamic answer for a sick friend. *"La'ba'sa tahurun insha'Allah."*

Roughly translated, it meant, "Don't worry, this illness will purify you from your sins."

Sadly, this was impossible, even if Marwan had truly been ill.

♦♦♦♦

A few minutes later, after reaching the outskirts of Damascus, Dave headed north on Tishreen Boulevard. When Marwan realized we were on the road leading up to Mount Qassioun, he grew agitated.

"Why are we going up to Qassioun?"

"You'll know soon enough."

"Have you been in touch with my wife? Is she well? Can I talk to her soon?"

"That all depends on you."

He held his hands out toward me. "Look, I've already agreed to work for you. Didn't Mr. Chessman tell you I signed the documents at Gitmo? What more do you want from me?"

I didn't respond, and, after a few seconds, he turned away from me and stared out the window.

After traveling north for another mile, Dave veered west and entered Arawdah Gardens, a once beautiful botanical garden located halfway up the side of Mount Qassioun. Now, after years of neglect and poor management, the bushes were overgrown, the shrubs were untrimmed, and the weeds in the flower beds appeared to be the garden's most notable feature.

As Dave drove deeper into the forested area, I silently commended Pike for picking such a deserted spot, not only because of its privacy, but also because Marwan seemed more and more distressed with every passing minute.

After driving past a faded marker, Dave hit the brakes, put the car in reverse, and turned onto a rutted dirt road. A few minutes later, he pulled up in front of a dilapidated wooden building with a marker above the doorway indicating the structure used to be the Arawdah Gardens Research Center.

"What are we doing here?" Marwan asked, staring out at the building.

"Waiting."

"For what?"

I moved closer to him, violating his personal space.

"I'm waiting for you to tell me what kind of advice Hassan Naballah wants you to give General Suleiman at the meeting on Saturday."

Dave, who'd followed my instructions to the letter and not uttered a single word or even looked at Marwan since he'd gotten inside the car, suddenly shifted his weight to his right hip.

Then, in one fluid motion, he turned around and leveled his pistol at Marwan's head.

To say he looked menacing would be an understatement.

Marwan immediately shrank back in the leather seat. "I told you in Buenos Aires. I don't know why Naballah wants me at the meeting."

"We both know that's not true, Marwan. While you represent Hezbollah's interests in Latin America, very few of those activities would be relevant to General Suleiman's upcoming visit. Somehow, I doubt if he's concerned about the shipment of arms to the Colombian rebels. On the other hand, the general might be very interested in how the drug cartels are bringing their product into the United States."

I backed off and gave him some breathing room. "Is that why

Naballah wants you at the meeting? Does he want you to educate Suleiman on how to use the drug cartels to move the gas canisters north?"

"Ah . . . I'm not sure."

"You're not sure?"

I pulled a black hood from my pocket. "You're about to take a short trip, and I'd advise you to use the time to remember why Naballah wants you at that meeting. When we talk again, the only thing I want to hear from you is the truth."

I tossed the hood in his lap. "Put it on."

Marwan took one final look at Dave before placing the hood over his head.

"My friend will be transferring you to another vehicle in a few minutes. He'll be with you the whole time, so I don't advise removing the blindfold."

Marwan shook his head. "You're nothing like Mr. Chessman. When we were at Gitmo, he always treated me with respect."

"You're right. I'm nothing like Mr. Chessman. Be grateful for that."

♦♦♦♦

Five minutes later, Finn and Pike drove up in the EAI van. As soon as Pike got out, I joined him, leaving Dave in the Renault with Marwan.

When I walked up, Pike immediately asked, "What did he say about Zaidi?"

"He claims Zaidi's worried about the general's visit, and that's why he asked Marwan to meet him at the mosque. Evidently, Zaidi's afraid Suleiman will blame him for Ahmed's death."

Pike nodded. "He's probably right." He gestured over at the hooded Marwan. "How's he doing?"

"He didn't appreciate being grabbed off the street, and when he noticed I was bringing him up here, he got even more rattled."

"Have you learned anything yet?"

"No, but I have a feeling he'll be ready to talk by the time we get him back down to the safe house."

"Let's do it."

I signaled for Dave to put Marwan in the back of the EAI van. Once he'd shoved Marwan inside, he got in himself, and then Finn immediately headed back towards the entrance to the gardens.

Pike and I followed them in the Renault.

As Finn navigated the mountain curves at a high rate of speed, Pike used a bunch of colorful words to describe Finn's driving, but I reminded him Finn was only following my orders.

Earlier, I'd told Dave and Finn not to speak to Marwan once he was in their custody, and I felt certain their silence, plus being blindfolded during the wild ride down the mountain, would mean Marwan would arrive at the safe house even more off balanced than he was when I'd grabbed him off the street.

Using this disorientation technique on Marwan hadn't been a difficult decision for me. His personality appeared to lend itself to the psychology of this method, and, as far as I could tell, it was working.

When I'd briefed Pike on my plans for Marwan, he'd voiced his skepticism of my methods.

He said he preferred to use force to intimidate his assets into subjection, or, if they'd already demonstrated their compliance, to shower them with cash.

However, Pike and I both knew it didn't really matter what he thought of my approach.

Even though he was the primary for the mission, the DDO had told Carlton running Marwan was my responsibility, and he'd given me permission to handle him however I thought best.

While I appreciated the DDO's apparent confidence in me, I knew his real objective was to make sure Pike's cover didn't get blown. He didn't want anyone in Naballah's organization knowing that Keever Pike the journalist was, in reality, Keever Pike the spy.

Pike understood all this. However, that didn't stop him from making suggestions.

"You need to push him harder on why Naballah wants him at the meeting. The asset I was running in Naballah's organization said Marwan knew all the big players in the Mexican and Colombian cartels. I'm betting Naballah is planning to use the cartels in the general's operation."

"I'll keep that in mind."

This wasn't the first time Pike had mentioned the asset he'd been running inside Naballah's organization. While I was curious about the asset's identity, the fact that Pike hadn't told me who he was or what his position had been in the organization was a pretty good indication this loss was affecting him.

He pointed at the EAI van just ahead of us. "What's Finn doing now? Why is he heading east?"

As we both watched Finn take a left turn out of Arawdah Gardens, I said, "He must be taking the loop over to Asaker Road and heading south from there. I told him to make sure Marwan's ride was a memorable one."

He nodded. "That's where he's headed then. Asaker Road should be a rough ride since the Syrian Air Force targeted that area two days ago. Evidently, they discovered a small enclave of rebel fighters occupying a city block there and completely destroyed the neighborhood with an air strike."

As soon as Finn turned south on Asaker Road, the damage inflicted by the Syrian Air Force was immediately apparent. All but two of the high rise apartment buildings in the area lay in ruins. The floors were sandwiched one on top of the other, and the vehicles parked nearby were completely demolished. Concrete dust covered everything.

I saw a few people sifting through the debris, but everyone else was either taking pictures on their cell phones or just wandering around.

After traveling about a mile down the rough road, the Agency phone on the dashboard started pinging. Within seconds, Carlton was yelling instructions at us.

"Get out of there now!"

"Is there a—"

Before I could finish the sentence, I heard the distinct *thump, thump, thump* of a helicopter, and Pike pointed up at a couple of objects tumbling out of the aircraft.

"Barrel bombs," he shouted, quickly spinning the car around and reversing direction.

As Pike sped away, I saw the bombs hit the last two buildings still standing amidst the rubble. The explosion shook the Renault and quickly enveloped us in a huge dust cloud.

I yelled, "We need to check on the van."

"We need to get out of here first," he said, driving blindly through the murky cloud of dust and debris.

When I heard the muffled sound of Carlton's voice asking for a status report, I realized the sat phone had been jarred loose from the dashboard and had fallen to the floor.

After retrieving it, I told Carlton what was going on with Pike and me.

"What about the van?" I asked. "Is it still on the Grid?"

"I don't think it's been damaged. Trudy's talking with Finn right now, and the Grid shows the van is moving in your direction."

"Is Marwan okay?"

"She hasn't told me otherwise."

Pike, who was still driving blind, asked Carlton. "How far are we from the main intersection with Asaker?"

"Maybe half a mile."

Seconds later, the dust cloud began to clear, and we were able to see ahead of us.

"We've got eyes now," I told Carlton.

"That's good."

"That's debatable," I said, looking at the scene in front of us.

♦♦♦♦

Directly in front of us, the Syrian army had set up a roadblock. More than likely, they expected to catch any of the rebel fighters, who were fleeing the bombing. As soon as we emerged from the dust cloud, the officer in charge began to flag us down.

After giving Carlton a brief synopsis of what was going on, I dropped the phone in my pocket and grabbed the PRESS placard out of the glove box, displaying it across the front windshield. I also pulled my press ID lanyard out from underneath my shirt.

It identified me as Donovan Bartlett, credentialed journalist. It included a thumb-size photograph, but it wasn't a very good likeness; the photograph made me look like a much older man.

As we watched the soldier approaching our vehicle, Pike made sure his own ID was prominently displayed. "This could get dicey. The guy looks a little jumpy."

When the officer leaned in the window to take a look at our papers, Pike spun him an elaborate tale about how the two of us were gathering material for a story on the rebel stronghold and had just happened to be in the area when the bombs exploded.

As he examined our documents, the officer, whose insignia identified him as a captain, suddenly looked off to his right and noticed all the people emerging from the bombed out area.

One woman, covered in white, chalky dust, was holding the hand of a small child, who appeared to be bleeding from a head wound. The man following her was carrying a crying baby covered in blood, and behind him were dozens of other injured people. Some were in worse shape than others, but all looked dazed and confused.

The captain quickly gave us permission to leave the area and began directing his men to help the injured. As he walked away, I saw the EAI van pull in behind Pike's vehicle.

Pike put the Renault in gear and said, "Well, that was easy."

"Yeah, but look behind you."

The captain had flagged down the EAI van and was directing Finn to pull off the main road and park on the shoulder.

"He'll be expecting the EAI staff to start handing out emergency supplies to these people," I said, gesturing toward the crowds. "He may even want them to use the van to transport some of the critically injured to hospitals. We need to get Marwan out of the back of that vehicle as quickly as possible."

"Let Douglas know what's going on. I'll try to squeeze in behind the van."

I took out my sat phone and told Carlton what was happening on the ground, while Pike maneuvered the Renault through the crowded street and over to the side of the road.

Carlton said, "Some of the EAI staff are en route to your location with a full load of emergency kits. Whatever happens, you *have* to get

Marwan out of there. I'll patch you through to Dave, and the two of you can work out the details of how you're going to make that happen."

As Carlton was connecting me to Dave's phone, I noticed one of the soldiers was already directing a group of people on the street over to the EAI van. Then, as Pike managed to park behind the van, Dave came on the line.

"What's your status?" I asked. "Make it quick because you're about to have company."

"He's out cold."

"You mean Marwan?"

"Yeah. When those barrel bombs hit the buildings, we got shaken up pretty good. I think he must have hit his head. He's been out ever since."

"Is he still alive?"

"Other than the bump on his head, he seems fine."

"Let's hope that's true."

# Chapter 40

Sometimes, in order to hide something, it's better to put it out there in the open where everyone can see it. That's what I suggested we do with Marwan, and Pike agreed.

Of course, there were certain risks involved in doing it this way, and as I considered those risks, I suddenly remembered the promise I'd made to Nikki.

*"Promise me when you're away, especially during those times when you're required to take risks, you'll remember I'm praying for you."*

I remembered.

I phoned Dave. "You and Finn grab the blankets I saw in the back of the van and start distributing them on the street. Leave the cargo doors open when you walk away from the van."

"Gotcha."

The moment Dave and Finn took the blankets out of the van and started walking up the street, Pike and I got out of the Renault, walked over to the van, and climbed inside.

Marwan was lying face up on the floor of the van with a large goose egg on the right side of his head. He was still unconscious, and I wanted him to stay that way, at least for now.

After Pike and I positioned ourselves on either side of him, we each grabbed one of his shoulders and pulled him into a sitting position, Then, we dragged him to the back of the van, where we placed his arms across our shoulders. At this point, we half-carried, half-dragged him back to the Renault.

Just as we laid him out across the backseat, I glanced up and saw the captain approaching the SUV.

"What's happening here?" the captain asked, looking inside the window.

"We found this man on the side of the road over there," I said, pointing in the direction of the EAI van. "He needs to see a doctor."

The captain stared down at Marwan, studying his face as if he might look familiar. "Judging from his appearance, he wasn't caught up in the blast. Do you know how he got hurt?"

I was counting on the captain thinking the unconscious man was a member of the rebel insurgency group. If that were true, I knew he would immediately check him for some form of identification.

Pike said, "We're not sure how his injuries occurred."

"Was there any identification on him?"

"Yes," I said, handing over Marwan's wallet. "it's all in there."

The captain riffled through the wallet until he came to an ID card showing Marwan was a member of Hezbollah's executive council. Once he'd spotted the card, he immediately returned the wallet to me and said, "Get this man to a hospital immediately."

The captain waved at the soldiers guarding the roadblock and told them to let us through the barriers. As soon as we cleared the area and headed south toward the safe house, Marwan began to moan.

A few seconds later, his eyelids began to flutter. That's when I realized I'd left the black hood in the back of the van, which meant there was a real possibility Marwan would recognize that Keever Pike the journalist was, in reality, Keever Pike the spy.

In turn, this created the possibility—or perhaps the inevitability—the DDO wouldn't be happy with me for allowing that to happen.

♦♦♦♦

As Marwan struggled to fully regain consciousness, I texted Carlton two short sentences updating him on our status. He immediately texted back he was sending Trudy over to the safe house to assess

Marwan's injuries.

Just as Pike pulled in the garage at the safe house, Marwan sat up.

He touched the knot on the side of his head. "What happened? Where am I?"

I put off answering his questions until we were inside the house, and then, the only thing I told him was that we were somewhere safe.

He nodded and didn't ask any more questions about our location. As a long-time Hezbollah operative, I figured he knew I'd taken him to one of the Agency's safe houses.

When we entered the kitchen, Pike stopped and grabbed some bottles of fruit juice out of the refrigerator, offering one to Marwan.

Marwan took the bottle, but then he walked over to me and pointed to the bump on his head. "Did you do this to me?"

At that moment, I was tempted to tell him he'd been knocked unconscious as a taste of what could happen to him if he didn't cooperate with us. After thinking about it for a moment, I decided it was time to stop playing psychological games with him.

"No, that happened when the van you were riding in happened to be on Asaker Road when the Syrian Air Force decided to dump a couple of barrel bombs on their own citizens. Those explosions shook the van and caused you to hit your head. You can blame President Assad for that knot on your head."

"Naballah has condemned President Assad for targeting the Damascus neighborhoods," he said. "Hezbollah would never do such a thing."

I seriously doubted his assertion.

Barrel bombs were simply large metal containers filled with high explosives and shrapnel and dropped out of helicopters. However, Hezbollah often used those same kinds of devices to target Israeli troops in Lebanon or American troops in Iraq. Instead of using helicopters, though, they placed the containers on trucks and drove them to a crowded location, using a detonator to explode the devices.

"Since you brought up the subject of Naballah, are you ready to answer my questions now?" I asked.

Marwan sat down on the sofa across from Pike and ignored me.

After staring at Pike for several seconds, he asked, "Aren't you the American journalist who's been reporting on the civil war for *The Times*?"

"The same," Pike said, seemingly unconcerned about being identified.

"Do you also work for them?" Marwan asked, pointing his finger over at me.

When Pike nodded, Marwan said, "I don't imagine they're holding your wife and daughter prisoner so you'll cooperate with them, are they?"

"No, I more or less volunteered for this job."

I said, "Your wife and daughter haven't been harmed, Marwan. I'll prove it to you once you've answered my questions about Naballah."

"Prove it to me? You mean you'll show me another video?"

"No, if you answer my questions truthfully, you'll be able to talk with them in real time." I glanced at my watch. "In fact, it's possible you could speak to them within the hour."

Marwan sighed and lowered his head a moment, looking as if he might be ashamed of what he was about to say.

"What do you want to know?" he asked.

I wanted to know everything.

♦♦♦♦

I reminded Marwan of the conversation we'd had in Buenos Aires on Friday when I'd asked him about why he'd been invited to the meeting with General Suleiman.

"I asked you what advice Naballah wanted you to give the general. At that time, you said you didn't know. That wasn't true, was it?"

He shook his head. "No, that wasn't true. When Naballah ordered me to be at the meeting, he said I needed to convince General Suleiman our partnership with the Zeta cartel is reliable. He also wants me to explain how this partnership has allowed our operatives to set up sleeper cells in the U.S."

"Are the cells connected to the general's plans for the chemical weapons?"

"I don't know anything about how General Suleiman plans to use the weapons. Naballah just told me I should emphasize how easily the cartel is able to move their product into the United States. He told me to discuss the cartel's delivery options and shipping methods, and he said to talk about their reliability."

"Did he tell you why you needed to convince the general of the cartel's reliability?"

"Naballah never gives me a reason when he issues an order."

Marwan acted as if he might be about to add something to his statement, so I waited a second before questioning him further. But, instead of saying anything, he grabbed the bottle of juice he'd been drinking and drained it dry.

When he put it back down on the table, I noticed his right thumb was twitching. It was the same nervous gesture I'd seen him make in Buenos Aires whenever I'd mentioned the chemical weapons.

Pike asked, "Would you like something else to drink?"

"Let's have Marwan finish what he was about to say first," I said. "What were you about to tell us about the gas canisters?"

Marwan looked surprised at my question, but then he nodded and said, "Naballah didn't have to give me a reason why it was important for the general to hear how reliable the cartel was. I already knew why he wanted me to emphasize that."

He took a deep breath.

Later, I knew that was the moment he'd decided to cross the deep chasm of betrayal from which there would be no return.

"As soon as Naballah made the agreement with the Iranians to take possession of the remainder of Syria's chemical weapons, he had me contact one of the lieutenants in the Los Zetas organization. The man's name is Franco Cabello. He's the—"

"We know Cabello," I said. "He's the mastermind behind Los Zetas' smuggling operations. Why did Naballah have you contact him?"

"The agreement Naballah made with General Suleiman when he acquired the weapons was that some of the canisters would be transferred to a small contingent of Hezbollah fighters stationed on Margarita Island. These were the recruits trained by Rehman Zaidi.

The general wanted them to smuggle the canisters into the U.S."

Marwan looked away for a second. I couldn't tell whether he was reluctant to give me this information or he was just trying to remember the details.

He continued, "Naballah didn't believe Suleiman's plan would work, though. The sheikh didn't think the Venezuelan recruits had the expertise to do the job. That's why Naballah had me contact Cabello. Once I started negotiations with Los Zetas, he realized they had the means to get the weapons into the U.S. without putting the entire Hezbollah organization at risk."

"So Naballah entered into a contract with Los Zetas?"

Marwan nodded. "It was strictly a cash for services agreement."

Up to this point, Pike hadn't said anything and allowed me do the questioning. Now, though, he put on his journalist's hat and proceeded to question Marwan himself.

"Just to clarify your point. Are you saying Naballah went against the general's orders and handed the chemical weapons over to the drug cartel instead of giving them to the Hezbollah fighters trained by Zaidi?"

"That's right."

"How many canisters are we talking about here?" Pike asked.

"The agreement was for two shipping containers, which would be two hundred canisters."

Pike raised his eyebrows as if he'd never heard this number before. "That's a lot of sarin gas. So tell me about the agreement you worked out with Cabello. How does he plan to take possession of the canisters?"

"After Naballah gave him the names of the ships carrying the chemical weapons and their approximate time of arrival in Cuba, Cabello refused to give out the specifics of his operation. He didn't give Naballah any details of the offloading procedure or how he planned to transport the canisters to the U.S."

"And Naballah agreed to this?"

Marwan nodded and looked down at his feet. "I'm assuming Los Zetas has already taken possession of those canisters by now. They're probably on their way to the States at this moment."

Pike and I made eye contact.

We'd come to a pivotal juncture in the interrogation process, and we both knew it. I also figured Marwan knew it, and he was just waiting for one of us to ask him the critical question. Once we did, he'd try to wring some more concessions from us.

I asked him the question."If Los Zetas has taken possession of the gas canisters, what happens next?"

Marwan looked me in the eye. "Before I give you that information, do I have your word you'll protect me and my family?"

I nodded. "You have my word."

We both stared at each for a few seconds; one of us wanting to believe the other; one of us willing the other to believe.

Finally he said, "Franco Cabello will call Naballah on Saturday morning, just before Suleiman arrives. At that time, he'll let him know the timing of when the canisters will arrive in Washington and the procedure for turning them over."

"I'm guessing Naballah wants you there with him so you can translate for him during that conversation?"

"That's right."

I tried to refrain from showing any emotion on the outside, but on the inside, I was doing cartwheels.

Forty-eight hours from now, we might not only know the details of how Suleiman planned to attack Washington, but also the location of the missing canisters.

Whether it was the stress of revealing this information, or the blow he'd suffered to his head, Marwan lowered his head and began massaging his temples.

"Could I have something for this headache?" he asked.

Although I hated to admit it, having access to this vital intel was totally dependent on one man, and, right now, he wasn't looking too good.

♦♦♦♦

When Pike got up to get Marwan some aspirin, the security system surrounding the outside perimeter of the safe house suddenly sounded an alert.

Pike and I both drew our weapons.

However, within seconds, we determined the alarm had been triggered by Trudy, who was standing at the front door holding her medical bag. She apologized as soon as Pike let her inside.

"I guess I should have let you know I was on my way over," she said, eyeing Pike's gun, "but I thought you knew I was coming."

"My bad," Pike said. "We were in the middle of something."

"You're just in time," I said, pointing over at Marwan. "Here's your patient, and he's complaining of a headache."

Marwan was less than enthusiastic when he realized Trudy was about to examine his head, but she ignored his skittishness and ran her fingers gently over the bruised area at the edge of his scalp.

After answering her questions, he appeared to relax a little. Second later, when Trudy got right up next to him in order to examine his pupils with her penlight, I saw the shadow of a smile flit across his face.

I figured Pike, who couldn't take his eyes off Trudy, had also observed Marwan's behavior, because he immediately asked, "So what's the verdict? Will the patient die any time soon?"

Marwan didn't seem to find Pike's question amusing.

Trudy put her penlight away and said, "I'm certain he's going to die one day, but, for now, he'll probably just have a headache for a few hours. As far as I can tell, he's fine."

"In that case," I said, "I believe it's time for us to make a phone call to Caracas."

Marwan looked as if he couldn't quite believe what he was hearing. "I can speak to my wife and daughter now?"

Before I had a chance to respond, Trudy looked over at me and said, "There's something we need to discuss first." She pointed up to the loft. "We should probably go upstairs to do that."

Pike remained in the living room with Marwan, while I followed Trudy up to the loft. As soon as we reached the landing, I asked, "What's wrong? Is Marwan really okay?"

"He'll be fine. This has nothing to do with Marwan."

Trudy walked over to a computer and typed in some numbers.

"The Ops Center will be updating Mr. Carlton in a few minutes, and he wants you in on the call."

"Has something happened?"

"I don't know the details yet, but I heard Ben Mitchell missed his last scheduled check in with the RTM Center. That was several hours ago."

I was running through some possibilities in my head and didn't respond. *What happened, Ben? Where are you?*

Trudy must have thought my silence meant I was worried about Mitchell.

"Don't worry. He could be following a lead on the missing canisters, or maybe he lost track of time."

"I'm not worried."

*What happened, Ben? Where are you?*

# Chapter 41

As soon as I sat down at the conference table, Carlton's face filled up the video monitor's screen. Within a few seconds, Trudy had changed the view to the picture-in-a-picture option, reducing Carlton's feed to a small square at the bottom of the video. The rest of the screen stayed blank.

Carlton must have sensed I was about to ask him a question.

"Don't start quizzing me about what's going on in Cuba," he said. "I won't answer any questions until after we hear from C.J."

"That's fine," I said, even though it wasn't.

"While we're waiting, give me an update on Marwan. Have you had a chance to question him? Is he okay?"

I answered both questions in the affirmative, and then I briefed Carlton on what Marwan had told me about Los Zetas' involvement in the acquisition of the two shipping containers.

Although he didn't show it, I thought he sounded pleased about the new intel.

"So the cartel's involved in the missing canisters. I guess that means we should give it up to Salazar for calling this one right. I'm sure Keever won't be too happy when he finds out he lost that argument."

"That's for sure."

I decided it wasn't a good time to tell him Pike had already heard this information from Marwan himself.

Carlton asked, "Now that you've had a chance to question him, what's your assessment of Marwan? Can we count on his cooperation?"

"As long as I keep reminding him of what's at stake with his wife and daughter, he's not offering much resistance. Whether that resolve will hold up when he meets with the general might be problematic. I understand Suleiman can be pretty intimidating."

"It's absolutely vital we learn all the details of the attack on Washington and what's happening with the canisters. If you have to put more pressure on Marwan, do it."

I was surprised to hear the harsh tone in Carlton's voice, and I wondered if it had anything to do with events on the ground in Cuba.

I didn't have to wonder long.

Seconds later, Salazar came online.

♦♦♦♦

In a repeat of the scene from yesterday's briefing, the camera was displaying a view of the Agency's RTM Center C, where Salazar could be seen seated at the main console.

This time, however, Katherine Broward was seated at the console next to him, along with a couple of other analysts from the ASA division.

As soon as Salazar made note of the operation's identification tag for the official record, he pointed out the obvious presence of Katherine, although he failed to mention the other analysts.

"Ms. Broward is here at my request, and she'll be briefing you on her findings shortly. First, though, I wanted to address the situation in Santiago."

He pointed to a street map of Santiago de Cuba on the wide-screen monitor just above his head.

In an area southeast of the city, near the docks, was a small blue dot. The map had a notation in the bottom right hand corner, which identified it as coming from the Schematic Tracking Grid.

Below the STG label were the words *Operation Citadel Protection, Component Two, Primary Location*, which meant the map was pinpointing the location of the primary operative running the mission in Santiago.

In other words, we were looking at Ben Mitchell's location on the Grid in Santiago.

Ordinarily, whenever an operative's phone or communication device was locatable, a small blue dot on the Grid blinked or pulsated occasionally.

Mitchell's blue dot was not blinking.

It had no pulse.

Salazar said, "Around four o'clock this morning, which would have been around eleven o'clock Damascus time, the Ops Center received a text message from Ben, along with a single photograph."

Salazar pointed to the blue dot on the screen. "The Grid had him at this location when he sent the message. Shortly after that, he went dark, and the Grid hasn't been able to pick up his signal since then."

I glanced down at the video at the bottom of the monitor to see whether Carlton had any reaction to this news. But, other than his pursed lips, his face remained impassive.

The monitor above Salazar's head changed to a screenshot of a text message from an Agency sat phone.

Salazar said, "Here's the message Ben sent to the Ops Center. It includes the photograph."

Mitchell's text contained just two words, "*Found them.*"

Directly below the text, was a dimly lit photograph of two orange shipping containers. The Hazardous Materials warning was stenciled across the sides.

The angle of the camera made it difficult to tell if the containers were in a warehouse or on a ship, but stacked alongside them, were a couple of pallets loaded with boxes, plus some wooden crates.

As soon as I saw the image, I felt an immediate rush.

Mitchell had located the missing containers! My euphoria was soon tempered by the realization of what the non-pulsating blue dot meant.

Salazar said, "As soon as the Grid lost contact with Ben, the STG system tried pinging his sat phone. At that time, there was no response, and there's been no response since then. Ben missed the mandatory update with the Center at seven o'clock this morning, and the rest—"

"What about the other members of his surveillance team?" I asked. "Have you been able to contact any of—"

"As I was about to say, the rest of the members of his surveillance team have been contacted and all of them are in place. Until we locate Ben, they've been told to keep a low profile."

Carlton started peppering him with questions. "Could they tell you anything about Ben's location? What about the tracks he left behind on the Grid? Was that message sent to anyone else on his team?"

As if he Carlton's rapid-fire grilling had overwhelmed him, Salazar hesitated for a few seconds, "Ah . . . Let's see . . ."

He picked up the blue operations notebook on the console and began reading from it. "Juliana Lamar said she and Ben were together at the safe house around midnight. She said he talked about investigating some of the warehouses located further away from the dock, even though he knew it was a long shot. Juliana said she agreed to go with him at first light, but she had no idea Ben had left the house, until she woke up this morning. The last time anyone else heard from him was around eight o'clock last night."

Salazar looked up from the notebook and asked the STG operations officer to upload the tracks Ben had left on the Grid in the hours before transmitting the text.

The map of Santiago reappeared on the screen, but this time, there were a series of red dots noting where Mitchell had been prior to uploading the photograph. The locations were only archived on an hourly basis, so it wasn't exactly a precise trail of where an operative had been.

Salazar used a laser pointer to mark the location of the safe house, noting that Mitchell was there until two o'clock, when the Grid showed him further west. At three o'clock, a red dot showed him about a mile from his final transmission point.

Salazar turned to his right and looked at Katherine. "Ms. Broward's findings will further clarify what the Grid is showing us on the map."

Katherine smiled at the camera and said, "Good afternoon,

everyone."

Once Carlton and I had greeted her, she picked up a remote mouse and clicked it once, using the laser pointer to draw an imaginary circle around the blue dot on Mitchell's last location.

"Ben sent the photograph and the text from here. We've identified it as a nightclub, Club Nocturno."

Katherine clicked the mouse again, and an image of the bar appeared on the screen. Like most Latin American nightlife establishments, this one had a colorful exterior with a garish neon sign and a large outdoor seating area.

I could easily picture Mitchell sitting at one of the tables, uploading his message to the Ops Center, and patting himself on the back for following through on his instincts.

*What happened, Ben? Where are you?*

"Club Nocturno is approximately a block away from this warehouse," Katherine said, bringing up an aerial view of a nondescript building covering almost a city block. "The tracks left behind on the Grid indicate he was here an hour before his last known location."

I saw Salazar smiling, so I immediately knew where Katherine's report was taking us.

She said, "This warehouse, Almacén Santiago, contains a variety of products, including farm machinery and canned goods, but most notably, it serves as a holding area for shipments of heroin and cocaine from Barranquilla, Colombia."

The next slide, an exterior shot, showed a gray concrete building surrounded by a high chain link fence.

"This is the front view of Almacén Santiago. It's owned by a high-ranking member of the Los Zetas drug cartel, and we believe there's a high probability this is where Ben took the photograph of the shipping containers."

Katherine turned to one of the other analysts seated next to her and had him explain the procedure used to examine the photograph Ben had sent. It sounded like mumbo-jumbo to me, but I understood enough to be convinced Mitchell had probably snapped the photo from there.

As soon as he was finished, Carlton said, "Titus interrogated an asset today who admitted Hezbollah has contracted with Los Zetas to bring the canisters into the U.S. That warehouse must be where they took the containers after offloading them from the ship."

Before Salazar responded, I said, "It seems pretty obvious the cartel must have caught Ben snooping around the warehouse, followed him to the bar, and then grabbed him after he'd texted you."

Salazar nodded. "That's our conclusion as well." He glanced at his watch. "The DDO said he'd be down any minute to discuss our options for dealing with the situation. I'll be recommending a SOF unit be deployed to Santiago immediately."

The Select Operations Force (SOF) was a specialized division of the Agency comprised of highly trained units of rapid deployment teams. They stood ready to respond whenever Agency personnel went missing anywhere in the world.

I had worked with a couple of SOF units before, and I felt confident they'd be able to locate Mitchell. I just prayed they'd find him before it was too late.

As Salazar signed off, he said, "At least we can rest a little easier tonight knowing those gas canisters are nowhere near Washington."

Was that really true?

I had my doubts.

♦♦♦♦

Immediately after Salazar terminated the conference call, Trudy changed the picture-in-picture option on the monitor in front of me, and Carlton's face reemerged on the screen looking bigger than life.

Despite that, when he began discussing the situation in Santiago, I found it nearly impossible to read the expression on his face.

On the one hand, he looked angry.

On the other hand, he looked depressed.

With so much at stake, I decided I had to know which one it was, and I interrupted him in mid-sentence and asked Trudy if she'd mind going downstairs and bringing Marwan up to the loft.

Once she'd left, I apologized to Carlton for the interruption, and he resumed the point he was making about Mitchell's missing status. It wasn't long before I began to notice he wasn't mentioning Mitchell by name. Instead, he was using "he" and "his actions."

When he'd finished, I asked him, "Do you know something about Ben you're not telling me?"

He looked surprised. "You heard the same intel as I did."

"I'm sorry, Douglas, but you're not answering my question."

Just in case he might be trying to hide behind a curtain of deniability, I said, "I'll make it easier on you by asking my question a different way. Besides C.J., have you talked to anyone else at the Agency about Ben?"

He looked away for a second.

That told me all I needed to know.

Now, I fully expected him to dodge the question.

For some reason, he didn't.

"Yes, the DDO let me know about Ben's status before I heard it from the Ops Center. I probably don't need to tell you what that means."

"It means Ben's disappearance has political implications."

Carlton nodded. "By law, the Agency must inform the Senate Intelligence Committee whenever an officer goes missing during an ongoing operation. As you probably know, the head of that committee is—"

"Senator Elijah Mitchell," I said, finishing his sentence. "Please tell me he doesn't know Ben is the missing operative."

He shook his head. "No names were given at the briefing, but should the situation not be resolved soon, the DDO believes the Senator will demand to know if the missing officer is his son."

"Of course he will."

Carlton's eyes widened. "I wasn't aware you knew the Senator that well."

"Ben and I have had plenty of conversations about his father. I think I know him pretty well."

"Then you'll understand the DDO's concern. You'll appreciate why he got in touch with me after the briefing."

I thought about it for a second. "I'm guessing the DDO isn't fully convinced the cartel has Ben. Is he thinking Hezbollah could have grabbed him?"

Carlton nodded. "That's what he's thinking, and he wants you to have Marwan bring up the subject with Naballah."

Although I tried to control my temper, I knew there had to be an edge to my voice. "You know that's not Marwan's role on the council. He can't bring up topics for discussion; he's strictly a consultant. If he acts otherwise, Naballah will get suspicious of him."

"I'm aware of that, and, more than likely, the cartel has Ben. I'm just hoping our SOF unit will locate him before the meeting on Saturday."

"If not, then perhaps Franco Cabello will mention Ben in connection with the canisters."

Carlton shook his head. "I think you're grasping at straws there. If Cabello's men discovered someone in their warehouse taking pictures, they wouldn't tell Naballah about it."

"What about those containers, Douglas. Does the fact they're still in that warehouse bother you at all?"

He looked away for a second. "Well, now that you brought it up, I guess it does. Since Marwan said the canisters should be on their way to the States by now, it seems strange Ben was able to photograph them in the warehouse this morning."

"That's my point. Even though Ben photographed what appears to be the two missing containers, I'm betting those containers are empty now."

"So you're saying the cartel has already removed the canisters from the containers?"

"That's exactly what I'm saying. I believe those weapons are on their way to the States right now, and Ben risked his life to photograph some empty shipping containers."

## Chapter 42

When Trudy brought Marwan up to the loft, I could tell he wasn't going to be comfortable speaking to his wife with another woman present, so I told Trudy I'd handle the uplink with Caracas myself, and she went back downstairs.

After she left, I warned Marwan, "Don't say a word to your wife and daughter about your location and don't say anything about when you might be seeing them again."

"No, of course not."

Yamina and Samira Farage appeared on the screen a few seconds after I initiated the call to the safe house in Caracas. For operational security, Marwan couldn't see Sam Wylie or any other Agency personnel who might be in the room, and the ladies weren't able to tell if there was anyone in the room with Marwan.

Although their conversation was emotional at times, I knew Marwan had to be reassured when he saw his wife and daughter were unharmed, even if they weren't happy about their confinement.

I allowed him to talk with them for twenty minutes—five minutes longer than I'd intended—and then I signaled Marwan it was time to wrap things up. As he tried to tell Yamina goodbye, she issued an impassioned plea for him to do whatever was necessary in order to end their ordeal.

By the look on his face, I could tell he was moved by her tearful petition, and I decided if I'd scripted the whole thing myself, I couldn't have wished for a better outcome.

When Marwan finally said goodbye, he turned to me and said, "I want to be on the next plane to Caracas as soon as I leave the meeting with the general."

"Do what you're told, and I guarantee that dream will become a reality."

He looked me in the eye. "I'm prepared to do whatever it takes."

I believed him.

♦♦♦♦

After taking a break for dinner, the four of us went back up to the loft in order to introduce Marwan to the gadgets he'd be using during his meeting with Naballah.

These technological marvels would be the only means the Ops Center had of observing what went on inside Naballah's compound on Saturday.

When I mentioned this to Marwan, he immediately protested. "As soon as I arrive at the compound, the security guards search me. They take away my cell phone and scan anything else I have with me."

"Don't worry. Everything I give you will pass their inspection."

I picked up a package wrapped in plastic and handed it to Marwan. "This is what you'll be wearing Saturday morning when you arrive at the compound."

He tore it open and pulled out a white *thobe*, a long loose tunic worn over a pair of trousers, the common attire of most Muslim men.

"Put this on," I said, "and I'll show you some special features of your new clothes."

Once Marwan had slipped the *thobe* over his head and buttoned up the opening, I nodded at Trudy who clicked a program on her computer.

"We're set," she said.

Stepping in front of him, I twisted the bottom button on the tunic opening, and then I took a couple of steps back.

The screen in front of Trudy pixilated for a moment, and then there was a clear shot of me, standing just a few feet away.

"Not a bad likeness," Pike said.

Marwan turned to his left, and the view on the computer screen changed to a shot of Pike, who was seated in the only comfortable chair in the room.

I walked over and twisted the button on the *thobe* again and the video disappeared altogether.

"A metal detector won't pick this up?" Marwan asked, removing the tunic and taking a closer look at the button.

After assuring him it was undetectable, he asked, "What about sound? I didn't hear any audio."

"The camera on the *thobe* will only broadcast video. Audio acquisition will require something a little different."

I picked up a couple of small purple boxes. One fit easily in the palm of my hand and reminded me of a velvet ring box, something a jeweler might use to display an engagement ring.

Just thinking about that analogy made me feel a little funny.

"Here are the gifts you'll be carrying with you when you arrive at Naballah's headquarters. You'll give one to Naballah, and the other one you'll present to the general."

Marwan's eyes narrowed. "I guess that means you're aware the council members often bring Naballah a gift when he calls a security council meeting?"

"Yes, we know about such practices."

This admission seemed to bother him less than I thought it would.

He opened one of the purple boxes.

Inside, was a gleaming gold nugget about the size of a quarter. It was nestled on a piece of black velvet.

"Oh, that's beautiful," Trudy said.

Along with the nugget was a label certifying the gold had been mined in Santa Elena, Venezuela, one of the country's most famous gold mines.

I opened the second box and revealed a similar nugget. "When you present these gifts, you should tell General Suleiman and Hassan Naballah you purchased the gold nuggets for them while you were vacationing with your family in Venezuela."

Marwan nodded, carefully looking over the box he was holding. "Is the nugget capable of transmitting sound?"

I shook my head. "No. The audio transmitters are actually embedded inside the boxes themselves. The men would have to tear the boxes apart to find the transmitters, but we don't think that will happen."

Marwan quickly closed the purple box with a snap. "You don't think that will happen? And what if it does? If they find the transmitters, I won't be allowed to leave the compound alive."

Before I had a chance to respond, Pike got out of his chair and walked over to where Marwan was seated.

"Nothing like that will happen," he said, sitting down beside him. "We've studied the psychology behind these gifts, and the results are indisputable. Even though the nuggets aren't worth all that much, just the idea of owning gold recently taken out of a mine creates such a visceral feeling of raw power, it's guaranteed to overwhelm all other emotions. Once these men unwrap their gifts, they won't be able to think about anything else."

As if he were quoting from an article he'd written, Pike explained how mankind's love affair with gold went back thousands of years and encompassed every ethnicity. He cited statistics, told a couple of anecdotes, and ended up giving Marwan a mini-lesson on the precious metal's history. Although I knew exactly what he was doing, he did it so well, I found it fascinating.

Of course, almost everything Pike said—except the history lesson—was a bunch of malarkey. However, Marwan appeared to be placated by this diversionary tactic, and, at that moment, I was optimistic he wouldn't have any more concerns about the transmitters inside the purple boxes.

Had Rehman Zaidi not called Marwan a few minutes later, I'm certain that would have been the case.

♦♦♦♦

As soon as I asked Trudy to put up an aerial view of western Damascus where Naballah's compound was located, Marwan's phone vibrated.

When he pulled it from his pocket, he glanced down at the screen and said, "It's Rehman Zaidi. Should I answer it?"

I nodded, "Put it on speaker. He probably wants to know how you're feeling."

After giving the traditional Muslim greeting, *"Assalamu alaikum,"* Zaidi inquired about Marwan's health.

"I'm much better now," he said.

"You sound better. What made you ill?"

Marwan looked up at the ceiling a moment, and then he touched the bump on his head. "I fell and hit my head in the stairwell of my apartment just as I was leaving for the mosque. I thought I might pass out."

I nodded at Marwan, letting him know I was pleased at how he was handling himself.

Zaidi said, "You won't miss the meeting on Saturday, will you?"

"I'll be fine by then."

"That's good, because if General Suleiman questions me about Ahmed's death, I want to be able to count on your support. I plan to tell him it was Roberto Montilla who killed him, and it wasn't my fault."

"Roberto killed my cousin. I'm sure of that."

"I've heard rumors the general was close friends with Ahmed."

"That's true. Ahmed once told me so himself."

"I'm sure you understand my concern then. The general might consider me his enemy because I didn't protect his friend. I could end up dead."

"Why would you think such a thing?"

"He's been known to take out his pistol and shoot someone who disagrees with him. I'm afraid if he believes I'm responsible for Ahmed's death, that could happen to me."

I noticed Marwan eyeing the purple boxes on the table. "You could be right," he said.

I was afraid Zaidi's paranoia was beginning to rub off Marwan, so I drew my finger across my throat, indicating he should cut the call short. I immediately regretted the gesture, but Marwan got the message.

He said, "I have to go now, Rehman. I'll see you on Saturday."

After Marwan disconnected the call, there was no mistaking the look on his face. It was clouded over with worry.

I quickly pointed to the aerial view of Naballah's compound and said, "I was just about to explain the plans we have for getting you out of the compound in case you run into a problem."

Pike looked surprised.

I assumed it was because Carlton had told us not to discuss those plans with Marwan.

♦♦♦♦

I pointed to a spot on the map just outside a cordoned off area around Naballah's headquarters. The whole section encompassed a city block and had been designated a security zone by the Syrian government.

I said, "While you're inside the compound, the three of us will be here on Bin Abdul Road."

He studied the map for a second and then nodded. "If we believe you're in trouble, we have the means to create a diversion and get you out of the compound immediately."

Marwan looked thoughtful for a moment. He pointed over to the *thobe*, which he'd carefully folded up and placed on the table. "But if something goes wrong with that camera, how will you be able to determine if I'm in trouble?"

I looked over at Trudy and said, "Show him the Grasshopper."

Trudy nodded and picked up a small gray box from the table beside her.

Inside the box was what appeared to be an ordinary Syrian locust, the most common type of grasshopper found in the Middle East.

She removed the brown metal bug from the box and placed it on the edge of the table. After picking up what looked like a mobile phone with a gamepad attached, she pressed a button.

The Grasshopper immediately took flight, and, as Trudy manipulated the controls on the gamepad, it began making a circular route around the room.

I walked over to the computer and said, "Here's how this works,

Marwan."

I touched an icon on Trudy's computer, and the monitor on the table in front of Marwan immediately displayed the Grasshopper's view of the room.

"As you can tell, besides the camera on your *thobe*, we'll have several other means of seeing inside the room. Don't act surprised if you see one of these insects land on a window during the meeting."

For the first time since speaking with his wife and daughter, Marwan smiled. "Oh, that's good," he said, nodding his head.

I wondered if Carlton would feel the same way about my disclosure.

♦♦♦♦

When I finished demonstrating the attributes of the Grasshopper, I asked Marwan if he usually drove his own car to Naballah's compound.

"No, that never happens. Tomorrow evening, I'll receive a phone call from Naballah's personal assistant telling me what time I should expect to be picked up the following morning."

"What's the assistant's name?" I asked.

Marwan hesitated. "Ah . . . his new assistant is Jamal Isa. He took Rasha Mansour's place after Rasha was accused of being an Israeli spy. You can probably guess what Naballah did to him after that."

I stole a quick glance over at Pike. I felt sure Rasha Mansour must have been the asset who'd been feeding Pike the intel about Naballah's inner circle, More than likely, he was the person identified as the UA in the transcript I'd seen during my briefing.

Although Pike had his eyes glued to a spot on the floor, it was easy to read the pained expression on his face.

I could identify with his loss. No matter how I felt about an asset while I was running him, I always felt terrible if he got caught, especially if I hadn't been able to warn him he was in danger.

I quickly changed the subject and moved the conversation from Rasha Mansour over to General Suleiman.

In an effort to keep it simple and lessen Marwan's anxiety, I told him we were primarily interested in three pieces of intel.

"We want to know the exact date of the planned attack on Washington, how the chemical weapons will be used, and where the weapons are at this moment."

Marwan nodded. "I should know all of that by the end of the meeting," He pointed over to the purple boxes. "Won't you also be able to hear what the general has to say?"

"You're right, of course, but if the general or Naballah fails to bring up one of the points I've just made, you'll be responsible for getting the answers for us."

Marwan looked worried. "How can I do that? I'm only there to give my opinion. Unless someone specifically asks me a question, I'm supposed to keep my mouth shut."

Pike spoke up. "Give Naballah and the general your opinion. Say something radical. Do something dramatic. Create a controversy. Start an argument with someone. You'd be surprised how much information you can get out of a person that way."

I figured Pike was speaking from experience, but his suggestion seemed to carry some weight with Marwan.

He nodded. "I guess I could do that."

On that positive note, I decided it was time to wrap things up.

I asked, "What happens when Naballah adjourns the council? Does the driver take you back to your apartment or do you call a taxi?"

"The same driver who picks me up always takes me back home or drops me wherever I want to go."

"Okay, that's good. Once you leave Naballah's compound, have the driver drop you off at Bakdash. Tell him you'll walk home from there."

Bakdash was a popular ice cream establishment in Damascus. It was famous for its pistachio-covered ice cream, and it was the perfect place to meet an asset, because it was always crowded.

Marwan seemed noticeably excited by this information. "Does this mean when I leave Naballah's compound I won't be going back to my apartment?"

"That's right. The moment you step inside Bakdash, you'll be on your way to Caracas. Order your favorite ice cream, find yourself a table, and wait for me to show up."

"You make it sound so simple," he said, shaking his head. "We all know it will turn out to be much more complicated than that."

He was right.

# PART FIVE

## Chapter 43

*Saturday, July 4*

On the Fourth of July, at nine o'clock in the morning, Pike and I arrived in the parking lot of an abandoned warehouse off Bin Abdul Road. The building was located about two hundred yards outside the security zone set up around Naballah's compound.

The warehouse belonged to Aramex, a parcel delivery service, but soon after the Syrian civil war had reached the outskirts of Damascus, it had boarded up its doors.

Even after leaving the city, several of their delivery trucks were still parked in the lot outside the warehouse, and Pike had maneuvered the truck we were driving into a spot alongside one of them.

While our vehicle had the Aramex logo on the outside and looked exactly like the other trucks in the lot, the interior resembled a mini version of an Ops Center control room. Lining both sides of the vehicle were four video monitors, and mounted below them were two computers and the rest of the tech equipment from the safe house.

Pike and I had been sitting inside the cramped quarters of the truck for about twenty minutes when all four of the surveillance monitors sprang to life.

Although Carlton had said the feed from the Ops Center would be available shortly after we arrived at the warehouse, I wasn't expecting to see anything on the screens until Naballah's driver picked Marwan up from his apartment—approximately twenty minutes from now.

Pike seemed as surprised as I was by the images we were seeing. But, after taking a closer look at the feed, we both realized we were only viewing aerial shots of Damascus from the two Agency drones flying overhead.

In addition to the drone footage, we could also see a live shot of the grounds inside Naballah's compound. This feed was coming from a camera on the rooftop of a residence located about three blocks away from us.

According to Pike, when one of his surveillance guys had scaled the outer wall to install it on the roof, he'd almost been discovered by the homeowner.

Pike pointed to an image on one of the monitors and said, "Monitor #4 is a view of the south gate. It's the one Naballah's driver will use when he brings Marwan into the compound."

Pike's explanation was primarily for Carlton, who was over at EAI headquarters receiving the exact same feed as we were.

The three of us, along with Trudy, were wearing headsets linked up to the Agency's secure communications system (SCS). Anything we said on the SCS network could be heard in the Ops Center back at Langley—unless one of us deliberately pushed the mute button.

Carlton immediately commented on Pike's statement. "From this angle, I believe we'll also be able to identify the general's entourage."

Trudy, who was two miles away from the Aramex warehouse and didn't have access to the images we were seeing, said, "I guess I'll have to catch that movie later."

Pike said, "The only movie I care about seeing is the one you'll be making with the Grasshopper."

Trudy was inside the Renault in a residential area overlooking Naballah's compound to the east. Pike had chosen the site because it offered the least obstructive route for Trudy to navigate the Grasshopper over to the second story window of Naballah's library, which was where we'd heard the general would be meeting with

Naballah in less than two hours.

We had received this intel on Friday, when the general had checked into his suite at the Sheraton.

Not long after General Suleiman's arrival, Naballah's assistant had called him to confirm the details of the meeting, and the listening devices Pike had installed inside the suite had picked up every word of their conversation.

Unfortunately, the general was either a man of few words or extremely cautious on the phone, and, except for the time and place of the meeting, we hadn't gained any new intel.

"Here we go," Pike said.

He pointed to Monitor #1, which displayed an aerial view of a black SUV pulling up to the front of Marwan's apartment.

As soon as the car arrived, Marwan hurried out of the building wearing his white *thobe*.

In his hand was a small plastic bag.

Presumably, inside the bag, were two purple boxes.

♦♦♦♦

We watched as the black SUV made its way through the city streets of Damascus and arrived at the south gate of Naballah's compound.

Even though the security guards must have recognized the driver and Marwan, they still carefully scrutinized their passes and looked inside the trunk of the vehicle. After that, one of the guards ran a long mirrored pole underneath the body of the vehicle to check for explosive devices.

Finally, after the gate slid open, the SUV was allowed to enter the compound. From there, the driver made his way around to the front entrance of Naballah's headquarters.

When he stopped in the circle drive, Marwan emerged from the vehicle and walked over to the portico of the building, pausing to straighten his white *thobe* before walking inside. The moment he'd finished adjusting his *thobe*, an image pixilated across Monitor #2, and now, we were able to see what Marwan was seeing as he entered the foyer of Naballah's headquarters.

Inside the high-ceiling hall, with its black and white checkered floor, was a metal detector manned by a couple of guards. They immediately took Marwan's cell phone and did a thorough scan of the contents of his plastic bag. They also insisted on removing a ballpoint pen they discovered in the pocket of his white trousers when they patted him down.

Since the Ops Center had not yet activated the audio devices inside the purple boxes, there was no sound to go with the images we were seeing on Monitor #2. Still, I could have sworn I heard Marwan breathe a sigh of relief when the guards waved him through the metal detector.

Once he'd taken the elevator up to the second floor, he was met by two additional security guards standing in front of a set of double doors. After one of the guards used his handheld wand to scan the plastic bag yet again, the other guard opened the door and ushered him inside.

Upon entering the room, Marwan paused a moment, and, although I had no way of knowing for certain, I thought he might be surprised to see he was the only person inside Naballah's library.

What surprised me, though, was the decision someone had made to call the room a library. That person was either unacquainted with the concept or was being factitious, because the room contained only one bookcase, and there were fewer than a dozen books on its shelves.

Next to the bookcase, was an oversized pedestal desk. Despite its name, it was obvious the room functioned mainly as a place to receive guests and conduct official business.

In addition to a half dozen overstuffed armchairs, there were two upholstered sofas, with a small wooden table at the end of each sofa. Except for the beautiful Persian rug partially covering the hardwood floor, the room was colorless and had a dull, utilitarian look to it.

To Marwan's left, behind one of the sofas, was a long table. On most days, it probably functioned as Naballah's conference table. Today, however, it held a variety of pastries, beverages, and fruit.

Marwan headed there soon after entering the room.

I thought I knew why he was drawn to that spot.

It wasn't necessarily because he was hungry.

Since the conference table had been set up underneath a picture window overlooking the compound, I figured Marwan wanted to see if the Grasshopper had arrived yet.

As he stood in front of the table, I knew he must have been disappointed when the only insect resting on the window pane was a large horsefly.

♦♦♦♦

The moment Marwan began dropping ice cubes inside a tumbler, I realized I could hear the sound of them clinking up against the glass, which meant the Ops Center had activated the audio transmitters embed inside the purple boxes he was carrying.

As obvious as that was, I heard Carlton say, "Audio has been activated."

Trudy, who was relying on Carlton to tell her what was going on inside the compound, replied, "Okay, thanks for letting me know. The Grasshopper is ready to go whenever you give the order."

Carlton said, "Stand by. I may not use it until the general arrives."

Since the Grasshopper's power source was limited, I understood Carlton's hesitancy in using it until he needed additional eyes inside the room.

Once Marwan had poured apple juice in his glass, he walked over and sat down in an armchair facing the door, placing the plastic bag on the floor beside him.

Almost immediately, a guard swung open the door, and Marwan jumped to his feet again, sloshing a few drops of apple juice on his *thobe* in the process.

"Let the games begin," Pike said, as Sheikh Hassan Naballah entered the room.

♦♦♦♦

With his cloak swirling around him, Naballah swept inside the room with a bit of dramatic flair. Walking a few steps behind him was his new assistant, Jamal Isa.

Jamal had a pinched, narrow face and was dressed in a white shirt and dark slacks. In contrast, Naballah was wearing a brown cloak or *bisht* over a dark gray *thobe.* Following the custom of most Shia clerics—at least those who claimed to be a descendant of the Prophet Muhammad—he was also wearing a black turban on his head.

After a few words of greeting, Naballah peered over his wire-rimmed glasses at Marwan and asked, "What happened to your head?"

Although I hadn't seen Marwan the previous day, I knew the bruise on his forehead must have turned purple by now, so Naballah's comment was understandable.

On the other hand, if the captain manning the roadblock on Asaker Road had reported Marwan's presence in the area, then it was entirely possible Naballah was asking the question for an totally different reason.

Marwan stuck to the answer he'd given Zaidi on Thursday and said he'd fallen in the stairwell of his apartment.

Naballah nodded, but the stern expression on his face never changed, and I found it impossible to tell if he believed him or not.

When Naballah walked over to the desk and sat down, Jamal immediately opened up the briefcase he was carrying and removed a black metal box.

As he began attaching it to the telephone on Naballah's desk, I realized it was an encryption device used to prevent electronic eavesdropping during sensitive phone calls, such as the one he was expecting to receive from Franco Cabello.

Naballah turned to Marwan and asked, "And your trip to Caracas? How was it?"

"It was good to get away with my family," Marwan said, reaching down and retrieving one of the purple boxes from the bag he'd placed on the floor beside him. "That reminds me. I brought you a gift from Venezuela."

Marwan walked over and placed the purple box on Naballah's desk. Although I saw his hand shaking as he pushed the box toward the sheikh, at that moment, Naballah was glancing down at his watch and didn't seem to notice.

"It's ten o'clock. We should be hearing from Franco now," Naballah said, picking up the purple box and lifting the lid.

Although the camera angle from Marwan's *thobe* made it impossible to see the gold nugget inside, it allowed us an excellent view of the surprised look on Naballah's face when he saw the nugget for the first time.

"Is this gold?" he asked, removing the nugget from the black velvet.

"Yes, it's from the Santa Elena gold mines," Marwan said, pointing to the notation on the inside of the box.

Just as Pike had predicted, the man seemed mesmerized by the nugget and ignored the purple box it came in.

A few seconds later, Naballah's phone rang.

It was Franco Cabello.

# Chapter 44

Nasrallah answered the call by identifying himself by name. Once Cabello was on the line, he pushed a button and put the call on speakerphone so Marwan could translate for him.

Among the many notations in the Ops Center's profile on Cabello was one indicating he'd been a chain smoker all his life. His low, gravelly voice reflected this bad habit, and the sound contrasted sharply with Naballah's higher pitched intonation.

Cabello said, "So, tell me, Hassan. What's the weather like in Damascus today?"

When Marwan and I had talked about what to expect during the phone call, he'd told me Cabello was extremely paranoid about security and always insisted on using a code phrase about the weather to make sure he was really speaking to the sheikh.

Naballah said, "It's hot and dry with no chance of rain in sight."

Cabello responded, "Sounds exactly like the weather here."

Once this identification process was over, Naballah wasted no time in asking Cabello about the status of the canisters.

As Marwan translated for the two men, I realized he was choosing his Arabic words very carefully, because the Los Zetas lieutenant was using a less respectful form of Spanish when addressing Naballah.

Cabello said, "Don't worry, Sheikh. Everything's proceeding according to schedule."

Naballah said, "It must have been a smooth transfer in Santiago. My men had no idea the containers were missing until several hours after the ships arrived in port."

"Did you know the Americans also had their eyes on the dock?"

"That doesn't surprise me. We knew they were tracking the ships."

"We took care of them."

I held my breath, hoping Naballah would ask Cabello to elaborate on this assertion. Instead, he asked, "Where's the shipment now?"

"That's not your concern, Sheikh. Once I've received confirmation your final payment has been credited to my account, I'll let you know."

"That's unacceptable. I need to know where the shipping containers are right now. Otherwise, I won't have time to get my men in position to offload the containers properly."

"Well, first of all, the shipment's been broken apart, so we aren't dealing with the shipping containers anymore. What we have now are four separate crates."

After hearing this, Naballah pressed him for more details on how he was handling the shipment. Finally, after going back and forth for several minutes, Cabello relented and explained the route the chemical weapons had taken since leaving the *Sea Star*.

As an American—especially someone charged with the responsibility of keeping the country safe—the way in which the gas canisters had crossed the border into the U.S. sent chills down my spine.

♦♦♦♦

Cabello described how the two shipping containers had been removed from the *Sea Star* and transferred to a warehouse in Santiago de Cuba. I wasn't surprised to learn the cartel had used the heavy fog in the area to camouflage their activities.

At the warehouse—which I had to believe was where Mitchell had taken the photo—the crates of gas canisters had been removed from the shipping containers and put aboard a chartered flight to Tijuana, Mexico.

From there, the crates had been transported to a furniture store in Tijuana where they'd traveled underground along an eight hundred yard tunnel and ended up in a utility shed in the parking lot of an industrial parts plant in San Diego, California.

In addition to its own elevator, Cabello said the tunnel included an underground rail system, and he gave Naballah a short explanation of how the cartel had been using the passageway to deliver tons of marijuana and cocaine into the States on a daily basis.

After mentioning how they'd smuggled people across the Mexican border through the same tunnel, Cabello added, "You might want to keep that in mind in case you need my specialized services in the future."

Naballah said, "I'm only interested in where the canisters are right now. Tell me what happened to them once they arrived in San Diego."

"I was getting to that, Sheikh. They were loaded onto a semi-tractor trailer full of industrial parts bound for Baltimore. Four days from now, your shipment should arrive on the East Coast, and according to my calculations, that date meets your deadline, which I believe was July 8th."

"That date is correct. Where will my men pick up the shipment when it reaches Baltimore?"

"Like I said before, once I've received confirmation you've wired the final payment to my bank account in Zurich, I'll give you a location. It's not happening before then."

Naballah said nothing for several seconds, causing Cabello to ask, "Are you still there? Can you hear me, Sheikh?"

Marwan replied, "We're here. Just one second."

Naballah removed his glasses and massaged the bridge of his nose. "If you continue your refusal to give me an approximate location, you won't see the money in your account on July 8th or any other day."

"Here's what you need to know," Cabello said. "As soon as I receive confirmation from my bank in Zurich, I'll text Marwan the name of the truck stop on I-95 where the semi will be parked. Along with that location, I'll give him the vehicle's license plate number. At that point, you'll have four hours to arrive at that location and offload the merchandise. Just have your men somewhere south of Baltimore, and there shouldn't be a problem."

After Marwan translated Cabello's instructions, Naballah said, "As long as the truck stop is near Washington, that's acceptable."

Cabello said, "Once I've heard from Zurich, I'll send Marwan a text." He paused a moment. "And now, Sheikh, I believe we're done here. *Adios*."

Cabello might be done, but I figured we were just getting started.

Immediately after hanging up the phone, Naballah got up from his desk and walked over to the large picture window. After staring out at the compound for several seconds, he pulled a bottle of chilled water out of an ice bucket.

Tossing the cap aside, he turned around and gestured toward Marwan. "Be back here next Wednesday. Once I've wired Franco the rest of the money, we'll see if he keeps his word and sends you the information."

"Of course, he'll keep his word. You can't doubt that."

Although Marwan's curt reply surprised me, I found it understandable.

Since Cabello hadn't revealed the exact location of the canisters and this was the type of intel we needed, I figured Marwan might be worried about his future.

To make matters worse, Naballah wanted him back at the compound in four days, and he didn't plan to be anywhere near Naballah's compound in four days.

"I'm beginning to wonder if Franco is all that trustworthy," Naballah said.

"There's nothing to worry about. If he doesn't keep his word, he knows you'll come after him. Plus, you won't use his services in the future. You heard him; he was offering to do business with you again."

"Let's hope you're right."

"I know I'm right."

Marwan's voice had a definite edge to it now, and by the look on Naballah's face, he could hear it as well.

I heard Carlton's voice in my earpiece. "What's he doing?"

"I wish I knew."

♦♦♦♦

Naballah didn't respond to Marwan's comment. Instead, he gave his attention to the pastry tray and selected a sweet roll for himself. A few seconds later, Marwan got up out of his chair and joined him.

As the two men faced each other, Naballah asked, "What's wrong, Marwan?"

"My daughter's birthday is Wednesday, and I had planned to be in Caracas to celebrate it with her. Now you're telling me I have to be here."

"I know how important family is to you, but our service to Allah is much more important than our families. Think about the service you'll be rendering Allah when we attack our enemy's capital."

"I can serve Allah in Caracas as well as I can in Damascus."

At that moment, I realized Marwan was taking Pike's advice and stirring up a little drama, trying to make sure he didn't have to stick around Damascus until Wednesday. I seriously doubted his daughter's birthday was next week, but even so, I wasn't sure this outburst would work on the sheikh.

Naballah's eyes narrowed as he looked at him. "What exactly are you saying?"

"I'm saying I don't have to be here on Wednesday. I can get Franco's text in Caracas as well as I can in this room."

Naballah took a bite out of his pastry and nodded. "I suppose you're right."

"Once Cabello gives me the license number of the truck and where it's located, I'll immediately send you that information. I could even call you, if you like."

Naballah popped the last bite of pastry in his mouth and wiped his hands with his napkin. "You're right, of course. You should go to Caracas. I'd hate for you to miss Samira's birthday, especially after the loss you've suffered with the death of your son."

Marwan bowed his head. "Thank you, Hassan."

"As soon as you send me the information from Franco, I'll notify the cell in Baltimore where they can pick up the canisters. But if something goes wrong, I'll expect you to drop everything and contact Franco immediately."

"Of course."

When Naballah returned to his desk, Jamal was just getting off his cell phone."That was General Suleiman's driver. He's leaving the hotel now and should be here shortly."

Naballah looked over at Marwan. "Wait in the foyer with the rest of the council members until I call you. I need to meet with the general before convening the council."

When Marwan picked up his plastic bag and turned to leave the room, Naballah added, "I've never heard you sound so passionate about something, Marwan. Make sure you're equally as passionate when you assure the general the cartel is reliable, and the canisters will be in Washington when he requires them."

"I'm prepared to do that."

The moment Marwan sat down on the wooden bench outside Naballah's library, Rehman Zaidi stepped off the elevator, and, after clearing security, he sat down on the bench next to him.

One of the purple boxes—the one destined for the general—was still inside Marwan's plastic bag, and we were able to listen in on the conversation between the two men.

But, since Zaidi only seemed interested in finding out more about the accident Marwan had suffered in the stairwell of his apartment, their chatter yielded nothing in the way of new information.

When Abdul Latif, Naballah's financial minister, arrived a few minutes later, the three men continued their idle chatter and avoided mentioning their impending meeting with General Suleiman.

Although it appeared no one on the bench was especially eager to meet with the general, I didn't share those sentiments.

♦♦♦♦

As Pike and I continued watching Marwan, we also had our eyes on Monitor #1, which was displaying the drone footage of the black Chevy Suburban transporting the general from the Sheraton over to Naballah's compound.

The moment the Suburban was a mile away from the compound, we heard Carlton tell Trudy to launch the Grasshopper.

A few seconds later, she said, "Okay, she's on her way. Activating camera now."

I suspected identifying the Grasshopper as a female locust was pure conjecture on Trudy's part, but whether the tiny drone was male or female, it hardly mattered to me.

All that mattered to me was having eyes in the room when the general arrived. I wanted to be able to read Suleiman's body language and get a feel for the man who was about to launch the attack on Washington.

Although we still had audio in the library, Naballah and Jamal were only discussing his schedule for the rest of the day, so when I heard that, I flipped the mute switch and asked Carlton a question.

"Douglas, you heard Cabello say he knew the Americans were watching the docks in Santiago. Doesn't this confirm the cartel grabbed Ben?"

"Not necessarily. I think we need to wait and hear the report from the SOF unit on the ground in Santiago before jumping to a conclusion."

Pike asked, "What about the reference Naballah made to the Hezbollah cell in Baltimore? Have the feds shared any intel with the Agency about its existence?"

Carlton said, "My sources tell me the Bureau is working overtime running down leads on Hezbollah's activities in the D.C. area following the Navy Yard incident, but I haven't heard anything about a specific cell."

I thought about my last conversation with Frank Benson, and the connections he was trying to make between Reyes Valario and Walid Khouri. Was Khouri involved in the Baltimore cell? Was the terrorist group one of Benson's missing pieces?

I said, "The type of operation required to transport those

canisters has to be pretty sophisticated. The logistics alone would seem to indicate some kind of central control in the Washington area."

Carlton said, "The feds are running down leads on the domestic front. It's up to us to get answers from here."

Pike pointed to Monitor #4 showing the general's arrival at the compound. "Here's the guy who has all the answers."

"Let's hope someone asks him the right questions."

# Chapter 45

When General Alizadeh Suleiman stepped out of the elevator on the second floor of Naballah's headquarters, the camera on Marwan's *thobe* captured the moment.

However, the moment only lasted a few seconds, since the general and his deputy were immediately ushered into Naballah's library without first having to undergo a security check.

During Operation Torchlight, when I'd lived in Tehran for almost two years, I'd seen Suleiman's face in the newspapers or on television on a weekly basis. He was a high-ranking member of the Iranian Revolutionary Guard Corps (IRGC) and head of the Quds Force, a unit of the IRGC responsible for military operations abroad.

Physically, he wasn't a very large man, but despite his stature, he had a powerful presence about him. It was the type of self-assurance easily captured on camera and envied by politicians everywhere.

Suleiman was in his late fifties with a full head of black hair and a closely cropped gray beard. His furrowed brow emphasized his brooding, intense demeanor, and his unsmiling face contributed to his reputation of being aloof.

Since taking control of the Quds Force fifteen years ago, Suleiman had reshaped the organization into a powerful clandestine agency and built a network of militant operatives dedicated to the general's admitted purpose of destroying his most hated enemy, the United States.

Now, unless we were successful in thwarting his plans, he was about to inflict some serious damage on Washington.

As I watched Suleiman enter Naballah's library, I breathed a quick prayer asking for success in discovering the general's plans.

I wasn't greedy, though. I'd be content with a hint or two.

♦♦♦♦

Moments before the general walked in the room, the Grasshopper had begun transmitting images from the window outside Naballah's library, The feed on Monitor #3 indicated Trudy had managed to position the insect at the top of the picture window, giving an optimum view of the entire room.

Unlike the drama employed by Naballah when he'd entered the library, General Suleiman simply opened the door and strolled in. Even so, the raw power exuded by the man commanded immediate attention, and Naballah hurried to his side.

"General Suleiman, welcome to Damascus."

In traditional Muslim fashion, the two men planted air kisses on each check and greeted one another with *"As-salamu Alaykum."*

Roughly translated the phrase meant "Peace be upon you," which I considered ironic since the men had come together to plan discord.

The general and his deputy immediately accepted Naballah's offer of food and beverages, and after they'd finished filling their plates, the general glanced up at the locust resting on the glass pane outside Naballah's library.

For a moment, I felt as if Suleiman were staring straight at me, his black eyes reading my face as easily as I could read his.

Seconds later, Naballah asked him about recent events in Tehran, and he turned his back on the Grasshopper and walked over to the sofa.

After a few minutes of small talk, General Suleiman set aside his empty plate and told his deputy to hand him his briefcase. Once he'd released the latches, he pulled out a file folder and removed a single sheet of paper.

"These are my requirements for the next recruits," he said, handing the document over to Naballah. "Look for young men and women willing to die for Allah. Make sure they know their lives will be martyred to bring down the Great Satan, and, of course, assure them their arrival in Paradise will result in great rewards."

Naballah looked down at what the general had given him. "There are many willing recruits at our training facilities on Margarita Island, and I'm sure you'll be pleased to know our cells in Latin America are gaining new followers every day."

After taking a moment to read through the list, Naballah asked, "Were you satisfied with what Reyes Valario accomplished at the military base in Washington?"

"I was hoping for more casualties, but he achieved my objective. Now I know what to expect when we drop the canisters on the city."

"My council member, Rehman Zaidi, personally recruited Valario when he was living in Caracas. He'll be pleased to hear you approved of his selection. Did your asset in Washington also find Valario useful?"

The general nodded. "Mohammed spoke highly of him. He said he was an exceptional soldier and followed his instructions without question."

"That's excellent. Rehman remains one of my best recruiters, but, to be honest, he's concerned you'll blame him for the death of Ahmed Al-Amin."

The general appeared to consider Naballah's statement a moment. "You must understand, Hassan; my focus is entirely on destroying the arrogant power of the United States. Mohammed and I have been working toward this goal for many years, and I won't be distracted by anything or anyone. Believe me when I say nothing is more important to me than the annihilation of the Great Satan."

"Yes, of course."

"That's not to say I didn't grieve when Ahmed was murdered, but his death hasn't interfered with my plans, so it's of no consequence to me."

After giving Naballah a lecture on how crucial it was to annihilate the "brutal repressive regime of America," the general removed a handful of documents from his briefcase and handed them over to the sheikh.

Although it was impossible to view the contents of the papers, it was clear from their conversation the documents outlined the funding of Hezbollah's activities by the IRGC.

While it didn't make much sense to me, I knew the analysts in the Ops Center would be overjoyed to hear the men discussing the budget items, and they'd be studying the numbers on Hezbollah's finances long after the meeting was over.

As the discussion seemed to be winding down, Naballah shifted gears and brought up his own personal budget, giving the general a detailed rationale for increasing it.

Suleiman replied, "Once the members of your security council have briefed me on how successful they've been in getting the chemical weapons into the United States, then I'll consider your request for more money."

"I'll bring them in now," Naballah said, gesturing at Jamal to invite the council members into the library. "I think you'll be pleased at what you're about to hear."

Pike and I watched as the three men in the foyer jumped to their feet when Jamal appeared.

As they were about to enter the library, Pike muted the sound on his headset and looked over at me, "Would you care to speculate on the identity of the general's asset, this guy he's calling Mohammed?"

"There's no need for me to speculate. I feel certain it's Walid Khouri."

♦♦♦♦

When Marwan entered Naballah's library, the first thing he did was glance over at the picture window again. Although his facial expression didn't indicate he'd spotted the Grasshopper, he followed my instructions and sat down in an armchair facing away from the window, giving us another view of the room.

When Naballah introduced the three men to the general, each one presented him with a gift of some nature. Suleiman didn't appear to be as impressed with Marwan's gift of the gold nugget as Naballah had been, but he set the purple box aside and didn't examine it further.

Once the introductions were over, the general said, "So tell me, Hassan, what's the status of the weapons?"

Naballah started off by telling the general the steps he'd taken to ensure the safety of the chemical weapons once he'd determined it was too risky to store them in Venezuela. He went on to explain how the Cuban government had been more than willing to allow them to use a warehouse in Santiago de Cuba.

The general acted as if he didn't consider these details important, waving his hand at Naballah dismissively. "I'm well aware the weapons have arrived in Cuba."

"I just thought—"

"I'm more interested in how you managed to get them into the U.S."

Suleiman turned to his right and addressed Zaidi. "That was your assignment, wasn't it, Rehman?"

Before Zaidi had a chance to respond, Marwan spoke up. "General, if you don't mind, I'd like to answer that question."

Although he appeared surprised at this request, the general nodded at Marwan. "Go ahead."

"What I'm about to tell you may sound disrespectful, but I assure you, I don't mean it that way."

Marwan paused a moment, but when the general showed no reaction to his statement, he hurried on. "When I heard about your plan to use Hezbollah recruits in Venezuela to bring the weapons into the U.S., I decided to explore a different possibility, one that didn't involve using the recruits. My intention was to protect Hezbollah's exposure should the canisters be discovered beforehand. I also wanted to lessen Hezbollah's blame after the attack."

Here was a side of Marwan I hadn't seen before, but, as I observed the look of approval on Naballah's face, I realized this was exactly what he was expecting Marwan to do. He wanted him to use his negotiating skills to sell the cartel to the general, even if it meant he had to take the blame for something the cleric had done.

Marwan said, "With that in mind, I contacted a member of the Los Zetas organization, someone who had partnered with us before on a weapons shipment, and he agreed to handle the canisters for us. When he—"

The general immediately cut him off and asked Naballah, "Did you approve of this plan?"

"I did," Naballah said.

He quickly added, "But it was only after being assured of its success. It seemed a viable option once the Americans had discovered we'd taken possession of the weapons."

Suleiman gave his attention to Marwan. "So has it been a success? Were they able to get the canisters across the border?"

Marwan nodded. "I just heard from my contact, and the canisters arrived in California yesterday. Right now, they're in transit, but they'll be in the D.C. area within four days."

The general addressed Naballah. "What arrangements have you made for the shipment once it arrives?"

"I've alerted the Baltimore cell to have a truck available for pickup, and they've rented a warehouse where they can store the canisters until you intend to use them."

The general looked over at Zaidi. "Did you train the members of the Baltimore cell? Are they your recruits?"

Zaidi seemed pleased the general had asked him that question. "Yes, I trained all of them in Venezuela, and I personally recruited their cell leader, Leandro Manolo."

"Will he follow orders?"

"Without question."

"Outstanding." The general gestured over at Marwan and Naballah. "All of you have done an outstanding job."

Naballah beamed, showering the general with words of appreciation. Following this show of gratitude, he instructed Latif, his financial secretary, to give Suleiman an accounting of the money they'd spent to do this outstanding job.

As Latif went over the numbers, the Grasshopper's feed started to break up, and Carlton asked, "Trudy, how much time before we lose the Grasshopper?"

"I think that was only a hiccup. Her batteries should last another thirty minutes, and the audio will probably hold out for at least that long."

Pike said, "That should be plenty of time. Suleiman just told the sheikh he was ready to go over the final phase of the operation."

"Let's hope it's not as final as he intends it to be," I said.

♦♦♦♦

General Suleiman looked intense as he sat on the edge of the sofa and reiterated his desire to strike a decisive blow on the U.S. capital.

"On 9/11, when Al-Qaeda brought down the Twin Towers in New York City, I'd just been named commander of the Quds Force. As I watched those images being broadcast and heard the officers outside my office cheering, I vowed one day I would bring that same type of chaos to Washington, D.C. That day is almost here."

Suleiman reached inside his jacket and withdrew a cream-colored business card. After handing it over to Naballah, he said, "Once you've received word the Baltimore cell is in possession of the canisters, call this number. It's a direct line to Mohammed, and he'll tell you what to do next."

Naballah glanced down at the card. Even though the camera on Marwan's *thobe* was facing Naballah, it was impossible to see the number written on the back of the card.

After Naballah had given Jamal the card and told him to enter the phone number on his contact list, he turned his attention to the general. "Does this mean you won't be directing the operation?"

"Mohammed is on site, and I have the utmost confidence in his abilities. A few months ago, after he acquired the aircraft necessary to mount the attack, we met together in Dubai and finalized the logistics of the operation. Now, it's simply a matter of getting him the canisters. He'll take care of everything after that."

Marwan spoke up. "So your plan calls for an aerial attack?"

While I applauded Marwan's effort to get us the intel we needed, I was afraid his question might make the general suspicious.

Instead, Suleiman chuckled and appeared to find it amusing. "Did you think we'd be attaching nozzles to the canisters and spraying Washington with nerve gas?"

Marwan shrugged, and the general used the opportunity to give a mini-lecture on how the weapons functioned.

"There's a disc inside the canister shell which separates two gas cylinders. In order for the gases to mix, the disc must be ruptured. That only happens when the canister is shot from a rocket or dropped from the air. Otherwise, no nerve gas is produced."

Marwan nodded. "I understand."

"I know you must have chosen a date for the operation," Naballah said. "Otherwise, you wouldn't have insisted I have the canisters in Washington by Wednesday."

Suleiman nodded. "The attack will take place on July 11th, one week from today."

Naballah smiled. "That would make it 7/11, the perfect match for 9/11."

"That's true, and while I find the parallel amusing and, to be honest, an added bonus, that's not why I chose the date. Since I doubt anyone in this room is a student of American military history, I don't expect you to know this, but on July 11, 1864, during the American civil war, a significant battle took place in Washington, D.C. If the South had pressed their advantage on that day, the U.S. capital would have fallen, and, more than likely, today there would be no United States of America. However, the Confederate general failed to use his most powerful weapon on the city, and, as a consequence, he lost the battle. That failure will not be repeated on July 11th this year."

"God help us," Pike muttered.

I felt certain he would.

## Chapter 46

The general continued lecturing his audience for several more minutes, demonstrating his extensive knowledge of U.S. history and pointing out what he considered to be America's many failures throughout the world.

When Trudy announced the Grasshopper's batteries were nearly depleted, Carlton reluctantly told her to withdraw the tiny drone. Unfortunately, she said we'd probably lose the audio from the purple boxes within the next thirty minutes, and Marwan's *thobe* camera wouldn't last much longer than that.

Shortly after the Grasshopper flew off, General Suleiman ended his lecture and stood to his feet.

It appeared the meeting was over.

Once the general had placed his newly acquired gifts inside his briefcase—including the purple box with the gold nugget inside—he invited Naballah to join him later at the Sheraton for dinner. After mentioning he'd be willing to discuss an increase in the sheikh's personal budget at that time, Naballah immediately accepted the invitation and personally escorted Suleiman and his deputy to the elevator.

When he returned to the library, he congratulated the three members of his security council on a job well done. Once he'd dismissed Zaidi and Latif, he asked Marwan to remain behind.

When the two men left, Naballah told Jamal, "Get Marwan one of the encrypted phones and make note of the number."

Turning to Marwan, he said, "You'll use this phone to call me after you hear from Franco on Wednesday. Jamal has already programmed my personal number into the contact list."

"I'll call you as soon as I hear from Franco," Marwan said.

I thought he sounded very sincere.

The moment Marwan took the cell phone from Jamal, we lost the audio feed and from that point forward, we had no sound to go with the video from Marwan's *thobe* camera.

"We've lost audio in the library," Pike said.

Carlton replied, "We've also lost the signal from Suleiman's box, but none of us should complain about the timing. The intel we've received has been solid."

The view from Marwan's camera showed Naballah speaking to him before he left the library. Pike seemed to think he was telling Marwan he'd done a good job with the general, but since I was lousy at lip reading, especially Arabic, I had to take his word for that.

When Marwan exited the building, Naballah's driver immediately picked him up at the entrance, and, as they drove out of the compound, Pike and I congratulated each other on achieving our objectives and executing a flawless plan.

However, as it turned out, those celebrations were premature.

♦♦♦♦

The moment Naballah's driver dropped Marwan off at Bakdash, a trendy ice cream shop in downtown Damascus, we heard from Carlton. He'd just arrived at the popular establishment in an EAI van driven by Dave.

"Marwan just entered Bakdash, and I'm right behind him," Carlton said. "I'll shadow him until you get here."

Pike and I were inside the Renault—after having exchanged vehicles with Trudy—and we were headed over to Bakdash as well.

"Is your security detail with you?" I asked.

"I'm equipped with a comms unit, and Dave and Finn are monitoring me from the van. I'll be fine."

Bakdash was a noisy, crowded place—more like a disco bar in the

States, minus the liquor—and that was precisely why Carlton had chosen it for our meet with Marwan.

It was an ideal spot for determining whether Marwan had picked up any surveillance, which wasn't an uncommon event after someone paid a visit to Naballah's headquarters—the Israelis always had the compound under surveillance—and the Bakdash location also offered us an easy exit out of the city.

Our plans were to meet up with Marwan at the ice cream shop and get him out of Damascus as quickly as possible. Although I had a feeling he'd be surprised to see Carlton—Mr. Chessman, as he knew him—I felt certain he'd be glad to have him around, considering he'd already told me Carlton was a much nicer guy than I was.

The Plan of Action (POA) called for Pike to drive Carlton, Marwan, and me to the airport in Beirut—a distance of approximately sixty miles—where the three of us would board a flight to Barcelona.

In Barcelona, we'd be met by Sam Wylie, who would be responsible for getting Marwan to Caracas and reuniting him with his wife and daughter. Once our asset had been handed off to Wylie, Carlton and I would board a flight for Washington.

After I hung up, I told Pike, "Douglas shouldn't be inside Bakdash without Dave or Finn."

"We're ten minutes out, and they're monitoring him on the security cameras. You're overreacting."

Maybe so, but from the moment Marwan had cleared the compound, I'd had a bad feeling.

That feeling wasn't going away.

♦♦♦♦

Pike and I drove along in silence for a few minutes. Once we got closer to the downtown area, I called Dave and asked him about the visuals inside Bakdash.

"Marwan's *thobe* camera isn't working anymore, but I've tapped into their CCTV security cameras. Is there something specific you wanted me to take a look at?"

"Nothing specific. Has Douglas made contact with Marwan yet?"

"No, it looks like he's still doing recon of the place."

"Give me a buzz if you see anything unusual."

As soon as I hung up, Pike returned to a subject he'd brought up with me earlier.

Namely, he was in disagreement with the POA.

"The plan is just all wrong," he said. "I should be flying back to Langley with you and Douglas. You could use my help ferreting out that cell in Baltimore or checking up on this Walid guy."

"You know it's up to the Bureau to locate the Baltimore cell. As for Walid, I'm not sure how the DDO will handle him, once he hears what the general had to say today."

"I know the feds will be in charge of the sleeper cell, but I thought I might talk to the DDO about doing an interview with Walid Khouri. I could contact him, tell him I'm doing a piece on famous photographers, and see what turns up."

"How would interviewing Walid help us determine if he's Suleiman's asset in Washington?"

"The general implied Mohammed was in possession of a plane capable of carrying the chemical weapons, and that he had an organizational structure with the means to do it. If Walid Khouri is really Mohammed, then there has to be some evidence of that at his residence or his place of business."

"So you're saying if you could get an interview with Khouri, you'd have access to those places? Just like that, he'd give you the keys and tell you to take a look around?"

"You'd be surprised at what people will do when they think someone has the means to make them famous. At the very least, I'd be able to snoop around his house without a warrant."

"Good luck with selling that idea to the DDO."

"I believe I could make him understand. It would just be a matter of—"

A call from Dave interrupted Pike's argument.

"You said I should call you if I saw anything unusual happening at Bakdash."

"And?"

"Well, this isn't really anything unusual, but a guy just sat down at the table with Marwan. They appear to know each other."

"Describe him."

"I captured a still shot of him. I'll send it to you."

"Where's Douglas? Do you see him anywhere?"

"Not right now, but I saw him a few seconds ago. He was on the other side of the room from Marwan."

"Keever and I should be there in a few minutes; we're not more than a mile away. Send Finn inside to locate Douglas and call me as soon as he does."

When I hung up, Pike said, "Marwan has lots of friends in Damascus. It doesn't surprise me he ran into one of them in there."

I took one look at the photograph Dave had sent me, and then I turned the phone around and showed it to Pike.

"Do you still think I'm overreacting?"

The camera had captured a full-face photo of Naballah's assistant, Jamal Isa.

♦♦♦♦

Bakdash was located near the end of a city block, with a large public parking lot on the west side of the building and a smaller employee lot on the east side. A narrow walkway ran behind the building and connected the two lots.

Although there was only one door into Bakdash, there were two exits out of the building; one on the west side and one on the east side. Both of them accessed the respective parking lots on each side.

As Pike pulled into the west parking lot, Dave called me back.

"Finn is inside the building trying to locate Douglas, but it appears Marwan and his friend are headed toward the exit door on the east side."

After a quick consultation, Pike agreed to drop me off at the back of the building, so I could head over to the east parking lot on foot, while he drove around the block and entered the lot from the other direction.

Before slipping into the alleyway behind Bakdash on the west side, I removed the Makarov from my holster. Then, I raced along the back of the building to the other side.

As I approached the corner of the building, I heard two people talking, so I flattened myself against the outer wall and cautiously edged my way forward.

When I peered around the corner, I spotted Marwan and Jamal standing next to a late-model Mercedes sedan.

They appeared to be arguing.

I crouched down and made my way past the first line of cars, until I arrived on the other side of the Mercedes.

I heard Jamal telling Marwan to get inside the car.

Marwan said, "If Sayyed Naballah wanted to see me, why didn't he send a car for me?"

"It was just easier for me to come and get you."

"You're lying to me, Jamal. I'm not going anywhere with you."

"After you lied to Hassan you're calling me a liar?"

"I didn't lie to him."

"Oh, but you did. Samira's birthday is not next Wednesday. Her birthday is August 15. I saw it on the computer."

"You have information about Samira on your computer?"

"Not on my computer; on Hassan's computer. I'm required to keep his database up to date, and when I recorded the number of the cell phone he gave you, I noticed your daughter's birthday isn't next week."

"When you told the sheikh, what did he say?"

"I didn't tell him."

Marwan appeared to take this as a good sign, and hurriedly offered an explanation of his actions.

"Thank you, Jamal. I realize we don't know each other very well, but if we did, you'd understand why I need to go to Caracas. My family means everything to me. I even relocated them to Caracas to keep them safe from the war. Now, I miss them and want to see them again. What I said was true. I can carry out my responsibilities in Caracas as well as I can here."

While I thought Marwan's answer might satisfy Jamal, I was still puzzled as to why he'd followed Marwan to Bakdash in the first place.

Suddenly, Jamal's voice took on a much harsher tone. "If your family means that much to you, then you'll be willing to compensate me for keeping quiet about the lie you told the sheikh."

Evidently, Jamal was simply engaged in a bit of old-fashioned blackmail.

Marwan asked, "What do you want, Jamal?"

"One of the gold nuggets you brought back from Venezuela."

Marwan was quiet for a few seconds. "I can do that. When I return from Caracas, I'll bring you one."

"No, you can't put me off. We're going over to your apartment. You can give it to me before you leave."

Marwan laughed. "You think I have gold nuggets just sitting around my apartment?"

"I'm sure you have at least a couple for yourself. If you want me to keep quiet about the lie you told the sheikh, you'll do what I say."

By this time, I'd crept around the Mercedes.

Now, I was crouched at the front bumper, and Jamal was just a few feet away from me. However, his back was to me, so when I stood up, he couldn't see me.

On the other hand, Marwan immediately saw me, and although he didn't give me away, he suddenly became emboldened. "Tell the sheikh whatever you want. I'm going back inside now."

With that, Marwan turned and started walking back toward the entrance to Bakdash.

Jamal immediately pulled a revolver out of his pocket and pointed it at Marwan. "Get in the car or you'll regret it."

When Marwan didn't even bother to look back at him, Jamal raised the pistol to a firing position and said, "Come with me, Marwan, or I swear I'll shoot you."

"Drop the gun," I said.

The moment Jamal whirled around and pointed the gun at me, Marwan turned and rushed back towards the Mercedes.

Everything seemed to happen in slow motion after that.

When he saw Marwan running toward him, Jamal immediately pivoted and fired a shot, barely missing his head. Meanwhile, I aimed my gun at Jamal and pulled the trigger.

Jamal slumped to the pavement in a pool of blood.

It wasn't my shot that killed him, though.

The Makarov had jammed on me.

Carlton had killed him with his Sig.

♦♦♦♦

As I bent down to check Jamal for a pulse, Carlton walked over. He still had the Sig in his hand.

"Is he dead?" he asked.

I nodded.

Marwan looked down at Jamal and then over at Carlton. "Mr. Chessman, what are you doing here?"

Carlton holstered his gun and immediately grabbed his phone, instructing Dave to come to the east parking lot. He never responded to Marwan's question.

I went through Jamal's pockets and took out his cell phone and his wallet. Inside his shirt pocket, I found the general's cream-colored business card.

On the back was Mohammed's phone number.

As I pocketed the card, Carlton asked, "Where's Keever?"

At that moment, Pike drove up in the Renault, jumped out of the SUV, and ran over to the Mercedes.

After taking one look at Jamal, he looked over at the Makarov in my hand and said, "Aren't you glad I insisted you take the Makarov?"

# Chapter 47

After Pike arrived, Carlton started issuing orders and giving instructions. Managing a crisis was in Carlton's wheelhouse, and he was at his best in such an environment.

A few minutes later, Dave drove off in the EAI van with Jamal's body inside, while Finn left in the Mercedes.

After Carlton pointed out there were no surveillance cameras in the parking lot and no witnesses to the shooting, he said he didn't believe the mission had been compromised, so we'd stick to the original POA and head for Beirut.

When we cleared the outskirts of Damascus, I gave Marwan a change of clothes, and he handed me his white *thobe*, along with the two cell phones he had on him. He spoke very little after that and eventually fell asleep. I suspected the events of the last few days had taken their toll on his psyche.

We were almost to Beirut before Pike brought up with Carlton his proposal to return to Langley with us. Carlton immediately shut him down and refused to even listen to the rationale for his proposal.

When Pike and I said goodbye to each other at the Beirut airport, he seemed genuinely confused as to why his persuasive arguments hadn't worked with Carlton.

I told him I was still trying to figure out the guy myself and couldn't help him.

After we shook hands, Pike said, "Thanks for putting up with me. I know I'm not the easiest guy to work with. Of course, people say the same thing about you."

I knew that couldn't be true, but I didn't have time to argue with him.

♦♦♦♦

When we met up with Sam Wylie at the airport in Barcelona, he assured Marwan he'd made arrangements for his wife and daughter to be at the airport in Caracas to meet him.

As happy as Marwan appeared to be when he heard that news, he seemed equally as pleased when Carlton told him the Agency planned to relocate him and his family to another country once the threat to Washington had been eliminated.

When he began quizzing Carlton about those plans, I pulled Wylie aside and asked him if he'd like to go grab a cup of coffee before his flight began boarding.

"Shoot, yeah. You know me. I never turn down a free cup of coffee."

"Did I say anything about free coffee?"

"I know you must want to pick my brain about something, so while you're at it, you should at least pay for my coffee."

I ended up paying for two coffees, and we sat down together in a corner of the snack bar.

"What's up?" he asked.

"Douglas won't tell me a thing about what's going on with Ben. Do you know what the SOF unit found when they got down to Santiago?"

He shook his head. "I don't think it's good news, amigo. They haven't located him yet, and you know what that means."

I nodded. "He's either dead, or the cartel's holding him for ransom."

"If I had to guess, I'd say it was the latter. A Senator's son would yield some mighty big bucks."

"Yeah, but the question is, would the Senator be willing to pay the big bucks?"

♦♦♦♦

When Wylie and I returned to the concourse, I walked over to say goodbye to Marwan, who was sitting all by himself in a long row of seats.

"Mind if I sit down?" I asked.

"Would it matter if I did?"

I ignored his response and sat down anyway.

"I want to thank you for doing an excellent job getting us the information we needed from the general."

"I didn't do it for you. I did it for my wife and daughter."

"I know that, and believe me, Marwan, if there had been another way to ensure your cooperation, I would have taken it."

"That almost sounds like an apology." He shook his head. "Even if it were, I wouldn't accept it."

"Doesn't the Prophet tell you to accept the apology of another?"

He looked surprised. "You know the Quran?"

"Until recently, I knew more about the Quran than I did about the Bible."

He seemed intrigued by my statement. "How do you compare the two?"

"They have much in common, but there are at least three things mentioned in the Bible that aren't in the Quran. If you were to believe them, you would join me in heaven."

"Only three?"

"I know the Quran presents Jesus as one who did great miracles, who was born of a virgin, and who was sinless, but what it doesn't tell you is that he died for our sins, he rose from the grave, and he ascended to heaven."

"Jesus was a prophet, nothing more."

"More than a prophet, he was a mediator. You remember when I showed you the pictures of your wife and daughter when I was questioning you in Buenos Aires and you begged me not to harm them?"

"How could I forget?"

"You were acting as a mediator then. You were intervening on their behalf. That's what Jesus did for us. He's more than a prophet.

He's a mediator. He intervened with God on our behalf."

Marwan didn't comment on my statement, but he did question me about some of the Quran's other teachings. I knew he was just testing me to see how much I really knew about the Quran, but I'm sure I passed the exam.

When I heard his flight called, I asked him if he'd ever read the Bible. He shook his head.

I challenged him to do so.

He didn't say he would, but he didn't say he wouldn't.

"Have a nice flight," I said, as he started to walk away.

He turned and faced me. "I know you were just doing your job, so I accept your apology."

I said a prayer for him as he walked away.

♦♦♦♦

There was a two-hour delay before our flight left for Washington. Carlton spent most of it on the phone with the Ops Center discussing the intel we'd received from Naballah's meeting.

Soon after leaving Damascus, I'd given him General Suleiman's business card, the one I'd discovered in Jamal's pocket with Mohammed's number on the back, and he'd already sent the number to Katherine's ASA office to see if the number was traceable.

I had a feeling it wasn't.

I suspected the phone was a burner, a one-time use cell phone paid for with cash and virtually untraceable. In that case, until someone called that number, there was no way of knowing if it belonged to Khouri or not.

When Carlton opened his briefcase to put away his phone, he looked over at me and said, "I know you have an idea about how you want the rest of the operation to play out, so you might as well tell me about it now. If it's feasible, I'll try to sell it to the DDO when we get back to Langley."

I pointed to Marwan's personal cell phone tucked inside Carlton's briefcase and said, "Franco Cabello said he would text Marwan on his cell phone in a few days. As long as the Agency remains in possession of that phone, then I believe the DDO can justify having the operation run on American soil. I realize the Legal Department will have to give their opinion on that, but let's say Legal gives the DDO the green light to continue running the operation from Langley."

"Let's say they do."

"In that case, I'd like to see the DDO propose a joint task force made up of agents from the Bureau, as well as Agency personnel. I know the Agency has no legal basis for confiscating the shipment of canisters or arresting the members of the Baltimore cell, so the feds could work that end of the operation, while the Agency goes after Mohammed."

"How would that work?"

I pointed to Marwan's phone again. "Once Franco Cabello texts the location of the truck carrying the weapons, we'll pass that information along to the Bureau. We'll do so with the understanding there won't be any news releases about the discovery of the chemical weapons or any publicity about the arrests of the terrorists connected with them until we locate Mohammed."

Carlton nodded. "You don't want Mohammed to know he's never going to see those weapons."

"Right. Mohammed expects to receive a call from Naballah after the canisters have arrived in the area. Once he receives that call, he'll tell Naballah where the canisters should be delivered. However, Naballah won't be making that call. Someone from the Agency will be making that call."

Carlton considered my proposal, rhythmically tapping his finger on his briefcase. "Your plan needs a lot of tweaking, but at least you've given me a framework I can use."

Despite what he said, I knew Carlton loved my plan.

# PART SIX

## Chapter 48

*Monday, July 6*

It had barely been a week since I'd last seen Frank Benson, but when I encountered him in Conference Room C on the ground floor of Agency headquarters, I could have sworn it had been much longer.

Benson was part of the Joint Task Force the DDO had hurriedly put together on Sunday once Carlton and I had arrived back at Dulles.

We'd come straight to Langley after receiving a message from the DDO telling the two of us to meet him in his office the moment we landed.

The meeting hadn't lasted long—at least not the one I was in.

He'd dismissed me as soon as I'd made the pitch to him about letting Operation Citadel Protection continue to play out on the domestic front.

After his curt, "you can go now," he'd asked Carlton to remain behind.

Later, Carlton had called to let me know the DDO had agreed with my proposal. He'd also told me to be back at Langley the next morning to meet with the DDO and the Joint Task Force he was putting together.

Following his call, I'd gone out to The Meadows and slept for twelve hours. I'd thought about calling Nikki, but I knew I was too jet-lagged to talk to her.

Now, after seeing Frank, I wished I had.

Frank had shaved off his scruffy-looking whiskers, and today he was dressed in a dark blue suit, white shirt, and blue-striped tie. I was dressed in more casual attire, and I felt shabby standing next to him.

"I see you survived Damascus," he said, stirring cream in his coffee with a swizzle stick. "Are things as bad there as I'm seeing on the news?"

"If you're seeing thousands of refugees and bomb-out buildings, then you're getting the true picture."

Although we were standing off to the side, away from anyone else in the room, Benson leaned in closer and whispered, "Nikki's had a tough first week, but she's doing a fantastic job. She's a quick learner, and I don't believe she'll have any problem passing the course."

I murmured something inane like "good" and moved away from him, wondering what I'd been thinking when I'd asked him to keep his eye on her.

The official name of Operation Citadel Protection's joint task force was Citadel Protection Joint Task Force Inter-Agency Collaboration, but everyone in the room was calling it the Joint Task Force.

It primarily consisted of Agency personnel and FBI agents, but once the meeting got started, two representatives from the Department of Homeland Security showed up.

One of the DHS people turned out to be Carlton's friend, Arnie, who didn't look too pleased to see me.

The feeling was mutual.

♦♦♦♦

The DDO himself chaired the meeting, but he did very little talking. Instead, he asked Carlton to summarize the intel the Agency had obtained when General Suleiman had met with Hassan Naballah to finalize his plans for mounting an attack on the nation's capital.

As Carlton outlined the facts, he didn't mention the intel he was sharing was the result of his own operation, or that the intelligence officer, who had been part of that operation, was sitting in the room.

Once Carlton had wrapped things up by explaining how the gas canisters had already made their way into the U.S., the DDO invited Frank Benson, who was serving as the FBI's spokesman, to address what the feds had found out about the weapons.

Since the Ops Center had already told the FBI about how the cartel had smuggled the canisters across the border through a tunnel in San Diego, that's where Benson began.

"At Deputy Ira's request," Benson said, gesturing toward the DDO, "we won't be shutting down the cartel's tunnel in San Diego until after we've secured the chemical weapons. For obvious reasons, we don't want to alert Los Zetas we're aware of its existence until then. And, along those same lines, we want to keep a low profile as we try to identify the semi-trailer truck transporting the canisters. At least fifty trucks go in and out of that industrial complex in San Diego every day, so we may not know which one it is until after Franco Cabello discloses the truck's license number."

When Benson reached inside his coat pocket and pulled out a folded piece of paper, I figured he was about to lay a bunch of his Egyptian hieroglyphics on the group.

Instead, he read off a list of names and explained these were people in the Baltimore area on the FBI's terrorism watch list. He said after learning a Hezbollah cell in Baltimore would be taking possession of the canisters, all the individuals on the list had been put under twenty-four hour surveillance, particularly their cell leader, Leandro Manolo, the person Naballah said he would contact once he'd heard from Marwan.

Benson sat down and the DDO addressed the group.

"As Douglas just told you, the head of the Quds Force in Iran, General Suleiman, appears to be the mastermind behind this attack. We believe his asset, a man he's identified as Mohammed, is, in fact, Walid Khouri, a Jordanian photographer who arrived in the United States ten years ago. I'm sure some of you may have heard of him."

Carlton gestured over at Katherine. "I've asked Ms. Broward, the head of our Strategic Analysis Division, to provide you with the data showing why we've come to the conclusion Walid Khouri is Mohammed."

Katherine was dressed in her lawyer-looking black suit today. She appeared more subdued than the last time I'd seen her, and it was difficult for me to tell if this was because of the group she was addressing or the sobering topic under discussion.

At any rate, there was no smile for me today.

As she briefly outlined the biographical facts on Khouri, I noticed Benson was listening to her intently, and, once she got to the part about Khouri's recent overseas trip, I saw him pull out his fact sheet on Reyes Valario and Walid Khouri.

Katherine said, "Khouri was recently in Dubai for a fashion shoot, and we believe he met with General Suleiman to receive his final instructions for the attack at that time. When Khouri returned to the States, a large sum of money was deposited in his Swiss bank account, and a few days later, he made contact with a Hezbollah recruit from South America, a college student at the University of Arkansas by the name of Reyes Valario. As I'm sure you're all aware, Valario has been identified as the shooter in the Navy Yard incident."

At this point in her presentation, I was surprised to see Katherine smile. I was even more surprised when Benson turned out to be the recipient of that smile.

She nodded at him. "Thanks to a very thorough investigation of Valario by an agent at the Bureau, we have a much better understanding of why Walid Khouri and Reyes Valario were in contact."

She picked up a thick plastic binder with CLASSIFIED stamped across the front of it. "Two days ago, the National Security Agency released the transcripts of the conversations between Khouri and Valario. I'll summarize those for you now, but if anyone wishes to read the conversations in their entirety, they're welcomed to see me after the meeting."

Outside of Benson, I seriously doubted anyone would take her up on that offer.

She said, "The transcripts show Khouri directing Valario to join the Razorback Century Club. This is a loosely organized collection of hobby clubs in Fayetteville, and some of the hobbyists provide their members with hands-on training in their field of interest.

"In their very first conversation, Khouri orders Valario to join the Aviation Club. While it's obvious a third party has initiated the contact between the two men, Valario still comments on the strange nature of the assignment. He argues with Khouri about how the club is connected to his desire to die for the cause of Islam.

"That's when Khouri tells Valario he wants him to learn to fly a UAV—he actually calls it a drone. Besides learning to fly the drone, he also needs to know how to equip it with a couple of cameras for taking aerial photographs. Then, Khouri directs Valario to call him immediately after completing each lesson and tell him what he's learned.

"Khouri explains how he plans to mount a camera on a drone he's recently purchased and use it to record a video of Valario and Alejandro Lovato carrying out their suicide mission at the Washington Navy Yard. He tells Valario he'll broadcast this video on the internet to a worldwide Jihadi network of followers once he and Lovato have become martyrs."

Katherine picked up the binder and read an excerpt from the conversation Valario had with Khouri moments before he entered the Navy Yard. In it, Khouri talked to Valario about becoming a selfless hero who would be defending Islam against the corrupt crusaders.

Katherine said, "He told Valario being martyred would send him to paradise immediately, where—I'm quoting here—good deeds erase bad deeds and jihad is the best deed of all."

Before Katherine sat down, she said, "Just to be clear. The FAA found no evidence there was a drone anywhere in the area when Valario and his partner entered the Navy Yard for his suicide mission."

When Katherine finished, Benson spoke up. "If I might add just a postscript to Ms. Broward's report?"

The DDO nodded at him.

"I've recreated the timeline of Khouri's activities the day of the shooting, and, if my calculations are correct, he was engaged in a wedding photo session on June 22, so there's no reason to believe he even tried to use the drone that day."

The DDO said, "That's not surprising. It was probably never Khouri's intention to use the drone for the suicide mission. I imagine he's saving it for something more significant, like taking pictures of gas canisters being exploded over the capital."

I asked, "What evidence do we have that Khouri even has a drone?"

Although the question needed to be asked, the DDO looked at me as if I'd committed a faux pas by asking it. Evidently, his agenda called for only the major players on the Joint Task Force—those wearing the suits and having long titles after their names—to be given the opportunity to speak.

Arnie cleared his throat and gestured at the DDO. "I believe I can answer that question."

Arnie was wearing a sports coat, so I wasn't exactly sure how he fit in with the DDO's agenda, but he was allowed to speak anyway.

"I'm Arnold Dawson with Homeland Security," he said. "The Director has appointed me to serve as the liaison between DHS and the Joint Task Force for this operation."

That meant Arnie was pretty high up on the food chain over at DHS, but since he was friends with Carlton, I'd already figured that out.

"Our office began looking into Walid Khouri as soon as we received evidence his phone number was associated with the shooting at the Navy Yard. Since we knew the Agency was examining his background, and the Bureau was concentrating on his association with Reyes Valario, we looked into his bank transactions, his tax records, and his property acquisitions. As far as we've been able to determine, there's no record of his having purchased a drone."

"What about an airplane?" Carlton asked. "General Suleiman said Mohammed was in possession of an aircraft capable of delivering the chemical weapons."

"Then Walid Khouri may not be Mohammed," Arnie said. "He doesn't own any kind of aircraft."

"Are you certain of that?" Katherine asked. "We know he's

provided aerial shots for some of his commercial clients before."

"While that may be true, his business records are pretty clear. He doesn't own any kind of aircraft."

Katherine said, "My office has also examined his business records, and what seems clear to me is that he knows a lot about creative accounting and encryption technology. Hidden in those records could be evidence he's in possession of a drone, or an airplane, or any number of suspicious items."

Arnie disputed her statement, and the DDO allowed them to argue the finer points of their respective analysis for several minutes. By the look on the deputy's face, he was enjoying their spirited interchanges.

Finally though, he put a stop to their bickering by asking Benson if the FBI's surveillance on Khouri had turned up anything suspicious.

Benson shook his head. "The guy leaves his townhouse around eight o'clock every morning and heads over to his studio. He goes out for lunch every day with someone on his staff or a client, and sometimes, on his way home from work, he stops by the construction site where his new studio is being built. He plays golf one morning a week, and on Friday afternoons, he plays tennis. He never attends a mosque, and he doesn't associate with any Islamic groups."

Although I wasn't sure anyone else had noticed, Benson had delivered this information without referring to his notes, which made me wonder if he had assigned himself to one of his own surveillance teams.

I could think of only one reason Benson would be doing this kind of grunt work himself—he must have discovered something about Khouri that wouldn't fit into one of his puzzle boxes.

I decided to ask him about that.

## Chapter 49

After the members of the Joint Task Force had been given their respective assignments, they were issued temporary passes to the Ops Center, where in two days, Operation Citadel Protection would go live in RTM Center C.

The protocol called for the FBI to move in and take possession of the canisters as soon as Cabello sent a text to Marwan's phone identifying the truck stop on I-95 where the weapons could be found.

The FBI's actions would be broadcast—via Agency drones—in real time to the RTM Center, and all the task force members would have front row seats to this action.

The DDO instructed Carlton to have personnel available—namely, me—in case Cabello suddenly decided to call Marwan instead of texting him.

Since Marwan had told us Cabello was paranoid about security and refused to talk on an unencrypted cell phone, I knew Carlton didn't really expect that to happen, but he assured the DDO he had that scenario covered anyway.

While the DDO was transparent about the role he was expecting the FBI and DHS to play in securing the chemical weapons, he was less candid about how the Agency was planning to handle Walid Khouri.

When one of the feds asked him about when a subpoena would be issued for Khouri's arrest, the DDO brushed him off and said he was still working out the details of how Khouri would be handled.

Seconds later, the DDO adjourned the meeting without allowing any further discussion.

♦♦♦♦

After the meeting had broken up, I caught up with Benson in the corridor outside Conference Room C. When I walked up, he was looking down at a message on his cell phone.

"Got a minute, Frank?"

"What's up?" he asked, slipping his phone inside his suit jacket.

"That's what I was wondering. Have you filled in all the boxes on your diagram of Walid Khouri yet?"

"I'm confident he's Mohammed, if that's what you're asking."

"I'm in agreement with that assessment, but we both know there's no evidence connecting Walid to the chemical weapons right now. While it's definitely his voice on the phone with Valario, a good lawyer could easily get those conversations thrown out of court."

As expected, my remarks caused Benson to pull out his diagram. As he was unfolding it, I got a text message from Carlton telling me to meet him in his office as soon as possible.

Benson pointed to the rectangle containing Walid Khouri's name. "What I find interesting is that every time Valario called Khouri to tell him what he'd learned about flying the UAV, the GPS coordinates show Khouri was always at his construction site. He was never at his studio. I'm bothered by that anomaly."

"I'm going to take a wild guess here and assume you've been following Khouri when he goes out to visit his new studio."

He smiled. "Yeah, that's right. But there's no way to get inside there without being noticed. I'd need a warrant to do that."

Same old Benson. Still the cautious type.

"Let me give this some thought, Frank. I might be able to come up with some way we could get in there and check things out. Right now, though, I'm headed upstairs to see Douglas."

"That's funny," he said. "So am I. When you walked up, I'd just received a text from his secretary asking me to stop by his office."

I didn't see anything remotely funny about that.

♦♦♦♦

When Sally Jo ushered us into Carlton's office, we were directed over to the left side of the room where there was a small conference table with four leather chairs around it.

Once Benson and I were seated, Carlton grabbed his legal pad and a couple of file folders from his desk and joined us.

The moment he sat down, Benson said, "I'll be honest with you, Douglas, this feels strange. I never thought I'd be sitting here again."

For a second, I thought Carlton was about to say, "Neither did I," but instead he said, "Thank you for agreeing to stop by."

After Carlton had placed his legal pad on top of the file folders and carefully aligned the edges, he looked up and said, "The DDO wants to keep the arrest of Walid Khouri as low-key as possible. According to him, doing so would be in the best interests of some Congressional members, and, I might add, a few highly-placed White House officials."

After making this statement, Carlton immediately glanced down at his legal pad, and I wondered if he found it embarrassing to be voicing the wishes of the DDO.

Benson said, "When you say low-key, I'm guessing the DDO doesn't want the Bureau calling up the press before we make the arrest?"

Carlton nodded. "That's correct. But it's also a bit more than that."

He opened up one of the file folders and pulled out a document. "I've constructed a couple of timelines demonstrating how events may unfold on Wednesday when we receive the text from Franco Cabello informing us where the canisters are located."

He turned the document around so Benson and I could take a look at it. The first thing that struck me was how clever Carlton had been to present Benson with such a diagram. It made me wonder if he'd ever seen some of Benson's own synopsis puzzles.

One look at Carlton's timelines, and I immediately recognized they were the same scenarios he and I had discussed at the airport in Barcelona before leaving for Washington.

I did my best to steer Benson in the direction I assumed Carlton wanted him to go.

"What I find worrisome about these timelines," I said, "is what Hassan Naballah will do when he doesn't hear from Marwan on Wednesday. Will he contact General Suleiman and tell him there's been a problem with the canisters?"

Carlton said, "I believe that's a likely scenario. And if Suleiman thinks the mission has failed, then he may immediately get in touch with Khouri."

Benson was nodding as he studied the document. "It's possible General Suleiman will be so spooked he'll tell Khouri he needs to leave the area immediately."

I said, "Or he might just tell him to go to ground for awhile. Either way, unless Khouri is arrested before Wednesday, we may lose him for good."

Carlton said, "The deputy and I have come to the same conclusion, and that means we'll need to find some connection between Khouri and the chemical weapons within the next 48 hours."

Carlton withdrew several pages from his second folder, and I immediately recognized the logo imprinted on the top sheet was from Katherine's ASA office.

He said, "What Ms. Broward didn't mention at the task force meeting this morning was that Valario's cell phone records included GPS data. What's interesting about the data, is that every time Valario called Khouri, he just happened to be at his new studio."

Benson immediately jumped in. "I had noticed that as well."

Carlton nodded. "That site is still under construction, so perhaps Khouri deliberately went out there just to make sure no one in his office would be able to overhear him talking to Valario."

Carlton handed us a couple of brochures.

"As you can see from this brochure, his new facility includes what he calls 'landscape ambience,' which are buildings he plans to use for backgrounds for his wedding photos and family portraits. Right now, besides the studio, the only other building on the property is an old barn, although the brochure promises there'll be other buildings, or at least the facades of such structures, when construction is complete."

I glanced at the brochure Carlton handed me. Besides a modern-looking photography studio, it showed a old barn with peeling paint, a medieval castle, a Western saloon and an antebellum mansion.

I asked, "How big is that barn? Could it hold a small plane?"

Carlton nodded. "According to one of the ASA image specialists, it could hold a large truck, a small plane, or any number of drones."

"Perhaps, when Valario was calling Khouri after a lesson, Khouri was inside the barn having some hands-on experience with his own drone." I pointed at the brochure. "I'd say that barn is definitely worth investigating."

Benson said, "I've seen that property myself. It's located in a heavily wooded area with only one way in, so it would be almost impossible to get on the site without having some reason to be there."

"Well, then," I said, "let's think of some reason to be there."

Carlton immediately reminded me I was operating on American soil. He said he couldn't condone, nor would he be part of any action that might jeopardize the FBI's case against Khouri in a court of law.

I knew he'd said this primarily for Benson's benefit, but he had sounded very convincing.

Convincing or not, the real question was, would Benson see this as an opportunity to redeem himself from past failures?

Or perhaps a better question might be, was he willing to take a chance in order to bring down a deep-cover operative? Say someone he might get credit for unmasking?

Benson said, "If Khouri invited us onto the property, then I don't believe there'd be a problem, at least not from a legal standpoint."

Apparently, Benson was willing to take a chance.

I said, "Well, if all it takes is an invitation, I may have a solution."

Carlton shook his head. "I don't want to hear the details. Just find some evidence we'll be able to use to get a search warrant from a judge, and the DDO will be happy."

By all means, let's make the DDO happy.

♦♦♦♦

After telling Benson to meet me at my Range Rover in the west parking lot in an hour, I left Carlton's office and walked over to Support Services in search of Josh Kellerman. I found him in the men's wardrobe section.

"Yesterday, when I turned in my Kit, I think I left some personal items inside the duffel bag. Have you had a chance to process it yet?"

"Since it was the weekend, I doubt it, but I can check."

We walked around the corner to a holding area a few feet away from the reception desk.

There, between a set of expensive-looking golf clubs and a ladies' briefcase, was the duffel bag I'd used in Syria.

"This is it, isn't it?" he asked, pointing down at the bag.

"That's it," I said, placing it up on a metal cart.

I was hoping Kellerman would leave the room while I dug through the bag, but he stood there and watched me while I worked the combination lock on the handle.

Although I knew it would cost me something, I sent him on an errand.

"As much as I hate to admit it, Josh, while I was in Syria, I misplaced the camera that was part of my Kit. Would you mind getting me the paperwork so I could report it?"

"Wasn't that a Nikon?"

"I'm afraid so."

He shook his head. "That was an expensive camera. I'll go grab the forms for you."

Once Kellerman had left the room, I unzipped the bag and found the wallet belonging to Donovan Bartlett, as well as the ID lanyard identifying him as an accredited journalist.

When I went out to the reception area, Kellerman asked, "Did you find what you were looking for?"

"No, it wasn't there".

He handed me a stack of forms. "I'll need to have these completely filled out and turned back in to me in two days."

"Are you kidding? Two days? This looks like a week's worth of work to me. Did I mention I was a little busy right now?"

He shrugged. "That's the price you have to pay for being careless."

♦♦♦♦

As soon as I got inside my Range Rover, I broke another Agency rule and made a call on my sat phone. Since I'd already broken several rules anyway, I doubted one more would make that much difference.

It was nine o'clock in the evening in Damascus, and when Pike answered his cell phone, I could hear loud music in the background.

"Partying without me?" I asked.

"Yes, we're definitely partying without you, but, come to think of it, I don't believe we ever partied with you when you were here."

"Who's we?"

"Trudy and I are having dinner together."

"Good for you."

"Well, one can only hope. What's up? Is this an official call?"

"Not really official; more like semi-official."

"In that case, I'll find a quieter place to talk."

As soon as I heard less noise in the background, I said, "Remember the scenario we discussed about getting an interview with a certain photographer?"

"Of course. Should I catch the next plane out of here?"

"No, I'm afraid that's not possible, but you could call the photographer up and ask him for that interview anyway. If he accepts—which I'm sure he will if you use your incredible powers of persuasion on him—then you should tell him you'll be sending another journalist, along with a photographer, over to his place to ask him some preliminary questions before you do a one-on-one interview with him."

"Can I assume this other journalist would be the world-renown Donnie Bartlett?"

"Correct."

Although it was obvious Pike wished he were stateside to take part in such an interview, he agreed to call Walid Khouri as soon as we were off the phone. I told him to emphasize Donovan Bartlett was only in Washington for a couple of days, so the appointment needed to happen immediately.

After telling him I'd be sending him Khouri's phone number, he promised to call me back once he got in touch with him.

A few minutes later, Frank Benson walked up and rapped on the car window.

After letting him in, I told him I had called Pike and asked him to set up an interview with Walid Khouri so we would have an excuse to get on his property.

He immediately sanctioned this plan, and he didn't balk at the idea of playing a photographer during the interview.

When I put the SUV in reverse and started backing out of the parking space, Benson asked, "So where are we headed now?"

"To a camera store. You'll need a good camera."

"I know nothing about cameras."

"A Nikon should do it, and I'm familiar with one of their better models."

"Are you also paying for it?"

"You're on official business. We'll put it on your FBI account."

## Chapter 50

After making the camera purchase, Benson and I stopped by a pizza joint to get a bite to eat. Once we'd finished, I gave him a brief lesson on how to use the Nikon.

He wasn't much of a techno nerd, and by the time Pike called me back, I could tell Benson was getting frustrated with the camera—not to mention irritated with me.

"He's agreed to do the interview," Pike said.

"When?"

"I couldn't pin him down. He said for you to call him, and he'd make the arrangements with you directly."

"Anything else?"

"As a matter of fact, he said he really admires my work. He even commented on several of my stories. To be truthful, he sounded more sophisticated than I expected."

"I'm sure he's a highly educated, well-read, intellectual kind of guy. Otherwise, he wouldn't be hobnobbing with the Washington elite."

"You should add charming to that list."

After I got off the phone with Pike, I had Benson get in touch with the surveillance team responsible for keeping a eye on Walid Khouri.

When he hung up, he said Khouri was still at his studio, but if he followed his usual pattern, he'd leave in an hour and stop by the construction site on his way home.

"It's getting pretty late," Benson said, "if you contact him today, he'll probably put off the interview until tomorrow."

"I agree. I'll call him in a few minutes. Perhaps, if I time it just right, I could catch him just as he's leaving work. He might even give me an invitation to meet him over at his new studio."

As soon as Benson left the table to get a refill on his diet Coke, Katherine called me, and by the time he got back, everything had changed.

♦♦♦♦

Katherine sounded excited. Along with her exuberance, there was an I'm-really-good-at-what-I-do tone in her voice.

"Douglas said I should call you."

"About?"

"What do you think? WK Photography. Walid Khouri."

"I'm listening."

"One of the encryption team members broke the code on Khouri's computer. When we got into his files, we discovered Walid Khouri is the proud owner of a drone. We traced the money from his Swiss bank account directly to the purchase."

She went on to make a few disparaging remarks about Arnie and his ineptitude at finding the drone purchase, and, admittedly, I didn't discourage her rants.

However, the moment she began winding down, I interrupted her and asked, "Is this the type of UAV Khouri could use for making aerial photographs? Would the drone accommodate a couple of cameras?"

"Are you kidding me? This is the type of drone that could accommodate just about anything. It's an Eagle Eye Model 918, developed by Bell Helicopter; it looks more like a mini-helicopter than a drone. I'm sending you a picture of it right now, along with some specs."

By this time, Benson had walked back over to the table, and I told him what Katherine had said as I waited for the image to appear.

When the Eagle Eye showed up on my screen moments later, we both studied it for several seconds.

I wasn't surprised when I heard Benson take a deep breath, because my heart rate definitely went up a couple of notches the longer I looked at it.

I said, "I haven't had a chance to look at the specs yet, Katherine, but from what I'm seeing here, I'd say this aircraft could be fitted with a payload, like maybe even some gas canisters. Is that right?"

"Oh, definitely, and more importantly, it's capable of reaching the altitude necessary to rupture the disc inside the canisters and mix the chemicals. When the weapons reach their target, depending on how hard the wind is blowing that day, the sarin gas could be spread over a wide area."

The Eagle Eye didn't appear all that ominous. The body of the aircraft was painted white, with red stripes across her nose, wings, and tail, which made the drone look more like a child's toy than a weapon of mass destruction.

However, I knew how deceptive the photograph was, so I asked Katherine to give me the highlights of the specs on it.

"It's a tilt rotor UAV, which means it's capable of vertical takeoff and landing, but during flight, her wings convert to a turboprop. It was developed by Bell in the late 90's for the Navy, but now it's sold commercially."

"What about its ground control system?"

"It's primarily a computer with a command module. One operator could handle it easily, and it wouldn't take up that much space either."

"How about transporting it? How big is it?"

"It has a wingspan of almost 18 feet with a height just under 6 feet. Transporting it would be fairly easy. It was designed to be broken down and moved in three sections."

I asked Benson if he had any questions for Katherine, and he nodded.

"Katherine, it's Frank. Do you see any connection between the type of training Valario was getting at the Aviation Club and this drone? I know he wasn't receiving instructions on this type of UAV."

"Yes, Frank, I've thought of that, and here's what interesting about the Eagle Eye. Its design is based on an earlier model Bell developed that didn't include a payload bay. Instead, that section of the fuselage was designed for a couple of cameras. However, the flight control system is exactly the same."

"So Valario trained on the earlier model and fed those instructions to Khouri?"

"I believe so. I'm having one of my analysts go over the transcript of those conversations to see if the instructions Valario gave Khouri would work on the Eagle Eye."

Benson thanked Katherine and handed the phone back to me.

"You're the best, Katherine. Thanks."

"Of course I am. I'm really good at what I do."

♦♦♦♦

We both agreed it was time to call Walid Khouri. However, I hesitated before making the call.

I wasn't sure why.

All I knew was that something was bothering me, and the plasma membrane inside my brain was frozen and wasn't allowing the neurons to communicate with each other.

Finally, something clicked, and I said, "Walid Khouri is a photographer."

"I believe that's what's known as stating the obvious."

"We need to switch roles. You should be the journalist, and I should be your photographer."

I opened the glove box and retrieved Donovan Bartlett's wallet, along with his press ID, and handed them both to Benson.

"I missed the part about why we're changing roles."

"One look at the way you handle the Nikon, and Khouri will immediately know you're clueless about photography."

Benson held up the press card. "I can't use this. It has your picture on it"

"You really think that looks like me? It could be anybody."

"It looks exactly like you."

"No, it doesn't. Besides, you probably won't have to show any ID."

"What happens if we both have to show some ID?"

"I've got that covered," I said, reaching back inside the glove box and pulling out a driver's license. "I'm Douglas Carlton. It says so right here."

♦♦♦♦

Before Benson made the call, I went over what Pike had told Khouri in order to get the interview. Namely, Pike said he was doing an article for a major magazine on photographers who took pictures of the rich and famous, and he wanted Walid Khouri to be the featured photographer.

When Benson made the call to Khouri, I had him put his phone on speaker so I could hear the conversation.

"Mr. Khouri, this is Donovan Bartlett. I believe you've been expecting my call?"

"Yes, of course. I spoke with Keever Pike earlier, and he said you'd be calling to set up an appointment. He mentioned he'd be sending his advance man and a photographer by to scout out some locations for the interview." Khouri paused and gave a short laugh. "Frankly, I was flattered he thought I merited an advance team."

It was Benson's turn to laugh, and he did a good job of making it sound authentic. "Well, Keever's a perfectionist, so he likes for things to go smoothly. Since I was here in D.C. for a couple of days, he thought I could stop by and go over some preliminary questions with you before he arrives in town to do the main interview. He'd also like for our photographer to shoot a few pictures, if you don't mind."

"That's fine, but I've already closed the studio for the day. Perhaps we could get together tomorrow. An afternoon appointment works best for me."

"That's certainly doable. Keever wants to include a special section on your new studio in the piece. Is it possible for us to meet there tomorrow afternoon?"

"Actually, I'm on my way over to the construction site right now. Would it be convenient for you to meet me over there now?"

Benson pretended to consider this for a few seconds, and then he told him he could be there within the hour. Khouri said he'd be looking forward to it and hung up.

"Okay, we're in," Benson said. "We should head over there now."

"First, we need to do something about your wardrobe. You look like an FBI agent."

Although Benson had shed his tie before we went in the store to buy the camera, he still had on his blue suit and white shirt.

"We'll stop somewhere and get you a different shirt," I said, "maybe a pair of jeans to go with it."

"You're right. I shouldn't look so respectable." He held up the press card of Donovan Bartlett. "I should look more like this picture, a little rough around the edges."

♦♦♦♦

The new home of WK Photography was located off Mt. Laurel Drive near Little Falls Park. After stopping off at a mall, where Benson purchased a pair of khakis and a sports shirt, we drove west on Mt. Laurel and then turned north onto a narrow drive leading up to Khouri's new studio.

While some clearing had taken place, the architect had obviously designed the building to incorporate the natural landscape, thus providing Khouri with plenty of ambiance to use as a backdrop for his award-wining photography.

In front of the rustic-looking studio, there was a small parking lot, and I pulled into a space next to a black Lexus, which Benson said belonged to Khouri.

"The studio looks finished," I said. "I wonder why he hasn't moved out here yet."

Benson pointed off in the distance, over to a construction site, where the front section of a Southern style mansion was being built. "That must be one of the facades the brochure mentioned. Maybe he's not moving in until everything's finished."

I picked up the Nikon and shot a few pictures. Then, I pointed the camera at an old barn at the back of the studio.

"That barn is definitely not a new construction. It looks authentically old."

"This used to be farmland out here. It could have been part of the original property."

The gabled barn was picturesque, like something out of a storybook. While it had obviously been painted red at one time, the sun had bleached the color to a soft rose now. However, the building itself appeared to be in good shape.

If the Eagle Eye was on the property, the barn was definitely the place I'd find it.

Before getting out of the car, I turned to Benson and said, "Even though you changed your clothes, I'm assuming you still have your weapon on you."

"Yeah, I've got my Sig. What about you? Did you bring the Glock you pulled on me the other night?"

"It wasn't necessary to remind me of that, but, yes, I've got my Glock on me."

One of the first rules the Agency drilled into new recruits at The Farm was never go into a situation without knowing what kind of weapon your partner was carrying.

Benson said, "I know you were just doing a weapons check, but just in case you had something else in mind, don't forget, we're only here to collect evidence linking Khouri to the canisters. That's it. Shoot some pictures, gather enough evidence for a warrant, and we're out of here."

"Speaking of shooting, here comes our target now," I said, pointing over to where the mansion's façade was being constructed.

When I'd parked the Range Rover in front of the studio, Khouri had been talking to a group of workers over by the site. Now, as the men were getting in their vehicles and leaving the property, Khouri was headed back towards the studio.

As I observed the man walking toward us, I understood why the DDO had been reluctant to tie him to the Navy Yard shooting, much less an attack on Washington.

For the first time, I questioned whether or not the photographer could really be Mohammed after all.

That was the last time I considered that question.

# Chapter 51

Walid Khouri bore little resemblance to any terrorist or deep-cover operative I'd ever met. He was dressed in a pair of designer jeans and an equally expensive shirt, and he exuded self-confidence, the type of exalted self-image usually only seen in career politicians or the very wealthy.

If a voice analysis hadn't positively identified Khouri as the person on the phone giving the orders to Reyes Valario, I would have had trouble believing he was in any way connected to Muslim extremists.

"Gentlemen," he said, gesturing all around him. "welcome to the new home of WK Photography. I'm Walid Khouri."

He smiled and extended his hand toward Benson. "Since you're the one without the camera, I have to assume you're Donovan Bartlett."

"That's right," Benson said, shaking hands with him.

"Douglas Carlton," I said, when Khouri offered me his hand.

Khouri more or less ignored me and gave his full attention to Benson, studying him as if he might be considering how to photograph that square jaw of his.

Benson appeared oblivious to this scrutiny and quizzed Khouri about the different venues he was building on the tract of land.

Khouri launched into a short explanation of how the property would be used to create family portraits and wedding photographs providing "exquisite memories lasting a lifetime."

As he pointed to different sites on the property and described his upcoming construction projects, I aimed the Nikon at the various spots and clicked away.

"Let's go inside, and I'll show you my new showroom and studio." Nodding his head at me, he said, "I'm sure you'll find it especially interesting."

I agreed with him; probably not for the reasons he thought.

The reception area of the studio was designed to be a showroom for Khouri's work. Thus, like the photographer I was supposed to be, I slowly made my way around the room scrutinizing every image and pretending to know all about lights and shadows and camera angles.

Pointing at an enlarged black and white portrait of a family standing in a field surrounded by cows, I told Khouri, "I love what you've done with the lighting in this picture."

Sweeping my arm around the entire room, I added, "In fact, I could spend hours here just studying your technique."

He gave me a brief smile, but I got the distinct impression he wasn't buying what I was selling.

Benson took my silly statement as his cue to get Khouri out of the room. "Before we start the interview, I'd love to see the rest of your studio."

Khouri nodded and gestured at me. "I'm sure you'll enjoy seeing it as well. My new equipment is all state-of-the-art."

"Do you mind if I finish looking at these photographs first?"

"Of course not," he said. "The studio's right down this hallway. Come join us when you're ready."

I waited until the two men had disappeared around the corner, and then I immediately slipped out the front door and headed down toward the barn.

I figured it would take me two minutes to get down there, two minutes to locate the Eagle Eye, and two minutes to get back to the studio before I was missed.

Those calculations were correct.

Unfortunately, I didn't take into account the locked door.

♦♦♦♦

Earlier, when I'd used the zoom feature on the Nikon to take a look at the barn, it had been impossible to see the details on the exterior doors.

Although I'd noticed they were sliding doors, typical of a horse barn, I wasn't able to see the locking mechanism located just above the door handles.

Now, that lock was staring me in the face.

A key was required to open it, but thankfully, it was a simple cylinder, so I began searching the area for something I could use to pick the lock.

According to my internal clock, I'd been away from Khouri's showroom for less than three minutes.

As I was about to give up any hope of finding anything, I happened to notice the camera strap around my neck. It had a thin strip of metal at the very end of it, close to the point where the camera was attached to the strap.

I immediately removed it and went to work on the lock.

A minute later, I was able to slide the barn doors open.

I'm not sure what I was expecting.

I knew there weren't any horses on the property, so it wasn't as if I were anticipating a barn full of hay and horse tack.

Still, because of the barn's age, I was at least expecting an onslaught of musty odors, perhaps the sight of bats hanging from the rafters.

Instead, the barn was pristine, with only a slight whiff of stale air, and, in lieu of bats, there was an unmanned aerial vehicle, a Bell Eagle Eye Model 918, parked in front of me.

The drone was painted white with red markings on the nose, wings, and tail, and it looked exactly like the photograph Katherine had sent me.

The shaft of light from the barn door illuminated the aircraft and bathed the wings in bright sunlight. The wings themselves were in their vertical position, looking very much like a couple of soldiers standing at attention.

I put the Nikon on continuous burst mode and walked around the UAV. As a way of documenting the drone's location, I also included the interior of the barn in some of my shots.

At least seven minutes had passed since I'd slipped out of the studio, and although I knew I should leave immediately, I couldn't do so until I'd taken a look at one last thing—namely, the vehicle parked behind the Eagle Eye.

I thought I knew what I'd find inside, and I wasn't far off the mark.

♦♦♦♦

It was a cargo van, similar to the Aramex van Pike and I had occupied in Damascus when we were monitoring Naballah's compound.

I opened the back door and climbed inside.

Katherine had told me the control system for the Eagle Eye was a command module attached to a computer, which sounded simple enough, but the setup inside the van looked a little more complicated than that. In fact, there were two computers and some additional equipment I couldn't identify.

Next to the second computer, I found a set of instructions. They were written in Arabic, and although I didn't have time to give them more than a cursory glance, I immediately recognized the second computer wasn't there to control the aircraft. Its purpose was to monitor the CCTV cameras around Washington.

Presumably, as Walid Khouri was flying the Eagle Eye over the nation's capital, bombarding the population with chemical weapons, he'd be observing his handiwork in real time on the second computer.

Since the control system for the drone was set up inside the cargo van, I had to believe he had plans to park the vehicle at a location far outside the kill zone on 7/11.

Even though I'd been away from the studio way past my self-imposed time limit, I took out my Agency phone and snapped a couple of photographs of the Eagle Eye as it stood alongside the cargo van.

I sent the pictures, along with a short message, to Carlton's phone.

My text said, "*Found them.*"

After sending it, I suddenly realized it was the same message

Mitchell had sent the Ops Center about the missing shipping containers—the last words anyone had heard from him.

On that ominous note, I quickly closed the barn doors and made my way back up to the studio.

♦♦♦♦

I half-expected Khouri and Benson to be waiting for me in the reception area. When they weren't, I breathed a sigh of relief and proceeded down the hallway to take a look at Khouri's studio.

While I knew I'd have to show at least a cursory interest in the new photography equipment, I was determined to let Benson know I'd found enough evidence for the feds to get a search warrant for Khouri's property, and it was time for Donovan Bartlett and Douglas Carlton to leave the grounds.

When I opened the door to the main portion of Khouri's studio, where his photography equipment was located, I was surprised to find the place empty.

At that point, I began to get a little uneasy.

I told myself it might be the stark white walls and the dead silence of the place that was making me uncomfortable. But then I noticed something out of place; something sitting on top of a white plastic cube.

I walked over and picked it up. It was an ID badge, Donovan Bartlett's press badge, the one with my picture on it.

I wasn't exactly sure what that meant, but I knew it couldn't be good.

I took out my Glock and reentered the hallway.

♦♦♦♦

The first room on the left was a feminine-looking dressing area, with two large makeup mirrors and some curtained changing rooms.

It was empty.

A similar room for men, in a much different décor, was across the hall.

It was also empty.

When I arrived at the last room at the end of the corridor, there was a sign on the door which read Walid Khouri, Photographer.

That room was not empty.

Although the door was shut, I could hear two people talking inside, and I quickly identified the voices as belonging to Benson and Khouri.

As I stood there listening to what Khouri was saying, I tried to envision where the two men were located in the room. I wanted to pinpoint specifically their position relative to each other and to the door.

Once I'd established that, I burst through the door, pivoted to my right, and aimed the pistol at Khouri, who was standing in front of a desk with a gun in his hand.

He was pointing it at Benson, who was seated in front of him.

The moment he saw me, he fired the pistol directly at Benson, and then he quickly turned and aimed the gun at me.

At that point, I shot him.

His left hand immediately clutched the center of his chest, and he fell to the floor.

He didn't move after that.

I rushed over to Benson, who was slumped over the chair.

"Where have you been?" he asked, holding onto his shoulder.

"How bad is it?"

"I'll live. He's a lousy shot."

"Either that or I startled him." I looked at the hole in Benson's shoulder. "You know he ruined your new shirt."

"At least I'm alive. He said he was going to kill me."

"Yeah, I heard that part."

After I ripped Khouri's shirt off his dead body and used it to apply pressure to Benson's wound, he called his division head at the FBI. Once he hung up, he said the feds were on their way, and they were sending an ambulance.

"Please tell me you found something inside the barn," Benson said, looking down at the blood-soaked shirt. "That way I won't feel so foolish."

After giving him the details of finding the Eagle Eye, I said, "Now, it's your turn. What happened after you left me in the showroom?"

♦♦♦♦

Benson said once Khouri had finished showing him the studio, he suggested they go over the background questions for Pike's interview.

"I was just trying to give you as much time as possible," Benson said, "but as soon as I brought up the interview, he asked me why I was pretending to be a journalist."

"He was on to us from the very beginning, wasn't he? I saw him staring at you when we were introducing ourselves."

Benson nodded. "Yeah, according to him he was."

"What did you say?"

"I held up my press badge, which wasn't very smart I guess, because he immediately grabbed it and made a big deal about it being your picture on the ID."

Benson paused and appeared to lose his train of thought. His color wasn't that good, and I thought he might be going into shock.

"Save your strength. I'll hear the rest of the story later."

"No, I can finish it. There's not that much left to tell."

He laid his head back against the chair cushion. "Before I knew what was happening, Khouri threw the badge back at me and pulled a gun on me. After that, he demanded I give him my weapon. When I asked him why he thought I was carrying a gun, he told me a newscaster had identified me as an FBI agent when they were doing live broadcasts of the Navy Yard shooting."

"Of course," I said. "I should have thought of that earlier. Khouri must have watched those videos numerous times. You were front and center on several of the news channels."

"Don't blame yourself. I didn't think of it either, and I'm twice the detail person you are."

"I can't argue with you about that."

"He demanded to know what we were doing on his property. At that point, I decided it didn't matter if I told him the truth, and frankly, I wanted to see how he'd respond. When I told him the FBI had evidence connecting him to the Navy Yard shooter, he seemed genuinely surprised at this information."

I glanced down at Khouri's body. "I'm sure he thought of himself as invincible."

"He didn't believe me about the evidence. He said if we had proof he was involved, we would have arrived at the property with an arrest warrant. He seemed convinced the two of us had gone rogue and hadn't told our superiors what we were doing. I denied it, of course, but I could tell he didn't believe me."

Benson grimaced, and I figured his body had started sending out some pretty heavy duty pain signals by now.

"He kept waiting around for you to show up, and when you didn't, I think he got a little spooked. When he said he was taking me to his office, I decided to leave the ID badge on the cube, hoping it might give you a heads up something had gone wrong."

"That's exactly what happened, Frank. I'm glad to see you've gotten a little more creative in your old age."

When Benson didn't respond to my comment, I knew he didn't have much fight left in him.

"Once we got in here, he shoved me in this chair and said he planned to shoot me whenever you showed up."

"I heard that part. I was standing outside the door by that time."

"I would say your timing was perfect, but—"

"Yeah, I know. You got shot."

When the ambulance arrived, I stepped out in the hallway and called Carlton.

"There's a situation. The DDO may want to get involved."

## Chapter 52

*Tuesday, July 7*

Stormy wouldn't leave my side. Last night, he'd been the first to greet me when I'd pulled in the driveway at The Meadows. When I'd left him to go inside, he'd remained at the front door, barking incessantly.

Despite Arkady's protests, I'd allowed him to come inside the house. Once Millie had gone up to bed, I'd even smuggled him upstairs and let him sleep with me.

Now, while I was sitting out on the patio enjoying a mug of Millie's delicious coffee, he was at my side watching Frisco chase a squirrel up a tree.

Stormy didn't seem the least bit interested in participating in the squirrel's antics, and I asked him, "What's going on, boy? You're not sick, are you?"

At the sound of my voice, he immediately looked up at me, tilting his head to one side as if he were considering how he should answer that question.

"Don't worry about Stormy," Arkady said, coming out the back door. "He's just fine."

Arkady sat down beside me and opened up a newspaper. "What about you?"

"What about me?"

"You don't look so good. I thought you looked pretty bad last night, but this morning, you don't look much better. That's the reason Stormy won't leave you alone. Dogs can sense those things, you know."

"It's been a rough few days, and the week's not over yet. That's about all I can say."

"Sure, I get it," he said, glancing down at his newspaper. "Hey, did you hear about this guy getting shot last night? It's all over the news this morning."

Before he turned the paper around and showed me the guy's picture, I thought for sure the Bureau had violated their agreement with the DDO and released the story of Walid Khouri's demise.

However, the headlines were about a rock star who'd been shot by a demented fan. "Sorry. Never heard of him."

"Not your generation, I guess."

His comment made me think of Benson, and I debated whether or not I should call the hospital and check up on him. I knew he had made it out of surgery because Carlton had texted me around midnight to tell me the doctors had removed the bullet, and he was expected to make a full recovery.

Carlton seldom texted me.

I'd never asked him why, but I suspected it had something to do with the way he communicated a message.

His verbal messages always involved *tone. Tone* was very big with Carlton, and it had taken me years to understand that. If I didn't get the *tone* right in his message, things could go very wrong.

Since Carlton had texted me about Benson, I had to believe he knew he'd portrayed his *tone* sufficiently when he'd viewed Walid Khouri's dead body.

Carlton had arrived at Khouri's studio after the ambulance had taken Benson to the hospital. He'd brought along a couple of suits from the seventh floor, who were there to represent the DDO in negotiations with the FBI.

Once everyone had heard my explanation and examined Khouri's body, they'd gone down the hallway to his studio and hammered out an agreement with the feds to keep Khouri's death out of the media—at least until after Franco Cabello had texted Marwan and the feds had been able to secure the chemical weapons.

The story they'd agreed to feed the press as to why an ambulance had been called to Walid Khouri's property was that a construction worker had been injured on the job.

After their confab was over, I took the whole crew down to the barn to show them the Eagle Eye. The feds seemed particularly upset with me after I told them my fingerprints would be all over the cargo van, but Carlton didn't say a word.

When the two of us were walking back up to the studio together, Carlton had turned to me and asked, "The description you gave about Khouri's death, would that be an accurate one? Was he about to shoot you? Were you the person who shot him?"

I stopped and stared at him. "Yes, that's exactly what happened."

He nodded. "That's what I thought, but I just wanted to make sure."

I hung my head for a second, but then I looked him straight in the eye. "Look, Douglas. I know why you felt compelled to ask me that, but I assure you, what happened in Caracas will never happen again."

He surprised me by placing his hand on my shoulder. "I know that, Titus, and, for what it's worth, the death of Ahmed Al-Amin was a good thing, no matter who pulled the trigger."

When we arrived back at the studio, I told him I was headed over to the hospital to check up on Benson.

"No, you should go out to The Meadows get some sleep. Frank knows you saved his life, and I'm quite certain he'll never forget it."

"Knowing Frank as I do, that might not be such a good thing."

"Personally, I think the fact you've finally forgiven him for what happened in Yemen is a good thing."

Was that true? Had I finally forgiven him?

I guess I had.

♦♦♦♦

Arkady and I were in the middle of a discussion about a couple of Russian jets buzzing a U.S. Navy ship, when my cell phone began vibrating.

The phone number on the screen wasn't one I recognized, but

since Carlton had told me someone from the Bureau would be contacting me for an official statement of Khouri's death, I took the call.

"Titus, it's Elijah Mitchell. Is this a bad time?"

"Ah . . . no. I suppose it's just as good a time as any."

Arkady must have realized I needed some privacy—the look on my face probably gave me away—and he picked up his newspaper and walked down the grassy slope towards the pool. Meanwhile, Stormy remained beside me.

"I'll get right to the point," the Senator said. "I've had my assistant put you on my schedule for today. Come by my office in the Senate Building at one o'clock."

"I can't think of any reason I'd need to come by your office. We have nothing left to discuss."

"We have plenty to discuss."

"Is this about my nephew? Brian told me you had hired him for the summer. If it—"

"It's not about Brian. It's about my son."

"What about Ben?"

"We'll discuss it when I see you at one o'clock. Don't be late."

On that arrogant note, he ended the call.

♦♦♦♦

I sat there for several minutes debating whether or not I should tell Carlton about the Senator's demand to see me. So far, Carlton had refused to discuss Mitchell's missing status with me, and I realized there was no reason to believe he would talk about it now.

In the end, I decided to play this one solo and see what the Senator had on his mind before informing him.

While I didn't call Carlton, I did make a couple of other phone calls.

The first one was to Nikki.

I caught her just as she was about to leave for her classes at Quantico, and she wasn't able to talk for more than a couple of minutes. When I told her I was free for the evening, we made plans for us to meet for dinner.

The second phone call was to Olivia. She answered immediately.

"Does this mean you didn't get killed in Damascus?"

"Hi, Olivia. It's nice to hear your voice."

"I find that hard to believe, but thanks anyway."

"How are you? Are you in much pain?"

"Why are men so concerned about pain? I'm not in any pain, and I barely took any pain medication after my surgery. If you want to know how I'm feeling, the answer is I'm feeling ugly."

"I know of no surgery that would ever make you ugly, Olivia. You know you're a beautiful woman. That's never going to change."

She didn't respond.

I tried to move on. "I read the note you left me, and I realize what a big step of faith that was for you."

I heard her sigh. "I might as well tell you, becoming a believer hasn't solved all my problems. I still don't understand very much, plus I have plenty of doubts about what I'm reading in the Bible, and I know it hasn't made me a nicer person."

"I think that's normal. While the decision itself is a one-time sort of thing, I'm just beginning to understand there's also a journey involved. In our line of work, we'd probably think of it as a course of action that moves from one point to another. As we move along, we get a little more understanding of the gospel message, and our faith increases at the same time. It's just a matter of taking baby steps."

"If that's true, then my journey has started out pretty slow."

"Join the club. As it stands right now, I seem to take one step forward and three steps back."

Olivia changed the subject and started quizzing me about Operation Citadel Protection. However, I wasn't comfortable discussing those details with her until she was back on active status, so I tried putting her off and telling her I'd get back with her in a few days.

She didn't like that one bit.

"I'm hanging up now because it sounds like you're giving me the cold shoulder. But hey, thanks for calling."

Always a pleasure, Olivia.

♦♦♦♦

The scene inside SR214 of the Russell Senate Building looked a little different than the last time I'd been there to see the Senator. The décor was still the same, but now, there were no constituents hanging around eating the Senator's refreshments or viewing his artifacts.

Instead, there was only a beautiful blond receptionist, who smiled at me when I gave her my name. She told me the Senator was expecting me.

As I followed her down the corridor toward his office, she asked, "You work for CIS, right?"

I nodded. "I'm a Senior Fellow there."

"I believe your nephew, Brian Simpson, is one of our new interns. He's out of the office right now, but I'll tell him you stopped by."

"Please do. I'm sorry I missed him."

"He seemed surprised when I told him you had an appointment with the Senator today."

"I can't imagine why."

She opened the door to the Senator's inner office and announced, "Mr. Ray is here for his appointment."

The Senator, who was seated behind his desk, immediately got to his feet and gave me a big smile. "I appreciate a man who arrives on time. Thank you, Shirley."

Once Shirley had left, his smile disappeared.

"A Mexican drug cartel has my son," he said. "I want you to get him back for me."

♦♦♦♦

I stood there in front of the Senator's desk, processing what he'd said for several seconds. Meanwhile, he sat down at his desk and turned his laptop around so I could view the screen.

"This picture was attached to an email message I received this morning." He used the touchpad to click open an icon on his screen. "It's obvious it was taken less than twelve hours ago."

I leaned across the top of his massive desk and studied the photograph.

It was Ben Mitchell; there was little doubt about that. He was facing the camera and holding what appeared to be the current international edition of *The Miami Herald*.

From a physical standpoint, he looked pretty good; clean-shaven, head erect, nothing to indicate he'd been tortured or injured in any way. However, his facial expression was blank; there was no fire in his eyes. That alone spoke volumes.

"It looks like Ben."

"Of course, it's Ben. I know my own son's face."

Although he hadn't offered me a seat, I sat down in the guest chair opposite his desk. "Tell me how you got this."

"Like I said, it came in an email. It's an address I primarily use for my personal correspondence, and, as far as I know, it's never been made public."

"Would this email address be familiar to Ben?"

"Sure. He uses it all the time."

"What about the message? You said the photograph was attached to an email message."

He nodded and used the touchpad to click on a different icon.

As soon as the message came up, he said, "Be forewarned. It reads like a bad movie."

He was right.

*"Your son is alive and well, but it's up to you to make sure he stays that way. We'll be in touch."*

The note was signed Z, which certainly made it appear as if it had come from the Los Zetas cartel.

The English translation of *Los Zetas* was "The Z's," and the cartel members used the letter Z as a means of claiming responsibility for their most violent crimes, including carving the letter on the torsos of their victims.

I pushed the computer back across the desk towards the Senator. "I'm sure you know the next message will include a demand for money."

"Forget the money. Let's talk about what's happened to my son."

Before I had a chance to respond, he began reciting the details of what he knew about Mitchell's disappearance, including some highly classified material I knew would not have been disseminated during a Senate Intelligence briefing.

The more he talked, the more I realized there had to be some high-ranking staff member at the Agency who was feeding the Senator his information.

The moment he said he knew Mitchell had been working with me in Buenos Aires, I had a flashback to a photograph on Ken Vasco's bookshelf at the embassy, and I immediately knew who his Agency source must be.

He said, "I've tried to be content and allow the SOF unit to locate Ben, but now that I know Los Zetas is holding him, I've decided to be proactive and find him myself."

"And how exactly would you go about doing that?"

"That's where you come in. I understand Operation Citadel Protection is about to reach its end point, and the Bureau will be able to secure the chemical weapons sometime tomorrow. Once that happens, I know the Agency will give you some time off, so I'd like to hire you to find out where the cartel is holding Ben. I assure you, I'll make it worth your while."

I shook my head. "Once the SOF unit runs out of leads to Ben's whereabouts, you should press the DDO to mount an operation to locate him. Using the Agency's resources is a better option than hiring one man to do the job."

He looked at me as if I'd insulted him. "No, Titus. It's obvious you don't understand the politics of my position as Chairman of the Senate Intelligence Committee. I've already asked the DDO to do me a favor once in regards to my son. If I do so again, I will have used up all my power chips with him, and that means I'll end up owing him a favor. That's a position I never want to find myself in."

"Not even for your son?"

He stared at me. "You're not turning me down, are you? I thought you cared about Ben."

"You're right on both counts. I do care about Ben, and I *am* turning you down. I won't do what you're asking me to do because I refuse to put Ben's life in even more danger. And, I assure you, Senator, that's exactly what you'll be doing if you try to mount a one-man operation to rescue him from the cartel."

I stood to my feet. "If you decide your son is more important than your political ambitions, then ask the DDO to initiate a search and rescue operation for Ben. When that happens, you can count on me being part of that mission. If not, we have nothing left to say to each other."

I stood there for a beat or two waiting for his response.

When there wasn't one, I turned and walked out the door.

## Chapter 53

During my conversation with Nikki earlier in the day, she'd suggested we meet for dinner at the Marine Corps National Museum in Triangle, Virginia, just a few miles down the road from the FBI Academy at Quantico.

I'd been surprised at the location, so I'd repeated it back to her just to make sure I'd heard her correctly. She must have known I was puzzled by her choice of restaurants, because after giving me the location again, she assured me I'd understand why she wanted me to meet her there once I arrived.

The Marine Museum was located off I-95, south of Washington, and I pulled in the parking lot at exactly seven o'clock.

When I got out of the Range Rover, I spotted Nikki sitting on a bench outside the entrance. She was watching a bunch of kids feeding the ducks at a nearby pond, and she didn't seem to notice me when I got out of my car.

As I walked toward her, I realized the sight of her sitting there had caused my heart rate to increase, and my palms to get a little sweaty.

Whether it was an illusion caused by the rays of light from the lowering sun, or simply the result of my imagination, there seemed to be an iridescent quality to her face, almost like a radiance from within, and I found myself wishing I could always remember how she looked at that moment.

A thought popped in my head that seemed so ridiculous it made me smile, and I was sure she would find it equally amusing, so I walked over to her and said, "If I were an artist, I'd have to paint your beautiful face in this light."

"Titus," she said, standing up and brushing her lips across my cheek, "what a wonderful thing to say."

Okay, I was wrong about that ridiculous part.

♦♦♦♦

Although the concrete walls of the museum's exterior were nondescript, the centerpiece in the middle of the structure was not. Ascending from the building's center section was a tall column of stainless steel meant to represent the raising of the flag at Iwo Jima during World War II.

The immense column was supported by a steel framework made up of hundreds of glass panels. The glass panels weren't all that noticeable on the outside, but, on the inside, they formed a gigantic skylight in the ceiling of the museum's lobby.

When Nikki and I walked inside, the effect of the sun shining through the multi-tiered windows produced a breathtaking effect.

Nikki pointed up at the ceiling. "Here's the reason I asked you to meet me here. Isn't this amazing?"

"It's beautiful."

"I was here over the weekend with some of my team members, and our tour guide told us to be sure and come back around sunset and eat dinner at The Overlook. She said the views would be spectacular."

The Overlook was located on the second level and was designed to resemble the cockpit view from a Marine Corps Harrier jet. When the waitress seated us, she said we wouldn't be disappointed in either the food or the view.

I looked across the table at Nikki. "How could I be disappointed in this view?"

The waitress smiled and tapped Nikki on the shoulder. "Honey, this one's a keeper."

Nikki nodded and smiled at me. "I'm beginning to believe that."

♦♦♦♦

As soon as the waitress took our orders, Nikki leaned across the table and squeezed my hand.

"Hearing your voice on the phone this morning made my day. I admit I've been worried about you."

"My assignment had its hairy moments, but you'll be happy to know I kept my promise and remembered you were praying for me during those times."

"You said you were headed to a dangerous place. Was it as bad as you thought it would be?"

I nodded. "In some ways it was much worse."

Like any good detective, she waited a few seconds before commenting, and I knew she was probably counting on the empty silence to elicit a more elaborate response from me.

When that didn't happen, she said, "I can tell it's been rough on you."

I laughed. "You're the second person today who's told me I don't look so hot."

She smiled at me. "I wasn't saying *that*."

It was my turn to smile. "Then you'll have to elaborate on your analysis."

She made an elaborate show of studying my face. "Okay, according to my expert analysis, you look emotionally drained, plus a little worried."

That pretty much summed up how I was feeling after shooting Walid Khouri last night and then hearing Ben Mitchell had been kidnapped by the cartel this afternoon. However, I was surprised to hear her say it.

"Well, Detective, it seems the feds have been perfecting your observation skills this week."

"So I'm right?"

I shrugged. "I admit I'm a little worried."

"In your line of work, if you're worried about something, I imagine all of us should be worried."

"No, my worries have nothing to do with a threat to our national security, at least not directly."

"Any day now, I should start receiving briefings on national security as part of my terrorism training. Once that happens, maybe you and I can discuss those threats."

Her remark gave me an opening to ask her about how her training was going, and she spent the rest of the meal describing her classes at the Academy and telling me how she felt about some of her instructors.

Nikki was in the middle of relating an incident that happened to her on the gun range, when our waitress came by and asked us about having dessert. Once we'd both ordered cappuccinos, she resumed her story.

The more I listened to her, the more I became envious of her freedom to tell me about all the things she was experiencing. Welling up inside of me was an overwhelming desire to share my own feelings with her, and, for the first time in my life, I resented the innate secrecy of a career that wouldn't allow me do that.

Almost immediately, I heard a voice inside my head—which sounded suspiciously like Carlton's—asking me what I'd tell Nikki if all the secrecy restrictions were suddenly lifted.

That was easy.

I'd tell her about being summoned to Senator Mitchell's office earlier in the day, and about the Senator's son being kidnapped by a Mexican drug cartel, and why I was so worried about that.

But that wasn't all.

I'd also share with her why I was forced to kill a man last night.

For some reason, I thought if I could just go over those details with her, I might stop thinking about it.

The urge to share my life with someone was an impulse completely foreign to me, but I suspected it was connected to the realization I was falling in love with Nikki Saxon, and I wanted us to have a future together.

The possibility of that happening seemed remote to me.

If I couldn't share my life experiences with her, or if I wasn't willing to open up and become more transparent about what I was thinking, how could we ever have an intimate relationship?

As Nikki finished telling me about the incident at the gun range, I remembered the advice I'd given Olivia about taking small steps. I decided if I really wanted to have an relationship with Nikki, I'd need to venture out of my shell and take at least one small step in that direction.

The problem was, I had no idea what that step might be.

A few minutes later, the problem was solved when Nikki brought up the subject of Frank Benson.

♦♦♦♦

After placing our cappuccinos in front of us, the waitress kept hanging around our table, and the minute I glanced down at my cup, I understood why.

The barista had used the foam on the top of the cup to create a set of matching hearts.

Nikki looked down at hers and laughed. "This is so sweet. Thank you."

The waitress shrugged. "What can I say? You two are obviously meant for each other, and I'm a born matchmaker."

As she walked away, I said, "I think the lady missed her calling. With those instincts, she would have made a good detective."

"Speaking of which, would you be surprised if I told you I was considering leaving the Norman Police Department and applying at the Bureau?"

I put my cup down. "Yes, I'd definitely be surprised at that."

She nodded. "I thought so."

"How long have you been thinking about this?"

"To be truthful, not very long. But I've had several conversations with Frank lately, and he—"

"Frank? You mean Frank Benson?"

She nodded. "Yes, Frank Benson, your friend at the Bureau. At least he still claims to be your friend, even though you pulled a gun on him."

"That was a misunderstanding."

She smiled at me and shook her head, making it obvious she knew

I still wasn't giving her the full story.

"Did you know your friend got shot last night?"

"Frank got shot?"

"One of our instructors said it happened during a training exercise. He's still in the hospital, but they said he'd be okay."

"Frank's a tough old bird."

Nikki suddenly morphed into Detective Saxon. "I don't believe you answered my question, Titus. Did you know Frank got shot last night?"

At that moment, the waitress came by and dropped off our check, which meant I didn't have to respond to her immediately. I bought myself even more time by removing several bills from my wallet and slowly counting them out before handing them over to the waitress.

After she walked away from the table, I glanced over at Nikki.

By the look on her face, I could tell she suspected I was deliberately avoiding the subject of Frank Benson.

It seemed an appropriate moment to take a small step, and I said, "Let's find a quiet place where we can be alone. There's something I need to tell you about Frank."

♦♦♦♦

Although the sun had nearly set by the time Nikki and I walked out of the museum, there was still enough light for us to make our way across the footbridge connecting the museum to Prince William Forest Park, a recreational area run by the National Parks Service.

The walkway led over to the park's visitor center, and, even though it was getting late, the place still looked busy. The park had an abundance of camp sites, not to mention several hiking trails, so I wasn't surprised it was crowded, especially at this time of year.

When I'd mentioned finding a quiet place to talk, Nikki had suggested we walk over to the visitor center, but, as we crossed over the bridge, we found ourselves surrounded by a large group of Boy Scouts, and I wondered if she'd heard me correctly.

"You heard me say I wanted to find a quiet place, right?"

"Trust me. When I was here the other day, I saw the perfect spot.

It's down this way."

I followed her over to a designated jogging path that meandered alongside a stream. We hadn't gone far before Nikki pointed over to a grassy area just off the pathway where the stream narrowed down to a trickle. Although there was a sign indicating no camping was allowed, the Parks Service had placed a picnic table in the clearing, along with a large trash barrel.

"Will this do?" she asked.

I took a quick look around. "It's perfect."

Something near the water's edge drew my attention, and while Nikki sat down at the picnic table, I walked over and picked it up.

It was a plastic toy, some type of super hero.

It looked as if the action figure had deliberately been placed behind a fortification built of rocks and then camouflaged with some mud and twigs. I decided a child had constructed the garrison, and then he'd forgotten about the hero or he'd intentionally left him out in the forest to make it on his own.

"Some kid may shed a few tears tonight when he realizes he left this guy behind," I said, sitting down across from Nikki and placing the figure between us.

She picked up the toy and gently brushed away the mud from his face. "Are you speaking from personal experience?"

"Not really. When I was growing up, I was mainly into sports."

"You didn't play with toy soldiers?"

"Definitely not."

"I'd love to hear about your childhood one day."

"Sure, as long as you like short stories."

"I'm mostly interested in the story itself; not the length of it."

"I don't believe you'll like the story I'm about to tell you. I'm certainly not proud of it. It involves you and Frank Benson."

♦♦♦♦

Whether it was my training or my desire to justify myself, I spent the next several minutes giving Nikki a thorough briefing on the circumstances that led up to when I asked Benson to make sure she passed the Quantico training course—a fact I didn't mention until I'd given her the background.

I began by telling her how my supervisor at the Agency—I never identified Carlton specifically—had forced me to confess I'd revealed my true identity to a detective in the Norman Police Department, a woman by the name of Nikki Saxon.

I went on to explain what the legal ramifications of my disclosure meant and my supervisor's no-nonsense approach to Agency rules.

Up to that point, Nikki had shown no visible reaction to anything I'd said. However, the moment I told her I suspected he was the person responsible for making sure she was invited to the FBI training course, I saw her flinch, as if someone had suddenly taken a swipe at her.

I quickly assured her she was expected to pass the course on her own, and my supervisor had only recommended her for the training because he knew her security clearance would protect me from being dismissed from the Agency.

"I don't believe passing the course will be a problem for me," she said. "I always thought Danny Jarrar had recommended me, but I guess if your boss cared enough about you to go to all that trouble, then I should be happy about that."

"I'm not sure what his motivation was. He's not an easy guy to read."

I paused and asked myself if there was some way I could spin the story without making myself the scapegoat, but she used the interlude to ask me an obvious question.

"How is Frank connected to this?"

I took a deep breath and told her the truth.

"That night you saw Frank at The Meadows, he'd followed me out there from Langley, hoping I'd share some information with him about a suspect. I was angry about that, plus the two of us have a history together, and, to be truthful, it's not all that pretty."

"That doesn't surprise me."

"I don't want you to think I'm using my anger as an excuse for what I'm about to tell you, because I know that's not the case. While I was upset with Frank that night, I was more concerned about my own future at the Agency, and when I saw an opportunity to make sure I wouldn't have to face any legal charges, I decided to make a deal with Frank."

Her eyes narrowed. "Did that deal involve me?"

"I'm afraid so."

"I see," she said, staring down at the action figure in her hand, "and what exactly were the terms of that agreement?"

My stomach churned. "I asked Frank to give you whatever help you needed in order to pass the Quantico course, and, in return, I promised to give him the information he wanted."

She kept her eyes glued to the super hero and didn't say a word.

"There's one more thing."

She raised her head and looked at me.

"I asked him not to tell you about our deal."

She immediately turned her back on me and got up from the table. Walking over to where the child had constructed his tiny castle in the dirt, she placed the plastic figure back in the mud. Then, she returned to her seat.

"I know you're angry, Nikki, and I have no right to ask you this, but—"

"Believe it or not, I'm not angry with you for using me as some kind of bargaining chip. I know I should be, but how can I be angry with you when you've just confessed to being a complete jerk?"

"If I could, I'd go back and—"

"No, Titus, listen to me," she said, reaching across the table and grabbing my hands. "I'm trying to tell you I'm glad you were honest with me. I want us to be able to share who we are with each other, and that includes the good, as well as the bad."

The tension I'd felt moments before suddenly dissipated, and I brought her hands up to my lips and gently kissed them. "Does this mean you've forgiven me?"

She nodded. "I've forgiven you, and I'll forgive you a hundred times over as long as you're willing to share things with me."

"That concept appeals to me on several levels, but you'll have to bear with me. The idea of being open and transparent isn't in the Agency's playbook."

"I'm not necessarily talking about Agency stuff. I'm talking about the insignificant stuff, stuff that isn't connected to your job."

I nodded. "You want to hear about what I had for dinner and how I slept last night?"

She laughed. "Well, that's a start. How *did* you sleep last night?"

I smiled. "I slept just fine thank you, and believe it or not, I let Stormy sleep with me. That was a first for me."

"Uh-oh. You've started something there. What did Millie say?"

"Arkady promised not to tell her."

"I guess that means you'll have to sneak him inside the house under cover of darkness every night. With your training, that shouldn't be too difficult."

I got up from the table. "Speaking of getting dark, we should head back to our cars while we've still got some daylight left."

I walked around and took Nikki's hand as she stood up. "I've enjoyed being with you this evening. It's definitely been the best part of my day."

"Mine too."

After putting my arm around her waist, I held her close and gently caressed her cheek. "While you're incredibly beautiful on the outside, it's the beauty inside you that's winning my heart. Thank you for your forgiveness."

She placed her arms around me and kissed me on the lips. When I returned her kiss, the intensity of our passion increased, and a few seconds later, she pulled away from me and said, "We really should go now."

"Not just yet," I said, leaning down and kissing her again.

Suddenly, the shrill sound of a young boy's voice shattered our intimate moment.

"Oh, yuck, what are you doing?"

Nikki and I quickly drew apart and glanced over at the jogging path, where a woman was clutching the hand of a small boy.

"I'm so sorry," the woman said. "We didn't mean to disturb you. Tyler forgot his—"

Before she could finish, Tyler broke away from her and ran over and picked up the action figure. "Nightwing," he said, "they didn't destroy you."

"It was touch and go for awhile," I said, "but your hero made it through."

Tyler shook his head. "He's no hero. He's a secret agent who defends the world against the bad guys."

"You're right. He's no hero."

# Chapter 54

*Wednesday, July 8*

Following Carlton's instructions, I arrived at Langley just after midnight on Wednesday. He tended to become paranoid whenever third-party deadlines were involved, and he said he wasn't taking any chances as to what Franco Cabello meant when he said he would send a text to Marwan's phone on July 8.

After checking in with security and having them inform Carlton I would meet him in the Ops Center, I walked over to the cafeteria and grabbed some breakfast. A few minutes later, Josh Kellerman from Support Services walked over to my table.

"Mind if I join you?" he asked. "I hate to eat alone."

"No, of course not. I won't be here long, though; I'm overdue in the Ops Center."

"That's okay. I'm a fast eater. I'll probably be finished before you are."

Agency personnel weren't specifically forbidden from discussing operational details in the cafeteria, but they seldom did. Kellerman didn't ask me why I was overdue in the Ops Center, and I didn't ask him why he was at Langley at midnight.

Instead, we discussed the previous evening's game between the Washington Nationals and the Pittsburgh Pirates, a game Stormy and I had watched together in my bedroom after I'd arrived back at The Meadows.

After Kellerman and I had rehashed the ump's bad calls, I gulped down the rest of my coffee and told him I had to head out, giving him the I-enjoyed-eating-with-you-and-now-I-have-to-rush type of social nicety.

When I picked up my tray, I also grabbed the camera Benson and I had purchased when we'd made the appointment to see Walid Khouri. I'd already sent the Ops Center all the photographs I'd taken, but later today, I planned to hand the Nikon over to one of the feds on the Joint Task Force, the person appointed to take Benson's place.

Kellerman gestured at the camera. "I see you found the Nikon. That's good. Now you won't have to fill out all the paperwork I gave you."

"Uh . . . no, I was just—"

"Since you're running late, why don't you just leave the camera with me? I'll return it for you."

I spent about twenty seconds having an internal debate with myself about the ethics of allowing the FBI to pay for my lost Nikon.

Did it matter whether it was the FBI or the CIA who paid for the expensive Nikon? In the end, wasn't it the U.S. taxpayer who was really footing the bill?

I left the camera with Kellerman.

♦♦♦♦

When I entered Room C of the RTM Center, Carlton was occupying the captain's chair, a slightly elevated seat in the middle of the room. On the console in front of him was the personal cell phone belonging to Marwan Farage, along with the encrypted cell phone given to him by Naballah. Both cell phones had a full battery charge.

Room C in the Real Time Management Center, was the largest of the six RTM centers, collectively referred to as the Ops Center.

Center C consisted of both an upper and lower section. The upper section had a seating area, and that's where the members of the Joint Task Force were seated; everyone that is, except Arnie, who was on the lower level standing next to Carlton.

A wall of high-definition monitors encircled the room, but the number of screens used for projecting real time video during an active operation depended on the type of operation, the amount of data coming in, and how many operatives were involved.

Today, six of the twenty screens were being used for real time video; the rest of the screens were connected to the computers of the RTM employees seated at consoles around the room.

Of the six screens displaying real time video, three were showing aerial shots from Agency drones flying around the Washington Beltway, but no one in the room was paying much attention to those screens. I knew that would change when the sun came up.

Two of the screens displayed the FBI logo. However, once Franco Cabello identified the location of the semi-trailer truck carrying the gas canisters, the FBI logos would disappear. Then, everyone inside RTM Center C would be able to view the live action video from the FBI's special reactionary force, the Critical Incident Response Group (CIRG), as it arrived at the truck stop and interdicted the shipment.

The last screen on the far right showed a residential street in Baltimore. The camera was focused on the home of Leandro Manolo, the Hezbollah cell leader who was awaiting a call from Hassan Naballah telling him where to pick up the chemical weapons.

Unless I totally blew it, Manolo would still receive that phone call from Naballah, and when he left his house to meet up with the other members of his cell to retrieve the weapons, the FBI would move in and start making arrests.

Unless I totally blew it.

My assignment—once Cabello had sent the text—was to call Hassan Naballah on the encrypted cell phone and pretend to be Marwan Farage.

When Carlton had first suggested this bit of play acting, I hadn't been enthusiastic about it, but he'd kept insisting I'd spent enough time with Marwan to fool Naballah for a few minutes.

I wasn't so sure about that.

♦♦♦♦

I was on my third cup of coffee when Marwan's personal cell phone dinged. The time was 7:47 a.m. The text message was from Jorge

Zamora.

I could tell the name didn't register with Arnie, but after Carlton adjusted his headset and announced Jorge Zamora was the alias Cabello always used in his business dealings, Arnie immediately nodded his head as if he'd known this all along.

Carlton cleared his throat and read the message aloud.

Nolan Wilson, who was acting as the RTM manager in Olivia's absence, quickly typed the words out on his computer screen, so everyone could view them on one of the video screens.

*"Calverton Travel Center; Exit 31; 5W69588."*

Once Carlton had finished reading the message, he said, "Target is acquired. Commence the operation."

RTM Center C sprang to life after that.

First, a map pinpointing the Calverton Travel Center was projected up on one of the monitors. It showed the truck stop was north of the Capital Beltway and thirty miles south of Baltimore.

A few seconds later, a drone was positioned over the location and everyone in the room was able to view the site in real time.

It looked like a typical truck stop. Semis were parked side-by-side along the outer perimeter, and several more were lined up at the gas pumps. Signage indicated there was a restaurant, driver's lounge, and other trucker amenities inside the sprawling building on the property.

The feds on the upper level of the RTM Center kept their eyes fixated on the drone feed, as they began issuing orders to the CIRG units on their cell phones.

Five minutes after Cabello's message arrived, the special agent in charge of CIRG unit #1 said he was ten minutes out from Exit 31.

Suddenly, Marwan's phone dinged again.

Carlton and I both looked down at the screen.

Another text had arrived from Jorge Zamora.

*"How's the weather there?"*

I said, "Cabello's paranoid about security. He's making sure it was Marwan who received his text. He's asking him for his code phrase."

"Well then, give him the code before he alerts the truck driver. If that happens, this operation could get very messy."

I looked down at the phone and tried to remember the exact words I'd heard Marwan say to Cabello in the library at Naballah's compound. I knew it had something to do with how hot it was and the lack of rain.

I wrote, *"It's hot with no chance of rain in sight."*

Seconds before sending it, I changed it to *"It's hot and dry with no chance of rain in sight."*

I pushed the send button, and Cabello texted back, *"Sounds exactly like the weather here."*

I handed the phone back to Carlton, who said, "I'm glad you remembered that phrase, because I certainly didn't."

"Perfect recall," I said, breathing a prayer of thanks.

♦♦♦♦

All three of the CIRG units arrived at the Calverton Travel Center within five minutes of each other. Once the last unit had joined the other two, they immediately surrounded a sky blue 18-wheeler with California license plate number 5W69588.

The moment the driver and his passenger were confronted by two dozen FBI personnel wearing black tactical gear, they surrendered without offering any resistance.

When that happened, everyone inside RTM Center C cheered and gave each other high-fives.

While I was enthusiastic about the peaceful takedown, my excitement was short-lived when I saw the FBI videographer moving around to the back of the truck in anticipation of opening up the cargo doors.

What if there were no canisters inside? What if Franco Cabello had double crossed Hassan Naballah and kept the sarin gas for himself?

The more I thought about it, the more I became convinced Cabello had done exactly that.

I knew the cartel wouldn't have any scruples about using the weapons to protect their drug empire, so this made perfect sense to me.

On the other hand, since Cabello was ultimately a business man, he could have decided to auction the weapons off to the highest bidder, say a terrorist group like ISIS or Al-Qaeda, and thus enhance his revenue stream.

I was conjuring up a third scenario, when one of the agents brought the driver around to the rear and had him unlock the cargo doors.

Once the doors swung open, all I could see were a couple of wooden crates, and I thought my worst fears had been realized. Then, two of the FBI guys hopped inside the truck and made their way down the aisle between the stacked crates. Seconds later, one of them appeared at the cargo door and gave the rest of the CIRG guys a thumbs up.

Not more than five minutes later, the Ops Center began receiving images of the pallets of gas canisters inside the truck. The grayish-blue metal canisters were nestled inside wooden pallets and appeared to be as harmless as a bunch of propane canisters sold at Walmart stores everywhere.

However, there was no mistaking the warning message written in Arabic on the outside of each of the canisters or the red and green chemical weapons symbol used by the Syrian military.

Once the feds on the upper level of the RTM Center saw the video coming in, they loudly congratulated each other on a job well done. For a brief moment, I thought someone was about to lead them in a cheer.

Carlton turned to me and said, "It's time for you to make that call to Hassan Naballah."

"I don't need a bunch of cheerleaders around me when I do it."

Carlton handed me the encrypted cell phone Naballah had given Marwan. "Go upstairs and make the call from my office. Mrs. Hartford will let you in."

In the elevator on the way up to Carlton's office, I congratulated myself on a job well done and gave Keever Pike an imaginary high five.

## Chapter 55

Sally Jo was waiting for me when I arrived in Carlton's outer office, so I had to assume he'd called ahead and told her I was coming.

I could have been wrong about that, because Sally Jo had a phenomenal intuition.

There were times when I even found it a little scary.

When she opened the door to his office, she said, "Now remember, Titus, if you move something out of its usual place, you'll need to put it back before you leave."

"Don't worry, Sally Jo. I know the drill."

"Of course you do, dear. I'll leave you alone now."

I sat down on Carlton's sofa and placed the cell phone beside me.

After closing my eyes and laying my head back against the seat cushion, I tried to recall Marwan's voice, the way he sounded when he'd spoken to Hassan Naballah. I needed to remember his exact tone.

Had he sounded deferential? Had he used formal Arabic or the less formal, more colloquial speech?

As I let those conversations play out in my head, I realized his Syrian dialect had been tinged with a Spanish accent. Should I try and mimic that?

I picked up the phone and made the call.

"*As-Salaam-Alaikum.*"

Naballah replied, "*Wa-Alaikum-Salaam.* Did Franco send you the text? Do you have a location?"

"It's Calverton Travel Center; Exit 31; 5W69588."

Naballah repeated the information back to me.

"That's correct."

"I've been studying the I-95 freeway near Washington. I believe Exit 31 is near Baltimore. That means Leandro and his men should have plenty of time to arrive at the travel center before Cabello's deadline expires."

"I believe so."

"Are you well, Marwan? Are you enjoying your visit with your family?"

"I am. And you?"

"I'm fine, but I'm worried about Jamal. He's been missing for several days now."

"Missing?"

"He left shortly after you did on Saturday, and no one's seen him since."

"Strange."

"While it may be strange, I don't find it surprising. He was always coming up with some scheme to make money. I imagine that's why he decided to leave so abruptly. Someone must have offered him a chance at a better life."

I doubted Jamal was enjoying a better life right now.

"Perhaps you're right."

"When you get back to Damascus next week, we'll be celebrating our great victory over the Americans. Once things have settled down here, I have something important to discuss with you. It's an opportunity General Suleiman offered me when I met with him last Saturday night. His plan also involves you."

Even with my short answers, I knew I'd already pressed my luck at pretending to be Marwan, but when Naballah brought up what sounded like an upcoming operation, I couldn't resist asking him for further details.

"What kind of opportunity?"

"We'll discuss it later. I need to call Leandro now and let him know where to pick up the shipment."

Since I knew the Ops Center was waiting for Naballah to make the phone call to Leandro, I didn't press the issue and immediately told him goodbye. *"Ma'aasalaama."*

"Go celebrate Samira's birthday now, Marwan. We'll all be having a celebration on 7/11 when we bring down the Great Satan."

Within the next twenty-four hours, Hassan Naballah would get the news the chemical weapons had been confiscated and the Hezbollah members of the Baltimore cell had been arrested. At that point, he'd realize there would be nothing to celebrate on 7/11.

Shortly after reaching that conclusion, he would reluctantly pick up the phone and tell General Suleiman his decade-long plan to rain down death on Washington had failed.

When that moment arrived, I'd give anything to have a Grasshopper in place to capture the general's reaction to that news.

♦♦♦♦

After disconnecting the call, I looked around the room to make sure I hadn't disturbed anything. Once I'd readjusted one of the pillows on the couch, I left Carlton's office and returned to the reception area.

I noticed Sally Jo was talking on the phone, so I simply waved at her to let her know I was leaving. She immediately shook her head and raised her hand like a traffic cop.

"Yes, sir," I heard her say to the caller, "I'll see that he gets the message."

Once she hung up, I asked, "Was that our boss? Was Douglas checking up on me?"

"That was definitely our boss, but it wasn't Mr. Carlton on the phone. It was the DDO, and he wants to see you in his office immediately."

"Now?"

She peered at me over the top of her wire-framed glasses. "He said immediately."

"Well then, would you get in touch with Douglas and tell him my phone call went well, and he should see activity at the house in Baltimore at any moment?"

"Of course. Anything else?"

"You might mention I'm on my way upstairs to meet with Deputy Ira."

She nodded. "I'm not sure why the DDO wants to see you, Titus. But, for what it's worth, he didn't sound angry."

I thanked Sally Jo, but I wasn't convinced her information was all that helpful to me.

Once the deputy had made up his mind about something, he seldom revealed his emotions.

♦♦♦♦

I was all alone as I rode the elevator up to the seventh floor. I was happy about that. It meant I didn't have to engage in social chit-chat with anyone, and I could use the time to figure out why the DDO wanted to see me.

What immediately came to mind was the death of Walid Khouri.

From the beginning, I suspected the DDO had been acquainted with Khouri on a personal basis, although I had no evidence to back that up. Nothing, except my own intuition. Granted, it probably wasn't as good as Sally Jo's intuition, but it was fairly reliable most of the time.

If my suspicions were correct, then I'd done the DDO a big favor by killing Khouri.

I'd spared him the embarrassment of having some Congressional committee investigate why the CIA's Deputy Director of Operations had been personally acquainted with an Iranian deep-cover operative, someone who had been just days away from dropping canisters full of sarin gas on the nation's capital.

Did I expect to receive a commendation from the DDO for helping him avoid such a scenario?

Hardly.

On the other hand, maybe I was being called up to the DDO's office to receive a condemnation. If so, it probably involved Keever Pike.

Perhaps the DDO would give me a blistering lecture for allowing my Hezbollah asset to find out Keever Pike the journalist was, in reality, Keever Pike the spy.

In the end, I had to admit I wasn't sure what to expect from the DDO, but, as I was escorted into his office, I thought I'd prepared myself for every possible scenario.

As it turned out, my preparation was less than adequate.

♦♦♦♦

Robert Ira occupied a corner office on the seventh floor of the Old Headquarters Building. Not surprisingly, he had a million dollar view.

The floor to ceiling windows overlooked several hundred acres of the Virginia countryside, which, at this time of year, resembled a lush Garden of Eden. As far as the eye could see, there were rolling green hills, thick forests, and an abundance of flourishing plant life.

Nevertheless, the room itself had a cold minimalist look to it. Unlike Carlton's office, there were no bookshelves full of books and there was no comfortable seating area. Instead, the room was dominated by Ira's glass-topped desk and a long black conference table.

When I stepped inside the room, the DDO was seated at the far end of that table.

Seated next him was Senator Elijah Mitchell.

The DDO gestured at an empty chair. "Have a seat, Titus."

While I was tempted to sit down at the opposite end of the table—as far away from the two men as possible—I walked around the table and took a seat across from the Senator.

When the DDO introduced me to Senator Mitchell, neither one of us referred to our previous encounters.

"It's a pleasure to meet you, Senator."

He nodded at me. "Deputy Ira was just telling me the missing canisters have been located. Congratulations."

"Thank you, sir."

The DDO said, "Yes, good job. There's no doubt you saved the lives of many here in Washington, and I'm personally grateful for what you've done. You're to be commended, Titus."

Although the DDO hadn't mentioned Walid Khouri specifically in his scant praise, I read a veiled reference to the man's fortunate death in his statement anyway.

"Thank you," I said, accepting his meager commendation.

As if he'd gotten something distasteful out of the way, the DDO immediately cleared his throat and took a drink of water from the crystal goblet in front of him.

After setting the glass down, he looked over at me. "One of the reasons I asked you here, Titus, was to let you know I'm pulling you off Operation Citadel Protection."

I figured the condemnation part was coming now.

As if he'd read my thoughts, he said, "This isn't a disciplinary action. We'll be closing the file on this operation in a few days anyway."

Opening the lid on his laptop, he said, "Ordinarily, you'd be due for some vacation time, but owing to some extenuating circumstances, I'm immediately assigning you to a new mission."

The DDO turned his computer around and for the second time in as many days, I found myself looking into the face of Ben Mitchell.

Ira went over the same facts the Senator had given me the day before, describing the email the Senator had received and showing me the cartel's brief message.

I pretended I was hearing about Ben's kidnapping for the very first time.

Once the DDO had explained what the SOF unit had been able to learn about Ben's disappearance in Cuba, he said, "An hour ago, I set in motion the protocols to rescue Ben, and Senator Mitchell has personally requested you be designated the primary for the operation."

The Senator spoke up. "Ben told me how the two of you had worked together on Clear Signal and Citadel Protection, and since he spoke so highly of you, I thought you would be the logical choice to head up the operation."

I knew that wasn't true, but the DDO had evidently bought the Senator's explanation.

"Has the operation been given a name yet?" I asked.

The DDO closed his laptop and said, "I'll leave the name of the operation up to C.J. Salazar. He'll be your operations officer. You'll receive your first briefing in the morning at ten o'clock."

I shook my head. "No, I won't. I won't be accepting this assignment."

The DDO glanced over at the Senator, whose face was a mass of contradictory emotions.

When he looked back at me, he said, "I realize you're not getting any down time, Titus, but the circumstances are such that—"

"I don't care about a vacation. What I do care about is the success of this mission. That's why I can't accept this assignment unless Douglas Carlton is my operations officer."

I leaned across the table and addressed the Senator. "If you want me to find your son for you, then I need the Agency's best operations officer assigned to this operation. That would be Douglas Carlton."

The Senator stood to his feet and looked down at the DDO.

"Give Titus what he wants."

He did.

♦♦♦♦

On Monday, July 13, three weeks after I encountered a shooter in the Washington Navy Yard on a summer day in June, I arrived in Cuba, determined to reunite Ben Mitchell with his father.

It would take me four months to do that.

## ACKNOWLEDGEMENTS

Although many people have given me support and encouragement in the process of writing *Three Weeks in Washington*, first and foremost, I wish to acknowledge the role my husband, James, and my daughter, Karis, have played in making my writing a success. They have continued to uplift me with their prayers, strengthen me with their love, and bolster me with their confidence.

This book could not have been written without the expertise, advice, and assistance of many people, especially J.D. Younger, Major, NPD, and Dony Jay, Detective, *(The Warrior Spy),* plus other sources who shall forever remain nameless.

I also wish to thank my beta readers for providing critiques and suggestions.

Saving the best for last, I wish to thank my faithful readers, many of whom I hear from on a weekly basis. Your love of Titus Ray Thrillers keeps me writing past midnight. May you never stop asking, "When is your next book coming out?"

All of you serve as my inspiration.

# A NOTE TO MY READERS

Dear Reader, Thank you for reading *Three Weeks in Washington*. If you enjoyed it, you might also enjoy Book I in the series, *One Night in Tehran*, along with Book II, *Two Days in Caracas*. All Titus Ray Thrillers are available on Amazon.

I'd love for you to do a review of *Three Weeks in Washington* on Amazon or on the Goodreads website. Since word-of-mouth testimonies and written reviews are usually the deciding factor in helping readers pick out a book, they are an author's best friend and much appreciated. Your review doesn't have to be extensive; a line or two is sufficient.

Would you also consider signing up for my newsletter? When you do, I'll send you a copy of Titus Ray's famous chili recipe, and you'll receive insider information, plus all my updates about Book IV in the series, *Four Months in Cuba,* due out in 2017. You can sign up at www.LuanaEhrlich.com.

Besides my personal website, you can find out more about Titus Ray Thrillers at www.TitusRayThrillers.com.

One of my greatest blessings comes from receiving email from my readers. My email address is author@luanaehrlich.com. I'd love to hear from you!

CPSIA information can be obtained
at www.ICGtesting.com
Printed in the USA
FSOW02n2123241016
26541FS